THE SHADOW PRIEST

ISBN-10: 1519356161
ISBN-13: 978-1519356161

Printed in the United States of America

ACKNOWLEDGMENTS

Many, many thanks to novelist Sue Grafton, who spent countless hours helping me hone my writing skills.

For invaluable assistance, advice, and encouragement along the way, I also owe a debt of gratitude to Holly Pemberton, Arland Digirolamo, Elaine Bilodeau, Art Bilodeau, Cheryl Kringle, Mickey Meece, Doug Kimball, Scott Lindsay, Paige Rivas, Jim Kemp, Elizabeth Goodman, Ellen Nason, Judy Pemberton, Jamie Mingus, Charlie Mingus, Julie Hawkins, Elizabeth George, Juanita Chen, Sue Campau, Norm Campau, Adrianne Hoadley, Kirsten Anderson, Christine Lyons, Amy Curtis, Assistant U.S. Attorney Karen Shelton, former Assistant U.S. Attorney Peter Katz, Special Agent Kory Casler, Special Agent Antonio Jasso, Special Agent Helena Chavez, Special Agent Brady Ipock, Hon. Judge Joan E. DuBuque, Professor Emeritus Malcolm A. Griffith, Professor Alexander Pettit, and the late Dr. Roger Salisbury.

Finally, I'm grateful to many authors and literary mavens for their priceless guidance over the years, including J.A. Jance, Kevin O'Brien, P.J. Alderman, Dr. Allen Wyler, Mike Lawson, Jane Porter, David Long, Greg Bear, Mark Lindquist, John J. Nance, Kelley Eskridge, Julie Paschkis, Jennie Shortridge, Dia Calhoun, Nancy Horan, Robert Dugoni, Nancy Pearl, Jess Walter, Stephanie Kallos, Royce Buckingham, Layton Green, and Rose O'Keefe.

For Holly and Haley

THE SHADOW PRIEST

Help me to discover Thy truth, O Lord,
and preserve me from those
who have already found it.

—*Goethe*

PART I

RIO DE LAS ANIMAS PERDIDAS

(RIVER OF THE LOST SOULS)

ONE

It was a clear autumn night, the dark sky full of stars, the crisp air smelling of fallen leaves. Special Agent Nathaniel Arkin and his partner, Special Agent Tom Killick, with faces painted and wearing ghillie suits, sat in an observation post surrounded by camouflage netting in the woods near Appomattox, Virginia. They wore radio headsets for communicating with two roadside surveillance teams and their command post down in Lynchburg. Killick watched a dilapidated single-wide trailer through a pair of high-powered spotter's binoculars mounted on a tripod, while Arkin, lying prone, watched through the scope of one of his own hunting rifles. He had agency-issued night vision binoculars as well. But while their subjects were clearly visible in the well-lit trailer, he preferred the higher power of his rifle scope.

Their target was a middleweight methamphetamine dealer and white supremacist named Raylan McGill. McGill was the prime suspect in the murder of an Ethiopian Jew convenience store clerk in Richmond. He was also the *de facto* leader of a conspiracy known to be in the final stages of planning a car bomb attack on the Holocaust Museum in Washington, D.C.

The directorate's teams had been watching McGill's trailer from this position—roughly 150 meters up the gentle slope of a forested hillside—in eight hour shifts for the past week and a half, looking out for any co-

conspirators they hadn't already identified. But so far, there'd been nothing. No visitors—not even a relevant phone call or email. The only noteworthy thing they'd seen was McGill drinking too much and slapping his wife around every couple of days. Tonight was different.

"Damn," Killick said. "He's really taking her apart."

They'd watched McGill and his wife drink most of a liter of cheap whiskey—from disposable party cups and with a splash of warm, off-brand diet cola—in the four hours since sundown. A moment earlier, the couple had been smoking cigarettes at a dirty kitchen table when McGill suddenly punched his wife square in the mouth, knocking her to the floor. He'd then grabbed her by the hair and yanked her up against the wall. There, he now held her by the throat, punching her in the side of her head while she did her best to shield her face with her forearms. Blood was running down her face and neck, onto her white tank top.

Arkin, who could hear Killick beginning to fidget, remained still as stone, though his abdomen was clenched as he watched through his scope.

"Are we going to let this happen?" Killick asked. "Nate, he could kill her." A pause. "Nate."

"Shit." Arkin keyed his microphone. "Harpoon One Actual, this is Harpoon Five. Over." Arkin waited. The radio remained silent. "Harpoon One Actual, Harpoon Five." All Arkin could hear was the rustling of dry leaves stirred by the breeze. "Harpoon One, how do you read? Over."

"Sheffield go out for a smoke, or what?" Killick asked.

"Harpoon Two, this is Harpoon Five. How do you read? Over."

"Harpoon Five, Harpoon Two reads you loud and clear. Over."

"Harpoon Two, interrogative. Can you make contact with Harpoon One Actual from your position? Over."

"Stand by, Harpoon Five."

McGill was now dragging his wife by her hair across the floor toward their bedroom as she held the top of her head with both hands as if trying to keep her scalp from being torn off her skull. Heat radiated from Arkin's face, fogging the edge of his scope lens. His pulse began to race. He did his best to counter his anger with controlled breathing exercises, with thoughts of the many lives they would save if they could roll up McGill's entire network, clearing a whole gang of potential terrorist bombers and murderers off the street in one fell swoop.

But a familiar sense of despair surfaced and held fast in Arkin's mind. How much of their agency's resources had they already burned up on this operation, pursuing someone who was almost certainly an irredeemable psychopath? And even if they rolled up McGill and his whole group, there would always be another. How could they ever prevail against such uninhibited evil, restrained as they were by their sense of morality? How could they ever prevail over the dark, never-ending flood of people like

3

McGill—people who were willing to do anything? It would save so much time and money and energy to just shoot him. And who would care? Who would ever be the wiser? His right hand moved up to the bolt lever of his rifle. He touched it with his fingertips, gingerly, as though expecting it to burn him.

As if reading Arkin's thoughts, Killick spoke. "You got a bead on the son of a bitch?"

Arkin continued to stare through the scope in silence, making a conscious effort to breathe through his nostrils, keeping his crosshairs lined up on McGill's skull through a flimsy trailer window. An easy shot.

"Harpoon Five, Harpoon Two. We can't raise Harpoon One Actual. Over."

"Copy that. Harpoon Five out. Damn it."

Arkin took hold of the bolt lever, chambered a .308 round with a fluid, well-practiced movement, and realigned his sights on McGill's head. McGill had his wife on her back on the bed. He straddled her upper chest and arms so that she couldn't raise a hand to block his blows, which by now were coming down on her unprotected face with cold precision.

"Ice the bastard," Killick said.

"It's tempting."

"You got the drop? Send it."

Arkin huffed.

"You think I'm joking? Drop the piece of shit. He must have a list of enemies 10 miles long. And that isn't even your service rifle. We'll dump it in the James River on the way home, and nobody on the outside will ever know or care. Shit, Sheffield would probably recommend you for an award."

"We aren't at war."

"Please."

"Our orders—"

"He's going to kill her, Nate. It's not part of our rules of engagement to stop a murder?"

"The bomb attack could kill hundreds if McGill or any of his people pull it off."

"Come on. We've already ID'd the whole organization."

"We don't know that."

"We have teams on every one of his people. You think this dope is still hiding something? Still has secret operatives we haven't seen yet? That's Headquarters bullshit, and you know it."

"Just stop talking."

For a moment, Killick was quiet. Then, "You know what? We're never going to win against these sorts of assholes unless we can cross the line over to the same side where they operate. Think about it."

Again, it was as if Killick were reading his mind. Arkin's surging rage and despair threatened to break his self-control. His index finger flexed over the trigger of his rifle. He felt the pressure of it against his skin. Felt the cold of its metal through the thin fabric of his glove. McGill had gone stationary. Arkin's crosshairs settled right over the man's ear hole. One shot would blow the contents of his head all over the Nazi flag on the bedroom wall behind him.

"Do it."

"Stop talking."

McGill's wife's face was so covered in blood that it was hard to tell she was Caucasian.

"Damn, Nate. This is fucked up."

Half a minute later, a long-barrel revolver appeared in McGill's hand. Arkin hadn't even seen where it came from. Maybe under a pillow. McGill was waving it back and forth over his wife's head, as though wagging a reprimanding finger."

"Nate."

"I see it."

McGill froze, staring down at his wife, an evil grin stretching across his face. He jammed the gun barrel into her mouth and cocked the hammer with his thumb.

"Nate!"

As it had on so many of his sniper missions, the world around Arkin seemed to go utterly silent as the decision point came. He would only have one chance. He exhaled slowly through his nose as his finger applied steadily increasing pressure to the trigger. *Smooth. Smooth. Almost there.*

Before the rifle fired, McGill pulled the revolver barrel back out of his wife's mouth and, to Arkin's immense relief, dismounted from her. He lurched back to the kitchen, got himself a can of beer from the refrigerator, and sat back down at the dirty kitchen table. Arkin kept his crosshairs trained on McGill's head for another moment, studying the man's impassive face and dead eyes, before finally taking his finger off the trigger. In his peripheral vision he could see Killick shaking his head, frustrated and disgusted.

"You should have taken that shot, Nate. You should have taken that damned shot."

Arkin felt ill.

SIX YEARS LATER

TWO

A dusting of new snow on the high peaks of the San Juan Range shone brilliant white in the midmorning sun, a lone red-tailed hawk circled in the deep blue sky overhead, and a gentle breeze carried the scent of dry sagebrush across the high Colorado Plateau in what was, even by Four Corners standards, a postcard of an October day. But for the next two minutes, nothing would draw Arkin's attention away from the small lump of brain tissue adhered to the wall in front of him.

He stood on a high wraparound porch on the north side of a cheaply constructed clapboard house, a few miles east-northeast of the small town of Cortez, Colorado, his back to the wide, wooden front stairwell as he examined the fragment—glazed, blood-speckled, and pale gray, no bigger than a dime—with a flat magnifying glass taken from the breast pocket of his dark wool suit. He wondered what it might have held only ninety minutes earlier when it was still part of an intact and functioning mind. Perhaps the cherished memory of a first kiss, or a wedding day, or the birth of a child. Perhaps some component of the victim's personality—part of the essence of who he was. Maybe it compelled the heart to beat or the lungs to draw breath.

Whatever purpose it served, it was now just dead tissue. An inanimate cluster of nonfunctional cells that would soon disassociate, reverting to simple, unorganized molecules. Atoms, particles, and the empty spaces between them. And Arkin couldn't help but wonder whether people were nothing more than molecules and particles in the end. Not the product of miracles or supernatural design. Lacking an immortal component. Lacking anything that would fly off to Heaven when all was said and done. The

7

thought made his chest tighten. Made it harder for him to breathe.

It didn't help that Arkin found a number of things about the crime scene acutely unsettling. It wasn't the blood and death. Experience had long ago given him a sadly high tolerance for such things. What troubled him was an improbable confidence in his familiarity with what he was seeing. A confidence that he'd encountered the same distinguishing evidence—the general context and modus operandi—more than once before. And he couldn't help but feel that an obscure and shadowed figure from his past was reaching out, from somewhere far away, as if to drag him back to a place and time he wished never to revisit. Dark memories of frustration, failure, disgrace, and exile surged into his mind.

Lost in thought, Arkin barely registered the crunch of gravel as an unmarked SUV kicked up a cloud of dust and roared to a stop in the unpaved drive at the base of the stairway. What did catch his attention was an untimely gust of north wind that blew the end of his tie so that it grazed the tacky oval spatter of drying cerebrospinal fluid and bits of human debris surrounding two large, dark bullet holes in the wall. *Oh—Oh, shit.* Snapped from his trance, Arkin noticed that at least a dozen flies were now buzzing around the scene, frenzied, their ancient instincts awakened by the smell of blood.

Doors slammed as two men emerged from the vehicle.

"Look at him there, Pratt," he heard Special Agent Bill Morrison mutter in the singsong, Mississippi-accented voice that tended to make him sound like he was always on the verge of laughing. "He's in his Dale Cooper trance." Then, louder, "Hey, douche bag. How'd you beat us here?"

"A good morning to you too, Bill," Arkin said, still facing the wall, his own voice as modulated as ever. "I didn't see the short bus pull up, or I would have been there to extend a glad hand."

"Shocking political incorrectness for a Yankee."

"Just trying to speak your language."

"What language is that?"

"Whatever they taught you at University of Larry the Cable Guy."

"Now that's just plain mean," Morrison said, smiling. "What's eating you?"

Arkin sighed. "Nothing. Except that I got brain on my tie."

"Your Andover tie?"

"Exeter."

"Whatever."

"Anyway, how did they motivate *you* to get out of bed this early? I didn't hear anyone say anything about free crawdaddies and cornpone."

"Nate, one of the secrets of being funny is not trying so hard. And I'm from Mississippi, not Louisiana. It's shrimp and grits that get me out of bed. But back to my question. The Company loan you a black helicopter? For that matter, why are you here at all?"

"I was already at McCready's picking up roasted chilies,"

"They open this early?"

"A patrolman in front of me in line got the radio call."

"And you just couldn't help yourself."

Arkin shrugged.

"And you just happened to be wearing a $1,200 suit to a dusty little dry goods store."

"I always wear a suit."

Morrison's smile broadened. "Yeah. And you're the only man within a 100 miles of here who does, not counting funeral directors. But then you *are* a bit of an odd bird, truth be told. For example, most people don't drive 45 miles to get roasted chilies when there are half a dozen sources closer to home."

"McCready's are Hannah's favorite. I wanted to surprise her."

"That's sweet."

"She might give you a plate of her chile rellenos if you play your cards right."

"Oh, shit yeah."

Arkin broke into a smile of his own and at last turned to face Morrison. "Shit yeah? Is that you're way of expressing approval of one of my wife's culinary masterpieces?"

"Shit yeah."

"Bill, you're what they call a paragon of crassitude."

Morrison spat chew tobacco juice out of the corner of his mouth. "Crassitude? That really a word? They teach you that at Andover?"

"Exeter, you backwoods hick. You would have been calling me out here about 30 seconds from now anyway. Come take a look at this."

"At what?"

"The big holes in this wall. The ballistic trauma to the victim's head," he said, gesturing down toward the body of Allan Charles Egan chalked out and lying on its side at his feet.

Hands jammed into his pockets, Morrison climbed the steps to the porch in a lazy gait that largely disguised his strength and dexterity. His brown hair was unkempt and his square jaw bore 36-hour stubble. He wore threadbare jeans, an un-tucked flannel shirt, and dusty old leather harness boots—a tarnished badge attached to his belt the only indication of his status as a sworn law enforcement officer. The one overt sign of his true hardness and experience in mortal arts was to be found in his penetrating, steel blue predator's eyes.

Side-by-side with Morrison, Arkin looked like a poster boy of federal law enforcement—the perfect fit of his suit matching his tight, neatly trimmed black hair, clean shave, and perfectly polished shoes. His taut posture exuded quickness and ready power, while the sheer gravity of his facial expression left little doubt that he was not someone to be trifled with. Yet he and Morrison did share one notable similarity of appearance: the fundamental quality of their eyes. While Arkin's were a dark brown, they had the same measuring, calculating, potentially ferocious look that Morrison's did. And even the most oblivious of passers-by would find it hard to miss that they smoldered with an anger or bitterness born of God only knew what. That they were the eyes of someone who had, perhaps more than once, descended into the abyss and seen the lake of fire.

"Yes, sir," Morrison said. "Those are some big holes in that wall."

"Not as big as the one in Mr. Egan here."

The limbs and abdomen of the body at their feet were unscathed. But the upper half of the man's head was gone, leaving an intact lower jaw, drying tongue, the open holes of his esophagus and windpipe, and a pulpy stalk constituting what remained of his brain stem.

"Holy shit."

"Quite."

Morrison stared for a moment, then grinned. "There's something almost comical about the way this guy looks."

"Only you would say something like that."

"What—you don't think so? It's like something out of a coyote and roadrunner cartoon. Like one of those ones where the coyote has a stick of ACME brand dynamite that blows his nose and jaw to the other side of his head or whatever." Morrison shrugged and looked up. "Hey, you got a stick of gum? Forgot to shave my teeth this morning."

"Judas!" said tall, blonde, and boyish Special Agent John Pratt, ascending the stairs after getting his crime scene camera out of the back of the car, looking spooked as he caught sight of the body. "What the heck bullet you think did that? .408?"

"Bigger," Arkin said, now staring at the smaller and cleaner of the two dark bullet holes in the wall, its diameter like that of a quarter. "And good morning to you too, Johnny-boy. Where are your Mormon manners today?" Sensing tension in Pratt's silence, Arkin switched tacks, and in a kindhearted voice asked, "How's the family?" hoping to distract the younger and less-experienced agent from the full horror of what was lying at his feet. Pratt was a tough kid, but anyone could be knocked off-kilter seeing a decapitated body for the first time.

"This callout interrupted banana pancake day. The kids are not happy with me." Pratt turned his wide eyes from the body to the bullet holes in the wall. "So, a bigger bullet than a .408?"

"Probably more like a—" Arkin stopped mid-sentence, his mouth hanging open in surprise as he turned to see Pratt wearing wrap-around sunglasses lashed to his head with a fluorescent orange neoprene eyewear retainer, his lips coated with bright white zinc oxide sunblock.

"Like a 12-gauge slug," a local officer shouted from inside the house, breaking Arkin's transfixion. "That's what Detective Cornell thinks."

Arkin looked over at Morrison who returned his glance before rolling his eyes.

"But you told me nobody in Egan's security detail saw the shooter," Arkin shouted back through the doorway.

"So?"

"So it stands to reason that the shooter was somewhere outside of the ten-foot-high walls of this compound."

"So?" the local said again, now emerging from the house wearing white latex crime scene gloves.

"The nearest possible firing point is hundreds of yards away," Arkin said, pointing to a brushy hillock in the distance, making a mental note of the direction of the breeze as he did so.

The officer stared blankly.

"What Sherlock is trying to say," Morrison said, "is that the nearest point from which someone could have taken a shot that would have cleared the walls of the compound is that little hill over yonder. And while it might be on the very edge of the maximum theoretical range of a 12-gauge loaded with slug, the chances of an accurate shot," Morrison said while making a pinching gesture with his thumb and index finger, "the chances of actually scoring a kill from that distance are smaller than Nate's already small testicles."

"That's an apples to oranges comparison," Arkin said.

"You wish it was."

"Were. I wish it *were*." He turned to the officer again. "How did Egan's security people describe the sound of the shots?"

"I don't know if anyone has asked them that yet."

Arkin nodded. "Well, regardless, you can tell Detective Cornell, with my compliments, that I'm certain this hole wasn't made by a 12-gauge slug."

They all stood staring out over the scrubland for a moment, wondering exactly where the shot had come from. Then the local shrugged his shoulders and went back inside. Arkin scanned the grounds of the surrounding compound, with its high cinderblock walls, its twin rows of perfectly trimmed ornamental shrubs planted in perfect straight lines to either side of the perfectly weed-less, perfectly level driveway. Evidence of the victim's greater-than-average efforts to prop up illusions of control, Arkin thought. But the illusions hadn't done much to save him from the bullet that blew his head off. They never saved anybody in the end.

"What do you think, Nate?" Morrison asked.

"If I told you, you'd think I was certifiable."

"Already do. So come on now, use that legendary Arkin ESP and tell us what we're going to find."

"Clairvoyance."

"What?"

"Clairvoyance, not ESP."

"Is there a difference?"

"Are you serious? Didn't you all sit around the bonfire telling top secret clairvoyance stories back at Camp Peary?"

Morrison smiled as he continued scanning the terrain to the east. "I wasn't a rich kid like you, Nate. I never got to go to summer camp."

Arkin smiled back. "Right."

"Where's Camp Peary?" Pratt asked as he snapped a photo of the bullet holes.

Morrison remained silent. "Virginia," Arkin said.

"Never heard of it."

"It's famous in some circles. But not for its s'mores."

"What do you mean?"

Arkin shrugged his shoulders.

Morrison, still smiling, shook his head without making eye contact with either of them. "Alright, then what does your *clairvoyance* tell you, smart guy?"

"That the late Mr. Egan here was ideological and charismatic. That his sphere of influence was growing rapidly. That he was probably about to burst onto the scene such that he would wield considerable power and command a much wider audience for his ideas. And that he was shot by a military-trained sniper with a .50 BMG round fired from a heavy rifle at what, to simple folk like Pratt here, would be considered ludicrous range."

Morrison nodded. "You just got here, right? You get all that just from looking at a couple of bullet holes and a body with no head?"

"Clairvoyance."

"That's good. Maybe you're funny after all, Nate. But really now."

Arkin shifted his weight, debating whether to say anything. "There are things here. . . ."

"Yes?"

"Things that remind me of something."

"What kind of something?"

Arkin didn't answer.

Morrison nodded knowingly. "Another Nate Arkin cliffhanger. You should write thrillers."

As they stood on the porch, a small black butterfly with double rows of blue and white spots running near the edges of its wings landed on the doorjamb near Arkin's foot. "Watch out there," Pratt said, pointing to it.

Arkin looked down. It was a beautiful thing to see, standing in stark contrast to the blood and debris all around it.

"You know," Arkin said, "the caterpillars of those things are ugly as sin.

And they feed on endangered local wildflowers. Devour them by the acre, in fact."

"No way," Pratt said, kneeling down for a closer look. "It's beautiful. Look at it."

Arkin studied Pratt's expression. He looked like a kid who'd just caught his first glimpse of Santa Claus after waiting in line at Macy's. It made Arkin smile. "John, your naïveté is heartwarming and horrifying at the same time."

"Whatever that means," Pratt said. The butterfly took flight and Pratt watched it until it vanished around the corner of the house. "So you think the shooter had a .50 caliber rifle?" he asked as the portly Detective Cornell came out the door followed by another local patrolman carrying little paper cups of coffee for each of them on a cardboard to-go carrier.

"Morning boys," Cornell said as he handed out coffee to any takers. "Who said anything about a .50 caliber rifle?"

"Nate's theory," Morrison said.

"And you think this because?"

"Because he's clairvoyant," Pratt said.

"Clairvoyant, or bat shit crazy," Morrison said.

"Just a hunch," Arkin said.

"A hunch? Really? Well, honk my hooter, Nate," Cornell said as he held up the clear plastic evidence bag he grasped in his right hand. It contained a bent metal fragment about the size of an adult human thumb. "That look like part of a .50 BMG bullet to you boys?"

Arkin noted what appeared to be traces of black paint on the tip, then glanced up to find Morrison shooting him a significant look.

"It sure does," Morrison said, his eyes locked on Arkin's. "An armor-piercing variant."

"Overkill for shooting someone," Arkin said.

"No shit."

"One of my guys just pried it out of the back side of Egan's cast-iron stove," Cornell said. "It went clear through the front of it. And that was after it went through Egan's head, as well as this here wall. Still trying to figure out where the other bullet went."

Morrison took a sip of his coffee and pulled a sour face. "This is terrible."

"You're welcome, dickhead," Cornell said. "I'm not your personal barista. Anyway, we're practically on the Utah border here. What do you expect?"

"Of you? You really want me to answer? Think, now."

Cornell grinned and shook his head. "Dick."

"So what do we know about the late Mr. Egan?" Arkin asked.

"*Reverend* Egan," Cornell said. "Reverend in his own eyes anyway, given that he was never officially credentialed as such by a recognized church. Born El Paso, Texas, August 2, 1967. Preaches to a fundamentalist congregation he founded after purchasing the old Cortez Grange building for next to nothing six years ago. Calls it White Road Church."

"Is it on White Road?" Morrison asked.

"Good guess, Bill."

"Creative name," Arkin said.

"Divorced. No children. Political nut job and bigot. Known for his vitriol against big government, homosexuals, Muslims, and illegal immigrants. The usual."

"Hey, at least the blacks and Jews get a break this time," Morrison said.

"Probably an oversight," Arkin said.

"Apparently his message resonates with some folks. His congregation has grown to over three thousand since its founding."

Arkin's eyebrows rose. "Three thousand? In a town of nine thousand?"

"He brings in the kooks from far and wide. Some drive all the way from Monticello, from Ridgeway, Farmington, even Moab. He promotes the church with over-the-top corny social media. Even broadcasts a radio show a couple of hours each day from a low-power antenna on the roof here. Favorite topics are the books of Leviticus and Revelation."

"Naturally. Licensed?"

"Yup."

Officially, Arkin's only reason for being at the scene was to document any use of military-grade weapons. But despite himself, he stood staring at the plain-view evidence, mentally cataloging, pondering the meaning of every last detail. "I presume Egan was exceptionally charismatic."

"Oh, yes. His flock thinks he can walk on water."

"Now maybe not so much," Morrison said.

"And I assume he was an advocate for the use of violence to achieve his ideological goals?" Arkin asked.

"Implicitly."

Morrison snorted and broke into a grin. "Implicitly? That's a big word for you, Cornell."

"Implicitly as in implied but not directly expressed, or implicitly as in without reservation?" Arkin asked.

"The first one. Or both, I guess. We never connected him or his group with any actual acts of violence, but he ran a sort of training camp out of here."

"Training camp?" Pratt asked.

"The usual backwoods wannabe type of thing. Bunch of fat fucks who were never in the military—or who, if they were, probably spent their careers as laundry workers at National Guard depots in the Dakotas—giving themselves hernias running around in camouflage BDUs, jumping over ditches, pretending to be Seal Team Six. Making videos of it to show their white trash buddies and girlfriends. That sort of thing. They have an obstacle course and gun range over there," Cornell said, pointing to a brush-free rectangle of dusty earth southeast of the compound. One of my guys just took a look at it and found paper targets done up to look like Bedouin Arabs pinned to stacks of hay bales."

"Charming," Arkin said.

"I reckon Egan's parents never took him on the 'It's a Small World' ride at Disneyland," Morrison said. "And if I were a betting man, I'd say he had control issues. His shrubs are trimmed to perfection, planted in perfectly straight lines. You saw that too, I noticed," he said to Arkin.

"What's his shrubs got to do with anything?" Pratt asked.

"Grammar, Pratt," Arkin said. "I beg you."

"You can know just about everything you need to know about a person by looking at their yard," Morrison said.

"Really?" Pratt asked.

"Your yard looks like the cover photo of an ad for a big-box hardware store. Simple. Square. Perfectly maintained, not a single weed to be seen, utterly lacking in creativity or character. You've adopted, wholesale, someone else's idea of a yard."

"Hey, I work really hard to—"

"Cornell's yard is probably a big empty pit strewn with off-brand beer cans. Then there's Arkin's. Exotic. Ideas adapted from other cultures, altered to his own tastes and vision. Over-thought, over-manipulated, over-controlled detail. Anal, from end to end."

"Whereas yours," Arkin said, "is a repulsive expanse of patchy weeds and bare compacted earth. An archetype for people who don't give a shit about anything."

"See?"

"I believe I do."

"Egan had fifty or so trainees out here, off and on," Cornell went on.

"Fifty trainees." Arkin repeated. "Why have we not seen this group mentioned in the JTTF hot sheets?"

"Because Cornell would have had to put it in," Morrison said, "which means he'd have to know how to read and write."

"He also posted a video clip on the internet advertising his camp, encouraging all patriots to prepare themselves for the coming struggle to defend our families and restore our great country or whatever the fuck. Nothing plainly illegal, mind you. Just paranoid and weird."

"And he was planning to run for office," Pratt said. Arkin and Morrison turned to look at him. "I read it in the Herald a few weeks back."

"The U.S. House of Representatives, no less," Cornell added. "Do you think that's a factor here?"

"Now that you mention it." Arkin scanned the horizon. "I think someone out there may have found the combination of Egan's ideologies, charisma, and potential political power to be profoundly distressing."

"Congress? This guy?" Morrison asked. "An openly racist Bible-thumper from Shitsville?"

"Hey," Cornell protested. "I live here, asshole. And it ain't like Durango's the center of the universe."

"It's Rome compared to this manure dust crap hole. Really though, what chance could Egan possibly have had?"

"He was set to run against Congressman Gary Sandoval," Pratt said.

"The guy who just got indicted for fraud?" Morrison asked.

"Yup."

"A .50 caliber bullet and an ideological target with surging power and influence, just as you guessed," Morrison said, shaking his head and smiling at Arkin. Clairvoyance, indeed. What do I always tell you, Pratt? This guy is a frigging bona fide law enforcement genius, though it pains me to admit it."

"So maybe Egan had a decent shot at winning," Cornell said.

"And maybe that troubled someone," Arkin said.

"Who?" Pratt asked.

"Local Mexicans, homosexuals, Muslims," Morrison said. "If we even have any Muslims around here."

"Or someone from elsewhere," Arkin said. "From over the horizon. Someone who watches for guys like Egan no matter where they sprout up."

"Why would you think that?" Morrison asked. "Clairvoyance again?"

Arkin didn't answer. He just stared out toward the mountains on the eastern horizon as the breeze returned, thinking. Though they invariably staked claims to this or that adamantine motive springing from religion, politics, social movements, or some other construct of human civilization, it was Arkin's long-held theory that the behaviors and actions of groups like Egan's were driven by something else altogether—perhaps by ancient psychological needs having nothing to do with anything that was ever incorporated into a coat of arms, anthem, sacred text, or manifesto.

"So what happened here?" Arkin asked at last.

"In short," Cornell began, "Egan's security goons were supposed to escort him to a meeting down at his church. As they stood here on the porch, waiting for one of their troupe to lock the door, the first shot passed right between them, missing Egan's neck by a hair, and put this hole right here," he said, pointing to the cleaner and rounder of the two holes. "Lead security guy said it sounded like somebody hit the wall with a sledge hammer. Of course, they didn't hear the gunshot until after the bullet had punched this hole. As to what happened next, near as I can guess from what these self-conscious security dipshits told my guys is that they all stood here startled by the unexpected, out-of-context sounds, their backs turned to the shooter as they stared in wonder at this giant bullet hole, trying to figure out what the fuck was going on. Then, in the five seconds they spent trying to collectively pull their heads out of their own assholes, the killer lined up a second shot that hit

Egan in the back of the skull, spraying some of his face and head on this wall here, and taking some of it through this second hole and into the kitchen. In the two hours since we got the call, my guys have been canvassing every dirt farmer, gas station attendant, and hotel clerk within 10 miles. So far, nobody knows shit."

"Have you questioned his security people yet?"

"Not in earnest. I'm holding them until we're done processing the scene."

"May I?"

"By all means. Egan had a five-man detail. Local knuckle-draggers except for the leader, Beckwith. He had some personal security and force protection experience in the Army."

"Is he a true believer?" Morrison asked.

"What do you mean?"

"I mean, some people march because they're true believers, and some march because it gets them laid. You follow me?"

"I. . . ."

"Might help us plan our approach to the interview."

"I'm sure it will be obvious," Arkin said. "Let's just go and see."

"Right this way, gentlemen."

THREE

"How do you want to play this?" Morrison asked Arkin as Cornell led them across the compound toward a small office built into a corner of Egan's massive hangar-like garage where Glen Beckwith, head of Egan's security detail, waited. "Good cop, bad cop?"

"Doesn't usually work on anti-government types. In fact, I'll bet you a case of beer this guy says 'fuck the federal government' in the first 60 seconds of this."

"You're on. But what's our approach? I'm up for a bit of theater. How about the two burnouts routine?"

"But you *are* a burnout."

"So?"

"You can't call it theater if you're just being yourself."

"Point. But can *you* hang with it?"

"What do you mean? I'm as much of a burnout as you are."

"Right."

"What's that supposed to mean?"

"You know what it means."

"No, I don't believe I do."

"Come on. Let's get into character."

"Hold on, hold on," Arkin said, stopping in his tracks.

"Are you going to argue with me about this? Look at how you're dressed." Silence. They stared at each other. Morrison nodded his head. "Right. So, can you pretend you don't still care? Or is your muse on spring break?"

More silence. Arkin gave him an irritated stare. "It's autumn."

"Okay then. Let's go in."

As they entered, they found Beckwith seated at a table, dressed in what looked like surplus navy blue U.S. Customs BDUs, fiddling with his cellphone. He looked up as they came in. "Who are you?"

"Mr. Beckwith, these are agents Arkin, Morrison, and Pratt," Cornell said. "They would like to ask you about the events of this morning."

"Are you feds?"

"After a fashion, yes," Arkin said.

"Fuck the government."

Arkin tried to suppress a grin. "Ah, which government exactly?"

"The federal government. Fuck the federal government."

Arkin allowed himself a tight smile as Morrison gave an exaggerated sigh.

"Really?" Morrison said. "You just cost me a case of beer, asswater. And that's such a clichéd thing to say."

"Fuck the government."

"Yeah. Great. Try working for them."

"I don't have to talk to you assholes. I know my rights."

Arkin snorted. "Your rights? Oh, well that's good. Did they teach you to say that back at Central Casting?"

"If you don't talk to us," Morrison said, "how are we going to break this case? And if we don't break the case, we don't get the stat."

"The what?"

"The stat, asswater! The stat! Our bonuses, our careers, our lives—all driven by the stats!"

Arkin and Morrison both lost it, breaking into half-stifled laughter.

Beckwith stared at them, confused. "Who are you guys with, FBI?"

"Fuck no," Morrison said. "Those poor sons of bitches work 12-hour days."

"We're from different agencies," Arkin said. "I work for one you've never heard of. A bureau within the Department of Defense tasked with tracking and prosecuting illegal distribution, possession, and use of military-grade weapons. Agent Morrison here is a jack-booted thug with the Bureau of Alcohol, Tobacco, Firearms and Explosives. And Pratt, in the back, well he's the underutilized and poorly positioned regional representative of an outfit called the Directorate for Counter Intelligence—DCI, for short—a post-9/11 inter-agency counter-terrorism task force that has more or less become permanent. Marginally constitutional charter. Real big brother stuff. It's his outfit that has the deep, dark holes we might drop you down if it suits us. Why Pratt is stationed all the way out here in the Four Corners area, instead of a place like New York or D.C., is anybody's guess. Probably some Colorado senator's idea of a jobs program he can take credit for. Boost those employment numbers."

"Again," Morrison said, "it's all in the stats."

"It doesn't matter," Beckwith said. "Ain't talking to you."

"The thing I can't figure," Arkin said, "is why someone would bother to shoot an irrelevant backwoods bumpkin like Egan?"

19

"Because the truth scares people," Beckwith said.

Arkin smiled mockingly. "The truth?"

"Egan spoke the truth, Nate," Morrison said matter-of-factly. "How refreshing."

"Well, there you go," Arkin said, turning to Morrison. "You know what? I've been searching for the truth my whole adult life. And here it was, all along, just down the highway in Cortez, Colorado."

Beckwith had gone quiet.

Arkin and Morrison stared at him for a moment, impassive. Then Arkin turned to Morrison. "He isn't supposed to clam up like this."

"No, you're right."

"It never went like this in the mock interviews back at the academy."

"No, it didn't."

"What are we doing wrong?"

Beckwith, hearing everything, stared at them.

"Oh, wait," Morrison said. "Remember, after we introduce ourselves, we're supposed to develop rapport."

"Rapport?"

"Chitchat. Find some common ground. That's supposed to prime the interviewee to talk, make him feel comfortable. And it establishes a behavioral baseline so that we know when he starts bullshitting us or whatever."

"Oh, right. Rapport. Man, we screwed that up already, didn't we? Maybe we should start over."

"That's a great idea. But how?" Morrison asked.

"Let me think. Ah! How's your golf game, Mr. Beckwith?"

"Go fuck yourself."

"Mine too. Morrison here thinks I'm holding back, not following through in my swing. But I think the bottom line is I'm just not getting out there enough, what with chess club, work, so on and so forth. Spread too thin. Seems like there's never enough time in the day."

"I ain't talking to you fuckers." Beckwith stared at them.

"Really?" Arkin said, feigning exasperation. "Even now?" He leaned back in his chair and looked over at Morrison. "I don't think it's working."

"No."

"Maybe my paralinguistics are off."

"Are off, or is off?"

"Are. Maybe we should try reverse psychology."

"You mean like say, 'Hey asswater, we don't want to hear what you have to say anyway.'"

"Something like that."

"I'm sitting right here," Beckwith said.

"You don't think he'll figure out that we're trying to play him?"

Arkin snorted. "This moron? No."

"Okay, let's try it."

"Okay."

"Hey asswater, we don't want to hear what you have to say anyway."

Beckwith crossed his arms and stared at them, silent, his bugged-out eyes jumping back and forth between them.

Morrison sighed. "This guy just don't get it."

"I don't get what?"

"You aren't reading between the lines," Arkin said. Beckwith squinted. "Sorry for the colloquialism. What I mean is, you're not getting the message—"

"That we don't give a shit," Morrison blurted.

"In as many words."

"We don't fucking care, buddy. Really. Why? We signed on, we drank the Kool-Aid, we waved the flags, we sacrificed for the team, and then we got shit on, time after time, over and over again. So now we're wise. Now we know there's nothing in this for us besides the paycheck. And we get paid whether you talk to us or not." Morrison leaned back in his chair and crossed his arms. "But what good will that do you? It won't get you your revenge. And let's be honest—we all know you ain't gonna get revenge on your own. You wouldn't know where to start, would you? You don't even know where the bullets came from. You have a good 40 or 50 million square foot search area out in the dusty scrubland out there. And even if you manage to find the firing position before winter comes, then what? You going to follow the footprints back to Colonel Mustard and Professor Plum?"

"Who?"

"Exactly."

Beckwith was beginning to look disconcerted. "I'm an Afghanistan veteran," he said in an almost pleading tone.

"Yeah. Join the club, dipshit," Morrison said.

A pained expression flashed across Beckwith's face. Arkin and Morrison both saw it. Time to shift gears. Morrison's voice softened. "We're just fucking with you, man. We fell for it too. You know what got me? It was those awesome commercials they played during halftime. Recon guys jumping out of helicopters and shit." He shook his head and stared at nothing in particular, lost in true memory.

Reading the man's eyes, Arkin was sure he could tell Beckwith's story with considerable accuracy. As with Morrison, half of Beckwith's personal motive for joining the military probably had to do with wanting to get away from an emotionally unavailable mother and abusive alcoholic of a father, or something along those lines. A turbulent and unpredictable childhood. A wretched home life. Heartbreaking feelings of irrelevance and inadequacy. Beckwith might not be able to recall specifically thinking it, but in his

THE SHADOW PRIEST

subconscious he probably figured that by signing on that line and putting on that uniform he'd finally get some sort of meaningful control over things— control over his tiny corner of the universe. All that training. All those weapons. All that power. But it didn't work out that way. It never did. Like so many who took that path, he found out, all too soon, that it didn't give him control. To the contrary, all being in combat did was drive home the horrible truth, the terrible secret that there was no escape. That he was still mortal. Still hurtling toward the infinite dark emptiness, just like everybody else.

They let the silence hang for a few moments. "Where were you based in Afghanistan?" Morrison eventually asked in a tone of comradely interest.

Beckwith didn't answer.

"I spent my first and last months at Bagram," Morrison said. "In between, Patrol Base Alcatraz, and some other places nobody has ever heard of. Places with really shitty food. Worse than Bagram. At least Bagram had a Pizza Hut. I must have ate Pizza Hut at least two meals a day for my last three weeks in-country. Got totally constipated. Arkin here, he was somewhere in the, what, Garmsir District somewhere?"

"Camp Dwyer," Arkin said. "But only for a couple of weeks for gearing up. After that, places nobody has ever heard of. But certainly not Pakistan," he added in a sarcastic tone. "No, sir. That would have been illegal under international law." He winked at Morrison.

"And the food at Camp Dwyer?"

"You haven't lived until you've tasted their goat demi-glace."

Morrison and Arkin exchanged a handful of brief stories about Afghanistan, covering noteworthy episodes of diarrhea, the video games they played while sitting around on base, and the difficulty of getting positive identification on plainclothes enemy combatants during firefights. They observed, in conclusion, that the country was a lost cause, and that the ISAF mission was mostly a giant clusterfuck.

"At least it was a clusterfuck with Pizza Hut pizza," Morrison said.

At this, Beckwith grinned weakly. So weakly it was barely noticeable. "Ghazni," he finally mumbled.

"Huh?"

"I was at FOB Ghazni."

"Ghazni," Morrison echoed. "Isn't that where part of the Polish brigade was based? How was the food?"

Beckwith shrugged.

"I heard Ghazni had decent food. Probably because Poles know how to cook."

"Come on," Arkin said. "The DFACs were all supplied and run by the same contractor."

"Still," Morrison said. "Some of them had cooks who gave a shit, and some didn't."

"Point."

Beckwith fidgeted. The defiance had melted from his face, replaced by sadness. Sadness, with hints of regret and, perhaps, of fear. His shoulders were slumped forward. "Fuck," he muttered through an exhale, slowly running his fingers through his hair. "Fuck it. Alright. What do you want to know?"

"Why was your security team here this morning?" Arkin asked.

"To escort Sam to a meeting with the church leaders. The deacon committee."

"What time was the meeting scheduled?"

"10 a.m."

"At White Road Church"?

"Yeah."

"Do they have that same meeting each week?"

"Every Tuesday and Thursday."

"Does it always start at 10 a.m., and do you always escort him from here to there?"

"Always."

"What's your procedure?"

"We arrive in the SUVs around 9:30. We bring them into the compound and close the gate. Then we go into the house to share a cup of coffee with the Reverend. He asks us how we're doing. How are families are. Has us update him on our own efforts to bring new followers into the church. Once we're all done, we step out onto the porch at the top of the stairs. I lock the door while the Reverend stands among the other four guys. When the house is secure, we go down the stairs, get into the SUVs and drive to White Road."

"Are the SUVs armored?"

"Yes," Beckwith said, clearly surprised to be asked. "Bulletproof glass. Kevlar plates. The works."

"What other routines do you follow through the week?"

"None, really. Aside from taking him to White Road for Sunday sermon. Besides that, he usually stays here."

"Doesn't go out much?"

"No."

"Why not?"

Beckwith shrugged.

"Who was he afraid of, Glen?"

At that, Beckwith bristled. "Afraid?" The resistance returned to his face. He sat up straight, re-crossed his arms and frowned. "Reverend Egan wasn't afraid of anybody."

"Right. That must be why he had 10-foot-high walls around his house, armored SUVs, and a five-man security detail in a town with two stoplights. Because he was fearless."

FOUR

Back in the main house, they watched as Cornell's people continued to process the scene. As they walked through the kitchen, Arkin spotted a pamphlet titled "Countering the Homosexual Threat to the American Family" lying open on the counter with certain passages underlined.

"I have to hand it to you," Arkin said to Morrison, "reminiscing about Afghanistan to get that idiot to talk was a smart play. I have to quit assuming you're dumb just because you have a southern accent."

"Yeah, and you almost fucked it up with your pompous reference to demi-glace. Did you see the look he gave you?"

"I did." Arkin smiled.

Morrison shook his head. "That guy's a cake from the same old recipe, ain't he?"

"Nothing like a little ignorance, confusion, and fear to drive the weak-minded into the hands of a guy like Egan."

"Preach it, brother. Still, he took it pretty well, didn't he? Usually meatheads like him are so desperate to believe that they go ape shit whenever anyone questions their prophet."

"Amen."

"We figured out where the other bullet went," a patrolman told Cornell as they entered the dining room.

"Where?"

"It hit right here at the edge of this area rug," the deputy said, pointing to a hole in the wood floor at the very edge of a brown bearskin rug, the fur of which nearly obscured it. "Renner found a hatch to the crawlspace in the closet."

"Is he down there now?"

"Hell no," Deputy Renner called from another room.

"Why not?" Cornell shouted back.

"Look down in there. It's dark and there's all kinds of spider webs and shit."

"Are you fucking kidding me?"

"That ain't in my job description. You're the detective."

They walked to the closet and peered down into the dark square hole of the access hatch.

"Oh. That *is* nasty," Cornell said as he peered through dense, dusty cobwebs at a packed earth floor littered with rodent droppings. "Definitely below my pay grade."

Arkin took off his jacket, pulled a pen light from the breast pocket, held it in his teeth, and began to lower himself down into the hole.

"You'll ruin your precious shoes, city boy," Morrison said.

Arkin had to crawl on hands and knees to keep from hitting his head on the floor joists. But in a few moments, he found the hole in the floor above, figured the likely trajectory of the bullet, slipped on a pair of latex gloves, and began digging in the dirt and rocks with his hands. The earth was more compact than he expected, and the tips of his gloves soon tore open. Dirt and grit lodged under his fingernails as he went. But five minutes and three ruptured pairs of latex gloves later, Arkin felt the bullet. It was around six inches deep. After loosening the earth around it, he drew it out with his fingertips. *Hello there, my little friend.* There was no doubt it was .50 caliber, intact and seemingly pristine enough to bear general rifling characteristics that might be of use in eventually identifying the gun from which it was fired. *Where did you come from?*

*****

Soon they were back on the front porch looking out over the surrounding land. At the nearest hillock, a couple of Cornell's people were searching for the sniper's firing point.

"Look, he's at it again, Pratt," Morrison said, gesturing to Arkin who was staring into the distance. "He has his all-seeing eyes turned on. Lord knows what he's really seeing."

"I think they're going to have to search farther out," Arkin said.

"Why do you say that?" Cornell asked. "Wouldn't the sniper have wanted to be as close in as possible for accuracy?"

"There's very little cover where they're searching, and the land slopes toward us. One of Egan's security people probably would have spotted the guy if he were positioned right there. Perhaps even before Egan was shot, while the killer was setting up and observing. Plus, that's only, what, maybe 400 yards out?"

"So?"

"With the right equipment, a good sniper can work from thousands of yards farther out."

"Thousands?"

"In March of 2002, in Afghanistan, a corporal of the 3rd Battalion of Princess Patricia's Canadian Light Infantry fired a .50 BMG round from a McMillan Tac-50 sniper rifle, scoring a kill on a Taliban combatant from 2,657 yards away, breaking the previous world distance record held by an American Marine."

"No shit?" Cornell said.

"Who's Princess Patricia?" Morrison said.

"How do you remember details like that?" Pratt asked, shaking his head.

"He sucks down Omega-3 fish oil like you suck down fruit punch or whatever fruity, kiddy thing it is that you drink," Morrison said.

"It also helped the shooter that we're at fairly high altitude here," Arkin said. The lower air density improves bullet performance. Stretches its effective range." He turned to Cornell. "Can we help you with the firearm identification?"

"That would be great. I'm pretty sure our forensics guy has never so much as seen a weapon like the one used here."

"I think I can get a high-priority turnaround from the lab in Albuquerque. And I'll get you a copy of everything as soon as I get it."

"Perfect."

"Do you have a plat map showing the location of roads in relation to the compound here?" Arkin asked Cornell.

"Yeah, in my car."

Arkin and Morrison examined the map on the hood of Cornell's vehicle while Pratt applied more white zinc oxide paste to his lips. As he rejoined the group by the map, Morrison said, "Cornell, man, your guys need to do a better job securing the crime scene."

"The hell you talking about?"

"Don't get defensive. I'm just saying you shouldn't let Cirque du Soleil performers just waltz around here like this," he said, gesturing to Pratt.

"I just read a thing on the internet about ultraviolet," Pratt said. "They had a picture of a dude with melanoma on his lip. Nasty. You have to really be careful."

"Apparently at the cost of fashion sense," Arkin said. "But thanks for the advice, Marcel."

"Who's Marcel?"

"Pratt, bless your heart," Morrison said. "This Christmas I'm going to get you a forehead tattoo that says 'douche bag.'"

"Yeah, well, we'll see if y'all are laughing when you have sunburned lips tonight."

"Point," Arkin said. "There's nothing funny about sunburned lips."

*****

Arkin, Morrison, and Pratt set off on foot toward a knoll at least 700 yards beyond and a few points east of the spot where Cornell's people were already searching. Pratt lugged an evidence kit in a heavy black duffel. From looking at the map, they knew a dirt road ran behind the knoll, alongside a defunct irrigation canal. As they drew near, Arkin, in the lead, turned so that they were headed for the north side of the knoll, and slowed his pace to a crawl, all the time searching the ground, sometimes dropping to his knees to look at something more closely.

"Are we going to be doing this all day?" Morrison asked. "I'm hungry. Let's go get some tamales at Ren's."

"Just stay behind me."

"You ask me, you're going around your ass to get to your elbow."

"What?"

"Wouldn't it be better if we fanned out?"

"And risk having you trample over evidence like some blind elephant? Anyway, I'm pretty sure I know where to go."

"Why don't you let Cornell's people handle this?"

"That's a good one."

Arkin kept moving, scanning the ground as he went.

"See, this is the type of thing I was alluding to earlier," Morrison said. "Obsessively combing the scrubland in a $1,200 suit and $500 Italian shoes when there are a dozen locals standing around with their dicks in their hands ready to do the same thing isn't the behavior of a quote-unquote burnout." Arkin tried to ignore him. "And maybe more interestingly, your behavior creates a paradox."

"Paradox?"

"Being a type-A, as you are—"

"I'm not a type-A."

"You're a type-A with a capital 'A.' Overachieving. Driven to perfection by an agonizing psychological deficiency need to fill an unfillable—"

"Please," Arkin groaned. "Am I going to have to listen to this all morning?"

"You don't see the paradox?"

"I'm probably missing all kinds of things, being distracted by your babbling."

"It's that your obsessive pursuit of perfection is, in and of itself, a profound personality flaw. An imperfection. You follow me?"

"You're a doctor of logic now."

"See, Pratt, the difference between Arkin and me is I know that nothing we do makes any real difference in the big picture, so I don't care. Whereas Arkin here knows that nothing we do makes any real difference in the big picture, but the poor fool can't let go. It's not his fault though. If you look at his childhood—"

"Please. Please, just give me a few minutes of peace and quiet here to find our firing position, and then we can all go back to our endless bitching about how meaningless everything is."

Pratt looked doubtful. "With all this territory, what makes you think the shooter would have been way out here?" he asked.

"The longer morning shadows afforded by the northwest facing slope, for one thing," Arkin said. "It would have made him harder to spot from the compound. There's also a decent amount of scrub brush for cover, and it's more-or-less downwind of the house."

"Meaning?"

"Meaning the shooter would have had minimal crosswind to contend with in setting up a long-distance shot. And, of course, there's the road behind the knoll. An egress route."

"Elementary," Morrison said.

After another half hour of painfully slow forward progress and sporadic backtracking, Arkin found the firing position marked by scuffing and faint depressions where elbows, knees, and toes had rested on the dirt. The marks had clearly been made by a man lying prone with his head and upper torso raised up on his elbows and forearms. Arkin hung his suit coat on a nearby tree branch, rolled up his shirtsleeves, and began a methodical examination of the area, starting where the toes of the man's boots had scratched small trenches into the earth, and noting every bent twig, every stone that seemed out of place, pointing out each discovery to his companions as he went. Pratt took photos and marked evidence with small, brightly colored flags stuck into the ground.

"There are the marks of a small tripod, there," Arkin said at one point, gesturing toward the ground to his left. "Probably for a telescope and laser range finder."

He searched every inch of ground with his pocket magnifying glass. At one point, he pulled out a set of tweezers to pick up fragments that he guessed were pieces of freeze-dried black beans. At last he reached the area where the gun's bipod would have stood, only to find the dirt brushed to obliterate the bipod's prints. Then Arkin, despite his delicate clothing, lay down on the bare earth in the impression left by the shooter, mirroring the position he thought the shooter had taken, and looked back across the high scrubland toward Egan's compound.

"Come on, Columbo," Morrison groaned, beginning to sound genuinely grumpy. "Let's pick up the pace. I'm starving."

"You could help track the guy's egress instead of standing there like a stroked out ape."

"Well, this stroked out ape has some dime store psychology that might do more to help you."

"Would it hurt your feelings, Bill, if I told you that even after all these years I'm still really not interested in your opinion?"

"Even if you break every case ever assigned to you, you're never going to rid the world of evil. And more importantly, you're never going to fill that bottomless hole in your heart. Those are, as we say in logic, impossibilities. So give it up. You'll sleep better at night."

Arkin, just as hungry as Morrison, turned and glared at him without a word. Despite his rant, Morrison began ferreting out and following the path of the shooter's escape. As he moved off, Arkin used a tape measure to record the length of the impression of the shooter's body, from elbows to toes. Then, as he began a wider grid search of the surrounding area, he saw something that made him freeze. *Oh, no.* Eight inches in front of his face, hanging from a twig of sagebrush, was a long, jet black strand of moderately curly hair. He reached out with his gloved hand, carefully removed the hair from the branch, sat back cross-legged, and stared at it.

"Is something wrong?" Pratt asked.

But Arkin didn't hear him. He stared down at the hair held between his fingers, his mind far away.

"Nate?"

"Hmm?"

"Are you alright? You look like you just saw a ghost."

"This is broken off short of the follicle," he muttered.

"What?"

"Could you hand me an evidence bag please?"

*****

Half an hour later, Arkin had placed several rocks and twigs in evidence bags in the unlikely hope they would yield a useable print. Then, as he was clipping leaves from which he hoped to extract gun powder residue, Morrison came waltzing back up the trail. "Our shooter was a big guy."

"Tell me something I don't know."

"Probably in the neighborhood of six-foot-four and 230 pounds."

"I'll say it again."

"Whatever gun and gear he was carrying probably added a good 40 to 45 pounds to his gross hiking weight. He wears size 13 military boots with moderate wear on the treads. He has high arches and an over-pronated stride. Best I can tell, it looks like he made the round-trip to his firing position four different times over at least a couple of days. His tracks run from here, about a quarter mile, to a dogleg in the dirt road we saw on the plat map. There, he parked his car, a full-size sedan, on a gravel spur that ends at a small abandoned sand pit out of sight of the road. New tires. Brand new."

"A rental car," Arkin said. "And our shooter had moderately curly, long, black hair. By the look of it, maybe Southern European. Maybe Black Irish or Circassian. Maybe Balkan." Arkin tried to beat some of the dirt off the front of his suit pants and shirt. "So, Marcel," Arkin said, turning to Pratt, "what do we deduce from all of this?"

"I don't know."

"We deduce that this guy is big and strong enough to carry a monster of a gun a quarter mile. That he's disciplined. Patient. A thorough planner. That he probably knew the direction of the prevailing winds. That he scouted the target over several days, studied his movements, established the patterns. That he was already prepared to fire at the very moment Egan came out of his house. That he was good enough to fire off two highly accurate shots, including a kill, with what was probably a bolt-action rifle, from more than 1,200 yards out. That he had good enough intel to know the job might call for a heavy, anti-material sniper rifle firing armor-piercing bullets, instead of a more common and lighter anti-personnel rifle firing ball, on account of Egan's armored car. That he was clever enough to lie here for days, take out his target, and then escape, on foot and then in a car, without being detected by anyone, let alone Egan's security detail, which included in its ranks an experienced, though apparently obtuse, military-trained personal security expert. That he knew the imprints left by his bipod might help us narrow down the type of gun he used. That he is a pro, probably military trained. And that he has done this before." Arkin looked up at the blue sky. "Yes, that he has certainly done this before."

"Bravo," Morrison said. "I tell you, Pratt, you should keep your eye on this guy. His cause is futile in the greater scheme, as I so enjoy reminding him. But the son of a bitch is good."

"We should ask about a big guy with long, black, curly hair at all the motels in town," Pratt said.

"He stayed out here," Arkin said. "Ate backpacker's food. Probably slept in the car."

"For days? Well, if he was out here for days, should we look for his urine and feces?"

"You can if you think it will help earn you your Eagle Scout badge. But he probably took it with him."

"Took it with him?"

"Like I said, he's a pro." For a moment, they stood quiet. "But everyone leaves some sort of trail. Maybe he was a local. But I doubt it. And if he wasn't, then he probably had to buy gas somewhere within a 150-or-so miles of here. Maybe he used a credit card."

"That would have been stupid of him."

"It's a balancing of risks. If he paid cash, he would have had to go into a gas station and be seen up close by a clerk, maybe even a security camera. Which option presents the greater risk?"

"I suppose it depends on how memorable the guy is," Pratt said. "If he looks funny or has a foreign accent or something like that."

"Which he very well could. Very good, apprentice. It might be worthwhile to subpoena some credit card data. Run some formulas. Look for patterns."

"Sounds like looking for a needle in a haystack."

"And then we'll cross-reference it against other data."

"What other data?" Morrison asked.

Arkin didn't answer.

FIVE

As they arrived back at their parked cars, Morrison said, "I might run over to McCready's too. Can you give Pratt a ride home?"

"As long as he removes that ridiculous neon eyewear strap and the white mime lipstick."

"You want anything from McCready's, Pratt? Some roasted chilies?"

"No, I'm good. Thanks."

"What about for your wife?"

"She doesn't do spicy."

"Are we still going to the range later?"

"Four o'clock," Arkin said.

"See you boys there."

Arkin and Pratt got in Arkin's G-ride—an old navy blue Crown Victoria, immaculate inside and out. Arkin held the keys in his hand but stared out the windshield without putting them in the ignition, taking a deep breath as he revisited the evidence in his mind, wondering whether the similarities between what he'd seen here and a case from years past, a case that still haunted him, were an unbelievable coincidence or, as he suspected and dreaded, something more.

Pratt sat in the passenger seat, a newly opened bottle of SunnyD orange drink held between his thighs, writing notes on a pad that looked to Arkin like a pink cartoon rendering of a monkey's face.

"What the hell kind of notepad is that? Is that what they're issuing in crime scene kits at DCI these days?"

"You don't know about 'Strawberry Monkey'? It's Kayla's favorite cartoon character. You're out of touch, my friend."

"Very professional."

"She gave it to me for Father's Day, so I have to use it. You'll understand when you—" Pratt choked off his statement. He shook his head and looked down at his own lap. "Sorry."

"It's alright."

A quiet moment passed.

"Oh, I almost forgot," Pratt said, "do you want a cookie?"

"Do I want a cookie?"

"A lady bug cookie." Pratt pulled it from his gun bag—a large, round sugar cookie in plastic wrap, its surface a mass of red frosting with black dots. "Ella baked them yesterday, and Kayla did the frosting. Kayla said I was supposed to give you the ladybug because you caught one for her at the park."

Arkin smiled wearily. "Thanks, but I'm afraid I don't have much of an appetite after seeing Egan's brains blown all over the place."

"Take it home then. You don't want to hurt Kayla's feelings."

"No, I do not." Arkin took the cookie and slid it into his computer bag. "I can't believe she's turning 5 already."

"You guys are coming to the party, right?"

"Wouldn't miss it."

Arkin selected a CD, popped it into the car stereo, and fired up the big 4.6-liter V8 engine. The quiet notes of a Chopin nocturne softened the road noise as they flew back down the country road toward town, passing open rangeland dotted with clumps of brush and scrub trees. But barely a mile on, as Arkin gave further thought to the crime scene, his eyes caught a flash of movement—something small and brown—crossing the path of their car. He stood on the brakes, locking them. The car began to skid sideways. Arkin turned into the slide, regaining control as they came to a roaring stop, gravel flying everywhere, an enormous dust cloud catching up with and enveloping them. He turned to see that Pratt had dropped his bottle of SunnyD as he reached for the dashboard to brace himself, and that most of the beverage had spilled onto his lap. Then Arkin, his heart pounding, frantically scanned the scrubland to the left of the car until he spotted a tiny, limping fawn just as it disappeared behind the trees. It couldn't have been more than a month old.

"Oh, that's nice. My pants are soaked. You out of your mind?"

"There was a baby deer."

"Yeah, I can see that. But why go all Starsky and Hutch like that? We could have gone off the road."

"I'm too good a driver."

"Whatever. That thing wouldn't have even put a dent in your bumper.

And it was limping."

"I didn't hit it."

"I didn't say you did. My point is that it was already injured or born with a birth defect or whatever. And it's lost or was rejected by its mother. So it isn't going to survive anyway."

"You don't know that. It could survive and be just fine. It could prove to be the next Donner or Blitzen."

"Gimpy, reject, motherless, month-old fawns don't survive, city boy. That's a fact of life."

"You don't know that."

"And to think you were smirking at me because of that butterfly."

"Alright, already."

"And why are you being grumpy? I'm the one who got his pants soaked."

"Because I'm starving."

"So eat something."

"I can't. I have to get a damned colonoscopy tomorrow morning."

"What's that?"

"Ask Morrison. He probably gets them for the fun of it." He took a deep breath to settle himself. "And come to think of it, why don't you take a turn driving, young buck. I need to read a file on the way home."

"I'm only five years younger than you."

"Whatever," Arkin said, tossing Pratt the keys. "Drive, Jeeves."

*****

As they drove toward Durango, just passing the entrance to Mesa Verde National Park on Highway 160, Pratt began telling Arkin about a bestselling novel he'd nearly finished, insisting that Arkin read it. *Khyber Recon* was about a Marine recon team that was watching for Taliban crossing into Afghanistan near the Khyber Pass. Pratt described several scenes to Arkin, asking him if the tactics described in the book were accurate and if the action was realistic. One scene involved the team getting pinned down, outnumbered 3-to-1 by a group of insurgents, then forced to retreat into a cave where they found themselves trapped.

"Well, for one thing," Arkin said, "a 3-to-1 ratio of Taliban to recon Marines is still a pretty good ratio as far as the Marines are concerned. So having them be allegedly pinned down and forced to retreat into a cave isn't realistic. But that aside, how did they escape?"

"I don't want to ruin it for you."

"Pratt, I'm not going to read it."

"Why not?"

"For the same reasons lawyers don't read legal novels and doctors don't read medical novels. And anyway, I don't read popular fiction."

"It's a best seller."

"Most best sellers are tripe. And I'll let you in on a dirty little secret. Some of the most popular best seller lists aren't even based on straight retail sales. They're products of corporate influence and rampant industry manipulation. Venerable illusions."

"I'm trying to do you the favor of recommending a good book, and you're thanking me with a lecture on corruption in the publishing industry?"

"I'm not going to read it."

"Alright then. What do you read in your snobby circles?"

"Literature," Arkin said in his best William F. Buckley, exaggerating each syllable.

"Oh, pardon me, but would you have any Grey Poupon?"

"Really, Pratt. Why do you read that crap? It's just cotton candy for your brain."

"I like cotton candy."

"You like war stories? Why don't you read *War and Peace*?"

"Isn't that, like, 10,000 pages?"

"It's epic. A masterpiece. The themes it addresses are timeless."

"Like what?"

"Like that a certain freedom lies in learning the limits of suffering and in the acceptance of death."

Pratt huffed, shaking his head. "Yeah, that sounds great. Sounds like a fun read."

"Suit yourself. Stay in your comfort zone of literary junk food, you Utah philistine yokel. Stay oblivious to the universe all around you. Just do me a favor and don't vote." A moment passed. Then Arkin grinned. "So how do they get out of the cave?"

"I should refuse to tell you out of spite."

"Come on."

"There's an earthquake that opens a new shaft to the surface."

Arkin rolled his eyes. "An earthquake? Really? Exquisite timing."

"You're being sarcastic."

"In my snobby literature circles, John, that's what we call *deus ex machina*."

"Day of what?"

"*Deus. Deus ex machina*. Latin for 'God out of the machine.' It's a plot device for authors who lack creativity. A difficult problem is suddenly and unexpectedly solved by something that comes out of nowhere. Like an amazingly well-timed earthquake that just happens to open an escape shaft for recon Marines trapped in an Afghan cave."

"Maybe it was divine intervention."

"Hence the expression *deus ex machina*. It's as if the author thought, 'wow, I've really written myself into a tight spot here. Now what? Oh, I know—I'll just have God fix everything.' It's too convenient. Too contrived. Lazy writing."

"Whatever."

A moment later, Arkin noticed Pratt casting repeated sidelong glances at him.

"What now?"

"Morrison calling you a law enforcement genius. I've been wanting to ask." Arkin didn't respond. "They were talking about you at last year's recurrent training at Tinker Air Force Base."

"They?"

"Some of the guys. A bunch of us were at lunch at some taco joint in town. They were talking about you like you were a legend."

"*They* tend to exaggerate."

"Said you broke every case ever assigned to you."

"Like I said."

"Said you were being groomed for a top slot, and that you were the director of ops' right-hand man."

Arkin took a breath. "Sheffield and I were close. We had similar backgrounds. He liked that."

"Similar backgrounds?"

"We were both shoved off to boarding school by our overbearing fathers. We both went to Annapolis, 25 years apart anyway. We were both recon Marines, bored lawyers, and finally intelligence officers seconded to DCI from different departments of the Defense Intelligence Agency after 9/11."

He might have added that Roland Sheffield, one-time DCI Director of Operations, deceased, had taken him under his wing from the day he was first interviewed. That they grew so close they went on joint family vacations. That Sheffield had stood in the Arkins' wedding. That he was possibly the first person in the world who had ever told Arkin he was proud of him. That aside from his wife, Hannah, Sheffield was the only person from whom Arkin was certain he had ever felt genuine affection.

"They also said you were the only person in DCI to ever receive the National Intelligence, uh—."

"National Intelligence Distinguished Service Medal."

"Yeah."

"It was a thousand years ago."

"What did you have to do to get that?"

"Have friends in high places."

"Come on."

"The nomination paperwork cited three cases I broke." Arkin shrugged.

"Are you going to tell me what they were?"

"For one, I led a team that broke up a ring of Yemenis who were planning a MANPADS attack at Andrews Air Force Base, presumably targeting Air

Force One."

"MANPADS"?

"Manned portable air defense systems. In this case, the SA-7 Grail, a Soviet-era shoulder-fired antiaircraft missile they'd gotten hold of from a corrupt supply sergeant in the Czech Republic. Lucky for us, the first one they got had a dead thermal battery, and they hadn't been able to find a new one by the time we rolled them up."

"What were the other two cases?"

"One involved a group of white supremacists out in Appomattox, Virginia, who were planning to detonate a car bomb at the Holocaust Museum in D.C. Then I bagged a guy who worked at DARPA—the Defense Advanced Research Projects Agency—who was trying to sell information about a breakthrough surveillance technology to the Iranians—a technology we could use to closely monitor the progress of their nuclear weapons program."

"What was the technology?"

"I could tell you. . . ."

"Forget I asked."

For a few minutes, they drove on in silence. Pratt looked increasingly ill at ease. "So what happened?" he finally asked.

"With what?"

"How did you end up assigned to Durango instead of a corner office on the seventh floor of headquarters? Why didn't you replace Roland Sheffield as director of ops after he died? And why did you quit DCI?"

Arkin's expression hardened. "You surprise me, John Pratt."

"I'm sorry. Forget it."

"No, it's alright. Like I said, it was a thousand years ago. I'm just surprised you've taken this long to ask. We've known each other for years. We work in the same building, and you work for my former agency."

"I didn't think it was my place."

"You're so proper," Arkin said, smiling weakly.

Pratt reconsidered for a moment. "So what happened?"

Arkin's eyes stared straight ahead, down the highway. He sighed. "Politics. Politics happened."

"Politics?"

"And a failure of character. It's a long story."

Arkin was rescued by the ring of his phone. It was Morrison.

"Hey, did you get that call?"

"Call?"

"Turn your radio on. One-fifty-five decimal five-thirty-five. County dispatch says Mesa Verde Park Police are 10-7 after chasing a couple of drunk assholes in a black Dodge Charger who just took a few errant shots at a fellow camper at Morefield. Last seen headed for the main entrance at high speed. You might be able to intercept."

"Why not." Arkin hung up. "Pratt, reach under your seat and grab my radio, would you?"

"Need me to plug it in?"

"I'll do that. You just drive."

"What's up?"

"How's your blood pressure?"

"What?"

"When's the last time you did a high-speed vehicle pursuit?"

A smile broke out on Pratt's face. "You pullin' my leg?"

"We'll see."

"Oh, shit yeah!"

"You Mormons aren't supposed to swear."

Arkin attached the radio to the dashboard bracket, plugged it in, and tuned it to 155.535 MHz. Just as he did, they heard a radio call from a Montezuma County Sheriff's Office helicopter reporting the position of the suspect vehicle.

"That's only a mile ahead of us," Arkin said. "Hit it, Opie." As the car accelerated, Arkin reached into the back seat, pulled a red and blue police light bar from a plastic utility box, and mounted it on a receiver frame on the dashboard. He turned them on a flash setting, then grabbed the radio mic. "Montezuma dispatch, unmarked unit, a dark blue Crown Victoria, dash lights on, is in pursuit eastbound US-160, just passing County Road 44, closing at 115 miles per hour. Air unit in sight."

"Copy that. Be advised, county unit intends to deploy a spike strip at the Highway 140 junction at Hesperus."

"Copy spike strip at Hesperus."

"Did you hear that?" Arkin asked Pratt. "That means you have about 14 miles to bag this guy, or you don't get credit."

"I'll get the son of a bitch."

"There you go again with the cuss words. You're going to have to wear your cilice to bed tonight to make atonement."

"You're thinking of Opus Dei."

"It's all the same to me."

"Which is just one of the reasons you're going to burn in hell."

"Great."

"There he is," Pratt said, pointing through the windshield at the black Charger coming into view, driving along at what looked to be the speed limit, give or take.

"Keep both your hands on the wheel there, Junior."

As the driver of the Charger spotted the police lights speeding toward him from behind, a blue puff of oil smoke in his exhaust gave away his intent to run, and the chase was on.

"You remember how to do a PIT maneuver?"

"I think so."

"Get up alongside him until your front wheel is just behind his back wheel. Ease over until you make contact. Then, when you're happy with your alignment, go hard over. As soon as he starts to lose it, tap your brakes and back off."

"Right."

"Don't wreck my car."

Pratt smiled. As they slowly closed the distance to the fleeing Charger, Arkin pulled a short-barreled Remington 870 shotgun from a rack behind the front seat and began loading it, alternating between 00 buckshot and slugs. Soon, Pratt was steering the front end of the Crown Victoria into the aft end of his quarry. The Charger turned sideways, finally skidding backward and disappearing in a cloud of dust. Pratt brought the Ford to a screeching stop, its nose pointing directly toward the Charger, now off the side of the road, two of its tires stuck in a ditch. Arkin and Pratt threw their doors open and aimed their guns through the gaps between the doors and body of the car as Arkin yelled out commands to the driver and passenger. Complying, the driver dropped his keys out his window. Slowly, the dazed-looking, dust-covered occupants emerged from the vehicle, turned several standing 360s, arms raised, as Arkin visually searched them for weapons, then obeyed Arkin's commands to assume a prone position, face down on the road with their arms out, palms up, legs splayed, and feet pointed outward. Arkin cuffed them and searched them for weapons as Pratt, grinning from ear to ear, covered him with his .45 from the six o'clock position. Panting, his body still quivering, Pratt muttered, "That was fffff—that was awesome."

"Good job not swearing. But don't forget to breathe, cowboy. And keep your finger outside that trigger guard. I only need one anus."

"Fucking awesome."

*****

Having handed their captives over to county officers, they headed back into Durango—an Old West mining and railroad town turned mecca for all things outdoors, situated on the edge of the San Juan Range and straddling the scenic Animas River. A town half-frozen in time, many of the buildings on its picturesque main street dating to the 1800s.

After a brief stop for lunch, and several congratulatory backslaps later, Arkin, Pratt and Morrison were loading three magazines apiece with frangible .40 caliber practice rounds. They had the dusty, outdoor range to themselves, and Pratt had already hung fresh targets. They planned to shoot the standard FLETC course of fire three times, then the shotgun course once. The late afternoon sun glinted off riffles in the Animas River, sliding along down in the valley to their left. The air was dry and unseasonably warm, the musky scent of the high country autumn hanging in the air.

"We gonna make this interesting?" Morrison asked. "I'm wearing my lucky briefs."

"You wear briefs?" Pratt said.

"He's from Mississippi," Arkin said.

"What does my being from Mississippi have to do with it?"

"There's no simple enough way to explain that to you."

Morrison smiled. "Schmuck. Usual wager?" Morrison asked as he slid his full magazines into the holders of his duty belt. "Loser buys the case of beer?"

"Pratt's LDS," Arkin said, playing along.

"Oh, right. Grape soda then?"

Pratt, his earmuffs already on, smiled as he flipped Morrison off from two stalls down. "Come on," he half shouted, deaf as he was wearing his ear protection. "Let's put some lead downrange."

"Shooters, are you loaded for duty-carry?" called the range master through the speakers from the control booth. They each gave a thumbs-up. "Two shots to center mass, one to the head. Shooters ready."

The targets turned 90 degrees to face them. Arkin drew his service sidearm, a Sig Sauer P229, extended his arms, fired three shots, and re-holstered, all in well-practiced movements made fluid by muscle memory. Over the next several minutes, they ran through the entire certification course of fire, shooting in different bursts, from ranges of 5, 15, and 25 yards, practicing emergency reloads, firing from the waist, and firing from a regular frontal stance. When the first round was complete, they removed their ear protection and the range master ran the targets back to the firing line so they could tally up their scores. Morrison rated "expert" on the FLETC scale. In fact, he hadn't missed a single shot. Arkin, who usually had perfect scores as well, had two shots hit outside the 5-ring.

"What the hell is wrong with you today?" Morrison asked, looking at Arkin's target over his shoulder.

"Preoccupied, I guess."

"Preoccupied, my ass. Just once, let me hear you say it."

"Say what?"

"That I'm the better shooter."

"Keep smoking that crack. Delusion is bliss."

"Say it."

"I'm sorry. I can't lie for the sake of your fragile self-esteem."

"Whatever. You're buying the grape soda."

"No, he still beat me by at least 20 points," Pratt said, totaling up his score to learn he rated "sharpshooter."

Morrison took a peek at Pratt's target. He'd fired a tight grouping, but it was centered slightly below and to the left of the 5-ring. "You're jerking the trigger."

"I know I'm jerking the trigger."

"You're not breathing through your eyelids."

"Shut up."

They shot their next three courses of fire, then fooled around with their remaining ammunition—Arkin at one point losing a bet, for a case of beer, that Morrison couldn't hit a nickel they'd taped to a target with one shot of a 12-gauge slug at 15 yards.

"Should we shoot a course with the AR-15s?" Pratt asked as things began to wind down.

"You pervert," Arkin said.

"Didn't bring the AR-15s today," Morrison said.

"Why not? I love those things."

"Didn't want any of your white lipstick to get on them. Anyway, we're practicing entries next Wednesday in Farmington. You'll get your jollies shooting the MP-5."

"Awesome."

Arkin smiled. "Gun freaks."

"Right," Morrison said. "Like you aren't."

SIX

By sunset, the trio was turning off the highway, up the long hill toward Arkin's house. A large, gaudy sign marked the entrance of the woodsy development of relatively new homes set on 10-acre parcels.

"Why do they call your neighborhood 'Beaver Hill'?" Pratt asked.

"Because of all the giraffes."

"Really, though. I've never seen one beaver here."

"I don't know, John. I'll look into it."

They pulled into the recently leveled gravel driveway of Arkin's flawlessly maintained craftsman bungalow. The home was surrounded by a Japanese-style garden of manicured bamboo, red maple, and pine trees, with a stone Toro lantern set among pathways of white sand, pebbles, and steppingstones. As they approached the house along the walkway, the tracks of a dog or large coyote drew Arkin's attention to the otherwise perfectly-raked white sand.

"Shit."

"What's wrong?" Pratt asked.

"I need to go get the rake."

"What did I tell you about people's yards, Pratt?" Morrison said.

It took Pratt a moment to figure out what Arkin was bothered by. "What's the deal?" he asked. "Does everything have to be perfect all the time?"

"Since you ask, this is a Japanese garden, incorporating elements of the

42

Chaniwa and Karesansui styles."

"Obviously," Morrison said.

"The raked sand simulates water, but if the grain is disrupted it ruins the effect."

"It's awfully orderly," Morrison said.

"What are you trying to tell me?"

"It's boring."

"Well, fuck you very much Morrison. Cold beer is in the basement fridge."

As he went around the side of the house to retrieve his imported Japanese rake, he heard Morrison shout, "Hey, good looking!" to his wife, Hannah, after he'd knocked and opened the front door without waiting.

After erasing the offending tracks and returning his rake to its proper rack in the garden shed, Arkin came around the corner to find Pratt reading his book on the front porch as he waited for everyone to join him. As Arkin climbed the steps, Hannah came out the front door. "I think Morrison is fouling our bathroom," she said with a repulsed expression.

Arkin couldn't put a finger on exactly why he thought so, but to his watchful eye, she looked worse. Maybe her skin had grown a touch sallow, or maybe she'd lost more volume in her eyebrows. He wasn't sure. But it worried him.

As Hannah handed a glass of lemonade to Pratt, she asked him, "What are you reading?"

"It's called *Khyber Recon*. It's about—"

"Ah! Spare me."

"You too? You're just like your husband."

"I'll slap you if you're going to insult me on my own front porch," Hannah said with a wink.

"She will," Arkin said, plopping down into a rocker.

"You shouldn't read pop fiction, John. It kills brain cells. If you like war stories, read *War and Peace*."

Pratt smiled. "See, now, that's exactly what your husband told me not two hours ago."

Her eyebrows arched. "Really? Usually I tell people that it's a bad idea to listen to him. But just this one time—"

"Ahhhhhh," Morrison groaned as he emerged from the house, stretching his arms above his head as he came through the doorway. "Lordy bees. That was *the* most satisfying—"

"Bill!" Arkin barked. "Spare us. Just grab a beer and sit down."

Hannah went back inside to work on an appellate brief due to be filed in district court at week's end while the guys sat on the porch looking down-valley to where a short stretch of the Animas River lay in view.

"October blue-wing olive hatch is coming off," Pratt said. "We should fish this weekend. I hear there's good action on the Animas, from the border down to Aztec. Huge rainbows and some nice browns. And the water is high enough that we can do a float."

"I was going to take my horses out and camp somewhere up on the Uncompahgre Plateau, but I could be talked out of it," Morrison said. "Arkin?"

"Hmm?"

"Are you in?"

"For what?"

"Man, where is your Ivy League head today?"

"I attended the United States Naval Academy in Annapolis, Maryland. Perhaps you've heard of it."

"Whatever. Do you want to hit the Animas this weekend?"

"Let me check with Hannah. And only on condition that Pratt promises not to wear his neon lanyard or creepy white lipstick."

"It's sunscreen."

"Sure it is." Arkin went quiet again, staring down at the river slowly disappearing in the twilight. "Hey, Pratt...."

"What."

"Mmmmmm—never mind."

"Come on. What?"

"Have you ever worked an assassination case like this Egan thing since you joined DCI?"

"Are we calling this an assassination already?" Morrison asked.

"No, I haven't," Pratt said. "Why?"

Arkin shook his head and leaned back in his rocker. "I don't know."

"Nate, come on."

"Well, it might be useful for you to look at the file of a similar case. You know, to see how the agency handled it. What investigative techniques were used and so forth. For comparison purposes. Might help."

"Sure," Pratt said before waiting for more. "And?"

Arkin took a deep breath. "Right before I quit DCI, I worked a case that might be good for you to look at. Target name: Bryant. File number 03-125A-MCE."

"You remember file numbers?"

"It was a memorable case."

"Tell me about it."

"Nah. I'm too tired. Read the summary of the electronic file in INDIGO tomorrow, see if you want to use it for reference."

"I will. Thanks."

They sat silently watching the moon rise and listening to coyotes cry to each other across the distant expanse of the darkening valley.

*****

After Morrison and Pratt went home, Arkin went inside to find that Hannah was already asleep. Not wanting to wake her, he added logs to the cast-iron wood-burning stove and poured himself a healthy glass of an exceptional Washington State cabernet sauvignon. Then he queued up the Seattle Symphony's version of the Tallis Fantasia on his stereo, loosened his tie, and kicked off his shoes. He slipped on his noise-canceling headphones, closed his eyes, and sank into his oversized leather club chair to reflect on the day.

Two glasses of wine and a half hour of music later, his thoughts at last left the real world behind. He pictured himself flying just above the jagged and snowy peaks of the San Juan Mountains in the pink dawn light of a clear winter sky, nature's grandeur all around him. The vision stayed with him until he fell asleep in his chair.

*****

Arkin woke close to 3 a.m., undressed, and crawled into bed, feeling his way in the dark. But his anxiety over the Cortez shooting returned with a vengeance, and he couldn't fall back to sleep. Just before 4 a.m., his fidgeting finally woke Hannah. She switched on her reading light, replaced the knit cap that had fallen from her bald head as she slept, propped her hand under her ear and looked at him. He stared at the ceiling.

"Can't sleep?"

"No."

"What's on your mind?"

"That scene we looked at today."

"Cortez?"

"Yeah."

"That bad, huh?"

"No, it's not the shooting, though it was gruesome."

"What then?"

"It brought up memories."

"D.C.?"

Arkin exhaled through his nose. "Yup."

"Nathaniel, that's all behind us. You're a duck. Let the rain roll off your back."

"I know."

"Our lives are so much better now, away from there."

"Yes."

"Why is it on your mind at all?"

"Pratt was asking me about what happened. How we ended up here.

Plus. . . ."

"Plus what?"

"There were some things about the crime scene that reminded me of the Priest."

"Nathaniel."

"I know."

"How many times have we talked about this? You have to let it go."

"I know. I have."

"Except that it's giving you insomnia again." She paused for a moment. "Do you think there's a connection?"

"No. I don't know. There were a few things—maybe too much to discount entirely."

"Really?"

"I don't know. What are the chances? It was years ago, and 2,000 miles away from here."

She turned on her side and massaged his forehead and scalp with her fingers. "Sleep, Nathaniel," she whispered. "Go to sleep."

"What time is your chemo tomorrow?"

"9:30."

"I'll go with you."

"No, Diane is giving me a ride. Go to work and save your leave for our next trip to Kauai." She squeezed his hand. He turned to look at her and she smiled. "We'll go for a month this time. We'll eat coconut-mango shave ice at Joejoe's and seared ahi at Cafe Coco. Then we'll hike to the Kalalau Valley, bathe under the little waterfalls, and pick ripe fruit from the vines and trees. Papaya, mangos, guavas, and passion fruit. Sunny skies, sandy beaches, palm trees, and warm blue water. Focus on that. And then dream about it. Our next trip to Kauai. To paradise." She smiled at him as she closed her eyes.

Arkin kept himself outwardly composed. But on the inside, as he gazed at his wife, ravaged as she was by her illness, his heart was breaking.

SEVEN

The next morning, Arkin stood in his office in Durango, sipping a cup of hot black coffee, looking out his windows, down onto a long curving reach of the Animas River where it was flanked by grassy flats. A kayaker was plying a small stretch of rapids. The gentle piano notes of a Chopin nocturne were barely audible, playing from impossibly small Bose speakers Arkin had bracketed up in each of the four corners of his ceiling. Though it was still early, he was already on his third cup of coffee, trying to revive himself from a near sleepless night.

Aside from the speakers and a gleaming chrome Breville coffee maker, Arkin's office was spartan, his old wooden desk bare but for a keyboard, flat-screen monitor and framed photograph of Hannah from before she lost her hair. He had a simple black chair and an old-fashioned standup coat hanger. On his window sill sat a miniature potted bonsai tree, its dark waxy foliage neatly trimmed into four flawlessly rounded spheroids. On one wall hung a framed, hand-painted map of the Four Corners region. On another, a print depicting the 16th match of the 1985 World Chess Championship between Arkin's favorite player in the world, Garry Kasparov, and Kasparov's long-time rival, Anatoly Karpov.

For the most part, the low-rise building was occupied by small contingents of Forest Service, Department of Energy, and Bureau of Land Management employees. For reasons lost to history, but no doubt having more to do with political favors and pork barrel politics than need, logic, or notions of government efficiency, the building also housed, against all odds, Bill Morrison of ATF, John Pratt of DCI, and Arkin, himself now an employee of the obscure Military Weaponry Administration—the three of them constituting the entirety of federal law enforcement officials stationed in Durango.

Arkin stood in the center of the room, good posture, rigid back, one hand in his suit pocket, the other holding his coffee, watching the kayaker negotiate the rapids as he described the Cortez crime scene, speaking into a wireless microphone he'd clipped to his lapel. Voice recognition software recorded his every word on the computer under his desk. "Firing point approximately 1,320 yards from target. Two shots fired four to five seconds apart. Likelihood of the use of a bolt-action rifle, considered in light of the speed with which two shots were fired, as well as their accuracy, suggests a high level of specialized training. Note to self: compare technique to that of DCI case involving—"

A knock on the door.

"Come in." Pratt poked his head through the door. "Morning, Opie."

"Morning, Andy."

"What can I do for you?"

"I checked INDIGO for that file you were talking about."

"Yes?"

"There's nothing in it. Or almost nothing."

"03-125A-MCE?"

"Target name: Bryant. That's the one. There's a tab for it in the index. But when you click the file open, there's basically nothing in it.

Arkin stood for a moment, his eyebrows furrowed, then removed his microphone. "Show me."

A minute later, they sat in Pratt's tiny, damp basement office, staring at Pratt's INDIGO terminal. On the screen, they looked at an electronic case file cover page. What would normally be an information-filled document describing the vitals of the case record was instead a page of unfilled blanks. At the very top, in the space normally filled by the name of the assigned case officer, was a notation reading "ALL INQUIRIES TO DIRECTOR OF OPERATIONS." With Arkin watching over his shoulder, Pratt scrolled through several other standard sections, labeled "reports of interviews," "evidence log," "grand jury materials," "telephone communications log," "scanned documents," etc.—with the same results. Each section was empty.

"That's odd," Arkin said. "In hard copy, this was an enormous file, with several volumes." He didn't mention that the current director of operations, Tom Killick, was his former colleague, partner, and friend.

"Oh yeah?"

"You know what probably happened here—they were just implementing

INDIGO, just getting it up and running, when I handed this file over. Before that, everything was in hard copy. They probably just have a huge backlog of old cases they still need to manually enter into the system."

"Makes sense."

"I would call Central Records and have them ship the hard copy of the file out to you."

"Is it worth the sweat?"

"It might be. After that, it might be worthwhile to call ViCAP and have them do an ad hoc query for similar cases."

Pratt grinned.

"What?" Arkin said.

"One time Morrison told me ViCAP is about as useful as teats on a bull."

"Yeah, well, bear in mind that Morrison's an ignorant hillbilly chawbacon, despite being an encyclopedia of Southern colloquialisms. Just send them a query."

"For sniper killings?"

"For shootings involving a .50 or other high-caliber rifle, in which the offender was lying in wait, in which no living person witnessed the offender's approach, in which the murder weapon was not recovered, in which the victim was a high-profile figure and Kool-Aid pusher with respect to some sort of extremist religious, political, social, or whatever sort of ideological movement. A victim whose popularity and influence was surging."

"Does ViCAP have that sort of detail?"

"It depends on the officer who submitted the report to ViCAP in the first place. They'll probably have to sift through quite a few cases, looking for unusual characteristics and details described in the textual overviews instead of just running a simple search string with straight variables. It might take them a little while. But give them a chance. They're good."

Pratt stood for a moment. "Do you think I'll even end up having jurisdiction in this one?"

"Don't want to bother?"

"Well, I mean, some local extremist creep, no wife, no kids, gets his head blown off. A hate monger. Who cares, you know? Maybe the shooter did everyone a favor. Anyway, why would I be involved? What's it got to do with terrorism?"

"Get the file, check with ViCAP, and we'll see."

"You don't sound very enthusiastic either."

"Yeah, well, let's just see what we find."

*****

That afternoon, Pratt stuck his head through the office door once again, this time finding Arkin sitting in his chair and staring at his blank computer

49

monitor. "ViCAP already got back to me with two cases."

His words seemed to startle Arkin from a trance. "That was fast."

"They were the only two they could find in the past three years that seemed at all like what you were saying I should look for."

"And?"

"The first one isn't similar as far as technique is concerned, but they sent it to me because of details in the text overview. Victim was a white supremacist in rural Michigan who burned to death in his house two months ago. Body was too toasted for a meaningful autopsy, but the fire was ruled an arson, started with kerosene. At any rate, the guy was an activist. Gaining in popularity. Head of a group of about 500 backwoods troublemakers. Advocated the use of force by the general citizenry for 'defending the constitution.' Plus he had a radio show that was starting to get picked up by redneck radio stations in the Bible Belt."

"Interesting."

"Now, the second case involved an Earth First guy out in Eureka, California. A regional honcho. Local law enforcement listed him as a suspect in a couple of pipe bombings of timber company vehicles. Getting more and more popular on the whacko granola lecture circuit until he was killed two years ago on his morning jog along the high cliffs of the Pacific Coast. But get this: He was sniped."

Arkin closed his eyes, exhaled and slumped forward in his chair as though punched in the gut. "What make of rifle?"

"Don't know. The locals didn't recover the bullet. The guy was shot when he stopped on the pinnacle of the trail for a breather, a bong toke, or whatever. Shot came from the east, so the locals figured the bullet flew out to sea. But they guessed it was of an awfully high caliber based on the size of the partially intact entry hole in the victim's skull."

"Have you sent out your credit card data subpoena yet?"

"No."

"Amend it to include the areas around these two killings, covering a period a week before and after each of them. Give it at least a 200-mile radius."

"Are you my boss now?"

"Your role model."

"Isn't this subpoena a bit overbroad?"

"It's legal. The data is relevant. Just limit your request to the card numbers, and the locations and dates of the transactions. If we identify a link, we can go back and ask for details on the account holders later."

"You think an AUSA will sign off?"

"Pratt, if you're worried about it, take it to Bramwell."

"Bramwell? Doesn't he mostly do civil side now?"

"Please. He still has a 'remember 9/11' flag flying from a 50-foot pole in his front yard. Just use the phrase 'possible links to terrorism' in your request. He'll sign off." Pratt looked dubious. "Look, we aren't asking for a truckload of documents to randomly fish through here. It's all electronic. If the clearinghouses or payment processors balk, we'll get a court order. My only concern is that their data might not go back far enough to capture the California information. Though in this day and age of endless terabytes of storage and automated backups, it certainly should. So get that subpoena out the door today, young man."

"Subpoena to AUSA Bramwell. Aye-aye, captain."

Morrison appeared in the doorway, empty coffee cup in hand. "Bramwell? Don't go to that chicken head."

"Why not?" Pratt said.

"He's the type of guy who would spend $500 for a bus ticket when he could spend $50 for one that would get him to the same place."

"Huh?"

"Morrison means he's a talker."

"I mean he never shuts his mouth. Takes 10 years to make a simple point. Drives me to tears."

"Pratt has a lot more patience than you do. Now, why don't you just help yourself to a perfect cup of aged Sumatra coffee, brewed at exactly 205 degrees, with a carafe temperature of exactly 195," Arkin said, smiling as it occurred to him that Hannah would call him an ass for being so pedantic.

"Only if it's at exactly 195." Morrison poured a cup, sipped, and sighed. "Damn, Nate. Anal or not, you brew a damn good pot of coffee."

"Where have you been all day?"

"Had to go over to Pagosa Springs to interview some asshole claiming his neighbor was running a still."

"Was he?"

"He was home-brewing beer. Needless to say, these neighbors aren't the best of friends. Sounds like it all started when one guy's dog started shitting in the other guy's yard."

"How mundane."

"Yeah, well. We still up for fishing on Saturday?" "Definitely," Pratt said.

"I'm out," Arkin said.

"Come on. Don't be a boarding school wuss."

"Hannah had chemo again today."

"Oh."

"I'll catch you next time."

*****

Just past 3 a.m., Arkin woke to the sound of retching. He scrambled from bed to find Hannah sitting on the tile floor next to the flushing toilet, bile dribbling from the corner of her mouth.

"Oh. Oh, no." He grabbed a washcloth, dampened it with warm water, and knelt down to gently clean her mouth.

"Help me back to bed."

"Are you all done?"

"I think so. For now."

*****

As they lay in bed, Arkin clenched his fists so hard his knuckles were white. They were both wide awake now.

"Ella Pratt told me the guys are going fishing tomorrow," Hannah said. "Why don't you go relax and have some fun."

"There is no way in hell I'm leaving you here by yourself."

"Diane is coming over."

"I'm not leaving you. You might need help. You might need someone to get you a glass of water or walk you to the bathroom."

"Diane can do all that."

"No."

"Listen, having you moping around all stressed out doesn't help me. If anything, it makes it worse. Diane and I are going to lie on the couches and watch chick flicks all day. It's just what I need. It'll help me get my mind off the nausea. And then I'll feel better, okay? It's just chemo. It'll get better. Go fishing. Have fun. Drink some cold beers with the guys and relax. You have to relax. I'll be okay."

I'll be okay. That was exactly what she'd said to him after he'd broken the news that he was being, in effect, banished from Washington, D.C., to Durango. She'd been a partner in a major law firm. Highly respected. A big gun. Yet she'd given it all up without a hint of regret—the career she'd worked so hard for—to follow him to this remote Colorado mountain town where she had no connections, status, or power. Where hardly anyone knew anything about her.

I'll be okay, she'd said. *Let's focus on you*, being the unspoken part of her message. And she *had* focused on him. She'd held his hand through the whole thing. The derailment of his career. The smoldering anger. The humiliation. She'd helped him de-emphasize his career, appreciate the beauty of what they had, and find a new sense of purpose in life. She'd helped him forget the city and open his eyes to the grandeur of nature—the mountains, rivers, woods, and high desert—in the Four Corners. Over time, though he'd always said as much, the focal point of his life honestly and truly became her. She became his main reason for living, and he wondered what he'd ever done to deserve her.

"By the time you get home with all your fish, I'll probably be feeling better and we can take a nice walk down along the river."

He took a huge breath. "Okay."

Hannah eventually fell back to sleep, but Arkin remained wide awake, unable to unwind. He thought about what fishing gear he'd need to assemble in the morning. Fly fishing always reminded Arkin of Roland Sheffield, not only because it was something Sheffield taught him to do, but more so because it had come to stand as a sort of symbol of the part Sheffield had once played in his life. And right on cue, Arkin's memory wandered back to a windowless government conference room in Washington, D.C., where a skeptical intelligence oversight panel sat listening to Sheffield's emphatic plea that Arkin, a junior agent sitting just behind him at the long table, be named lead agent of a major investigation involving a terrorist cell that was plotting a machine-gun attack on commuting employees queued up at the front gate of the National Security Agency headquarters in Fort Meade, Maryland.

"I'll remind you that it was Agent Arkin who did *all* the footwork, found and recruited our key informant, and developed the intelligence that put us onto this group in the first place," Sheffield said. "Add to that the fact that he's a Naval Academy grad, a lawyer, a decorated recon marine, and, by the way, has enough brains in his skull to be a bona fide chess master. What the hell more could you people possibly want?"

"Investigative experience," one of the others muttered in a tone that suggested he was near surrender.

"Well, believe me, this is one of those times when brains, fire in the belly, and sheer ability trump experience," Sheffield answered. "Speaking of experience, in my experience, experience often equates to complacency. Come count the number of rotund specimens around the conference table at the two o'clock case managers meeting this afternoon." The panel was silent. "Look, I believe in him. That should be good enough for you."

Five weeks later, a day after Arkin's team rolled up the entire cell, disrupting a major terrorist plot and chalking up seven federal indictments in the process, Arkin stood in Sheffield's corner office with its peek-a-boo view of the Washington Monument. Sheffield had just spent five minutes gushing about how proud he was of Arkin. How he'd taken a gamble on him, and his gamble had paid off beyond his wildest dreams. "So what do you want?" Sheffield asked.

"What do I want?"

"You just broke the biggest case our fledgling outfit has ever seen. You get a reward. What do you want? A bonus? A choice assignment? Some time off?"

Arkin thought for a moment. "I'd like to try fishing."

"*Try* fishing?" Sheffield said with a smile. "You've never been fishing? And you call yourself an American?"

Despite himself, Arkin had winced. "My father. . . ." He'd held his tongue. But his mind had kept going. *Never took me fishing. Never played catch with me. Never came to watch my baseball games or chess matches or piano recitals. Not once. He was always too busy growing his empire, of which I was nothing more than a subsidiary, only valued to the extent that I made the emperor look good.*

Sheffield had stared, his expression changing from teasing to sympathetic. Even to understanding. "I'll take you myself."

And he did. Well before dawn on the very next Saturday, he picked Arkin up from his apartment—the back of his SUV loaded with fly fishing gear, bags of salami sandwiches, and a cooler of beer—and drove him out to a tributary of the Shenandoah River that flowed off the Blue Ridge. Two hours later, they stood, each in a pair of Sheffield's hip waders, in shin-deep water.

"This is a blue-ribbon trout stream," Sheffield said. "Or so they say. Fishing tackle shop owners are a bit like political appointees. They tend to tell you whatever they think you want to hear."

"So which of these do I use?" Arkin asked, picking through a small box of artificial flies.

"Get that little tan-colored one in the lower-left corner. That's a caddis. I've had good luck with those out here this time of year. You know how to tie an improved clinch knot?"

"Remember, Roland, I was deprived of a normal American boyhood. I don't even know how to tie an *unimproved* clinch knot."

Before long, Arkin, with Sheffield's close supervision and constant instruction, was casting out into the creek.

"An easy way to start is with what they call the ten o'clock to two o'clock casting arc. But really, the key to a tight loop and accurate casting is to make sure your rod tip is traveling straight, and that you're patient and let the line roll out behind you before you cast forward."

Despite Sheffield's simple instruction, Arkin kept starting his forward casts prematurely.

"Patience, Nathaniel. And a lighter touch wouldn't hurt. We aren't whipping the bulls of Pamplona here."

Arkin tried again, his cast landing short, his line falling from the air in random curves.

"You're jerking. Again, smooth acceleration to an abrupt stop."

Eventually, Sheffield rigged another rod and began fishing himself, just downstream from Arkin. They fished for two hours, twice pausing to change flies, Sheffield landing half a dozen fish, Arkin not getting so much as a nibble. Finally, as Arkin began to get into the groove, began to feel as though his casts were landing where he wanted them to, his fly disappeared from the surface with a small splash. He raised his rod tip as Sheffield had instructed, only to see it bend downward from the pull of a fighting fish.

"I have one!"

"You're supposed to say 'fish on.'"

"Fish on!"

"Good. Take it slow."

"I think it's big. Look how the pole is bending!" Arkin half laughed, grinning from ear to ear, feeling every bit of the fight through the light three-weight rod.

He reeled in and brought his rod tip over to where Sheffield waited with a net. Sheffield scooped into the water below his fishing line and pulled out what Arkin first took to be a small stick. *He missed him*, Arkin thought.

"A whopper!" Sheffield said, pulling the fish out of the net by the shaft of the tiny hook caught in its lip. He held out an olive-colored trout, with distinctive red and yellow spots, that couldn't have been more than four inches long. Arkin wondered how the thing had even fit the hook in its mouth.

"That, young Nathaniel, is a beautiful specimen of *Salvelinus fontinalis*, better known as the eastern brook trout."

"It's smaller than I expected."

"Well, now. You could do worse for a first fish. Mine was nothing but a damned grass carp. Be proud."

"Proud?"

"Let's have a celebratory beer and salami sandwich."

They'd spent the next hour sitting on boulders next to the stream, trading Naval Academy stories. Trading war stories. Talking about favorite movies, restaurants, wines, and bourbons. They even touched on the fact that they'd each, as children, been more or less ignored by semi-absentee fathers who largely neglected their emotional needs. Arkin was surprised at how much they had in common. To his astonishment, Sheffield was even an avid chess player, and, like Arkin, essentially idolized Grandmaster Garry Kasparov. They pledged to play each other at least once a week, perhaps over lunch on Fridays.

They fished more, drank more beer, and eventually got back in Sheffield's car and drove up onto Skyline Drive to watch the sun set from a nearby viewpoint just inside Shenandoah National Park.

*****

The sound of distant thunder brought Arkin back to the present. He got out of bed, slipped on a robe, and went down to the desk in the finished section of their basement. There, he pulled a large leather-bound photo album off a high shelf. He clicked on his reading lamp, sat down at the desk, and began flipping pages until he found what he was looking for—a spread of pictures he and Hannah took during a weekend trip to the Sheffields' beach house in North Carolina's Outer Banks. There they all were, in happier times—Arkin, Hannah with a full head of beautiful hair and glowing skin, and the late Mr. and Mrs. Sheffield, she in white linen, he in a seersucker suit—grazing over a large silver platter of clams casino and oysters on the half shell, strolling a sandy Nag's Head beach at sunset, standing on the balcony with the Atlantic surf crashing across the beach behind them, raising their wine glasses in a toast, all smiles. The wine, Arkin recalled, had been a Haut-Brion '82—a superb vintage from one of the Premiers Crus of Bordeaux—that Sheffield brought out of his cellar to celebrate Arkin having just rolled up the terrorist cell planning the MANPADS attack at Andrews Air Force Base. It had paired perfectly with Claudia Sheffield's beef Wellington—a dish that Roland confided was her signature.

It all couldn't have been more than seven years ago. But so much had changed since. What he wouldn't give to go back. To have everyone back, happy and healthy.

He stared at one shot in particular—a close-up of Sheffield, taken by Hannah—that he always thought really captured his old boss's essence. It was the expression on his face. One of deep intelligence, compassion, empathy. He was one of those rare birds who could see things in you that you couldn't even see for yourself. He got people. Understood what made them tick. Saw their hidden strengths and weaknesses. Knew how to help them heal their wounds.

Hannah had taken the photo just before he and Sheffield had a long discussion in the study while the ladies cleaned up from dinner. In the photo, Sheffield sat smoking a Dominican cigar at his teak desk with an original Brinkman oil painting of the frigate U.S.S. Constitution hanging on the wall behind him. Arkin remembered sitting on the brown leather couch, a 20-year-old Islay Scotch with three ice cubes in a crystal tumbler in his hand. They'd ended up discussing their relationships with their late fathers—Sheffield's a rear-admiral, Arkin's a federal judge. Sheffield was surprisingly forthcoming about his tumultuous relationship with his own father. But what really stuck in Arkin's memory was Sheffield's certainty that the late Judge Hon. David Arkin—however hard, however demeaning he might have been, however warped and driven to cruelty by his own self-esteem issues—had been very proud of his son. Arkin could rest assured that, deep down in his heart, his father had loved him. "Trust me on this," Sheffield had said, though he'd never met Arkin's father. "You're as much as anyone could ever want in a son. If I'd had a son, I'd want him to be you."

Arkin remembered that his abdomen had clenched as he tried to stifle its convulsion—tried to stifle the cathartic sob that wanted, so badly, to come out. It was as close as he'd come to crying in many years. Sheffield's words had filled him with both great, body-warming joy and heavy, dark sadness. He didn't know which way the surge of emotion would take him, and he found the lack of control profoundly disconcerting. "I love that painting of the Constitution," he'd said, gesturing toward the wall behind Sheffield, desperate to change the subject, his voice tight.

Sheffield, no doubt knowing exactly what Arkin was thinking, had nodded. "Why don't you pair that scotch with a nice cigar from the humidor on the shelf there while I go tie down the kayaks for the night?"

EIGHT

Arkin was just emerging from the front door, fishing tackle in hand, when Pratt pulled into the driveway in his truck. Hannah came out onto the porch to see them off. She was wearing her brunette wig, which wasn't too far off her pre-chemo hairstyle. But Arkin still didn't think it looked right, probably because her eyebrows were almost gone.

"John, you tell that little princess of yours that we loved her ladybug cookie," she shouted down to them.

Pratt smiled and tipped his hat. Arkin threw his gear in the bed and they set off for Morrison's house, deep in the forest, several miles up Florida Road.

"Why doesn't the ape meet us down in town?" Arkin asked. "We're just going to have to double back."

"No big deal. It's my turn to drive anyway."

Morrison lived in an honest-to-goodness log cabin that he'd built himself. A simple affair of rough-hewn logs, thick chinking, a few square windows and a simple tin roof. It was only four finished rooms and a basement, but he'd built a separate garage at the top of his driveway, set back 100 feet from the road. Around the back, he'd built a corral for his two horses—one Arabian, one mustang caught by the Bureau of Land Management and auctioned off. It was isolated, but that was how he liked it.

Pratt and Arkin parked the truck and followed the sound of Morrison talking to his horses around back to find him working with his Arabian, a beautiful dark brown stallion. A magnificent horse of a quality Arkin had rarely seen. On its flank was an odd, swooping brand that looked to Arkin like a modified character from the Persian alphabet. Morrison was standing on the lowest board of his four-board fence, brushing the stallion's mane with one hand, feeding it a carrot with the other.

"That's a beautiful horse," Pratt said.

"Thank you," Morrison said after spitting what looked like half a cup of tobacco juice out of the corner of his mouth.

"Where did you get it?"

"Texas."

Pratt stepped forward for a closer examination. He ran his palm down the animal's impressive shoulder, then along its body until his hand came to the brand which he partially traced with his index finger. He grinned. "Texas, my ass."

Morrison grinned too. "You're not half as dumb as you look, Spanky."

"Are you ever going to plant anything in this weed patch of yard?" Arkin asked. "Couple of rose bushes? Anything?"

"Rome wasn't built in a day."

As they made their way to the front of the house, Arkin spotted a powder blue toilet lying on its side in the back of Morrison's old pickup, strapped down with yellow nylon cargo webbing.

"What's with the toilet?"

"That's no mere toilet, sir."

"No?"

"It's a 1975 American Standard Cadet with a 3.4-gallon flush. Made in the U.S. of A."

"Do I even need to ask?"

"I take it you aren't privy to the dirty little secret of the 1992 Energy Policy Act."

"Enlighten me."

"It made it unlawful to install toilets using any more than 1.6 gallons of water per flush. And that, sir, simply will not do."

"For some of us."

"The Act forced normally upstanding but large-coloned people to literally smuggle new toilets in from Canada."

"So it's contraband."

"It's the Cuban cigar of shitters. And the law is unconstitutional on its face, since it discriminates against the large-coloned."

"So now the large-coloned are a constitutionally protected class."

"As the founding fathers intended. Benjamin Franklin had a huge colon."

"Really?" Pratt asked.

"It's time we came out of the shadows and held our heads high."

"Good for you," Arkin said.

"You're being sarcastic."

"Me?"

"You're mathematically inclined. Let me ask you something. If you can flush a 3.4-gallon toilet once, but have to flush a 1.6-gallon toilet three times, who's winning if we go with the 1.6? Mother Nature or the robber barons of the toilet water industry?"

"An excellent question. Did you go to Canada for this?"

"Some 34-year-old retired Microsoft millionaire from Seattle is remodeling a Victorian down on 3rd. I salvaged it."

"A decades-old used toilet."

"That's right."

"You're a very strange man, Morrison."

"Compared to you?"

"Can we go fishing?" Pratt said.

*****

They put in at the end of a dirt road a few miles south of the New Mexico-Colorado border, dragging Pratt's river dory down to the left bank of the Animas, loading their fishing tackle and a cooler of food and beverages, then shoving off. The river ran swift in this stretch, but Pratt was an experienced boatman and guided them around several hazards before the water widened and slowed. They floated past a handful of small, dusty, fenced-in pastures, then pulled off at a right bank sandbar under a rocky ridge a quarter mile downriver from the put-in. There, they popped open some beers and fished a riffle after tying small blue-wing olive flies to the ends of their lines. The water was cold and clear, and the air smelled of dried wild grasses. Before long, they'd each landed a rainbow trout—Morrison's a whopping 22 inches long. As it was another unseasonably warm day, they were soon wearing nothing but T-shirts under their chest waders. At one point, Morrison lost his footing and fell in. After that, he wore nothing but the waders while waiting for his shirt to dry on a convenient tree branch. Pratt spotted a tattoo on his left shoulder. It was a small dagger with the number "86" written next to it.

"So what's the story with that tattoo?" Pratt asked.

Morrison turned completely around, revealing his right shoulder. It bore the letters USMC. Morrison looked down at it, then up at Pratt. "You really don't know what that means?"

"The other tattoo, wise guy."

"What other tattoo?"

"What do you mean 'what other tattoo'? The one on your other shoulder. Right here," he said, gesturing to the same spot on his own shoulder.

"Oh, that. I don't know."

"Come on."

"Ah, some guys talked me into getting it when I was really drunk. I don't even remember why."

"Bull."

Morrison didn't respond. His face had taken on a certain hardness. Pratt let it go.

Three beers later, Arkin hiked up the riverbank to urinate, and then, his curiosity getting the better of him, climbed the steep slope of rocks and eroded soil, up toward the top of the ridge, to get a better look around. The higher he climbed, the wider the blue sky became, and the better he began to feel—about everything. He wasn't normally given to sentimentality, but had to admit that moments like this one—where he was surrounded by the grandeur of the deep blue sky above, the crystal clear river winding through the valley below, breathing in warm air laden with the aroma of the sagebrush and dry wild grasses of the high open country stretching to the horizon in every direction—filled him with an undeniable sense of awakening. Sharpened his perceptions.

As he pushed his way through a dense thicket of sage and rabbit bush near the top of the slope, he came upon a bare rock face veiled in deep shadow just below the overhanging rim of the canyon. On it was a pictograph, remarkably well-preserved. He'd long known the area was rich with such archaeological marvels, but he'd never before seen a pictograph that wasn't cordoned off in a well-trodden park or preserve and explained by a plastic placard. The immediate surroundings of this one probably hadn't changed much in a thousand years. And while he was sure he wasn't the first Anglo to see it, given all the nearby farming and ranching activity, and given the popularity of this stretch of the Animas with local trout fishermen, he was still genuinely awestruck by his discovery.

It was a painting of people. A group of them, maybe one-third life size. Long, dark, shadowy figures. There was very little detail to them—just elongated bodies and rounded heads. No limbs or facial features. But at the center of the group, a taller figure stood out, its body decorated with broad vertical and zigzagging stripes, its dark head adorned with two pair of protruding, antennae-like spokes that could have been a crown or symbol for beams of light. The eyes of the tall figure caught and held Arkin. They were large, round, and empty, devoid of pupils or irises. But red. A glowing, menacing red. And despite the many centuries the painting had no doubt withstood sun, wind, rain, and snow, the red paint of the tall figure's eyes was still sharp. Taken as a whole, the dark figure did not look the least bit kind or happy. If anything, he looked threatening. Not necessarily angry, but cold and dangerous. Cold, despite the red color of his eyes.

Who was he? He looked to be someone of great importance. Perhaps a great chief, a god, or an Anasazi holy man—a priest.

61

Arkin returned to the river, told Pratt and Morrison of his discovery, and led them back up the ridge for a look. After that, they ate a riverside lunch of salami sandwiches, apples, and cheese, then shoved off to find a fresh spot to fish further downstream. As they drifted along, the wall of the ridge on the right bank grew sheer and drew closer until it was no more than a dozen yards from the river's edge. Up near the rim, faces of bare rock, undercut by many millennia of erosion, formed large overhangs. And as they navigated a curve in the river, a short box canyon opened on their right, running straight off the apex of their turn, revealing an unusually large, smoke-stained overhang in its far rim, maybe sixty yards from the boat. In the shadow of the overhang, Arkin spotted a small cluster of cliff dwellings tucked up in a sheltered horizontal crevice. Anasazi ruins, many hundreds, perhaps even thousands of years old, built of stone and mud, their short, narrow doorways impenetrably dark. Perhaps one of them was the ancient home of whomever had painted the pictographs upriver.

As they floated by the ruins, Arkin pondered what had become of the once vast and complex culture that gave rise to these structures. Their kivas, cliff dwellings, villages, and far-flung trading centers. What had happened to the Anasazi? Where had they gone? What became of their chiefs, holy men, heroes, and great thinkers? Their many thousands of families? Their religious clans and gods? All their names and faces, the stories of their struggles, triumphs, and tragedies, now lost to time. Nothing but scattered pockets of sad, crumbling shelters to indicate that they—the thousands and thousands of them—ever even existed.

Arkin stared up at one of the short, dark doorways, wishing his eyes could see through the blackness. He'd always wondered at these doorways, standing silent, open, and ominous. It was easy to imagine that one could step through them and into another world, as if they were the very portals through which their long vanished builders disappeared so many centuries earlier, perhaps leaving this dry country for one of lush green lands. Perhaps the other world was looking back through the dark doorways at him. But Arkin was a rational man, a skeptic, not at all inclined to embrace superstition—and he already knew better. On one of those rare occasions when he'd let the last vestiges of his subconscious not yet yellowed by cynicism to run wild, he'd fallen for it, risking his neck climbing up to such ruins, full of illogical hope that he would find something—some amorphous thing that he no longer had the fortitude to dream about. He'd poked his head through the doorways, only to discover, in each instance, empty rooms. Empty rooms of crumbling masonry, rodent droppings, and dust, long since stripped of anything else by grave robbers and looters. And the longer he'd lingered, the emptier the rooms had seemed, and the more he'd felt it likely that the vanished Anasazi had simply been wiped out by disease, starved out by drought, or had pillaged the land until it could no longer provide the resources to sustain their population and had moved on, dispersing across the region in fractured and diminished bands, perhaps following the ancient Animas down to greener country. He recalled how strangely lonely these thoughts had made him feel.

*****

When they were done fishing, Morrison volunteered to jog back up Highway 550 to recover the truck, and by midevening, they were back in Durango. After a quick dinner, Arkin eating a bowl of cornflakes, Hannah drinking a smoothie, Arkin drove Hannah down to Schneider Park for the promised stroll along the river. Hannah was still feeling the effects of chemo, and her pace was slow. But it was a pleasant walk all the same, Arkin just happy to be with his wife.

As they walked along, silent, hand-in-hand, Arkin remembered how, when they first moved to Durango, he would stroll this very trail almost every day, watching the swift-moving river, amazed at the idea that these very waters flowed on for hundreds and hundreds of miles, merging into the San Juan, then the Colorado, running through the Grand Canyon, and on out to the Gulf of California and Pacific Ocean. Thinking about it had always comforted him, but for reasons he never fully understood. Then, one gray and dismal afternoon, Morrison told him the awful secret: sapped by irrigation and drinking water systems in Arizona, Nevada, and California, the mighty Colorado River trickled to a brackish dead end in a lonely basin of dusty Mexican desert. It did not make it to the sea. When Arkin learned this, he didn't sleep for three days.

NINE

"Put on your vest and strap on your pistola," Pratt said as he intercepted Arkin in the hallway on his way out to the parking lot at the end of the day.

"And why would I want to do that?"

"Because Cornell found our man," he said, thrusting a sheaf of printouts into Arkin's hands.

"Cornell?" Arkin asked as he began flipping through the papers. "Get real."

"One of his guys was canvassing the town of Green River, Utah, yesterday. Gas station attendant remembered a guy gassing up in the late morning the day of the Eagan shooting."

"Yeah?"

"Well over six feet tall. Long, curly, black hair, and a funny accent. He was wearing a hat pulled low, dark sunglasses, acting all squirrelly. Look here." Pratt turned to a page consisting of three black-and-white security camera images. One was of the suspect sitting in his sedan in the fueling bay. It was taken from overhead, and the man's face was blocked from view by the roof of his car. But through the windshield, the camera had caught a picture of a large chin flanked by long, curly, dark hair. The other two images consisted of a view of the man from behind as he exited the station's mini-mart—unremarkable aside from helping establish his height—and, critically, a blow-up of his car's license plate.

"Whose car is it?"

"DMV sheet is in there."

"Come on."

"Paul Milford. Portland, Oregon. Age 35. Height 6-foot-4. Black hair. Weight 285."

"He doesn't weigh 285 in this photo."

"Maybe he goes to Weight Watchers now. NCIC has him down for two arrests for public indecency."

"Of what flavor?"

"Doesn't say."

Arkin examined the rest of the documents as Pratt stood waiting. "Hmmm."

"'Hmmm,' what? We going to have a word with this guy or not?"

"In Oregon?"

"He's at a motel in Walsenburg."

"Walsenburg, Colorado?"

"No, Walsenburg, Germany, genius."

*****

Three hours later, Pratt and Arkin—wearing body armor, but in plain clothes—sat in Arkin's unmarked car on the edge of the dark parking lot of a dusty, 1950s-era Walsenburg motel, having just arrived from Durango, their eyes locked on the door and window of Paul Milford's room. Milford's sedan was parked in front of his door. Dim light could be seen around the edges of the drawn blackout curtains. Three local patrol cars were parked just out of sight on the street fronting the motel. Each held three members of the local county's special reaction team, in full tactical gear. Cornell and one of his deputies were in another unmarked car parked in front of the motel office, just within sight of Milford's door.

"Manager told Cornell that Milford's been there a week," Pratt said. "They haven't seen him leave his room."

"At all?"

"Nope."

"Interesting."

"Interesting, he says. I'll tell you what else is interesting. This body armor is gonna be about as good as tissue paper against .50 caliber armor-piercing bullets."

"Well, let's not give him time to set up."

"Shouldn't we let the SRT guys take him down?"

"I have a gut feeling we should just try talking to him first."

Pratt looked doubtful. "Talking to him?"

"Yes."

"You're the law enforcement genius."

As Pratt said this, the light in Milford's room went out. Then his door opened, but only an inch.

"Are you guys seeing this?" Cornell asked over the radio.

Arkin keyed the mic of his radio. "We're on it." Then, to Pratt, "Let's go."

Pratt radioed the other units that they were initiating contact. They each chambered rounds into their guns and re-holstered them, got out, shut their doors as quietly as they could, then crossed the parking lot as Milford's door clicked shut again. As they reached Milford's sedan, Pratt placed a large wooden chock behind the right rear tire while Arkin scanned its interior and ran his hand over the hood to see if it was warm from recent use. It was cool. Reaching the door to Milford's room, they stood to either side of it, ready for action but doing their best to look nonchalant. The air smelled of cigarette smoke. Pratt knocked.

"Who's there?" someone asked. Something about the voice struck Arkin as unusual. But it wasn't an accent. It had more to do with the tone.

"Police," Pratt answered.

"Hold on."

The door opened a crack. Nervous, yellowed eyes peered out at them.

"You're police?"

"Yes, sir," Pratt answered, pushing the door open wider to reveal a tall, slouching, anxious looking man with sallow skin and long, dark, curly hair tied back in a ponytail. He held a half-burned brown cigarette in his hand, wore pink terrycloth slippers, a cherry-red silk robe embroidered with flowers, and ruby stud earrings in each ear. The air that flowed through the open doorway was humid and smelled of iodine, expensive cigarettes, and some type of cheap perfume. Arkin thought he recognized Lucille Ball's voice coming from the antiquated tube television set. As he processed the scene, he turned to see Pratt looking utterly revolted—almost to the point of anger. Milford saw it too, and his face betrayed a sudden terror.

"You don't look like cops," he said, his voice tense, as he took a step back.

Programmed by training, as Milford stepped back, Pratt stepped forward. At this, Milford's eyes went wide. He dropped his cigarette and began reaching behind his back.

"Gun!" Pratt shouted as he sprang forward. In seconds, they had Milford disarmed, in handcuffs, and flat on his belly, Arkin having wrenched a small, stainless steel, fake pearl-handled .25 caliber semiautomatic from the man's hand as he'd tried to pull it from the silk belt around the back side of his robe. Milford was moaning as if in great pain.

"What's your problem, pervert?" Pratt shouted, his knee pressed into the small of Milford's back as he held tight to the handcuff chain.

As Arkin radioed Cornell and the locals to move in, he scanned the room, seeing clear evidence of an extended, shut-in stay. Empty boxes of Chinese delivery. Empty cans of generic diet soda. Full ashtrays and empty cigarette packs. Clothes—women's clothes—flung about. On the dresser, half a dozen open prescription bottles of pills.

"Didn't see the 'no smoking' signs, right friend?" Pratt asked, his voice still loud, now dripping with sarcasm. "And I'm sure those are all legal prescriptions."

"I'm recovering from surgery," Milford said meekly.

Arkin rose, walked over to the dresser, and began examining the bottles of pills as Cornell and the locals came in. A painkiller, an antibiotic, an anti-inflammatory, two drugs Arkin didn't recognize, and a bottle of estrogen capsules. Each bottle with a legitimate looking prescription label, bearing Milford's name, from a pharmacy in Trinidad, Colorado, 40 miles to the southeast.

"John," Arkin said. "John, ease off."

"Why?"

"What's that smell?" Cornell asked, helping Pratt raise Milford to his feet. Pratt came over to where Arkin was examining the medicine. A quart-sized specimen jar stood at the back corner of the dresser. It was filled with an amber liquid in which floated something Pratt thought looked like cherrystone clams.

"What's this?" Pratt asked, picking it up.

"That's me, asshole," Milford said, sounding equal parts resigned and agonized.

As the wires connected in Pratt's brain, he slammed the jar down, looking nauseated. "Why do you have this?"

"Religious reasons. My whole body is supposed to be present at burial when I die."

"The hell whacko religion is that?" Pratt asked, turning a venomous stare toward Milford.

"The Long Island Congregation of—"

"Never mind, never mind," Pratt moaned, rolling his eyes and holding his palms up.

"John," Arkin said, placing a hand on Pratt's shoulder. "Let's go for a walk. You look a bit disconcerted."

"I look what?"

"Come on. Let's get you some air."

*****

Pratt and Arkin sat in Arkin's car after grabbing burgers and root beers at a nearby drive-in.

67

"Sex-change surgery?" Pratt said. "That has to be baloney, right?"

"You saw his testicles."

"Yeah, but here?"

"Much to the chagrin of the more conservative members of the community, Trinidad, Colorado, just down I-25 from here, is known in some circles as the sex-change capital of the world because of its famous and highly respected surgical clinic."

"You're kidding me."

"Nope. But the title is an exaggeration. Far more sex-change surgeries are performed in Thailand and Iran than in Trinidad—or the U.S. as a whole, for that matter."

"Iran?"

"Who knew, right?"

Pratt looked dumbfounded. "And you know all of this because?"

Arkin smiled as his cellphone rang. "Arkin." He spoke with Cornell for a minute, then hung up. "Milford's story checks out. He says he's just staying here until he feels well enough for the return drive to Oregon. The sex-change clinic refused to confirm that he's a patient until we give them a court order. But the night pharmacist at the Trinidad drugstore said the prescription bottles were legitimate."

"So why did he go for his gun?"

"He didn't believe we were cops. Thought we were rural Colorado bigots there to beat him up. Says he's been the victim of hate crimes before and always carries a gun now."

"So it's a dead end?"

"I have to admit, when you first came to me, I didn't think it smelled right."

"Huh? What about a tall guy with a funny accent and long, curly, dark hair gassing up near the crime scene on the same day as our shooting didn't smell right?"

"You said the gas station attendant described Milford as acting 'squirrelly.'"

"Wouldn't the average man be a little squirrelly while gassing up after blowing someone's head off and fleeing the scene?"

"That's just it. We aren't talking about the average man here."

"Huh?"

"If the shooter is the pro that his handiwork suggests he is, then he probably has liquid nitrogen for blood."

Pratt stared at him for a moment. "You could have mentioned that before we spent three hours driving over here just so that I could be traumatized."

"Don't be such a baby."

"Nate, I—"

"Just because someone doesn't fit one of the two or three white-bread human archetypes you learned about growing up in hayseed hillbillyland doesn't mean they're evil. For just one moment, try not to be a walking caricature of the vanilla tough guy law enforcement officer. Everybody can see through the façade anyway."

"What's a façade?"

"We're all just faking it, Pratt. Some of us are better at faking it than others. All of us scared of being singled out. Hoping for dear life not to have whatever it is that makes each of us different exposed for the world to see."

"Remember when you told me to tell you when you're being preachy?"

"Well, if you're going to play the outraged country bumpkin. . . ."

"Nate, I just handled a jar full of someone's balls."

"For free. A lot of people pay good money just to see a low-resolution photograph of something like that on the internet. And don't pretend you weren't titillated."

After a moment of apparent deliberation, Pratt half chuckled and smiled as he seemed, finally, to relax. "Shit."

"Don't cuss, Opie. Let's go home."

TEN

Arkin sat cross-legged on the floor of his office, halfway through the weekly ritual of polishing his perfectly cared for Salvatore Ferragamo shoes, sipping at a perfectly brewed cup of single-origin Rwandan coffee and waiting for his opponent in an online chess game to make his move. His chess opponent, a mathematics professor playing the white side, was supposed to be the University of Salzburg champion three years running. When the game opened, Arkin reasoned that an Austrian academic—an establishment man in what Arkin thought of as a frightfully backward country—would have conservative chess habits tending toward those of the classical school. So far, the tactics Arkin adopted to counter what he expected of his opponent had paid off in spades. After only five moves, Arkin was already certain he'd win. The fool had taken the bait—hook, line and sinker—on Arkin's version of Alekhine's Defense, deploying four white pawns in pursuit of Arkin's roving king's knight. Now to spring the trap.

He'd hoped for more of a challenge to get him warmed up for his approaching online match against Gregori Zhukov. Zhukov was a retired Ukrainian national champion—still one of the finest players in the world, and one of the few champions who still accepted challenges from well-respected amateurs like Arkin. Arkin had played him three times now, losing each match. But he'd done better each time, and he'd continued to study Zhukov's famous games, analyzing his tactics and tendencies, pinpointing his weaknesses. Sooner or later, he knew he would win. And he wouldn't quit issuing challenges until he did. The only catch was that a lot of people wanted to play against Zhukov, so Arkin had to wait nearly six months between matches.

Three moves later, and Arkin had the Austrian's queen trapped. A knock on his door broke his concentration. *Now what?* "Yes?"

Pratt stepped in. "Our data came back."

"Data?"

"From the credit card payment processors."

"Oh—right, right. Good." Arkin sent an instant message to his opponent requesting a pause in the game, hoping the man wouldn't, in the interregnum, realize his colossal blunder and devise an improbable but effective recovery. "What did you find?"

"I haven't found anything yet. There are more than 380,000 entries."

"Americans love their credit cards."

"What should I do with it?"

"Cross-reference the different data sets, looking for matches."

"What kind of matches?"

"Any kind. Think about it—if we have the same card being used in relatively close proximity to murder scenes that were more than a thousand miles and several years apart, well, that would be worth examining further."

"So how do I do that?"

"Write a formula or two in Litmus and run the data through it."

Pratt stood staring.

"You don't know how to do that."

"No."

Arkin shook his head. "When they first found you in that cave, were you completely naked, or had you at least figured out how to cut animal skin into a loincloth?"

"Cave?"

"You need to get on the ball, Opie. Data mining's the wave of the future. That's how they found D.B. Cooper."

"They found D.B. Cooper?"

"Pratt, you're killing me."

*****

In the basement a few minutes later, Pratt watched as Arkin sat at Pratt's computer, typing what to Pratt looked like quasi-mathematical gibberish: a long formula of letters, symbols, and numbers written in the language of Litmus data processing software.

"So let me make sure I understand the universe of what we're looking at here," Arkin said.

"Okay."

"These three datasets cover all credit transactions within 200 miles of the Eureka, rural Michigan, and Cortez killings, covering a range of days that includes a week before and after each?

"I—yes, I think so."

"Can you follow what I'm doing here by looking at this formula?"

"No."

"I'm polling for any account numbers that turn up in more than one of these datasets."

"Okay."

Arkin finished up, hit return, and they both watched as the program spit out a list of four account numbers. None were used near the Michigan killing. But all four were used near both Cortez and Eureka in the timeframe they were examining. Two were used at a Redding, California, retailer called Shasta Fishing Lures, as well as at grocery stores and fast-food restaurants in Telluride and Bayfield, Colorado. "Those first two are probably just mail-order purchases," Arkin said. "Colorado fishermen ordering lures from an outfit up there in Redding. We can probably rule those out." But the third and fourth account numbers were used for purchases of gas. In fact, there were two gas purchases made under each account number within easy driving range of each crime scene. "Look at that," Arkin said, pointing at the screen.

"What?"

"This pattern. For the Eureka data set, the first gas purchase on each card was made on Wednesday the 11th, and the second on each card was made on the 19th—the exact date of the Eureka shooting."

"You don't think that's a coincidence?"

"For the Cortez data set, the first gas purchase on each card was made on the Sunday before the killing, the second on the day of the killing."

"Okay, I suppose that is a little weird."

"What's the average range of a car on a full tank of gas? Maybe 300 miles?"

"Something like that. Unless it's a hybrid."

"Do you have an atlas in here?"

Pratt pulled a U.S. highways atlas out of one of his cubicle cabinets and handed it to Arkin. Arkin turned to the page covering the whole of the Lower 48 as Morrison walked in.

"You peckerwoods are as busy as cats burying shit on a marble floor. Anyone up for a run over to Carver's? I'm craving eggs."

Arkin held up a *wait a minute* finger without breaking his concentration on the map. "Okay, look here. For this first account number, on the 11th, the cardholder looks to have gassed up here," he said, his finger on the map, "in Gold Beach, Oregon. Then on the 19th, he gasses up in Grants Pass. Both towns just about half an average car gas tank to the north or northeast of

Eureka. Meanwhile, the second cardholder gasses up in Redding and Shingletown, California, each about half a gas tank east of Eureka. You follow me?"

"Uh-huh."

"Then we jump ahead two years, and here is that same first cardholder gassing up near Crescent Junction, Utah, half a gas tank's drive northwest of Cortez, on both that Sunday and the following Friday on which Egan was shot. And that same second card paying for gas on those same days, but in Pagosa Springs, probably less than half a gas tank east of Cortez, on the way in, and in Alamosa, a little more than half a gas tank away, on the way out. And look—neither card has been used since."

"What do you think it means?"

"Maybe nothing. Maybe it just happens that two different people happened to be in fairly close proximity to two eerily similar killings two years and 1,200 miles apart. Maybe it means a couple of people just happened to move from Oregon and California to Utah and Colorado. Or maybe it means that two people were involved in both of these assassinations, that they gassed up as far away as they could going to and from the assassinations, and that one of them is based to the north of Eureka and to the northwest of Durango, while the other is based to the east."

"Nate, stay here. I'll be right back," Morrison said.

"Where are you going?"

"To get the equipment."

"Equipment?"

"The bag and tubing and so forth. For your enema."

"But wait," Pratt said. "Look at these purchases here on the day *after* the Cortez shooting. Each of the cards has another gas purchase. The first one bought gas in Montrose, the second one in South Fork. Those towns are each *closer* to Cortez than either Crescent Junction or Alamosa."

Arkin examined the data again. "Huh." Indeed, it did appear as though the cardholders were driving back and forth, first away from, but then back toward Cortez.

"That kind of shoots down your theory that the cardholders were fleeing the crime scene, doesn't it?" Morrison asked. "Or do you think they maybe just forgot to pack their Neiman Marcus toiletries before checking out of the Assassin Motor Inn, and were doubling back to retrieve them?"

"Those toiletries are expensive," Arkin said, as he wondered whether perhaps it wasn't all just a coincidence after all. Perhaps the cardholders really were just locals. Or maybe truck drivers or delivery people. Whatever the case, odds were they weren't connected to the Cortez shooting. Arkin didn't know whether to be frustrated or relieved. He exhaled through his nose. "Well, Morrison, I reckon you had better go ahead and rig up that enema for me."

"Lilac or lavender scented?"

"Lilac." Arkin smiled. But the data still troubled him, and he couldn't let go of his hunch that, despite the likelihood of their irrelevance given the back-and-forth movements indicated by the gas purchases, the two credit card accounts in question were somehow important. "You know what? I still think you should send out a follow-up subpoena for details on these two account holders," he said to Pratt.

"Really? You think it's worth our time?"

"Come on, Nate," Morrison said. "Give the kid a break." "It'll take five minutes to draft. Let's just see what there is to see."

Morrison shook his head. "You've never been one to accept defeat gracefully."

"Thank you."

"That wasn't really a compliment. Sometimes you just got to chuck it in the fuck it bucket and move on."

"You make your point as eloquently as ever."

*****

That afternoon, Arkin slipped out of the building, alone, and drove the 45 miles back to the Cortez crime scene. It was an unusually blustery and overcast day, and the gray sky seemed to leech the color out of everything below it, leaving the mountains, the forests, and the rivers all looking flat and cold. Winter was coming.

Arkin turned off Highway 160 and zigzagged his way up a haphazard network of country roads to the long driveway of Egan's remote compound. He pulled up and parked at the partially open gate, was greeted by a gust of cold and dusty wind as he opened the door of his car, walked the 50 or more yards to the house, and climbed up onto the porch. There were no lights on inside or out. The place already had the lonely air of abandonment. Things had been cleaned up. The body was gone, as were the blood and brains. The bullet holes were still there. But otherwise nothing remained to indicate that a man's life had ended in spectacular fashion, on that very porch, only a few days earlier.

In fact, it had been barely a week since the shooting, but Arkin could already see signs of neglect and decline in the property. The porch, which had been spotless—aside from Egan's body and brains—when Arkin had been there last, was now coated in a film of tan dust. The leaves of the perfect little ornamental shrubs lining the driveway were curling for lack of water. And the driveway itself, which had been hand-raked to a flawless and level grade, was a crisscross of ridges and ruts left by the innumerable vehicles of police, the coroner, the media, orphaned followers, and nosy neighbors.

"Anybody here?" Arkin called. No answer came. All he heard was the cold north wind whistling across the plateau, and the rap-rap of a loose, wind-blown screen door repeatedly banging against its frame over at the tiny garage office where they'd interviewed Egan's chief of security.

Arkin peered through the nearest window, shielding his eyes from the dull glare of the overcast sky. Empty. He peeked through the hole left by the killing bullet. It framed a small view of the living room, including Egan's old cast-iron wood stove, black and cold. Seeing nothing of interest, he turned and gazed out over the surrounding land, at first scanning the horizon from north to south, then bringing his focus back to the little valley—more a trough—where Egan's killer set up to shoot him. The spot, already hard to see in the low light of an overcast evening, was veiled in the deepening shadow cast by the small knoll to its southwest.

Is it you? Arkin wondered. *Or am I chasing a shadow?*

He continued to stare, his hands jammed into his suit pockets and his arms drawn tight against his sides, as the north wind buffeted him, penetrating his clothes, sending a chill up his spine. The sky slowly grew darker with the approach of dusk. But still he stood and stared out across the land.

*****

Returning home that evening, he opened the front door to discover an infant sitting reclined and eyeballing him from a brightly-colored bouncer seat. A little girl—maybe 3 months old—with beautiful Native American black hair and dark brown eyes. She was studying him intently, having no doubt turned when she heard the sound of the heavy wooden door opening.

"Hello there," Arkin said softly, dropping to a crouch so as to appear smaller and hopefully less threatening. "I'm Nate. What's your name?"

"This is Faith," Hannah said, rounding the corner with a bottle of formula and a small towel.

"Hi, Faith," he said, smiling as he did his best baby wave.

"Her mom is my client at Legal Aid. She had to go in for emergency surgery. Complications from diabetes. Don't ask."

"Uh-oh."

"So Faith is going to stay at our house for a couple of nights, aren't you?" she said, tickling the child's foot, getting her to smile. Arkin caught Hannah wincing as she lifted Faith from the bouncer. She sat down on the couch, gingerly, and cradled the child in her arms while she hand-fed her formula—as naturally as though she'd raised half a dozen children of her own. Faith's eyes locked on Hannah's, and in their warm expressions Arkin read unspoken messages of mutual unconditional affection and happiness.

"And how are *you* feeling?" Arkin asked, hoping his worry didn't show through.

"I'll manage."

He forced a smile and shook his head.

ELEVEN

Arkin, Morrison, and Pratt spent the morning in Farmington with a handful of ATF agents up from Santa Fe, sweating in body armor and full tactical gear, practicing dynamic entries at a sandbag-lined raid training house set up in a derelict military housing rambler at the National Guard armory. They took turns knocking the doors in with rams and leading six-agent entry teams as they cleared rooms and blew human-shaped cardboard targets to shreds with their pistols, short-barreled shotguns, and MP-5 machine guns.

Back in Durango after wolfing down a lunch of drive-through burgers en route, they sat around the long table of a conference room they borrowed from the Forest Service, listening on speakerphone to the ring of a call Arkin placed.

A man with a deep baritone voice answered. "Hubbard."

"Good afternoon, Dr. Hubbard. This is Nate Arkin. I have Pratt and Bill Morrison with me here in Durango, and I believe we now have Detective Cornell on the line from Cortez."

"Afternoon, gentlemen. Where shall we begin?"

"Perhaps with the bullets."

"Certainly. As you suspected, your victim was indeed killed by a .50 BMG round."

Arkin wondered why forensics people always used the word "victim" in place of the victims' actual names. Perhaps it helped them maintain a psychological buffer from the horror of what they analyzed every day.

"An enormous and powerful bullet. Variations of it have been around since before any of us were born. It's currently in use in militaries all over the world. In the United States, it's even available for purchase by the general public. But I've never analyzed one quite like this before." Dr. Hubbard sounded like a kid describing his first trip to Disneyland. "A 752-grain low-drag bullet, with a muzzle velocity of around 3,000 feet per second, delivering roughly 15,000 foot-pounds of energy. To give you some sense of proportion, the bullets you guys load in the .40 caliber handguns you're issued are between 150 and 200 grains, have a muzzle velocity of around 1,100 feet per second, and maybe deliver 400 or 500 foot-pounds of energy, depending on the brand. And the variant that killed your victim wasn't your usual .50 round. It was an armor-piercing round, designed for anti-materiel applications. But the real eyebrow-raiser here is that the composition of the residues we got off the surrounding leaves and brush you sent in indicates the round was of a type only available to the American military. I won't bore you with the details of its chemistry, but in short, it was loaded with a special powder that increases the kinetic energy of the round to a level significantly exceeding that of any other .50 round I've ever seen or read about. Fascinating."

"An American military bullet," Arkin muttered, staring through the far wall, his mind miles away. "How did he get hold of that?"

"Why would anyone need that much bullet to kill a man?" Cornell asked.

"The sniper may have been anticipating the need to shoot through cover," Arkin said. "He knew Egan's compound was surrounded by walls. He probably knew Egan's car was armored. Or maybe the .50 caliber is just what he was trained on and is most comfortable with. Who knows?"

"Well, it certainly got the job done."

"Dr. Hubbard, you have alarmed the peasants," Morrison said.

"Sorry about that."

"It's okay," Arkin said, "as long as you don't tell us the bullet was fired from a Zastava rifle."

Hubbard went quiet.

"Dr. Hubbard? You still with us?"

"Who said that? About the gun, I mean. Arkin?"

"Yes, sir."

"There are dozens of widely available weapons, long guns and handguns, capable of firing the .50 BMG round. May I ask what on Earth would make you guess it was fired from something as uncommon as a Zastava rifle?"

"You don't want to know."

"Well, it was."

Arkin barely nodded as Morrison and Pratt turned and stared at him, their mouths hanging open, their eyebrows furrowed. Then Morrison looked over at Pratt and mouthed the word, "clairvoyance."

"My colleague came to the same conclusion independently," Hubbard continued. "Given the twist as well as the number and dimensions of the land and groove impressions—that is to say the combination of these characteristics unique to the model of gun—we can say with utter certainty that the bullet was fired from a Zastava M93. The 'crna strella,' or 'black arrow' in English. A bolt-action sniper rifle of Serbian manufacture, in service since 1998, mostly used by special units of a handful of militaries, including those of Serbia, Bosnia-Herzegovina, Macedonia, and Montenegro. Like most heavy sniper rifles, it is designed to be fired from the prone position, supported by a folding bipod. Unaltered, the variant designed to fire the .50 BMG round has an effective range of more than 5,000 feet, weighs in at over 35 pounds, and is damn near 5 ½ feet long. An absolute monster of a gun."

Morrison, again staring at Arkin, couldn't hold back. "How the fuck did you—"

"Did you run it through Drugfire?" Arkin asked.

"I did. In fact that's where I obtained the general rifling characteristics for the Zastava. I'd never encountered the handiwork of one before."

"I should think not. Did Drugfire give you any matches for your striations?"

"No, it didn't. But I sent our scans of the fragments off to the Bureau's Firearms/Toolmarks Unit. They may still come up with something that isn't in their database as yet."

"If you forward copies to me, I'll direct them to the appropriate officials with Defense Intelligence as well. Sometimes their records include—well, sometimes they have data that supplements that of the Bureau."

Five minutes later, Pratt, Morrison and Arkin hung up and faced each other across the conference room table.

"So what does all this titillating information tell us that we hadn't yet deduced, neophyte Pratt?" Arkin asked.

"Hey, I've been in this job for years now."

"It tells us that our shooter, in addition to being a professional, is quite possibly a veteran of a Balkan military, trained therein as a sniper, and discharged no earlier than 1998. There's a chance, albeit a slim one, that our Belgrade station can obtain a copy of the rolls of their special forces and snipers active in the 1990s."

"So, are you finally going to let us in on the big secret?" Morrison asked.
"Big secret?"
"Don't play dumb with me, you boarding school degenerate."
Arkin smiled. "Maybe we should brew another pot of coffee first."

*****

Back in the conference room after their pause, Arkin and Morrison sipped hot coffees, Pratt a bottle of SunnyD, as Arkin explained how he'd anticipated the make of the murder weapon.

"About six months before I quit DCI, maybe five months before they moved me to Durango, I was assigned a 'go nowhere' case. A dog. At the time I was given the file, the only real witness was already dead. Killed. Worse, the leads provided in the transcript of the half-assed and only interview of the deceased witness, conducted by an uninspired Customs agent, largely involved information and events that were already more than thirty years old."

"Why did DCI even have a case like that?" Pratt asked.

"An excellent question. It was of interest to the agency for two reasons. First, because it allegedly involved an international terrorist group—in this case one that was orchestrating philosophically motivated assassinations, and second—"

"Philosophically motivated?" Pratt asked.

"I'll get back to that. And second, because one of the group's victims was being watched by one of our own surveillance teams at the very moment he was assassinated. Suffice it to say, the Agency's curiosity was piqued by the group's apparent ability to go utterly undetected in both tracking and killing someone who was under surveillance by the agency's own specialized and highly trained personnel."

"I heard something about this," Pratt said.

"So, backing up a bit, more than two years before this dog of a case landed on my desk, there was an Egyptian national, a person of interest to us, named Hassan al Nefud. Big-mouthed, self-described imam who had a sizeable and growing following back home, as well as a few obnoxiously vocal disciples in some strip-mall shithole neighborhood of Newark, New Jersey. The usual thing—bunch of mopes spooked by their insignificance in the universe, thinking that the louder they shout about their beliefs, the likelier it will be that theirs encompass the one true path."

"Path to what?" Pratt asked.

"Paradise," Morrison said.

"You mean Newark isn't?"

"Al Nefud's rhetoric bordered on the edge of an outright call to arms against the United States, and was already well over the line with respect to Israel. Nevertheless, to the considerable surprise of the press and great consternation of the Embassy of Israel, the State Department granted him a visa, ostensibly because he'd been invited to address the Middle Eastern Studies Program at Johns Hopkins. In truth, Johns Hopkins only extended their invitation after being prodded to do so by Homeland Security, which had, with the help of Treasury and NSA, uncovered a suspicious flow of money—from Geneva to cities including Cairo, Newark, and Islamabad—for which al Nefud appeared to be the facilitator. Bottom line, several agencies wanted to take a closer look at al Nefud to see what he was up to. And what better way to do that than give him a hall pass in a very closely watched hall. Hence, the invitation from Johns Hopkins."

"So, DCI is assigned point. That is to say, we had the primary responsibility to watch al Nefud from the moment he unbuckled his seatbelt at Dulles Airport to the moment he re-buckled it three days later on his way home. We even had agents sitting in front of and behind him on his flight from Cairo. Anyway, the whole time he's in the U.S., we have the dogs on him. A 14-person surveillance team. Big operation. Full eavesdropping. Full surveillance. Eyes and ears, 24/7. Of course, we're hoping he'll make contact with someone here so we can flush out any related homegrown threat. He never does. He goes straight from Dulles to his Baltimore hotel, orders room service, and turns on pay-per-view."

"Porn, right?" Pratt said.

"No—a Victorian period romance film, of all things. Anyway, the next day, he goes to Johns Hopkins to make his speech, then goes right back to his hotel room and more pay-per-view. Doesn't even make a phone call. Then, on the morning of his third day here, just as he's leaving his hotel to head back to Dulles Airport, walking to his limo while we have no fewer than five personnel with eyes on inside a 60-foot radius of this asshole, somebody blows his head off with a high-powered sniper rifle. All those eyes, and not one of our people sees the shooter or so much as a puff of smoke. Nobody even hears the shot until half the contents of al Nefud's skull are already decorating the stucco walls of the hotel's carport."

"And he was shot by a Zastava," Morrison said.

Arkin turned to Pratt and grinned. "Check out Morrison trying to think." Then, turning back to Morrison, "My hat, sir. He was indeed shot by a Zastava. A different model that time. Still a sniper rifle, but a smaller, older design called the M91, firing a 7.62 x 54 round. Like the M93, it's used by a handful of two-bit Balkan armies. So, long story short, to DCI's considerable embarrassment, their quarry was sniped right out from under their noses, and they never found the shooter. Best they were able to do was locate the spot from which the sniper shot al Nefud and identify the make and model of the gun based on a bullet fragment they found lodged in a floor joist supporting the mezzanine above the hotel's lobby. Otherwise, they never found jack for evidence, aside from a single long, black, moderately curly hair stuck on a bush the shooter hid behind. Needless to say, our deputy director for surveillance was sacked shortly thereafter. And all we ever put together was that one other person of similarly surging popularity and extreme views, a right-wing Odessa, Texas, radio host, was sniped by a Zastava M91 shooter a year earlier. Curiously, in that case, the shots were fired by a different M91, indicating either that the shootings were done by different killers, or by a single killer with a personal stockpile of Serbian guns. The other thing was that in each case, there were certain things—fingerprints, shall we say—indicating the involvement of particular groups. But it was odd."

"How?" Morrison asked.

"Like in the case of al Nefud, there was certain peripheral evidence that suggested the involvement of a particular foreign intelligence service. In the case of the right-wing radio guy, there were fingerprints—literally fingerprints, on the victim's car door—of a rather militant homosexual rights advocate who'd recently disappeared. Yet in each of these cases, the evidence just didn't smell right, and what there was of it was never enough to lead us anywhere."

"What are you saying?"

"Somebody was leaving us red herrings. Throwing us off the scent. Somebody with an exceedingly rare knowledge of the methods of certain foreign intelligence services, for example."

"Hey," Pratt said, "that reminds me—in the Eureka investigation, they found a piece of notebook paper bearing the logo for the local timber mill with the victim's license plate number written on it in the tank of a portable toilet at the trailhead near where he was shot."

"And Cornell will probably end up finding a threatening but curiously untraceable email sent to Egan from an anonymous user of a militant immigration, gay rights, or Islamist web site, or something like that," Arkin said. "And as with the sheet of timber mill notebook paper, it will seem just a hair too obvious vis-à-vis the otherwise thoroughly professional appearance of the shootings."

"So what does all that mean?" Pratt asked.

"One thing it means is that someone involved had, at least at one time, access to high-level intelligence information. That whoever is behind these killings is sophisticated."

"Not that sophisticated if they're killing people with the same model of an unusual Serbian gun," Morrison said. "Any idiot could see that a pattern like that would jump right off the page if anybody ever looked in the right places and began connecting the dots."

"I agree," Arkin said. "Using Zastavas is curiously sloppy tradecraft. But maybe the shooter was set in his ways. Maybe it was the gun he was trained on. Or maybe the shooter or his masters were confident nobody would ever be able to trace them anyway. Regardless, the al Nefud case went stone cold and was soon put in mothballs. At the time, everyone figured that was the end of the story. But a couple of years later, the case came back on us through an improbable channel. Exactly two weeks before al Nefud was killed, an illegal alien from Belize was caught jaywalking, of all the trivial things."

"They still cite people for jaywalking?" Pratt asked.

"In Seattle they do. Guy has a funny accent and no ID, so the street cop grabs him and SPD eventually turns him over to Immigration and Customs Enforcement. The guy tells ICE he has information on an international terrorist group. Nobody takes him seriously. ICE assumes from the start, and quite understandably, that the guy is just grabbing at straws, looking for leverage to avoid deportation. Nevertheless, they're obliged to at least interview him because of his claim. So they put some overworked probationer on it, he takes the interview, and this Belizean jaywalker proceeds to tell him that an unnamed 'international terrorist group' has penetrated the upper echelons of the intelligence and law enforcement communities of numerous countries, including the United States, that they are in the business of assassinating political, religious, and social extremists, and that their leader is, of all things, a former Catholic priest from Baltimore, Maryland."

"A priest?" Pratt asked.

"A Jesuit priest."

"A lapsed Jesuit priest running a star chamber type of thing," Morrison said in a tone of wonder. "A star chamber targeting hatemongers. That would make a damned good movie."

"Or novel," Arkin said.

"Please. Who reads anymore?"

"Point. Anyway, the probationer ICE agent writes his report of the interview, which is graded as bullshit by their analysts before the ink has even dried, and promptly files the paperwork to deport this nut job back to Belize. Customs probably wouldn't have given it another thought, and would never have forwarded the laughable report of interview to us—allegations of terrorism or not—."

"Except," Morrison said.

"Except that 10 months after he was sent home to Belize, someone blew his head off with a high-powered rifle as he stood at a bus stop in Belmopan."

"With a Zastava?" Pratt asked.

"We don't know. The locals never recovered the bullet. At any rate, as a courtesy, the Belizean government sent ICE the locals' report of investigation a couple of months after the fact so that ICE could close their file. ICE eventually forwarded a copy of their file to us because of the dubious reference to terrorism. At DCI, the case rang old bells. Eventually, someone noticed the similarities with the killing of al Nefud. Then it landed on my desk. And to my absolute astonishment, this dead Belizean had, in his ICE interview, specifically named al Nefud as a target for imminent assassination by the group. Again, the ICE interview was conducted two weeks *before* Nefud was killed."

"Holy fuck," Morrison said.

"Indeed. That little tidbit, considered in light of the method by which the Belizean himself was later killed, gave him a new smell of legitimacy to say the least."

"So what did you do?"

"The ICE report of the interview was painfully light on detail. The guy was probably holding back on his good stuff until ICE took the bait and offered him asylum. Of course, that never happened. So all I had to go on was a few scraps of information on a Jesuit priest from Baltimore who supposedly faked his own death in Kentucky in 1974."

"Did the guy at least give you a name?"

"Father Collin Bryant."

"Did the name check out?"

"There was such a man at one time."

"And?"

"And he grew up in Baltimore. Born Saint Agnes Hospital, July 20, 1941. Color of hair, black. Color of eyes, blue. Height, 6-foot-4. Weight, at the time he renewed his last known driver's license, 240 pounds."

"You really remember all this?" Pratt asked. "Like, from your memory?"

"You want to know something strange?" Arkin said, ignoring Pratt's question. "Half the background section of Bryant's dossier reads just like Osama bin Laden's. You could switch their names and religions around on their files and fool half the profiling unit. Guy from a huge family, starved for love and attention from his absentee father, predictably ends up wrapped around the axle over his existential anxieties and runs straight for the comfort of the nearest available black-and-white fundamentalism, right?"

"If you say so."

"Collin was the eighth of ten children of the owner of a hundred-and-fifty-year-old family-owned commercial fishing company based in Baltimore. Grew up working summers on the family's long-liners, up and down the Atlantic seaboard, from the Grand Banks to the Outer Banks. At age seven, he lost his older sister, Mary, after her grueling three-year battle with leukemia. Mary was, by all accounts, the Bryant sibling he was closest to. His best friend. Just three years his senior, and despite her own illness, she was credited by their other siblings as doing more to take care of young Collin than his own parents did. At any rate, after Mary's death, Collin fell into a depression that his mother described as lasting an unnaturally long time. Given that his mother grew up in a generation that just didn't talk about this sort of thing, it must have really been something for her to think it was worth mentioning to me decades later. By his 8th birthday, at his mother's insistence, he began an on-again-off-again pattern of psychiatric treatment—to match his on-again-off-again bouts with what would these days be diagnosed as acute depression—that would last until, at age 15, he declared his intent to enter the priesthood. At that point, his disposition, from his psychiatrist's point of view, seemed to stabilize rather abruptly. And he began to thrive."

"During his junior year, he won a State of Maryland essay contest with a wave-generating story about the unequal treatment of African Americans at the hands of the Baltimore Police Department. He was valedictorian of Mount Saint Joseph High School and captain of the football team as a senior. A handsome fellow. One acquaintance even described him as having, quote, fashion model good looks, unquote. In a nutshell, your stereotypical apple pie eating, all-American young man, at least on the surface. Went to Jesuit seminary straight from high school. Following ordination, his first assignment took him to Appalachia. A small coal town, up-hollow in a forgotten corner of the Maryland panhandle. After he cut his teeth there for two years, he was sent to start a new parish in Royburg, Kentucky—a small, dirt poor black town on the Mississippi River, near the Tennessee border. A town that happened to be just across the river and downwind from what was, at the time, a secret factory that manufactured HD for artillery shells."

"HD?" Pratt asked.

"Distilled mustard agent. A chemical weapon of biblically horrific effect. Like something out of the dark ages. Anyway, Father Bryant, being a bright and charismatic young priest, got his new parish up and running in short order. Holy Trinity Catholic Church. The community embraced him. They celebrated mass in a borrowed elementary school cafeteria. He heard confessions in the kitchen, set up his rectory in a little shotgun house next door, and things were going along swimmingly."

"Then, one sunny Tuesday afternoon in the summer of 1968, when the kids were all walking home from school, slinging backpacks and kicking balls down the road, a yellow cloud blew into the southern half of town from across the river. The kids played in it as if it were a winter fog. People who were indoors came out to see what the hubbub was about, walking around in the vapor, wondering at its odd garlic odor. The cloud lingered for an hour or so before the afternoon breeze kicked up and blew it east. Things went back to normal. Folks went home, fixed their suppers, kids did their chores, and everyone went to bed."

"But the next morning, people's skin began itching. By midday, large blisters of yellow liquid were appearing on their skin and their eyes were swelling shut. By evening, several dozen were coughing blood. And by nightfall, just as the first ambulances were finally starting to arrive from Paducah and Mayfield, 17 people—12 of them members of Father Bryant's fledgling parish—were already dead, with 12 more to follow over the next two weeks, succumbing to everything from sepsis to pulmonary edema. They were essentially suffocating on their own blood. A scene beyond most people's worst nightmares."

Arkin could still vividly recall the stuffy, rotting, dimly lit shotgun shack in Royburg where, years earlier, he'd interviewed Lucricia Burris—a 60-year-old widow who looked 90 as she neared the inevitable end of a two-year battle with lung cancer. She was the sole surviving confidant of Father Collin

Bryant in the whole of the parish community. The others had long since died of lung cancer, in all likelihood caused by their exposure to mustard gas from the industrial accident that sent the deadly yellow cloud through their small town decades earlier. Every few seconds, Lucricia had to take a breath from a plastic mask fed by a green oxygen tank next to her filthy armchair. The stale and overly humid air in her house had the sweet-sour smell of sickness. Of approaching death. Arkin remembered sitting on a terribly uncomfortable wooden piano stool, though there was no piano to be seen, as Lucricia did her best to answer his questions, her skin faded from deep brown to a sickly ashen, her exhausted eyes sunken back in their sockets. Every few minutes, overwhelmed with sorrow for those who'd been lost, she would shake her head and wipe the streaming tears from her eyes, as though it had all happened only yesterday. Yet whenever Arkin asked if he could make her more comfortable, or offered a sympathetic word, she brushed him off with a polite comment like "oh, don't worry about me, young man. This is just the way life goes." No denial. No bitterness. Just calm acceptance. Arkin couldn't fathom it.

"Of course, Father Bryant was devastated by the loss of life," she'd told him. "The loss of parishioners and other townsfolk he'd grown close to, as if they were his own blood. But what really got to him was what happened afterward."

"Afterward?" Arkin had asked, gently drawing her forward.

"The response. And the lack of response."

Arkin remembered nodding silently, patiently, despite his unease with the decay and reminders of death all around him, knowing in his gut that what was to be found between the lines of Lucricia's story held the keys to his case.

It had taken hours for the first ambulances to arrive, she told him. While waiting for help, Father Bryant had folks set up beds in the school cafeteria and tried to take care of people, tried to comfort them as best he could, between reading last rites. He'd kept a stiff upper lip, doing what needed to be done. But then, someone carried in a young boy of five, name of Gladman Mathis, a boy whom Bryant had befriended soon after arriving in Royburg. Like Bryant in his own youth, Mathis had an absentee father—in Mathis' case, because his father had been drafted into the Army and was stuck in Vietnam. Bryant took it upon himself to stand in, as best he could, for the father. They were often seen playing catch together. Bryant even bought him a baseball glove as a fifth birthday present. When they carried the disfigured, dying boy into the cafeteria and lay him on a cot, Bryant went to his side and never left. It was as if no one else existed for him anymore. He tried to sit the boy up, to help him clear the fluid from his lungs. But when he did so, Mathis choked, trying to scream from the pain of Bryant touching his raw, burned, blistered skin. So Bryant just held the boy's little hand. Held it for more than two hours, as the boy stared up at him in agony, terrified, gurgling as he struggled to breathe. Held it until a bubbling froth of blood rose up in his windpipe and spilled down his chin as he finally went limp. Then Bryant reached down and gathered the boy's body up in his giant arms and held him. Just held him in his arms, resting his own forehead against the top of the boy's head, for a long, long time.

In the aftermath, dozens were taken to Paducah for treatment, several of them never to return. Twenty-four dead in less than a week. Yet there was no mention of it in the national news. None. And not only that, but nobody came to explain what happened, let alone apologize. All they said was that there had been an accident at a factory on the other side of the river. People died, ambulances came and went, and that was that.

"You know," Lucricia said, "at Father Bryant's next mass, he didn't know what to say at sermon. He just stood there at the altar in front of what was left of us all, and when he tried to speak, he wept. But the next week we invited him to our house for chicken dinner and he was different. He was quiet. He seemed very angry. He said things would have gone differently if Royburg was a rich white town. He said they never would have built a dangerous factory across the river from a rich white town in the first place. Said he was going to call the archdiocese and the papers and the TV news stations and make people take notice."

"So Father Bryant did what he said he was going to do, called and wrote, and wrote and called every public official and news source he could, even after the archdiocese ordered him to stop. For a long time, nothing happened. But finally one day, oh, maybe three months later, a man from the Army shows up and goes door-to-door telling everyone we're going to get something special to recognize our sacrifice. So a week after that, we all assemble in front of the general store where they've set up this little stage with a big, new American flag hanging behind it, and this supply colonel from Fort Campbell gets up there and tells us about the cost of freedom, and how that plant across the river is important to our national defense, and that the whole country, from our soldiers in Vietnam to our factory workers back home, must make sacrifices to safeguard America. He asks us to never again speak of what happened here. He says we are heroes for being brave through the terrible tragedy and asks us to accept medals of patriotism on behalf of a grateful nation. Then his assistant brings a big cardboard box up to the stage and the colonel opens it and begins, one-by-one, having us come up to the stage to receive a little silver-colored aluminum star pin set on a 2-inch piece of red, white, and blue ribbon. We each take a pin, and the colonel shakes our hands. Then he leaves in his big black car while his staff stays behind to take down the flag and the little stage. And all this time, Father Bryant stands in the background watching, his skin burning red and sweating like he has fever."

"After that, things slowly got back to normal. Well, not normal, because a lot of people were gone, and others continued to have breathing troubles. Things were never the same. But we carried on. Father Bryant said mass every Sunday, did confession, baptized our babies and such. But something was different with him. For one, he stopped trying to bring new people into the parish. Just up and stopped. And there was something different about his sermons. They'd started to sound sort of hollow. Like he was reading them from a book. Like they weren't coming from the heart."

"He was going through the motions," Arkin offered, his voice soft.

"Yes, sir. Going through the motions. And he let his hair and beard grow long and crazy. Look," she'd said, pulling a grainy, bent, black-and-white photograph from the very back of a worn Bible sitting on her end table. Bryant stood in Easter habit at the center of a line of parishioners dressed in their Sunday best, two youngsters in altar boy regalia. "That's me right there," Lucricia said, pointing to a beautiful woman of 30, standing to Bryant's immediate right. All but Bryant were smiling. He alone looked somber, hard, his beard and hair grown long and wild. Something about his eyes held Arkin. It could have been an anomaly, a product of distortion in the low-quality film, but Arkin doubted it. His gut told him that it was anger. Fuming, burning anger. Then it hit him—Arkin was looking at the eyes of a newborn fanatic. Or perhaps, more accurately, a fanatic emerging from a lifelong gestation.

"He took to going on long paddles in his canoe out on the Mississippi," she continued. "He'd paddle way out to the middle, and then just sit there like he was in a trance, sometimes for hours." She took another breath from the mask. "I could watch him from my sun porch, just sitting out there, rain or shine, hot or cold. I worried about him. So one day I find him sitting on an old leather chair in the rectory's screened-in porch, just staring out at the sunset like he was a thousand miles away, and I finally ask him, I say, 'Father, what is troubling you? Is it still the accident? Because if it is, you got to let it go or it will break your heart, and that would serve no purpose.' Imagine, me saying this to a priest." She chuckled before drawing another breath from the mask. "But he just sat there like he didn't even hear. 'We need you here,' I says. 'You got to know there wasn't nothing you could have done to stop it. There wasn't nothing you could have done.' That seemed to wake him up a bit. He at least turned to look at me. Then you know what he says to me? He says 'Lucricia, I really don't know that that's true.' I don't understand what he's trying to say. Then he says, do I remember when the Army came and gave out those little aluminum star pins. Of course I remember, I tell him. Do I remember the flag, he asks me. The big, beautiful flag that hung behind the colonel. Looked like it was made of a very fine silk. Yes, I say. I remember that beautiful stars and stripes. Biggest flag I ever seen. 'You know,' he says, 'at the end of the ceremony, they folded that magnificent flag up and took it with them in a shiny new protective steel case. And all they left us was the little aluminum star pins.'"

*****

"And then," Arkin said to the rapt Pratt and Morrison, still sitting in the conference room, "in November 1974, Father Collin Bryant, founder and rector of the ill-fated Holy Trinity Parish, Royburg, Kentucky, disappeared from the face of the earth."

"Disappeared?" Pratt asked, snapping Arkin from his storyteller's trance.

"Needless to say, the police didn't respond to the townfolks' missing persons report for days. When they finally did, at the behest of an alarmed archdiocese, all they found was his swamped canoe stuck in overhanging branches along the left bank of the Mississippi, about three miles downriver."

"He drowned?"

"That's what everyone thought."

"But. . . ."

"But," Arkin echoed with a weary sigh, "I need some espresso."

"Oh, hell no!" Morrison said. "You aren't going to leave us hanging like that."

"You can both read the hard copy of the file when it gets here. I need a double-shot with a plate of chorizo and eggs. Anybody want to go to Carver's with me?"

"For someone who's as militant as you are about fitness and nutrition, I'm perplexed by your weakness for Carver's Mexican scramble. All those egg yolks? All that chorizo?"

"It's my kryptonite."

"It'll be the death of you."

"There are worse ways to go."

"Yes, sir. Yes, there are."

*****

That afternoon, Arkin locked up his office, went to the basement locker room to change clothes for his daily ride home, and slipped out the service entrance with his mountain bike. He chose one of his favorite routes—a trail that climbed high above the river just to the west of town, then dropped back down to Highway 550 north of Trimble. It was a trail he'd been riding since first moving to Durango. As usual, he timed himself.

The trail was unusually dusty, probably because it hadn't rained in many days. He blew past several casual riders, huffing and puffing, as the trail climbed out of town. At one point, he thought he might have seen a bobcat out of the corner of his eye. But he couldn't be sure. He was too focused on the trail, on his exertion, to be aware of much else.

Soon his thighs began to burn. Then his calves. Then his lungs. His watch beeped at one-minute intervals. He kept count. Ten minutes. Twenty. Twenty-five. His personal best time to the trail's apex—a point marked by an informal viewpoint on a boulder outcropping—was 27 minutes and 16 seconds. From somewhere within, the urge to beat the record rose inside him. He always rode with intensity. But now he stepped it up. His ride became a race. A race against time. It was going to be close.

He rose higher on his pedals. Put more energy into each down-stroke. Twenty-six minutes. His lungs ached for mercy. His mouth was utterly dry and dusty, his tongue feeling fat, like a foreign object in his own mouth. Twenty-six-thirty. As it sometimes did, his late father's voice echoed through his mind. *Come on! Your effort's pathetic!* Twenty-seven. A pinhead hemorrhage appeared astride a tiny burst capillary in the corner of his left eye. His thighs and calves began to lose strength, still burning. He began to lock his knees on the down-stroke to let his weight take some of the burden from his failing muscles. His breathing became wide-mouthed gasping. *Come on, you damned weakling!*

He crossed his imaginary finish line and hit the stop button on his watch timer at 27 minutes 32 seconds. He fell from his bike, crawled from the trail and into the brush on his hands and knees, and threw up. After a minute or so, he caught his breath and sat up. He looked at his watch, saw the figure on the timer, then fell onto his back in the bushes. *You lose again. You disappoint me again. Are you sure you're my son?*

TWELVE

Hannah had to sit down halfway through wrapping Kayla Pratt's birthday present. Nate got her a glass of apple juice and insisted that she lie down on the couch while he finished the wrapping job. Then he suggested they just stay home. The Pratts would understand. But she said she wouldn't miss Kayla's birthday come hell or high water, so Arkin helped her to the car and drove across town to the party.

Kayla ran to the door to greet them, and they each knelt down—Hannah wincing as she did so—to receive her hugs and kisses. She smelled like coconut, probably from a kids' shampoo. Arkin couldn't believe she was already 5. It seemed just yesterday he and Hannah were driving John and Ella Pratt home from the hospital with their new baby. He hugged Kayla tight, wishing he could protect her from the whole world. But life didn't work that way. She wasn't even his child. He didn't have one. He and Hannah couldn't. The thought left him cold.

"How is our beautiful princess?" Hannah asked

"That's a big present," Kayla said, eyeballing the large box they'd brought.

"That big present is for *you*," Arkin said, tickling her with a finger poke to the belly.

"Can I take that to the gift table for you?" Ella Pratt asked as she entered the hallway. "Thanks so much for coming."

Pratt came in dressed like he was ready for a round of golf at the cheapest golf course on Earth, handed Hannah something he described as "a vitamin-rich smoothie just for you," then grinned as he shoved a bottle of grape soda into Arkin's hand.

"Thanks, John."

Over the next two hours, Morrison and several other families with young children from the Pratt's LDS ward arrived. Everyone milled around as Arkin and Morrison stood outside watching Pratt grill two dozen hotdogs.

"How come I don't see any Dr. Seuss books in your house?" Arkin asked Pratt. "How can a kid grow up American without reading Dr. Seuss?"

"Dr. Seuss is a tree-hugging left-wing elitist who poisons the minds of children."

"You're mentally ill. And it's bad luck to disparage the dead."

Pratt winked at him as he continued to work the barbeque. Everyone ate hotdogs and birthday cake until they felt bloated, then watched Kayla open her birthday presents. She opened the large box from the Arkins to reveal a stack of books—the entire Dr. Seuss collection. Seeing it, Pratt gave Arkin a grin from across the room, then shot him a middle finger disguised as a scratch of his forehead.

Hannah tried to help Ella clean up, but Ella wouldn't hear of it and made Hannah sit in a comfortable chair in the kitchen and talk to her while she stood and did all the dishes. Meanwhile, Arkin and Morrison followed Pratt into the backyard where he was keeping an eye on his newly walking son, Jake. Jake puttered around, squatting here and there to pick blades of grass from their perfect yard, at one point squealing with delight at the discovery of a small caterpillar.

Pratt, his face bearing an odd expression, turned to face Arkin. "Hey, uh, Nate," he said, sounding hesitant.

"Hey, uh, what?"

"Ella and I were talking—"

"Uh-huh."

"Well, we just want you to know we're here for you. Anything you need. Really."

Deep down, Arkin knew exactly what Pratt was getting at. But he refused to let his understanding come to the surface easily. "What are you talking about?"

"You know, if Hannah—well, if she gets worse. If things get worse."

"Ah."

Morrison turned on his heels and faced away from Pratt and Arkin, as if meaning to give them some modicum of privacy even though they all stood in a fairly small triangle. He jammed his hands into the pockets of his jeans, pursed his lips, and stared down at his own boots as though contemplative, uncomfortable, even sad. He kicked at a small gray pebble that had been knocked into the grass from an adjoining gravel drainage trench.

"We could set up a bed for her in my den so that Ella could keep an eye on her during the day while we're at work. We can move my desk out of there, move a few of the kids toys, no sweat."

"That's very. . . ."

"The kids will try to make her have tea parties with them, but Ella can keep 'em mostly corralled."

Arkin cleared his throat. "You are both very kind."

"Well." Pratt searched for the right expression. "You're both like family."

His well-intentioned words hit Arkin like a punch in the gut. He'd been trying to convince himself that Hannah was doing just fine, and that her degraded appearance the night they came back from the Cortez crime scene was nothing more than an illusion caused by the feeble porch lighting at their house. But if the others thought she looked worse, then she probably did. His heart sank and he began, once again, to worry.

A welcome distraction came when Pratt's son picked up a rock and threw it an impressive distance out into the yard.

"Did you see that?" Pratt said. He smiled, picked his boy up and gave him a squeeze and a kiss on the head. "My boy. He's gonna be the next Ty Detmer."

"Kid's got a gun," Morrison said.

"Hey, you guys want to see him laugh like crazy?"

"Sure."

"Here, stand here and here," he said, directing Arkin and Morrison to points of a triangle roughly five feet on each side. "Now catch," he said, tossing his son, front first, to a startled Morrison. As soon as Morrison caught him, Jake burst out laughing. The unrestrained, mirthful laugh of a blissfully happy child.

"Holy shit, Pratt."

"Don't be teaching my boy cuss words. Here, give him a toss to Arkin."

Morrison, looking unsure, tossed Jake to Arkin, and the boy burst into laughter again. It was infectious. They went around the triangle with him for several minutes, the boy laughing hysterically. At one point, Ella saw them out the kitchen window, opened it and called out, "John Pratt, you be careful with that son of yours." Arkin felt a warmth in his chest and realized he was smiling.

*****

On their way home after the party, Arkin and Hannah stopped at Trimble Hot Springs to unwind. They sat in an open-air pool, gazing up at bright stars in the crystal clear autumn night sky. They had the pool to themselves for the moment.

"So it really is the Priest?" Hannah asked.

"Probably." Arkin sounded grave. Resigned.

"Unbelievable. Think about the odds of encountering this again."

"I know."

"You don't have to get involved."

"I know."

"You can just tell John what you know. Give him a little direction. Then leave it to him. Your jurisdiction is peripheral anyway, right? Limited to the weapons stuff?"

"I know."

"But you're tempted. Don't say 'I know.'"

"It's just floating around out there, unresolved. I wish Roland were here. I wonder if he would let it go or go after it."

"Nate, I need you here with me."

"I know you do. I'm not going anywhere. If someone has to travel, it will be Pratt. Believe me, I wouldn't leave you right now if they put a gun to my head."

She didn't seem to hear him. "I don't want you off chasing down leads from here to Zanzibar. And I don't want your mind running off to Zanzibar even when I have you here in body, alright? I need the whole you."

"Understood.'

"Anyway, even if one day you break the case, what does that get you? Peace of mind? A sense of vindication over the whole DCI debacle? Closure?" She turned to face him. "Is it going to fill the void for you? You know the answer to that as well as I do." She gathered up and held his hands in hers and looked him square in the eyes. "Let it go."

Arkin stayed quiet. But even in the dim starlight, Hannah could see the heartbreak in his face.

"Nate."

"I know. It just—dealing with it brings back a lot. Dark memories."

"Exactly. And you think catching the Priest will help you bury them?"

"Maybe."

"What if you don't catch him?"

Arkin shrugged.

"Nate, the more distance you've managed to put between yourself and what happened with DCI, the happier you've been. The happier we've both been. And even if you catch your Priest, it isn't going to fix the past. It isn't going to bring Roland back. It isn't going to put you back where you were in D.C. It isn't going to undo any of what happened."

"Yeah," he said, sounding dubious.

"It was years ago. We're happy here. Happy for having given up the race. Happier than we ever were in D.C., and you know it."

"But what happened to me—"

"No, no. Sometimes things just happen in life. Sometimes it's just a matter of luck. Random accident. Like this cancer."

Arkin closed his eyes and frowned. "Can we please not talk about that right now?"

"Do you think if you could go back in time and make me eat more leafy greens that this wouldn't have happened?"

"Please, let's not—"

"Nate, come here."

"Where."

"Come float on your back right in front of me here."

He took a deep breath, spread his arms and legs, arched his torso up to the surface and did his best to float on the hot, steaming water, staring straight up at the starry sky. Hannah moved to support him with her arms, and turned so that her face hovered nearly over his.

"I'm sinking."

"You're not sinking. You're floating. I'm holding you. We're going to perform a little ritual here."

"What?"

"Take a deep breath. As deep as you can."

He complied.

"Now hold it, hold it, hold it. Now let it out, slowly, through your nose."

She had him repeat the cycle seven times. Each time he exhaled, she described how the stress was being pushed further and further out from the center of his chest, until it moved down his limbs and eventually out his fingers and toes. As she did so, he pictured a glowing red line, marking the edge of tension, moving further and further out toward the ends of his appendages. He swore he could actually feel the stress leaving his body.

"Are you relaxed?" she asked at last.

"Yes." All he saw above him was the brilliant night sky and his wife's dimly lit face hovering on the edge of his field of vision.

"I want you to repeat after me, I'm going to let go."

"I'm going to let go."

"I'm not going to get involved, and I'm going to be okay."

"This is silly."

"Nathaniel."

"I'm not going to get involved."

"And you're going to be okay."

He paused. "And I'm going to be okay."

As he said this, Hannah removed her arms from under his back and eased away. He floated free, seemingly in space, totally relaxed. But without her support, as he let out the deep breath he was holding, he began to sink, so he jerked an arm back to support himself, to keep his head from going under.

THIRTEEN

"I got the data from our second subpoena," Pratt said as he strolled in through Arkin's open office door.

"Are the account holders located in Wyoming?"

Pratt stood dumb for a moment. "How—" He shook his head. "Yes. They are both Wyoming LLCs. One called V-TAC, one called Star Dynamics. I did some quick poking around on Lexis-Nexis and so forth, and it looks like both companies only exist on paper. No places of business. No contact information. No advertising. Nothing. Straw companies that don't appear to engage in any sort of business aside from being holders of our two suspect credit card accounts."

"Just like Beartooth Expeditors."

"Who?"

"I'll tell you later."

"Why Wyoming?"

"Wyoming doesn't require that you disclose the names of LLC owners or managers in the articles of organization or annual reports that have to be filed with the secretary of state. The only information available to the general public, and to databases like Lexis-Nexis, is the name of the agent for service of process."

"A dead end then?"

"We should still get the state records. Each LLC has to file an annual report each year. Maybe between the annual reports and the original articles of organization, we'll find that somebody screwed up and left some information in there we can exploit. A name. An address or phone number. A postmark. Anything."

"So are we taking a road trip to Wyoming?"

"Just send them a subpoena. It'll take a few more days, but it sure as hell beats a visit to Cheyenne."

"I like Cheyenne."

"Of course you do. Anyway, while you're at it, subpoena security camera footage for the gas stations, motels, and anywhere else those cards were used. If there was any, it's probably gone by now—the digital memory overwritten by more recent recordings—but it's worth a shot. And there's always a chance they started using the cards again. Might be worth subpoenaing more recent transaction data." Pratt stared at him, as if debating whether to speak. "What is it?"

"You sure like subpoenas."

"Hey, I'd interview a witness if we had one." Now Pratt looked downright glum. "John, you would have loved my last job. There was almost no paperwork, and you got into gunfights and high-speed car chases almost every week."

"Really?"

"No."

Pratt grinned.

Arkin looked out his window. "John, listen. I'll set you on your course here, but I really can't be involved in this one."

Pratt looked puzzled. "What are you talking about? This is your case. Your baby from back in the day."

"My jurisdiction ends with identification of the weapon and bullet."

"All that means is you aren't the primary. It doesn't mean you can't be involved."

"There's more to it than that."

"What do you mean?"

"It's hard to explain. This was the last case I ever worked for DCI. I'm not—I just need to stay on the sidelines for this one. You know what you're doing. You have the whole agency to back you up. I need to step away, alright?"

Pratt looked like a kid who just found out there was no Santa Claus. "If you say so."

"I'm sorry. Look, just subpoena the Wyoming Secretary of State's office for the articles of organization, annual reports, and whatever else they have on record for those two companies. Find out who owns them, then follow the trail on up the chain as far as you can go."

"Okay."

"Have you read through the hard copy of the file you got from headquarters?"

"I haven't got it yet."

"When did you send the request?"

"Oh, I guess last Tuesday."

"Eight days ago?" That was typical, Arkin thought. Whether it reflected conscious or subconscious decisions, records requests from field offices always seemed to be treated with lower priority than requests that came from within headquarters. "Is Mike Chase still running Central Records?"

"He is."

"You should give him a call to follow up."

"I called him two days ago."

"So why is it taking so long?"

"I don't know. He was kind of weird about it. Said he was really busy."

Shit. "Alright, I'll give him a call too. See if we can't light a fire under his lazy headquarters ass."

"Thanks."

*****

After calling and prodding his old drinking buddy, Mike Chase, on Pratt's behalf—only to learn from an embarrassed and awkward-sounding Chase that he hadn't even put the Priest file in the mail yet—Arkin spent the rest of his day focused on other cases, typing up a report of an interview from some two-week-old notes and organizing grand jury material for a Ute man who'd been caught with a fully automatic FN-FAL rifle on the back seat of his car during a traffic stop near Chama, New Mexico. He spent his lunch break beating, in only nine moves, a mid-ranking online chess player from Montreal. It was Hannah's yoga night, so he asked Pratt and Morrison to join him for dinner at the Ore House, and, feeling he needed a little fresh air, walked the half mile along the Animas River to downtown. As he was walking along Main Avenue a few minutes later, just a block from the Ore House, he approached a parked car with heavily tinted windows. A full-sized sedan, maroon in color. What caught his eye was the extra antenna stuck to the trunk with a magnetized base. It was of a sort often used by law enforcement officers when they didn't want to draw attention to themselves, like on unmarked patrol cars being used in speed traps, on surveillance vehicles, et cetera. But Arkin didn't recognize the car as one used by any of the locals he knew. The car appeared to be occupied. As he passed, he thought he could see the shape of a hand-held Motorola radio—another favorite tool of surveillance teams—sitting on the passenger seat. But he couldn't be sure given the dark tinting of the windows. He wondered if somebody might be in town running an operation.

The restaurant was dimly lit and smelled of baking potatoes and beef being grilled over open flame.

"Grape soda?" Morrison asked Pratt.

"Water, asshole."

"Wine?" Morrison asked Arkin.

"Of course."

"Perhaps you should—"

"Yes," Arkin said, reaching for the wine list. "Ah! This is a surprise. They have a four-year-old Tempranillo-Monastrell blend from a very reliable bodega of the Rioja Alavesa."

"The what?"

"A Spanish AVA with a terroir that lends a—"

"Wait a minute, wait a minute," Morrison said, holding up both hands, palms facing Arkin. "Are you fucking kidding me? 'Terroir?' Let me ask you something—did they beat your ass down at Camp Pendleton when you used words like that?"

Arkin eyeballed him, paused. "It goes well with meat."

"Okay then."

Arkin unfolded his napkin and spread it out on his lap. "Hey, have either of you been told about anyone running an op in town?"

"What sort of op?" Morrison asked.

"Any sort. I think I spotted a surveillance-fitted car about a block up Main."

"The maroon Impala?"

"Yes."

"I saw that too. But I haven't heard anything about anyone running an op."

"Some joker from Albuquerque taking his G-ride on vacation, I shouldn't wonder," Arkin said.

"But did you see the radio sitting on his passenger seat?"

"I did."

"So he probably isn't alone."

"Maybe I'll call around tomorrow. Inquire with the locals. See if anyone has declared."

They were soon devouring their steaks—rib-eyes for Morrison and Pratt, Arkin opting for an eleven-ounce filet topped with the Ore House's spin on au poivre—all of them medium-rare.

"So you never finished your story from our drive home from Cortez," Pratt said to Arkin.

"What story?"

"About what happened at DCI. I mean, you know, why you quit."

"Damnation, Pratt," Morrison said. "Do you really think the man wants to talk about that kind of shit over dinner?"

Pratt flushed. "Oh."

But Arkin was feeling unfettered by the half bottle of Spanish wine already in his belly. "No, to hell with it. I'll tell you what happened."

Pratt shook off his embarrassment. "I was just wondering. You said it was because of politics. Politics and a failure of character."

Arkin took a deep breath, then a big pull from his glass of wine. He set his glass down on the table and gazed at it. "About the time I started making some real progress in the Priest case, I was unexpectedly TDY'd to Indonesia to help with consular security in the aftermath of a big earthquake there. Nothing to do with counter-terrorism. They just needed as many agents with security and PSO training down there as they could get, to protect our assets, escort diplomatic personnel, and so forth. There was all sorts of rioting and looting taking place in the post-quake disorder. I was assigned to a four-person team tasked with essentially chauffeuring the family of the chargé d'affaires. For reasons that were never made entirely clear to me, I was made subordinate to a DCI agent who had a bad reputation for being incompetent. Matter of fact, Tom Killick, who is now your director of operations, was the coworker who warned me about this guy, telling me about a case he'd worked with him in which he'd done a number of unethical things trying to cover his own ass when he messed it up."

"You know Killick too?" Pratt asked.

"We're old friends, of sorts. Go way back. We were in training together at FLETC, Fort Belvoir, and other places that shall remain nameless. Ran a lot of cases together."

"You know everybody."

"Anyway, Killick really should have reported the ethical problems of this agent he was warning me about. He didn't. But that's another story." Arkin waved at the air in front of his face as if clearing away smoke. "The point is that this rotten egg of an agent was our team leader for two weeks in Indonesia. Things went badly from the start. It was obvious he didn't know what he was doing. He'd screw up basic things like route planning and end up leading motorcades into narrow, dead-end streets. One time he actually radioed a command for a motorcade to depart a dental clinic before the chargé's wife had even gotten in the car, leaving her and me standing on an exposed street corner like a couple of target dummies. On top of that, there were the ethical issues. For example, on our second day in-country, he ordered one of the guys on our team into a hot riot zone to find him—I shit you not—a Starbucks latte. Another time, claiming he had to follow up on a lead concerning the burglary of a State Department employee's house, he took a consulate vehicle on an 80 mile trip to a tropical beach resort, leaving the rest of us high and dry for three days."

"You're kidding," Pratt said.

"True stories. But the thing that took the cake was what he did with my

100

laptop computer."

"Which was what?"

"He claimed he left his at home because its hard drive crashed. So he asks to borrow mine. Fine, I say, just don't take it outside the consulate because it has sensitive national security information on it, right? Standard procedure. So what happens? First thing I find out after borrowing it back for an hour is that he has been using it to log onto NCIC. No big deal, right? Except that he told another woman on our team that he was querying NCIC to check the backgrounds of a couple of women he met through an online dating service. I don't say anything because I'm not sure how to approach it yet in light of the chain of command issue. I just figure I'll resist letting him borrow it again. When he eventually did ask, I made up some bullshit about the hard drive acting up. But he said he'd deal with it, and ordered me to let him use it. Exactly what happened next remains a mystery, but that same day, while he's out on the town doing heaven knows what, he probably left it in his car or on a table somewhere and it got stolen. On the hard drive were files containing documentation on our order of battle in a couple of ongoing investigations, lists of suspects, even the dossier of a confidential informant."

"Holy shit," Morrison nearly shouted.

"Quite. But does he fess up to having lost it so that CI-IS can deal with the security breach? No, sir. When I told him I needed it back to draft my daily report, he feigned ignorance, claiming he hadn't borrowed it after all, but left it on my makeshift desk in our little command center." Arkin shook his head. "A lie. I watched him take it. Unhappily for me, there were no other witnesses."

"Needless to say, when I called headquarters about it, the shit hit the fan. The team was recalled three days later. Internal Security interviewed each of us the day we got back. They didn't even let us go home from Dulles Airport to take showers first. Ordered us to come straight in. At that point I figured I had to lay it all out—the incompetence, the ethical violations, the lot. The other two members of the team provided corroborating evidence on much of it. But in the end, he got off without so much as a letter of admonishment. In fact, soon thereafter, he was promoted. Now he's the agent-in-charge of the Miami field office. The rest of us were formally reprimanded based on trumped-up nonsense like 'going outside the chain of command in reporting issues,' as if we were supposed to report his ethical violations to *him* instead of to headquarters. And I was all but accused of being a racist."

"What?" Pratt said. "You, a racist? That's almost funny."

"How the hell did he come out of it unscathed?" Morrison asked.

"The final decisions came from the political appointee level."

"So?"

"As fate would have it, he happened to be an Iraqi-American. Born and raised in Lubbock, Texas, and as American as Dick Clark, but never mind.

Through no fault of his own, DCI made him into their poster child for post-9/11 cooperation between the Arab-American community and federal law enforcement. For obvious reasons, DCI wouldn't have wanted to mar the facade, which I'll admit was an important one to maintain."

"And he could have played the minority card if they'd tried to remove him," Pratt said.

"He never gave the slightest hint that he would have."

"But management couldn't have known that he wouldn't."

"I don't go there."

"You wouldn't," Morrison said. "It's not in your programming. That's one of the reasons you're here and they're there, if you follow me."

"All that matters is that political considerations trumped logic and ethics."

"Say it ain't so," Morrison said.

"What happened?" Pratt asked.

"This is conjecture, but I'm guessing that the deputy attorney general for DCI, a political appointee, weighed all the evidence we gave him. At the end of the day, doing what was right constituted a greater risk to his own continued, untroubled promotion than did siding with an incompetent agent who also happened to be a liar and thief. So he took the safe path."

"Couldn't Sheffield protect you?"

"He went to bat for me. But it was at the political level. Above his station."

"So then what?"

"About a week later, I was recalled from the field to be informed of the results of the inquiry, and to be told I was being denied an annual promotion that was due me. The personnel director, an incompetent buffoon if there ever was one, said he couldn't, in good conscience, let my promotion paperwork go through given my proclivity to insubordinate behavior and possible racist attitudes."

"You've got to be shitting me," Morrison said. "Bastards."

"That's what I thought. A few days later, I was told I was being redeployed to Durango."

"Redeployed being a polite euphemism for banished and ostracized."

"Exactly. At that point, I was ready to hire a lawyer. But Sheffield told me to roll with it. He said Personnel was threatening to 'out me' as a racist if I tried to resist."

"That's absurd," Pratt said. "On what grounds?"

"It was never made clear to me. But it hardly matters. Sheffield said I should just go to Durango and bide my time because political appointees came and went. We'd no doubt have a new deputy AG and new personnel director before long, this would all be forgotten, and then he would see me returned to Camelot with all the fanfare due me."

"Laurels on your head, rose petals at your feet," Morrison said.

"But you quit and went to work for MWA."

Arkin nodded. "A month after we moved here, Sheffield died. I suppose you could say that my hope for redemption died with him. I flew to Arlington for his funeral, saluted as the Marine Corps honor guard fired their volleys, buried his empty coffin, and handed in my resignation. Finito."

They sat quietly for a moment. Then Pratt asked, "Do you believe the rumors that Sheffield killed himself?"

Arkin paused before answering. "No. They found his Mercedes convertible underwater in the mouth of Little Hunting Creek, off the George Washington Parkway down near Mount Vernon. He probably had a heart attack or stroke, went off the road, and then the current carried his body on down the Potomac."

"They said he was despondent over the death of his wife."

"He was."

"But you don't think—"

"No."

Pratt let it go.

FOURTEEN

"Arkin," he said, answering his office phone.

"It's me," Pratt said. "I got the Priest file."

"Great."

"I'd like to show you something in it."

"I'd really rather not."

"I know. I'm sorry. I just really need your advice on something."

A minute later, Arkin walked through the doorway of Pratt's basement office. A thin, pastel green file folder of the type always used by DCI's Central Records Unit lay open on Pratt's desk.

"Where's the rest of it?"

"This is it."

"What?"

"Yeah. And take a look at this," Pratt said, pointing to something in the file.

The tab was labeled with the proper case number: 03-125A-MCE. But the file contained only one sheet of paper. At the top of the sheet, in all capital letters of large point size, just as in the electronic file in the INDIGO database, were the words "CLOSED FILE--ALL INQUIRIES TO DIRECTOR OF OPERATIONS." There was nothing aside from the case number to even indicate that it was the Priest file.

"What the hell?"

"You tell me."

"Did you guys open some sort of ultra-secure, separate records room for the really sensitive cases or something?"

"Not that I know of. Maybe they just decided to start purging the hard copies of old files."

"No. They can't. Not for a certain number of years, anyway. Not unless they changed the classified records retention rules government-wide, which you and I would have heard about."

"Maybe there are other files for this case that the Central Records guys didn't see."

"Maybe."

"How big was this file when you worked the case?"

"Big. At least seven full file folders, and several boxes of hard evidence down in the vault. Bank records. Parish account books. Bryant's high school yearbooks. And fragments of bullets."

"So what's the deal?"

"I don't know."

"Well, I hate to ask, but can you help me? I feel like I've been badgering those Central Records guys every other day for two weeks now. I don't want to burn any bridges."

"No, you sure don't." Arkin thought for a moment. "Okay. Let me make a couple of phone calls."

*****

Back in his own office, Arkin sat at his desk, leaning forward and propping his forehead on the heels of his hands, his mind a jumble of thoughts and emotions. Was this a simple mistake by the records unit? No. If one of the many files had been left out, then maybe. But this was far too big an error for them to miss. So had the Priest file been purged? It was looking that way. But why? And did Hannah look worse this morning, or was it just his imagination? And why on Earth had that dishonest, incompetent creep been put in charge of his Indonesia security team? How did he ever get hired in the first place? How could anyone with a drop of honest blood in their bodies have sided with him after he lost the laptop and then lied about it?

His heart pounding, he stood up, took a deep breath, clapped his hands together, then left the building for a walk along the river in the cool, crisp autumn air.

He walked and walked, breathing deeply, trying to bring discipline to his mind. But his thoughts remained in shadow, focused on his wife's decline, reflecting on his fall from grace within DCI, on Sheffield's death, thinking back to the Priest case and all that it implied. Hearing distant shouts, he turned to see, on a riverside playfield in the floodplain below the walking path, two teams in a game of flag football. His eyes followed a receiver sprinting down the far edge of the field until they came upon a lone player standing still on the sideline watching the action. An extra. Arkin was too far away to see his face. But he was sure of the expression it bore. And all at once, as Arkin's gaze drifted to the hills beyond the playfield, he was back in any one of the several hometowns of his childhood, standing idle on the sideline of any of their playfields. The late-blooming "ethnic" kid in the WASP neighborhood. Newly arrived after yet another surprise relocation for the sake of his father's insatiable desire to move up to neighborhoods that were supposed to confer ever-higher status. The undersized, underdeveloped outsider and oddball. Forgotten, marginalized, and left on the sideline to ponder his inadequacy.

From there, his memory inexplicably jumped to his father's federal court chambers. Arkin had just graduated from law school, with honors, and his father, sitting in a massive leather chair and still wearing his black judicial robe more than an hour after adjourning court, had mentioned that he was having his will updated by the trusts and estates section of his former law firm in Manhattan.

"You know, I could update your will for you. You don't have to hand over thousands of dollars to some random lawyer in your old firm. I'd do it for nothing, with a level of conscientiousness you're only likely to find amongst family."

"You think you could handle it?" his father had said dubiously, shaking his head as he asked.

"Why not?"

"I'm not some Ford assembly line worker with a crude proletariat pension. You think you'd have any clue how to treat all the different assets in my estate?" he'd asked rhetorically. "No, I think I'll stick with the professionals, thank you very much."

As he was crossing the footbridge over the Animas and into town, the land all around seemed to darken. It was far too early for sunset, so Arkin at first thought it was his overactive imagination playing tricks on him again, seeming to add shadow to his vision to reflect his mood. But then he heard a deep rumble of thunder, and, turning to face the west, saw the leading edge of a tall, black storm cell just cresting the mountains, approaching town. *Damn.*

Gauging the speed of the clouds, he guessed he had about four minutes before the downpour hit. He was, as usual, in a dark wool suit. But he had no coat or umbrella as it had, until then, been a clear and sunny day. He turned around and headed for the office at a trot. Along the way, he passed the usual mix of walkers, runners, and bicyclers. Even a woman on rollerblades being pulled along by her tethered Great Dane. They all moved with an apparent urgency, no doubt mindful of the imminent need to seek shelter from the storm. As he neared the office building, he passed a man walking in the opposite direction, dressed in common khaki pants and an un-tucked flannel button-down shirt. But it was the man's beautiful brown suede oxfords that caught Arkin's shoe lover eye. They looked to be of high-quality. Yet curiously, the man wasn't making for shelter, but seemed headed for the open and exposed river trail. He was going to ruin a fine pair of shoes, Arkin thought. Senseless.

A lightning strike on the mountainside above drew Arkin's attention back to his journey. When he was 200 yards shy of the office building, the sky opened up, unleashing a deluge over top of his head. *Damn.* He ran for it. Nevertheless, by the time he reached the front door, he was soaked. *Damn it.* He stripped off his wet jacket and tie as he climbed the stairs to his floor and strode into his office. Realizing he was suddenly cold, he started a new pot of hot Rwandan coffee before collapsing into his chair. He took a handkerchief from a desk drawer and wiped the rain from his face. Though it was barely after four o'clock, the land outside was so dark in the shadow of the storm cell that it could have been mistaken for dusk.

Arkin closed his eyes, his mind somewhat calmed by his exertion, but still troubled. The feeling reminded him of his last days in D.C., when so many things seemed to be going against him. He remembered it feeling as though he were caught in some sort of dark and terrible whirlwind created and fed by an almost unbelievable chain of events. Random events. Events and consequences that all seemed to defy logic. None of it in his control.

The smell of coffee brewing brought him back to the present. He opened his eyes, unlocked a file drawer with a small key, and pulled the drawer all the way out until the very last file in the far back of it was accessible. From this, he drew out an unmarked file folder and laid it on his desk. A flash of lightning accompanied a simultaneous flickering of his office lights. A thunder clap. Another flash of lightning and the electricity went out. All was dim. Arkin let his eyes adjust, then flipped the file open. There, in a grainy old 5x7 black-and-white print copied from Lucricia Burris, was the Priest. He stood in the center of a group of people, a good six inches taller than anyone else, in full habit, looking grim. His hair and beard grown long and disheveled. Another lightning flash surged and faded, briefly illuminating the photo. And in the flash, Arkin focused on Bryant's eyes. Those crazy fanatic's eyes.

So much of what had gone wrong in Arkin's life seemed to happen when he was working the Priest case. What strange fortune. He returned the photo to its storage place and slammed the file drawer home. He lifted the receiver of his phone and dialed a number he hadn't dialed in several years.

"Killick."

"Hello, Tom."

"Nate?"

"Es correcto."

"Hey, you old pariah! How are you?"

"Older. How's trade?"

"Same old bullshit. You?"

"Closing in on D.B. Cooper. How's the family?"

"Grace is good. Starting to work part-time again now that the twins are in preschool. I still haven't built the garden shed she's been bugging me for since you lived here."

"Still? You're worse than me."

"I seriously doubt that. I remember you still having Christmas lights up on April Fool's Day. And you don't even celebrate Christmas."

"Who doesn't like Christmas lights?"

"How's Hannah?"

"Okay at the moment. Pretty worn down by the chemo, but she's a tough cookie."

"Give her our best."

"Look, Tom, we are really overdue to catch up."

"You're right about that."

"But I'm actually calling you about a case."

"A case? An MWA case?"

"No. One of yours. I'm peripherally involved by virtue of the murder weapon."

"Oh?"

"Cortez, Colorado. Shooting of a high-profile lay minister. A firebrand."

"I don't think I've been briefed on that one. But what can I do for you?"

"Your man out here, Pratt, has been trying to get hold of an archived file that might help him in his investigation. He was running into the usual Central Records Unit indifference. When he finally got the file, it was empty."

"Empty?"

"All it has in it is a note directing all inquiries to the Director of Operations. That's you."

"That's me."

"So where are the case materials?"

"Are you going to tell me what case you're talking about?"

Arkin paused. "The Priest."

"The Priest? Nate Arkin's holy grail? Are you shitting me?"

"You've always had a gift for creative verbs."

"Nate, seriously, what the hell does the Priest case have to do with a shooting in Cortez, Colorado?"

"There are just some similarities I think your man should look at. If nothing else, it will give him some guidance on useful investigative techniques given that the cases are so similar. But why the special treatment, Tom?"

"Special treatment?"

"Why is the file empty? Why does it direct all inquiries to you?"

"I have no idea. Maybe Roland put that in there before he died." Killick was quiet for a moment. "Look, Nate, I don't mean to be an asshole, but isn't this going a bit over the line for you? I mean, you looking through *our* files, and for a case you aren't involved with anymore?"

"Okay. As I said, I'm involved in the Cortez investigation by virtue of the murder weapon, a .50 caliber Serbian military sniper rifle. So everything is kosher. I'm not overstepping any boundaries."

"Nate, you know perfectly well how—"

"Look, I'm just trying to help your guy, Tom. Given my past involvement, I know that the Priest file would be a good thing for Pratt to look at. Believe me, it's the last thing in the world I want to reread."

"Alright, alright. I just don't want you to get into trouble, that's all."

"Hey, thanks for looking out for me, Tom."

"Nate—"

"I'll tell you what—you find the case file and send it to the kid, and I promise I won't even look at it. Scout's honor."

"You were in the Boy Scouts?"

"Fuck no."

After an awkward silence, Killick promised to look into where the case materials had gone, and to see if he couldn't have them shipped to Pratt. He told Arkin he would personally oversee a search of the archives. From there, the conversation degenerated into forced talk of other things going on in their respective lives. When he finally rang off, Arkin realized that his hand and forearm ached from holding the telephone handset so tightly.

*****

Morrison threw Arkin's office door open.

"Don't you ever knock?"

"Worried I'll catch you waxing your ass crack? Come on, it's five o'clock somewhere. Are you up for—"

"A pint. Yes."

"Steamworks?"

"Perfect."

"Should we ask the Mormon?"

"It would be the polite thing to do. Just give me five minutes to finish this guy off," Arkin said, gesturing to the chessboard on his screen.

"Our tax dollars hard at work."

"Go piss up a rope. I've been on the clock for 10 hours."

"Some days you lose your charm faster than a buttermilk biscuit. Who's your opponent?"

"Some minister of economics in France."

"France, eh? If memory serves, I believe there's a place in France where the naked ladies dance."

Arkin's face was blank.

"You don't get the reference? A place in France where the naked ladies dance? See, Nate, you've been so insulated all your life, surrounded by chess-playing Andover dorks who hide behind academics because they can't get laid, that you're culturally illiterate."

"Exeter dorks. Exeter. And, as usual, your prose is as awkward as the day is long."

*****

Soon they were walking to the pub after having to park Morrison's car down on Main Avenue. Though it wasn't yet Thanksgiving, many of the shop windows were already decorated for Christmas. By autumn, Arkin usually began hoping for an early, heavy snowfall. But this year, given Hannah's condition, all he cared about was being able to drive her to the hospital if he needed to.

As they passed a candy shop, Pratt said, "Hold on, fellas. I want to look at something in that window."

"The marzipan vegetables?" Morrison asked. "And you call yourself an American?"

"No, not that crap. It looked like there was peanut butter fudge on the silver tray on the left."

"Fudge?"

"Yessiree."

"You live up to your nicknames, Junior."

As they doubled back, they passed a man wearing frayed blue jeans and a puffy black down jacket. As he slipped by them, keeping to the inside edge of the sidewalk, Arkin happened to catch a look at the man's shoes. The brown suede oxfords again. Arkin looked up to see the man's face, but he was turned away, as though examining something on the wall of the building he was walking past. The only thing on the wall was a standard no parking sign.

The tiny hairs on the back of Arkin's neck stood up. What were the chances of his passing two different pairs of identical suede city shoes in this out-of-the-way western town on the same day? And if it was the same man, what were the odds it was a coincidence that Arkin would run into him again, and that the man would be wearing a completely different outfit even though barely an hour had passed since their first encounter? Durango was a small town, but still. Arkin stopped and turned around for another attempt to see the man's face, but the man was walking away from him. There was a motorcycle parked five feet away. Arkin hopped over to it and pressed a button to sound its loud horn. He held it down, the bike's horn filling the street with its obnoxious din. Yet while he wasn't more than 20 yards away, the suede-shoed man didn't turn around to see what the noise was about. He kept walking. Arkin let go of the horn and watched as the man rounded the corner and disappeared.

"The fuck are you doing?" Morrison asked, looking half amused.

"That guy who just passed us."

"What about him?"

"Ever see him before?"

"I didn't get a good look. Why?"

Arkin didn't answer, but watched the street corner, hoping the man would come back around. He looked up and down the street, eyeballing each pedestrian, looking for anything odd. Looking for the maroon Impala he'd seen by the Ore House. Nothing stood out. Against his better judgment, he took off after the man. But when Arkin finally rounded the corner, the man was nowhere to be seen.

*****

They grabbed a booth. Arkin and Morrison each ordered a stout and a glass of bourbon. Pratt asked for soda water with grenadine.

"So what was that about, your little scene there back on Main?" Morrison asked Arkin.

"Paranoia."

"Over what?"

"Being surveilled."

Morrison's eyebrows rose. "It's funny you say that."

"Is it?"

"I've had the old tingle myself. Nothing solid. Just a feeling."

"Where?"

"Well, on the way here, for example. I swear I saw just the tiniest pause in a couple of pedestrians as we doubled back to the candy shop. That watcher's 10th-of-a-second, involuntary pause of contemplation. You know the one."

"I do. But you didn't see it in the guy I was eyeballing?"

"No. Not him. But I wasn't focused on him. It was a woman following behind him by about twenty yards, and a man on the far side of the street. What caught my eye was that they both did it simultaneously, the little pause."

Arkin told them about the brown suede shoes. "Like I said, I'm probably just being paranoid."

They sat silent, drank their drinks, and ordered another round along with two dozen hot wings. All the while, unwelcome theories, implications, and fears began to take shape in Arkin's mind.

"So what do I do about this file?" Pratt finally asked as he licked buttery hot sauce from his fingers.

"Oh, I meant to tell you, I made some calls. If there's anything to be found, it'll be found tomorrow and shipped to you."

"You think you'll get better results than I did?"

"I called Killick."

Pratt's eyes popped wide. "You called the director of ops, for me? I'm going to remember you come Christmas, Nate, even if you are a heathen."

"Don't count your chickens."

"About you being a heathen?" Morrison asked. "Has Pratt finally convinced you to convert?"

Arkin smiled.

"You don't think they'll find anything." Pratt said.

"I don't know. Maybe not. It's all very odd."

"So what if they can't find anything?"

"Then I can at least tell you the rest of what I know about the case."

"Let's have it right now," Morrison said. "Your overuse of cliffhangers is getting just a little bit too irritatingly cute, even for you."

"I don't have the energy."

"Come on, you big pussy."

Arkin sat slumped.

"What the hell is wrong with you? You look like shit."

"Thanks."

"No, really. What's going on with you?"

"I don't know. I haven't been sleeping very well. This case—" He shrugged.

"The Priest case? What about it?"

"It brings back a lot of dark memories for me." Arkin paused. "And Hannah—" He shook his head. "I think she looks worse. I think she might be going downhill."

Morrison's expression softened. He slid his own tumbler of bourbon over to Arkin. Arkin caught it in his right hand, looked at it for a moment, then drank it and slammed the empty glass back down on the table. *Hell.* He sat up straight, a new intensity filling his eyes as he stared at himself in the large mirror that hung behind the old wooden bar. He lay his arms flat on the table. "Father Bryant was officially reported drowned in 1974."

"Drowned," Morrison echoed. "Case closed. And then?"

"And then, decades later, I did some poking around. To my astonishment, the archdiocese let me take a look at their archived records without a subpoena."

"That has to be a first."

"I copied the books covering the early years of the Royburg parish's existence and did a rudimentary audit. Pretty simple accounting. At any rate, what I found was eye-opening to say the least."

"Do go on."

"Over a period beginning three months after the industrial accident and ending the very month of Bryant's disappearance, the per capita tithing of the parish was almost exactly fifteen percent below what it was during the first years of the parish and in the years after Bryant was replaced by a new priest."

Morrison nodded. Pratt looked perplexed.

I crunched the numbers and figured that from 1968 to 1974, Bryant skimmed more than $12,000. A tidy sum in those days."

"You think he walked away with the cash?" Pratt asked.

"Not exactly."

"What do you mean?"

"I mean it would have been hard to travel inconspicuously with a burden of $12,000 in small bills pilfered from the collection basket. I took a guess that he'd opened a bank account somewhere. Somewhere he could go in his regular civilian clothes, and where folks wouldn't recognize him. So on this hunch, I visited all the banks I could find within about thirty miles of Royburg, figuring he wouldn't want to go farther than a single hitch-hiked ride of reasonable duration. Of course, many of the banks that were around in the seventies had long since gone belly up. Some had been taken over by larger banks. Most all had long since purged their records of old, dead accounts. And most had long since dumped all old paper records in introducing computerized systems. But to my absolute disbelief, I found a tiny, tiny, stand-alone bank in the little town of Acuff—about 27 miles east of Royburg—that not only had a plain old 'Mister' Collin Bryant as a customer, they actually had the paper records from his account. The bank was founded by Great Depression survivors who had a policy of keeping everything— literally every record or document they or their relatively small circle of customers ever generated—in boxes in their basement. They never threw anything away."

"And?"

"And Bryant had closed his account in 1974, exactly three weeks before his disappearance, wiring the balance of his $12,223 savings account to the account of a 'Collin Brant,' no 'y,' at a bank in Nanaimo, British Columbia."

"Nanaimo?"

"Vancouver Island. Hometown of Diana Krall, the jazz pianist. But here I hit a dead end. On the Canadian side, we could find no surviving records of the account or the wire transfer, and the only Collin Brant who ever lived in the province was a different guy. A lumber mill worker from Prince Rupert, younger than Bryant by seventeen years. So best I could figure, Bryant worked up some form of fake ID to facilitate the wire transfer, then dropped it and went underground with his big pile of money. Unfortunately, that was as far as I could track him.

"So that was it?" Pratt asked.

"Did you really just say that?" Morrison said to Pratt. "Did you really just ask Arkin, our resident clairvoyant and winner of the National Intelligence Distinguished Service Medal, if 'that was it'?"

"Well, I mean, I—"

"—am an ignorant Utah hillbilly? We know."

"Not seeing a way forward, I backtracked. Dug back through the case file. In fact, I did exactly what you're doing now," he said, turning to Pratt. "Got credit card data, found a pattern of gas station stops within a couple hundred miles of three Zastava shootings and involving the same credit card account number, and then traced the account to a Wyoming LLC: Beartooth Expeditors. I subpoenaed the articles of organization and found that it was owned by another company. A Canadian company—PPK Packers of Port Hardy, British Columbia. Also on Vancouver Island. With the help of our Canadian liaison, I was granted permission to go up there for a covert look. All I found at the address of record was an empty, rotting, long-abandoned salmon cannery. It had obviously been boarded up for years. I walked all around it, not knowing what to look for." Arkin's eyes were fixed on a something far away as he told the story. "Then, on the back corner of the building, in an area of gravel driveway overgrown with weeds and blackberry vines, I saw them."

"Saw what?" Pratt said.

"New fasteners."

"Fasteners?"

"Screws. Quite unlike the regular nails that had been used to board up all the other windows and doors. The nails were all thoroughly corroded. But the screws holding the two-by-fours into place over this tiny, nearly hidden fire door were practically new, spray painted flat black to hide their shine. But I spotted them. I ran to the nearest hardware store to buy a screwdriver, came back, unscrewed the boards, picked the simple doorknob lock, and stepped inside. The place stunk of the stale air of disuse, of rodent excrement, dampness, and mildew. There were dead flies everywhere—on the windowsills, more scattered about the dusty floor."

"And there were footprints in the dust. Many sets of footprints, some older, some new, all from the same sized foot, and all leading from the fire door to a tiny side office partitioned off from the greater interior of the warehouse. In that office, under a tarnished brass mail slot cut through the outer wall, lay a pile of unopened mail, free of dust, with cancellation dates no more than two weeks old. Most of it was junk. But there was also a postcard with nothing in the text section but a series of three ten-digit numbers, as well as one sealed phone bill addressed to 'PPK Packers.'"

"Was there a phone in the building?" Pratt asked.

"No."

"Maybe they'd forgotten to cancel their phone service when they went out of business."

"But if nobody was paying for the line, the phone company would have cut it off in short order and sent the amount due to collections," Morrison said. "And this place had been out of business for years. So who was picking up their mail and paying the bill?"

"Exactly. I figure someone was using the number to communicate via remote electronic voicemail. Somebody calls the voicemail system and leaves a message. Someone from somewhere else retrieves it. I held the phone bill up to the window to try to see what I could see through the outer envelope. Most of the text was of such a small point size that I couldn't make it out. But the total amount due looked to be either $54 or $64 and change. I put everything back just as I'd found it, resealed the door, then staked the place out from the woods across the road. After five days of eating hideous freeze-dried food and sitting bored out of my mind in a clammy plastic camouflaged poncho out in the never-ending British Columbia rain, watching the place through binoculars, a man finally appeared. An Asian man, maybe 5-foot tall. He was jogging, dressed out in a runner's typical rainy day garb. He made one pass, running on down the road, around the bend and out of sight. But then he doubled back, slowed, turned into the narrow gap between the building and the encroaching brush, and disappeared."

"He could have been taking a leak," Pratt said.

"It would have been a long leak. All in, he spent about as much time in there as I figured it would have taken him to unscrew the door, grab the mail, and reseal the place. He wasn't holding anything in his hands when he emerged, but his pockets bulged as though filled with papers. Needless to say, I tracked him home and forwarded his address and license plate number to my Canadian liaison. Came back as a Zhang Zhou, Canadian citizen granted asylum from mainland China 22 years earlier. A refugee of some sort. Clean record up north. Anyway, in an unbelievably bad stroke of luck with respect to timing, within hours of dictating the report of my discovery to headquarters via telephone, I was bluntly summoned back to headquarters by the director of personnel. I was to appear before a board of inquiry formed to review my conduct in Indonesia. I returned home, and immediately asked our Canadian liaison to subpoena Zhou's bank and phone records, as well as the phone records for PPK."

"And?"

"And the only calls made to PPK's number were from burners. Unregistered, disposable cellphones, purchased from convenience stores or shopping mall cart vendors, pre-charged with however many minutes."

"Shit," Morrison said.

"But," Arkin said as he held up a finger, "I also found a deposit to Mr.

Zhou's main checking account, in the amount of $64.33, made exactly one day after he'd paid his mysterious visit to the abandoned PPK cannery."

"Get out!" Morrison said, his face breaking into a smile. "Did I not tell you he was the fucking best there ever was?" he said to Pratt. "So who made the deposit?"

"Another Canadian company, this one in Vancouver."

"What was it called?"

"Something with an 'S.' Or maybe an 'F.'" Arkin's expression changed. He looked Pratt and Morrison each in the eye, in turn, then turned his own eyes downward. "I can't remember."

"What?" Morrison asked. "You, mister steel trap for a memory? You can't remember?"

"Nobody's perfect."

"Nobody's perfect? Are you shitting me? You? With something *that* critical?"

"I got the call from my Canadian liaison," he said, sounding deeply frustrated. "I wrote the name of the company down on the very top line of the very first sheet of paper in a brand new yellow notepad. I used a red pen. After the liaison rung off, I put the pen in my right-hand desk drawer and took a long sip of hot coffee from my Exeter mug." Morrison and Pratt sat rapt. Arkin shook his head, looking suddenly quite worn down. "Then I got a rather distracting phone call from the deputy attorney general's office bluntly ordering me to a meeting, right then and there, to discuss the results of the personnel inquiry."

"And then what?" Pratt asked.

"Then nothing. *Then,* in my agitation over the ominous and urgent summons to the personnel inquiry meeting, and not anticipating the immediate need to do so, I failed to record the name of the Canadian company in my memory. *Then,* I was suspended for two weeks without pay. *Then,* I was escorted from the deputy's office straight to the back door, without a chance to stop by my office, after having my badge and gun taken and my coat and umbrella all but thrown at me. Before the suspension was up, I was issued orders to redeploy to Durango, and all the cases I was working for the D.C. office were taken away from me. The deputy attorney general himself ordered me to keep my nose out of them. And I never again saw the yellow notepad with the name of the Vancouver company on it. The most I ever learned after that was that the new agent the Priest case was assigned to did a couple of months of follow-up before the case was closed out for 'lack of actionable evidence.'"

"They didn't even let you go back to your office?" Pratt said. "So you couldn't get or even see your yellow pad with the name of the Vancouver company? The timing!"

"One of the more rotund building security goons met me and the security goon who was escorting me down from the deputy's office at the back exit with a box containing my personal cellphone, my sack lunch, and my travel coffee mug. And, as I mentioned, they gave me my coat and umbrella. That was it. No yellow pad. Nothing to do with any of my cases. Just an acid glare for the road from each of the guards as I stood on the sidewalk, half in shock, looking back at them as they pulled the door shut behind me. You'd have thought they told those guys I'd been downloading child pornography on my work computer. Don't call us, asshole—we'll call you."

"That must have pissed you off to high heaven."

"It was a thousand years ago."

Morrison grinned hearing this. "Oh sure. You can tell yourself that all day."

"I still have a copy of that photograph though."

"Exactly," Morrison said.

"Copy of what photograph?" Pratt asked.

"Of the Priest. The one Lucricia Burris gave to me. It was the only thing I kept from the file."

"Why do you still have it?" Pratt asked.

Arkin shrugged.

"Because it was a thousand years ago and he doesn't care anymore," Morrison said, still grinning. "So what did he look like?"

"The Priest?"

"No, Mr. Bojangles. Yes, the Priest."

Arkin raised his tumbler of bourbon up to the light, his now angry eyes studying the amber liquid as he swirled it in his glass. "He looked like Rasputin. A 6-foot-4, 240-pound Rasputin."

*****

An hour later, Morrison and Arkin were starting to get drunk, with Pratt dutifully keeping them company—more to keep an eye on them than anything else.

"Hey, why don't we try to track down this Zhang Zhou guy?" Pratt asked, clearly excited that he came up with the idea.

"Oh, Johnny boy." Morrison said. "Now you're going to insult Nate's intelligence?"

"That's a good idea, John," Arkin said. "Except that about a year after we moved here, I tried to do just that."

"Ha!" Morrison shouted. "See, Pratt? He couldn't let it drop!"

"As soon as I was set up with MWA, I tried to run him down through all the usual databases. There were dozens of Zhang Zhous in the U.S. and Canada. Old ones, young ones, fat ones, thin ones. Tons and tons of information on them in our billions of dollars worth of law enforcement and intelligence computer networks. But could I find *my* Zhang Zhou? No, sir. Not in any of our vaunted databases. In fact, there were no traces of his ever having existed. It seems he dropped off the face of the earth with dazzlingly perfect timing," Arkin said, his voice seething with bitterness.

Wondering at Arkin's tone, Pratt asked, "How did you end up in law enforcement anyway?"

"Huh?"

"He means, with all your pedigree, and connections, and law degree, and other special shit, how did you end up in a thankless, low-paying crap job like this? A job that makes you and all the rest of us so bitter." Morrison said.

"Maybe I like the work."

"That isn't why," Morrison said.

"No. No, it isn't."

"Why didn't you stay a lawyer?" Pratt asked.

"Do you know what being a lawyer is like? It's like arguing about minutiae of the rules of Monopoly all day, every day, for the rest of your life, and you aren't even the one playing the game. You're the sorry schmuck sitting on a hard stool looking over someone's shoulder while everybody else plays. You're the custodian of other people's problems."

"So why did you go to law school in the first place?"

"Nobody knows what it's going to be like until they're doing it."

"I didn't ask why you didn't not go. I asked why you did go."

"Again with the grammar. You're making my head hurt."

"And you went to law school because?"

"Because, Pratt, when I was little, I was a nobody. No friends ever called me to come over and play. I had to call them. Ever since then, I've been trying to find ways to feel important."

"You're screwing with me."

"If you say so," Arkin said, grinning weakly. "Did you know my father was a named partner in a giant Manhattan law firm, and eventually a federal court judge?"

"I did not."

"Oh, yes. A very important man. Big-time power broker."

Pratt nodded stupidly.

"I'll tell you something he said to me on one of those rare days when he actually stooped to spend time with me. He said 'Nathanial, nobody in this world is worth the paper their diploma is printed on except a top lawyer from a top school in a top firm. Everybody else is just pretending, wishing they were the masters instead of the marionettes.'"

"I see," Pratt said, for lack of anything better.

"Of course, if I'd followed the career path he wanted me to take, joined his old firm and whatnot, I'd probably be a multimillionaire by now."

"A miserable multimillionaire," Morrison said.

"He shipped me off to boarding school when I was 12 years old."

"Sounds like a dick."

"Yes. You have to cut him some slack though. His own father was a Holocaust survivor whose sense of brotherly love for his fellow man was probably lessened by his experiences in a barb-wired rectangle of countryside northwest of Munich in the 1940s. So I imagine my father didn't have the happiest upbringing."

Talking about it reminded Arkin of the profound sense of loss he felt not when his own father died, but when Sheffield had. Sheffield—the one person who really seemed to know Arkin, to understand where he was coming from and what he needed. For weeks after they'd found Sheffield's car in the river, Arkin had reeled in a rudderless despair and crushing sense of emptiness. In stark contrast, when he'd stood alongside the Manhattan hospital bed that held his dead father, he'd felt detached and emotionless, and wondered how soon he could leave without it looking improper. His father's body had struck him as little more than an inanimate object, no more important than the plain furniture of the hospital room.

"You realize that in chasing the Priest, you're chasing another version of yourself, right?" Morrison said, his eyes glassy, a devilish smirk on his face.

"Shut your hillbilly mouth."

Pratt thought about ordering a fourth soda, decided against it. He was already bloated to the point of discomfort. "So how do you think they managed to lose the file?" he finally asked, eager to change the subject.

"Don't jump to conclusions," Arkin said.

"What do you mean?"

"Maybe someone lost the file, or maybe someone *lost* the file."

"You mean maybe someone got rid of it on purpose?" Pratt asked.

"Or is blocking access. Maybe keeping an eye on me too."

"Come on, it's clear as day, Pratt," Morrison said. "The U.S. government is now in the business of blowing the heads off of two-bit lay preachers from Cortez, Colorado, because of the obvious danger they pose to global security. They've hired this phantom priest's group to do their dirty work. A lapsed Jesuit priest whose henchmen make Blackwater look like a bunch of clumsy altar boys. And now they're tracking Nate, their old nemesis, because y'all's inquiries are ringing old bells. They're having their unbelievably well-positioned flunky operators stymie your requests for files from the moldy sub-basement records room of DCI Headquarters because you and Nate are a threat to their great transnational conspiracy. Right? Am I on target, Nate? I love this shit. I think it's ready for talk radio."

"Go ahead and exaggerate. But you're the one who said you picked up on the surveillance earlier."

"I said I had a *feeling*, Nate. A tingle. Nothing definite."

"Fine. But turncoats and rogue operators with their own agendas aren't unheard of in the intelligence fraternity."

"So then why don't they just kill you too?" Pratt asked. "Why go to all the trouble to hide files and surveil you if you're a threat to them?"

"That's the smartest thing you've said all week," Morrison said.

"But I'm not really a threat yet." Arkin said. "I mean, I don't know anything useful, do I? And as for the presumed surveillance, maybe they're still trying to ascertain whether or not I do know anything."

"Still," Pratt said. "Why wait around for you to turn over the right rock when you're obviously hell-bent?"

"Maybe they're reluctant."

"Why would they be?"

Arkin shrugged his shoulders. "An excellent question. Maybe they don't want any more attention. Or maybe it's something more complicated, like a philosophical issue for them. A moral code. A desire to avoid killing unless they believe it is absolutely necessary. Think about it. If these guys are assassinating fledgling extremists—murderous despots of the future, or whatever—then they're trying to *do good*, quote-unquote. There's a philanthropic ethos to their endeavor, however twisted it may be."

"Yeah, that's it," Morrison said. "It's because they love you. Lord alive. This just keeps getting better. Exhale and step away from the bong, Nate."

"No offense," Pratt added, "but it all sounds pretty far-fetched."

Arkin sipped his drink. "Maybe. But I'll say this. There is a curious regularity with which people who have any interest in the Priest case seem to get doors slammed in their faces or rugs pulled out from under them." Arkin's eyes burned with intensity.

"Look at you," Morrison said. "It was years and years ago, and you're still wrapped around the axle over this shit."

Arkin glared at him. "We can't all be you."

"You can try. None of it means shit in the end, but you've heard me say that before."

"*Ad nauseum.*"

"Why are you so cynical about our work?" Pratt asked Morrison.

"Here comes a Morrison rant," Arkin muttered.

"Pratt, bless your heart. It's the same shit, over and over again. Don't you see that yet? All you have to do is change the names of the countries, the religions, the political or social ideologies, the law firms, or whatever. A never-ending cycle of horrors. Always led or driven by head cases desperately seeking ways to fix their crap self-esteems, fill bottomless holes in their love-deprived limbic systems, or delude themselves out of their above-average terror of post-death oblivion, no matter what their pamphlets or banners or sacred texts say. Well I don't buy in. It's all a bunch of irrational, egocentric bullshit."

"Limbic system?" Pratt said.

"You should learn to read, Opie."

"And you're saying all religions are the same?"

"In the context of what I'm talking about here, they're heartbreakingly identical."

"That's ridiculous."

"The alleged gift is always the same, Pratt. It just comes in different wrapping."

"Maybe you're the one who should learn to read. And why are you always ragging on religion?"

"Because it needlessly divides people. People who are, where it actually matters, all the same. People who are all driven by the same things and headed for the same dark place, whether they want to believe it or not."

Arkin rolled his eyes as he and Pratt waited for more. "Wait, was that it?" Arkin asked. "Was that the whole rant? Hallelujah!"

"So then what *do* you believe in?" Pratt asked Morrison.

"Food and shelter."

"Come on. Really now."

Morrison looked genuinely thoughtful for a moment. "An absence of anxiety, I guess. After all, all any of us really want, deep down, is just to be able to sleep at night, right? To not be afraid. The rest of it's just frosting."

"That's impressive philosophy coming from someone who's as drunk as you are," Arkin said.

"I'm the smartest guy I know. You should listen to me more."

"You think about this stuff too much," Pratt said. "It's messing with your head."

"Well, maybe I'm not quite as unconcerned with my helplessness as you've fooled yourself into being with yours."

"I'm not helpless," Pratt said.

"We can always hope." Morrison turned to Arkin. "Come out to the Uncompaghre with me this weekend. Unplug. It will help you put things back into proper perspective. I'll saddle up both horses."

"Hannah needs me here."

"What do you do out there anyway?" Pratt asked.

"Quiet my mind, I suppose." Morrison turned his head as his eyes followed the progress of two short-skirted women toward the restroom. "Sometimes I don't really know what I'm doing out there. Maybe hoping some messenger will come down from the skies and tell me that I don't need to be afraid."

"What are you afraid of?"

"Nothing."

"You aren't making sense. You're afraid, but of nothing?"

"Exactly. That's it exactly. Just like you, John. Just like everyone. Afraid of the big nothing. Or the nothingness, I guess. Does that make more sense? Usually my diction improves as I drink. Tonight maybe not so much."

"Morrison, sometimes—" Pratt let his statement hang. "But if you're looking for messengers from the skies, then you believe in something after all."

"No. See, that's the joke. The longer I'm out there, the more I realize I'm on my own. It's just me, alone, under the endless, empty, uncaring universe." He shrugged. "There's a big difference, young Pratt, between hope and faith."

*****

They ordered one last round—Pratt switching from soda to, of all things, milk.

"Listen," Morrison said to Arkin. "I'm going to keep an eye on your house tonight."

"You're what?"

"I'm going to watch over your house. Counter-surveillance. Then we'll get to the bottom of whether or not somebody is watching you."

"Why would somebody be watching Nate's *house*?" Pratt asked.

"Well, assuming for the sake of argument that someone's watching him and you at all, and that he isn't just crazy, then maybe to monitor y'all's progress on this case. Or to know that you and Nate are safe at home, tucked in bed, as they rifle through your offices. That sort of thing. Come on, Opie. Where's your sense of imagination?"

"Wait—watching *me*?"

"It's your case, smart guy. Technically, anyway. And you're the one making the phone calls and inquiries."

"Dang. I don't want these jokers watching me."

"Tell you what—tomorrow I'll watch your house. But tonight I'm gonna watch Nate's."

"Morrison," Arkin half groaned, "don't do that. I don't want your stupid drunk ass sitting in the trees out there, peeking down on my windows like some old pervert."

"I've got your back, buddy. You won't even know I'm there."

"You're drunk. We're probably being paranoid anyway."

"Let's find out."

"I can take care of myself."

"You can take care of yourself by finally getting a good night's sleep knowing I've got your back."

"I'm going to sleep better knowing a whacko nihilist survivalist is out there watching my house though binoculars? And it would give Hannah the creeps. She already thinks you're a kook."

"Don't tell her."

"Morrison, I'm not fucking around. I don't want you out there."

Morrison stared down at his empty glass, his eyebrows arched, his lips pursed.

"Promise me you aren't going to set up an observation post next to my house."

"It's only five o'clock. Let's have one more round."

"Morrison."

"Alright, alright. Shit."

*****

Pratt dropped Arkin at the end of his gravel driveway and sped away. Hannah was still out, and aside from the porch light the house was dark, which was normal. Nevertheless, despite his being drunk, and despite the fading light of dusk, Akin could tell something was amiss. He couldn't put his finger on precisely why, but he had a gut feeling that someone else had been in the house, or was quite possibly still there.

Arkin unsnapped the thumb break on his holster as he tiptoed up his front steps. The door was locked, but that certainly didn't mean a person with the proper skills hadn't broken in this way. He wished his paranoia had come on stronger, and sooner, so that he might have had time to set up some detection traps—wedges in the doorway, hairs in keyholes, and so forth—to determine, with certainty, whether someone might have broken in and snooped his home. Too late.

He unlocked the door, stepped inside without closing it, and stood listening. Stood waiting for his senses to catch up. But for a solitary and perfectly normal ping from the ducting above the wood burning stove, the house was silent. Nobody was there, Arkin was sure of it. But still he stood, waiting for the vestiges of any uninvited guests to reveal themselves. Then one came. The slightest trace of an unfamiliar aroma, so faint and ephemeral he couldn't tell what it was. Was it flowery? Soapy? Perhaps from an intruder's laundry detergent, shampoo, or bath soap? He couldn't say. It was so faint that if he hadn't been on alert for it, he wouldn't have even noticed. But one thing was certain—someone had been in the house. It might have been hours earlier, but someone had been there.

He was tempted to call Morrison and give him the green light to keep an eye on the house. But then again, if Hannah ever found out, she wouldn't be very happy to learn that he'd been out there in the dark watching, no matter how benevolent his intent. Plus, he figured this wasn't anything he couldn't handle himself.

He went around the house, taking stock of their private papers, bills, passports, and so forth. Nothing appeared to be out of place. There was nothing to hint at what they might have been looking for. They were pros—

no doubt about it. They knew how to pick locks. They knew how to search a house without being caught, and without leaving traces that any ordinary person was likely to catch. But they weren't perfect. They'd underestimated the abilities of a fellow professional, his senses sharpened by surging paranoia, to sniff out their presence. Still, Arkin was perplexed as to why they would break in. Did they really expect to find, in his home, clues as to how far the investigation had progressed and what he'd found or not found? It seemed an inordinate risk to take, breaking into his house, given the ostensibly low probability of finding anything enlightening. Were they just that thorough? Could there be something else they were worried about? Something Arkin wasn't yet aware of?

Going to bed with Hannah four hours later, he stacked empty aluminum cans in front of each door, secured the windows, and set a .40 caliber gun on his nightstand, a round already racked into the chamber. When she gave him a quizzical look, all he said was, "Don't ask."

*****

That same evening, Morrison, still half drunk, having hitched his horse to a tree a quarter mile away, took up station in the woods across the street and just up the hill from Arkin's house. He was in full camouflage. BDUs, wool cap, makeup, the works. And he was armed—a black Sig .45 caliber, loaded for duty-carry in his hip holster. He sat perfectly still—a night's worth of water and rations to one side, his regular and night vision binoculars to the other—in perfect position for counter-surveillance.

He'd been there just about an hour already. In that time, thirty-two cars had driven by. One had passed by three times, but Morrison wrote it off as a friendly because each time it passed it had a different number of high school kids in it, and the driver couldn't have been a day over 17. Regardless, by habit forged through long, terrifying, sometimes tragic experience, he'd taken down the license numbers and descriptions of each and every vehicle that drove by. He'd run them at the office tomorrow.

There was also one man who'd jogged down the road in full running regalia during the first hour. Morrison watched him carefully, jotting down a thumbnail description of his features. His outfit looked normal. His jog looked natural. The only peculiarity Morrison could pick out was that he appeared to be missing his left pinkie finger.

The man hadn't turned to look directly at Arkin's house, Morrison was sure of that. But he also knew that a well-trained watcher on a well-disciplined surveillance team wouldn't overtly turn his head to observe his target for fear of being burned by just the sort of counter-surveillance Morrison was now conducting. No—they'd just observe out the corner of their eye, concentrating on the edges of their fields of vision. If they were looking to see if Arkin's car was in the driveway, that was all they'd need to do.

Morrison took a big bite of his homemade pemmican, shifted on his already sore ass, pulled the lens covers off his night vision binoculars and mounted them onto a tiny tripod. It was already almost too dark to see anything without them. That would complicate things just slightly. Cars would be easy enough to see coming because of their headlights. But he'd have to be quick in adjusting the direction and focus of his binoculars in order to catch the numbers on the rear license plates. As for people on foot, Morrison figured it took a walker two minutes to cover the distance from the curve in the road to the north, all the way to the house. Probably a minute and a half to do so from where a person would first come into view from the south. Half as long from either direction for a jogger. So he figured that if he shifted his binoculars between north and south every 45 seconds or so, he'd pretty well cover both approaches. Unless, of course, someone came down through the woods as he had. But it was the best he could do as one man with one set of night vision gear.

*****

Oblivious to Morrison's nearby vigil, Arkin was lying in bed, restless and unable to sleep, as seemingly random thoughts raced through his mind, many of which involved the old Priest case, or the evidence Pratt was gathering. In his youth, he might have blamed his insomnia on caffeine or his self-diagnosed tendency toward excitability over investigative work. But he'd been through this sort of spooled up borderline mania often enough to know he should pay close attention to what his mind was up to. Through long experience, he'd come to have great respect for the power of his subconscious to lead him in the right direction.

So what was it up to now? Was it picking up on things his conscious mind had yet to perceive? Threads linking the present to the past? He didn't know. He was all but sure that the two Wyoming-based credit card accounts were somehow tied to the whole conspiracy. But the back and forth movements of the cardholders perplexed him. He was missing something. Something he was sure would prove critical.

FIFTEEN

"I've been thinking that we should test your theory," Morrison said, as he, Pratt, and Arkin convened at the office water cooler the next morning.

"What theory?" Arkin asked.

"That you're being surveilled."

"I told you, it's more than a theory."

"You were pretty drunk when you got home last night."

"True. But somebody had been there."

"So let's do a clean-off. If someone really is following you, maybe we can catch them *in flagrante* and get a look at who we're dealing with."

"Now?"

"Why not? Get your blood pumping."

"Where?"

"Ah! Now, I'm so glad you asked. Because we can use this as an excuse to go get a proper breakfast at Carver's. On the way, I'll run ahead to the General Palmer Hotel. Give me two minutes lead. I'll set up in the lobby. You and Pratt just come through the front door and go right on up the steps. After the fun, we'll go get you some of your chorizo and eggs."

"I already had breakfast."

"Get a coffee then. Don't be difficult."

Fifteen minutes later, Arkin and Pratt strolled through the hotel lobby where Morrison sat in a Victorian armchair in a far corner while watching the door and pretending to read the paper. They climbed up to the third floor and waited. Ten minutes later, Morrison called Arkin's cellphone.

"You're clean, as far as I can tell. Nobody followed you in. And I took a sniff around outside after you came through. Didn't pick up on anything."

"They could be really heads-up. They could have suspected the trap and broken off."

"Well, if there is anybody, there has to be a pretty-good-sized team of them, and they're awful damn good."

*****

Later, Arkin was gulping down his last bite of ham sandwich, having just finished off his lunchtime internet chess opponent, when his phone rang.

"Arkin."

"Nate, it's Diane."

Diane was Hannah's best friend and colleague at the legal aid office. A shiver went up his spine. *Oh, no.*

"Nate, Hannah collapsed in her office. The ambulance just took her to the hospital."

He dropped the phone and ran for the door. In seconds, he was in his car and racing toward the hospital, driving well over the speed limit.

Halfway there, he got stuck at a red light. Waiting, squeezing the steering wheel and willing the light to turn green, he caught sight of Pratt standing on the sidewalk next to a parking meter. He began lowering his window to shout that he was on his way to the hospital when he realized Pratt was talking to someone. Arkin did a double-take. It was the man with the brown suede shoes. Pratt was pointing up the road, as if giving the man directions. Arkin rolled his window back up, faced forward, and drove on toward the hospital as soon as the light turned green as though he hadn't noticed a thing.

*****

By midafternoon, Hannah was stabilized. They'd moved her from the emergency room to the radiology lab, and, at last, to a regular room. They chalked up her collapse to a combination of dehydration and exhaustion, probably brought on by the chemo. But they'd run some diagnostic scans as a matter of routine. Shortly thereafter, Hannah's oncologist showed up at her room, looking somber, only to inform them that Hannah's cancer had spread to her liver. That it must have metastasized before they surgically removed her ovary three months earlier. That it was inoperable. She said she was sorry, and then left them alone.

Arkin held Hannah's hand and stared at the ceiling as she lay in bed. He did his best to be stoic, but his face betrayed his agony.

"Inoperable doesn't mean we don't have options," he said. Hannah just looked at him. "I thought the chemo was supposed to keep it from spreading."

"It doesn't always respond," Hannah said very matter-of-factly. "And some cancers respond to some drugs but not others."

"Then they can switch to a better drug."

"We'll see."

"Or radiation. Can they try radiation? Maybe we should move you to Denver."

"They know what they're doing here."

"Or Johns Hopkins."

"Nate."

Arkin shook his head.

"They said I can probably go home tomorrow, after they watch me for 24 hours. You're squeezing my hand too hard."

"Sorry."

"Nate, look at me." He did. "Do you remember that hike we took in July, northwest of Silverton?"

"Ice Lake Basin."

"Right. It was a warm, sunny day. The sky was so blue. And those high alpine lakes, in that green grassy valley high above the trees, the peaks still with snow on them towering above."

"We took a picnic lunch," Arkin said, "and we ate on the shore of one of the tiny lakes." He smiled, his mind's eye revisiting the place, the day, his nostrils filled with the fresh scent of alpine grasses, his ears taking in the gentle sounds of meltwater trickling down from receding ice fields. "And we talked about Shakespeare. *A Midsummer Night's Dream.* I hate that story."

"And you teased me because I like it, and insisted that I explain why."

"A beautiful place."

"The most beautiful place I've ever seen. A beautiful day, and a beautiful memory."

Oh no.

"I want you to spread my ashes there."

Arkin's face fell and went pale. He felt nauseated. "Hannah, they didn't say—" He couldn't finish his statement.

Hannah shook her head, still looking at him. She smiled. An understanding smile, as though Arkin were the one who needed sympathy. "Nate, you can't let this destroy you too, or I'll never forgive you."

"We're not going to talk about this." His voice cracked. He took a breath, mastered himself. "You are going to fight."

"I am fighting. But you have to accept that this is out of your hands."

"The hell it is. There are options we can still—"

"Nate, it is out of your hands. The only thing you can do, the only thing I want you to do, is to hold mine. That's all. Just hold my hand."

SIXTEEN

Two days later, Hannah was still in the hospital, her physicians monitoring the levels of some unpronounceable chemical in her blood. But after the first night, with a restless Arkin noisily rolling around in the recliner next to her bed the whole time, and asking her, almost hourly, how she was feeling, she insisted that he go home and return to work. Insisted that it would be easier for her to sleep, and to recover more quickly, if he wasn't sitting in the room fidgeting every night. He could visit during the day. It would be better for both of them. When his resistance finally began to anger her, he donned his jacket, kissed her forehead and, with great reluctance, let himself out. But he didn't go home at first. He stopped at a park bench under a great sycamore tree on the side of the street opposite the hospital, sat down, and, for the better part of an hour, stared up at Hannah's window as yellow leaves fell all around him in a stiff and chilling afternoon breeze that poured out of the high San Juan Mountains, down the long valley of the Animas River.

He actively avoided confronting the fact that Hannah might not beat the cancer. But in doing so, all he really did was confirm to himself that it was a serious possibility. As he struggled to refocus his thoughts, to distract himself, his mind wandered back in time, to a scene in the dark wood-paneled study of Roland Sheffield's house on the southern shore of the Potomac, barely a mile upstream from Mount Vernon. Arkin had just flown in for the funeral of Sheffield's wife, Claudia. He sat in Sheffield's old leather chair, in his freshly pressed black suit. Sheffield sat at his desk, his back to the giant picture window revealing large old oak trees framing an expansive view of a broad, brown stretch of the great river. They were drinking warmed cognac from snifters. An ancient bottle someone had given the Sheffields on the day of their wedding in 1964. The sun had set and the sky was growing dark. Below them, the broad Potomac was glassy. The starboard running lights of a small sailboat were visible out near mid-river. Sheffield looked broken and pale, slumping in his chair, dark bags beneath his downturned eyes.

"Ah, Nathaniel," Sheffield had said in a voice weighed down by alcohol and sorrow as he stared at the warm amber liquid in his snifter. "We may grieve. We may feel the loss. The emptiness left behind. But we mustn't fear death." Arkin sat quietly, watching and listening. "There's no reason to. Oblivion holds no pain. No suffering." But his voice cracked as he said this, leaving Arkin to wonder whether Sheffield truly believed the things he was saying, or was just trying to convince himself. "We mustn't fear it. It's our only hope," he added, taking a sip of his cognac as his face seemed to harden just perceptibly. He shook his head slowly. "So much fear."

Back in the present, still sitting on the park bench, Arkin realized he was getting cold. But he didn't like the idea of going home to an empty house. Not today. Not yet. He headed for his office instead, making his way down to the river trail and turning south. Soon he came to the pedestrian bridge, where he stopped, mid-span, to watch the water slide by. At one point, a magnificent cluster of bright yellow aspen leaves, a foot wide and at least 30 feet long, came floating downstream. Arkin wondered at the innumerable little chance happenings that must have come to pass for the cluster to have taken shape. Leaves falling here and there along the riverbank. Then riffles, micro-currents, and eddies bringing them together to form this beautiful accident, this brilliant yellow stripe slipping along the surface of the clear river water.

He followed the progress of the leaf cluster, as it floated down a broad calm reach and on toward the small rapids near the edge of town. There, the current quickened, the water grew rough. In the blink of an eye, in the churning rapids, the great yellow cluster of leaves broke up and was scattered until its unremarkable constituent parts were too small for Arkin to see with his naked eye.

*****

Back at home that night, Arkin couldn't sleep a wink. He worried about Hannah. He worried about what options they had, what choices they faced. He worried about the implications of Pratt talking with the suede shoe guy. He worried about getting sucked back into the Priest case, and reflected on how his one-time obsession with it became so unhealthy.

Revisiting the past, he wondered whether things might have turned out better—better for him, better for Hannah—if he'd just made one or two different choices at key decision points. If only he'd done a better job of negotiating the minefield of his career. If only he'd had the foresight or intelligence to set a course for a happier future. But deep down he knew that he'd made the right choices, done the right things, and that what had happened to him was as unpredictable as it was arbitrary. It was never in his power to look out for or control. Knowing this brought solace on one level, but strong anxiety on another.

In the middle of the night, he gave up on sleep, got up, turned on the outdoor floodlights, and went about trimming every single bonsai in his Japanese garden to shapely perfection before raking the decorative pebbles into an even, orderly plain.

SEVENTEEN

The next day, Arkin sat in his desk chair, his radio off. He was fatigued to the point of feeling dumb and had no desire to work. He didn't even want to play chess. Yet thoughts of the Cortez shooting kept popping into his mind. The last thing he wanted to think about was the Priest case. But it kept jumping to the forefront of his consciousness. It didn't help that he again had the feeling he was being followed on his commute to work.

It also didn't help that he now had to worry about Pratt. There could have been any number of innocent explanations for Pratt standing on a sidewalk talking to the man with the suede shoes. Maybe their meeting was just a coincidence, the guy just asking for directions. Maybe the guy wasn't even involved—just someone who was in the wrong place at the wrong time when Arkin was being paranoid. On the other hand, maybe Pratt was involved somehow. If not as an actual conspirator, then maybe as someone who, thinking he was doing the right thing, was simply following the orders of a DCI traitor. Or maybe Pratt *was* a part of it. Maybe he'd been put in Durango to keep an eye on Arkin. It wasn't out of the realm of possibility. After all, it didn't really make sense for DCI to keep an agent in the region—especially now that 9/11 hysteria had largely subsided such that every frightened small town in America wasn't demanding that their senator get them their fair share of federal protection from terrorists. Didn't make sense, that is, unless there was some undisclosed reason for keeping him stationed here. He was almost certain he was being paranoid. But it didn't pay not to be.

Time slipped by as he thought about it. He might even have nodded off for a moment, for suddenly, it seemed, Morrison was standing in his doorway.

"You look like shit," Morrison said.

"And you always manage to say just the right thing."

"When was the last time you had a decent night's sleep?"

"Come in here and shut the door for a second." Morrison did. "I need you to watch Pratt for me."

"Wow. You really do need some sleep."

Arkin explained what he'd seen, and Morrison agreed to do what he could.

They were interrupted when Pratt knocked on the door. Pratt and Morrison asked Arkin to join them for a joint defensive tactics practice session they'd scheduled with a handful of locally stationed state police at a nearby gym.

"I can't."

"Come on. A little fresh air and exercise will do you good."

Arkin thought about it, took a deep breath, and grabbed his gym bag. As they approached the exit, he stopped. "I want you guys to watch my back, alright?"

"Are you sensing surveillance again?" Morrison asked.

"On the way here this morning. Nothing definite. Just a feeling." He watched Pratt's face and body language for any telltale signs of deceit. But none materialized.

*****

Five minutes later, they were at the gym, suiting up to practice defensive tactics on the padded training floor. Arkin paired up with a young, short, muscle-bound state trooper—5-foot-3 at best—who might have been trying to puff his chest out. Never a good sign.

Things started out professionally enough. They took turns practicing handcuffing a resistant suspect, moved on to gun retention, then to moves for countering high and low tackles.

As time passed, it became more and more obvious that Arkin was the vastly superior practitioner, as he repeatedly got the better of the state trooper. The more obvious it became, the more intense the state trooper's expression grew, and the harsher his movements grew.

Given that the level of his competition didn't demand much in the way of focus, Arkin's exhausted mind began to wander to the perplexing lack of information in the Priest file, to the question of whether or not he should move Hannah to a big city hospital, to bitterness over the fact that if they had still been in D.C., she would have had access to cutting-edge, possibly lifesaving medical care from the very outset of her treatment. But whenever his mind tried to really delve into these pressing matters, the state trooper jerked him back to the present with an unnecessarily harsh yank, shove, or squeeze. Arkin started to think of the trooper as a horse fly. An annoying distraction from more important things.

They donned riot helmets with face shields and began practicing scenarios in which the officer was down flat on his back with an assailant mounted on his upper chest, landing blows on the officer's head and face. The officer's goal in the exercise was to use his hands and arms to defend his face and head from the blows, and then to execute a move that would bounce and roll the assailant off to one side. The state trooper's practice blows bordered on being inappropriately hard. Arkin knew it was the right time to take a break, to let the trooper's surging bitterness dissipate. Instead, he let his thoughts return to options for Hannah's care. Meanwhile, he dislodged the state trooper, with embarrassing ease, three times in a row. As they set up to practice the scenario a fourth time, he remembered that there was an acquaintance of his from his Naval Academy days who was an oncologist at Mass General. As he tried to remember the doctor's name, the trooper landed a palm heal strike to the bottom edge of Arkin's face shield that came down so hard it bent the plastic until it hit Arkin in the chin, knocking his teeth together with a jarring pain. In the blink of an eye, he bucked the trooper forward, locked the man's left arm down against the floor, rolled him onto his back, and jammed both his thumbs, with full force, up and against the trooper's hypoglossal pressure points. The trooper grabbed hold of Arkin's arms, let out a long, agonized scream through his clenched teeth, then appeared to pass out.

"Out of role! Out of role!" he heard Morrison shout, the words half drowned out in the loud rumble of blood rushing through the vessels around his eardrums. Arkin disengaged and stood up over his victim, noticing a large wet spot on the crotch of the trooper's sweatpants. He looked around, meeting the troubled faces of the other officers. He took off his helmet and bent down to check the trooper's pulse, finding that the man's heart was racing from an adrenaline overload brought on by the pain. He sighed and stood up.

"I'm sorry," he said, gazing down at his unconscious victim. "I'm really sorry, everyone." He grabbed his duffel and left as another of the state troopers cradled the head of his fallen comrade and broke open a bindle of smelling salts under his nose.

*****

Arkin spent the rest of the day with Hannah, who seemed weaker than ever. "It's just the muscle relaxer," she said, trying to allay his obvious fear. "I was having muscle spasms in my leg."

At 10 p.m., Hannah ordered him to go home. He arrived at his cold, empty house to discover that there were nine voicemails waiting for him on their land line. Most were from friends inquiring after Hannah's condition, wishing her a speedy recovery and so forth. One was a recorded message from a local politician, warning the electorate that some sort of unspecified doom was at hand if they didn't stop such-and-such incumbent by voting for his ouster. The ninth and final message was from Pratt.

"Hey, Nate. I didn't want to bother you by calling your cell while you were at the hospital, and I'm sorry to bother you even now, but Bill and I wanted to let you know that we found a roster spot for you in a great anger management class up at Fort Lewis College." He laughed. "I'm just kidding. Actually, the troopers said to tell you not to sweat it, and that the dude you manhandled is a total asshole and that they've hammered him themselves on occasion. But the real reason I'm calling is to tell you that I'm heading back to the office. I was talking about this case with one of my old buddies from FLETC who's now in the Detroit field office, and he told me I should double-check a section of the INDIGO case file called 'miscellaneous case notes.' It's a sort of backwater section that was built into the half-hidden second-tier directory of the generic INDIGO case file structure, so every case file has it. But it's a redundant thing agents aren't even trained to use under normal procedures, so it never occurred to me to look there. Point is, this buddy of mine said that sometimes headquarters administrative personnel will use it as a place to add random things that come in after a case has been officially closed and archived. He said that once in a while he finds things in that section like late-arriving court filings, letters from witnesses, and documentary evidence that was misplaced or misdirected before finally being routed to the right file. That sort of thing. So I'm going to run down to the office and take a peek. Probably a long shot. But I'll let you know if I find anything. Oh, and the follow-up credit card data and security camera footage—such as it is—came in today. I didn't have time to look at it, but we can go over it in the morning. Still waiting on the State of Wyoming. Carry on sir." End of message.

EIGHTEEN

The next morning, Arkin woke to a vague anxiety that he was missing something critical. As he lay in bed, allowing himself the small luxury of a gradual wake up, his fear began to take shape. His intuition told him that someone—some hidden player—had indeed deleted the contents of the Priest file from INDIGO. And worse, that that someone had done so with a malicious intent that might pose an ongoing threat to their investigation. The implications were troubling. Someone at headquarters had an interest in making the Priest investigation go away. Probably a high-ranking someone at that, since only IT specialists and officers above a certain rank had the sort of access to INDIGO that would allow them to purge information from a case file.

In the wake of his epiphany, a new fear gripped him. For a number of reasons, most having to do with security, whenever field agents used the INDIGO system, their queries were logged and indexed at headquarters, such that certain staff and officers could monitor exactly who was working in which electronic files, and when. Whoever had been trying to extinguish the Priest case might still work at headquarters, and might even be aware of the exact extent of Pratt's inquiries—aware of any discoveries Pratt may have made.

A further realization made him sit straight up in bed. *The credit card data!* The date of the reversal of direction, back toward Durango, of the two suspected members of the Cortez assassination team coincided exactly with the day that Pratt, on Arkin's recommendation, first queried the Priest file in INDIGO.

Oh, shit.

As Arkin reached for his phone, he flinched at the unmistakable sound of a high-caliber rifle shot echoing out over Durango. It rattled the bedroom windows. He dialed Pratt's cell. It rang five times, then went to voicemail. He redialed. Same result. *Fucking hell.* He dialed Pratt's home phone. Same result. He kept trying, dialing each number in turn. By his eighth attempt, he heard the sirens. One ambulance, and at least three police cars. With the wild, echoing acoustics of the Animas River Valley, there was no way for Arkin to pinpoint the direction from which the sirens came. But he knew in his gut that they were converging on Pratt's home.

*****

Arkin had been friends with Durango's senior detective, Paul Regan, for years, and they had a deep mutual respect for each other's abilities, so Regan had no problem admitting Arkin to the scene as his team was finishing up. The FBI agents dispatched from Farmington hadn't arrived yet anyway. So Arkin was more or less free to examine the scene as he wished. The only problem was that he couldn't think. It wasn't that he was overcome with emotion. If anything, he was surprised at how numb he felt, given that his friend had just been gunned down in front of his family. Despite his personal connection, Arkin was somehow maintaining the cool, calculated distance he'd put on in innumerable, horrific crime and combat scenes of his past. It was more that his brain felt slow, as if he'd been studying civil court procedure for hours, to the point where his mind simply started to shut down. Almost as if he were mildly drunk, but without the comfort of an accompanying buzz.

Ella and the kids were at the home of another family—friends of theirs from their LDS church. And Pratt's body had already been consigned to the coroner's care. All that remained of him in his family home was a lot of his blood and tiny fragments of his head, scattered across the floor and left wall of the entryway, across from the breakfast nook where his children had been eating pancakes when it happened. According to Regan, all they could get out of an hysterical Ella was that Pratt had opened the front door, and then, like he did every morning, turned around to blow each of them kisses before he stepped out to leave for work.

But there was little mystery to what happened. Someone had set up with a heavy rifle—no doubt the same .50 caliber sniper rifle used in Cortez—on the scrubby hillside across the street from Pratt's house, probably no more than 80 yards away. As soon as Pratt opened his front door to go to work, a single round entered the lower left quarter of the back of his head, blowing more than half his brain out the other side and completely obliterating his face. The bullet had then gone through a window and out the far side of the house, probably landing somewhere in the brushy field behind Pratt's lot. It would take a while to find.

Arkin gave Regan the suspect credit card numbers, explaining their relevance. But he very much doubted the assassins would be foolish enough to use the same cards again. He wished they'd had a chance to run down information on the cars the credit card holders were driving—from gas station security camera footage or anything else. There were, after all, only four roads leading out of Durango—one for each point of the compass. It would have been easy to set up roadblocks. But they could hardly do so on the basis of what they had to identify a suspect—a mere hunch that one of them was tall with long, dark, moderately curly hair.

Arkin had been wandering the house and immediate surround in a daze. He returned to the present to find himself staring down at the dark red pool of blood on the entryway floor—blood that had drained from Pratt's head. It was quickly drying in the arid, high country air. He stared for a moment, then realized what he had to do.

"Regan," Arkin called.

"Yeah, Nate."

"A quick word?" He led Regan out the front door, out of earshot of his team. "Paul, I don't have time to give you a full explanation, but I need to ask a big favor."

"Anything."

"When you guys find that bullet, it's probably going to be a .50 BMG."

"Like in Cortez?"

"Probably fired from the same gun. In a nutshell, I think Pratt's involvement in the Cortez case is what got him killed. And what's more, I think he was compromised by someone in his own agency."

"A traitor? In DCI?"

"I hope not. But when you find that bullet, do me a favor, will you? I need you to keep it out of federal hands until after the state lab has had a chance to run its own analysis. Pretend not to find it. Pretend there's a mix-up in the evidence locker. Anything. Bottom line, we need to see the analysis before the feds take the bullet away."

"I understand. I'll do my best."

Arkin remained on the front porch after Regan went back inside, wondering at his own lack of emotion. He'd never been a particularly emotional person. But his lack of feeling here, in the immediate aftermath of the murder of his good friend, was disconcerting.

His gaze drifted across the road, over toward the hill where the assassin had no doubt taken his shot. He scanned the area for likely firing points.

Then something occurred to him. When the Priest case was taken away from him before his banishment to Durango, his Canadian liaison, an affable RCMP officer named Brian Tremblay, had, at least in theory, still been trying to run down information for him. It was possible that Tremblay had eventually—perhaps after DCI had closed the Priest case—sent DCI courtesy copies of whatever he'd found for Arkin. If Tremblay had done so, the documents he sent to DCI would probably have included the name of the Vancouver company. And given what Pratt's voicemail had told him, it was entirely possible that one of the DCI administrative staff, upon receiving documents from Tremblay concerning a case which was by then closed, had scanned the documents and entered them in the miscellaneous case notes section of the archived INDIGO case file for the Priest case.

If, as now seemed probable, someone had gone in and deliberately removed the file contents, then perhaps whoever had done so never bothered to check back to see if anything had been subsequently added. There would have been no reason to expect a significant addition of information after the case was closed, after all. Indeed, there would have been little reason for anyone to check the miscellaneous case notes section specifically unless, as he now suspected, someone had been monitoring Pratt's INDIGO queries. But this was conjecture, at best. He could only guess at the true story of what happened. Still, in his gut, Arkin had a feeling that Pratt had found something in the INDIGO file. Something critical. Perhaps the name of the Vancouver company. Whatever it was, it had probably gotten him killed.

Certain that Pratt's office had already been cleaned out—including any useful information that might have come in because of the subpoenas—Arkin nevertheless got in his car and headed toward their office building.

*****

Shutting off his car, Arkin scanned the parking lot of his office building. Not seeing any unfamiliar vehicles, he made his way to the back entrance, and once inside the rear stairwell, drew his gun and chambered a round. As he emerged on the basement level and made his way down the hall toward Pratt's office, he could see that a small round hole had been cut in the window of Pratt's door, probably with a simple glass cutter. He bent down and peeked through the hole. The office was vacant. He ran his fingertip around the edge of the hole, as if doing so might tell him something useful. When it didn't, he pushed the door open, stepped inside, and closed it behind him.

In the air he caught the faint smell of Pratt's cheap drugstore aftershave. Scanning the room, Arkin confirmed what he already expected to see. Pratt's INDIGO terminal and computer were gone. All they'd left on the desk was the monitor, mouse, some dangling wires, and the Strawberry Monkey notepad Pratt's kids had given him for Father's Day—its top page blank. Even the printer, fax machine, and antiquated phone with its built-in voicemail recorder were gone. Arkin flopped into Pratt's chair and began examining all of Pratt's files—having to pick the locks of three different file cabinets to do so—all the while knowing perfectly well that he wasn't going to find anything useful. Whoever had taken the computer would have been damn sure to take any paper files too.

An hour later, having found nothing, he was done. He picked up Pratt's desk phone, but then, thinking better of it, hung it up, went down the hall and picked up the phone on the vacant security officer's desk. He dialed a Washington, D.C., number. "Myers," a voice said.

"Hello there, Danny boy."

"Who's—Nate?"

"Good. I'm glad somebody remembers me."

Dan Myers, a respected field agent at one time, was now director of INDIGO integration—a paper title, given that he had no employees and no authority. Like Arkin, he'd been demoted—in his case, in the wake of a political power struggle within the agency, where his name ended up being too closely associated with the losing cabal. Now he sat at a dented metal desk in a windowless, low-ceilinged office and proofread information entered into INDIGO by other agents.

Arkin took a few minutes to catch up with his old friend before breaking the news about Pratt, and then explaining the real reason for his call.

"The bottom line is that the critical information I need, the information Pratt was getting for our case, was probably in INDIGO yesterday, in the miscellaneous case notes section. It may very well have been deleted by now. But if you have access to a backup or a cache memory where it might—"

"Whoa, daddy. Are you kidding me? I can't share that with you, even assuming I can find it."

"It isn't for me. Given that one of your agents was killed for it, we need to secure the evidence."

"Why wouldn't it be secure here?"

Arkin almost told him why, but stopped himself, knowing it would be foolish to advertise his suspicions until he had more information. Until he knew exactly who he could trust. "You know how much better I feel when I have something in my hand, Dan. Anyway, it's a joint investigation with a consolidated grand jury file."

"Nate, you know damn well that without an MOU to cover my ass, they'd put my severed head on a spike on the Key Bridge. Plus. . . ."

"Plus what?"

"Nothing."

"What?!"

Myers groaned. "This stays between you and me, Nate. Cross your heart, and all that shit."

"Sure. Anything."

"I've been ordered not to give you any information. I mean you, specifically."

Arkin digested this. "Ordered by whom?"

"Trlajic."

"Who?"

"Dragoslav Trlajic."

"Throw me a bone, Dan. I've been away for a few years. Who the hell is Dragoslav Trlajic?"

"Killick's senior policy advisor."

"Is he Serbian?"

"He ain't Irish."

"When did he go to work for Killick?"

"Pretty much just after you left."

"Does Killick know about this?"

"About Trlajic's order? I assumed it was coming from Killick."

"I doubt that very much."

"Well, regardless, Trlajic didn't say, and I didn't ask. He's a serious asshole. Territorial and insecure. Doesn't like anyone questioning him on anything. If he even found out I was talking to you. . . ."

"I understand. In the meantime, you can at least secure the information on your end."

He hung up with Myers, and then called his own supervisor at MWA, Scott O'Neil, to apprise him of his intent to work the Pratt case with the FBI, and to request a memorandum of understanding between MWA and DCI to appease Myers.

"I can't assign you to that. And I can't forward the request for an MOU."

"Why not?"

"We don't have the resources."

"Resources? Are you shitting me?

"Nate—"

"I only have seven active cases. I spend half of each work day dusting the empty shelves in my office. Anyway, two weeks ago you were telling me to use up my budget on new office furniture before the end of the fiscal year so that it wouldn't look like we didn't need as much funding next year."

"It isn't our jurisdiction."

"We're talking about a close friend of mine."

"And think about how that looks."

"A friend of mine who was working the case jointly with me—with us. The same case that got him killed."

"You don't know whether—Look, Nate, I appreciate where you're coming from, but it's outside our jurisdiction."

"How is a .50 caliber Serbian military-grade weapon outside our jurisdiction?"

"We don't know the gun that killed Pratt was a .50."

"It was."

Silence. "Nate. . . ."

"Scott, this isn't like you. What the hell is going on?"

Arkin could hear O'Neil breathing through his nostrils, deliberatively.

"Scott."

"Look, Nate, we've been briefed on this. It's hands-off for MWA."

"What?"

"We can't touch it."

"This case, in particular?"

"Yes."

"How the hell—"

"We were briefed barely half an hour ago. Apprised of our previous joint involvement with DCI, and then instructed to stand down. It came from the political level. The deputy director's office."

"Did they say why?"

"No. They probably want to steer clear because it will be so hot, politically, since we're talking about the murder of a federal agent."

"Shit. Well, what if—what if we. . . ." He was at a loss.

"You know how these guys are. It's dead in the water, Nate."

*****

By noon, Arkin was back at the hospital, lying in the recliner next to Hannah's bed, staring at the ceiling of her room. She'd been weeping for Pratt since Arkin's arrival half an hour earlier. "What are you going to do?" she finally asked, unable to mask her fear.

"I have to secure that evidence—the name of that company. It's the key to all of this. To Pratt's murder. Maybe even to my being banished."

She just stared at him, her face the picture of worry and agony. He knew exactly what she was thinking.

"Hannah, look, I'm not going to take up the mantle of the Priest case, alright? But I have to secure that evidence before someone makes it disappear. Before they can cover their tracks and move their whole apparatus, hide and hair, to somewhere where we'll never catch the scent of them again and lose them forever, if they haven't done so already. I have to secure it for whoever is going to take up the case from here."

*****

An hour later, having reluctantly talked himself into doing so, and seeing no other option, Arkin went to one of the few payphones still functioning in

Durango and placed a call to the automated DCI headquarters switchboard. Following the prompts, he entered the ten-digit code to direct his call to Killick's private encrypted line.

"Nate, I've been waiting for your call."

"I'm a little surprised I didn't hear from you first."

"What the hell happened?"

"You haven't been briefed?"

"Don't be an asshole. Of course I've been briefed. But not by anybody who had the background to read between the lines with this. What the fuck happened?"

"The Priest."

"What does the Priest have to do with it?"

"Pratt found the name of the company, Tom. The Canadian company we tracked the Priest assassinations back to years ago."

"You're kidding."

"It's what got him killed."

"How?"

"You have a mole."

"In DCI? Someone working for the Priest? Bullshit. We never even figured out if there really was a Priest, or if it wasn't our paranoid imaginations making connections that weren't really there."

"The only way I can figure this happened is that someone in DCI caught wind that Pratt was querying the Priest file in INDIGO, watched him, and then, when they saw what he'd found, decided he had to be taken out."

"You're out of your tree."

"It's more than plausible. And you need to handle this."

"Alright, alright. So what's the name of this mysterious Canadian company? Let's start there."

"It died with Pratt."

"Oh, come on! You are shitting me!"

"I don't have the name," Arkin said, his voice rising. "I don't have the address, the phone number, or even so much as a first initial."

Arkin told Killick about Pratt's voicemail. Then, without mentioning his earlier conversation with Myers, or his alarm over the orders communicated to Myers by Dragoslav Trlajic, he told Killick to task his INDIGO people with securing the information by any means necessary—even if they had to trawl every backup memory cache in the building.

"I'll do that. Okay, so where does that leave us?"

"It leaves you needing to watch your back until we can figure out a way to flush out your traitor."

"How do you propose to do that?"

"I need to think on it. The first thing you should do, after getting hold of the name of that Canadian company, is find out exactly who in your apparatus has the access they would have needed to be able to monitor what Pratt was looking at in INDIGO. There can't be that many. On my end, I'll run down every possible lead if it kills me."

"Now hold on, Nate. Don't go getting yourself into any sort of jurisdictional trouble."

"There's no issue. Pratt was killed with a .50 caliber. No doubt the same one used in Cortez."

Killick was quiet for a moment. "I think that, right now, you should let us handle this. Leave it to the cool heads. I'll keep you in the loop all the way, alright?"

"You'll give me the name of that company if you find it." It sounded more like an order than a request.

"Yes, yes."

"Okay. Alright. I'll hold off," Arkin said, sincerely hoping he could.

But he couldn't. Not entirely. That afternoon, the product of Pratt's last known subpoena arrived from the Wyoming Secretary of State. He opened it the moment he found it and began examining each and every annual report and filing document for both LLCs. But as he expected, there was nothing of apparent value. The sole named member/manager was the long-vanished Zhang Zhou. And there were no useful addresses or phone numbers. Just the name of a registered agent for service of process—a private company whose only relationship with the LLCs was to be contracted to accept legal and business documents on behalf of each. Probably some second-rate accountant in Cheyenne who was trying to prop up his business by holding himself out as a registered agent for hire. Another dead end.

NINETEEN

Seventy-two hours later, Morrison found Arkin staring out his office window.

"Hey, buddy. You doing alright?"

"I don't know, Bill. I really don't." He turned to face Morrison. "You try so hard to find something you can believe in. And then, when you think you have, you throw your heart and soul into it." He shook his head.

"Remember the big picture, Nate, for the sake of your health and sanity. Because in the end—"

"Spare me your existential despair today, will you? Go fast in your sweat lodge, or flagellate yourself, or do whatever it is you need to do to shake it off. Please. I'm already loaded down with as much as I can bear." He exhaled. "Sorry."

"It's alright."

"Want to know what's eating me?"

"In addition to the obvious?"

"Would it surprise you to learn that DCI still hasn't sent a team out here? Still hasn't sent anybody to help the FBI with the investigation of the murder of one of their own agents?" Morrison looked troubled. "What is it?"

"They were here yesterday."

"What?"

"I saw them going through Pratt's office. Two guys. Young. Really young. I just assumed they met with you at some point."

"Where are they now?"

"Came and went, far as I know."

"That can't be right."

After Morrison left, Arkin, with gut-wrenching reluctance, called Ella Pratt, only to learn that Morrison's suspicions were dead on. A team of two DCI agents had come and gone. They'd asked her very little. What had she seen? Did Pratt have any known enemies? Had they received any strange or threatening phone calls, or noticed anything out of the ordinary in their neighborhood in the days leading up the to the "incident." Was there any chance that Pratt could have been involved with drugs? Then they'd thanked her for her time—all of about 20 minutes—and left for the airport.

After hanging up with Ella, Arkin sat bewildered. By all indications, DCI had sent a two-man team of probationers out for a one-day survey of witnesses. That was it. After one of their own men had been gunned down, and when all indications were that he was killed by the very targets of a DCI investigation, that was all they'd bothered to do. They hadn't even spoken with Arkin—Pratt's close friend and joint case officer on the Cortez investigation. It was insane. Thirty seconds later, he was back on the phone with Killick.

"Have you lost your mind?"

"Calm down."

"You sent two neophytes out here with an eight-hour window to poke around? That's it? Are you kidding me?"

"The FBI spent two hours briefing them, and gave them a complete draft of their report. It's comprehensive."

"Oh, my ass. One of your own men was gunned down, Tom. What the hell is the matter with you?"

"There's no need to reinvent the wheel here. The FBI—"

"Please! Enough about the FBI. You know damn well Sheffield would never have left the investigation of the murder of one of his own people in the hands of those frat boys."

"Nate, get off your high horse. There are practical—"

"This is a damned disgrace."

Killick let the comment go. But the difficulty he had in constraining himself was evidenced by his heavy breathing, clearly audible over the phone.

After a few moments of silence, Arkin spoke. "I'm sorry. I'm sorry, Tom. I'm dealing with a lot."

"I know. How's Hannah?"

"She's not good."

"You guys are in our prayers."

"Thank you."

"Look, I have to run over to the Hill to testify before the Senate subcommittee on anal retentiveness, or some such thing. But call me tomorrow and I'll give you a rundown of a couple of the Bureau's 302s that you might find interesting."

"Alright, Tom."

"And get some sleep. You're a real dick when you're fatigued, you know that? All your proper Andover talk goes out the window, and you start cussing up a storm."

"Exeter, fucknuts."

"Whatever. All I'm saying is that you might as well have flushed all that prep school tuition money right down the fucking toilet if you're gonna talk like a redneck like me."

Arkin halfheartedly grinned into the phone, lacking the energy to laugh. But when he rang off, his face turned to stone as he looked out his window onto the dull grays and browns of the overcast late autumn day. The landscape looked dead, but for the never-ceasing movement of the river. He closed his eyes and soon fell asleep in his chair, his chin resting on his chest.

*****

More than an hour later, he awoke, with a stiff neck, to a gentle knock-knock and turned to again see Morrison standing in his doorway, now dressed in a dark suit and wearing a polished ATF badge, with a band of black tape across it, on his belt. "You ready?"

Arkin rose without a word.

They strode up the river trail in silence, crossing the Camino del Rio Bridge, and eventually arriving at the queuing area on 5th Street, just around the corner from Main. Both 5th and Main were closed to traffic. They shook hands with the rest of the honor guard pallbearers, and assumed their positions to either side of the cart that bore Pratt's flag-draped coffin.

As a troupe of bagpipers at the head of the procession began playing "Amazing Grace," Arkin looked around, astonished. Including the pallbearers, Pratt's honor guard was made up of at least forty officers. But that wasn't all. At least 200 officers, all in full dress uniforms, stood in formation behind the coffin cart. Arkin had never seen anything like it, even in the military. In addition to all the locals, the entire police force from Pratt's hometown of Eden, Utah, was on hand, along with strong contingents from towns as far away as Alamosa, Shiprock, Telluride, and Moab. Arkin had seen plenty of death in his lifetime and had borne witness to too many solemn memorial ceremonies to count. But the overwhelming tribute assembled in honor of his friend John Pratt brought tears to his eyes.

As they began the slow march up Main, lined on both sides with throngs of Durango's citizens, Arkin felt the weight of dark truths bearing down on his shoulders. Pratt was dead, and probably wouldn't be if Arkin had not directed him to the Priest case. And his sweet Hannah was suffering terribly. Was looking worse by the day. It was hard to imagine how things were ever going to get better.

*****

Later that afternoon, Arkin was back in his office when he got a frantic call from Paul Regan. "Nate, the state lab. Someone broke into the state lab."

"Did they get the bullet?"

"No. They tripped a motion sensor. Responding officers must have scared them off before they found it. But they were close. They'd started to rifle through the exact evidence locker it was in, but got chased off before opening the right drawer."

"Holy shit. Where is it now?"

"In the bombproof vault."

"Good. Good. How soon until they finish their analysis?"

"Two days. It's not on expedited status because, to cover our tracks, I didn't identify it as evidence for the Pratt case. But I have a buddy over there who is making it an unofficial priority. He says two days."

"Okay." He took a breath. "Okay. Good." But privately, he worried that two days wasn't soon enough.

*****

Almost at the same moment he hung up with Regan, his phone rang again. It was Scott O'Neil.

"Can you guess where I was just at?" O'Neil asked.

"Your grammar is atrocious, Scott, even for a hillbilly. Never finish a sentence with a preposition."

"No, really. Do you know where I just was?"

"Where were you?"

"I was in the deputy director's office, getting my ass handed to me by the interagency liaison, that cock Bruckmeier, along with the deputy director himself. And do you know why?"

"Because of your grammar?"

"Because I didn't communicate to my agents in the field that the Pratt investigation was hands-off. Which is funny, because I'm pretty sure I did."

"Scott—"

"Yes, I'm quite certain that I *did* communicate that message to my agents in the field. You know, I think that was the first time I've ever heard the deputy director use my name. In fact, I wasn't even sure if he knew my name, until now."

"Scott, I *have* been hands-off."

"Oh, yeah? Like when you opened a package of subpoenaed grand jury materials that were addressed to Pratt?"

How the hell did they know about that? "Those documents were for a joint grand jury file for the Cortez case."

"Yeah. And you had no ulterior motive in opening it. Nothing whatever to do with the Pratt case."

"Scott, come on."

"Yes, I thought so." O'Neil sighed as he spoke. "Like I said before, you know how these guys are. They didn't get to that level by doing what's right."

No, they did not, Arkin thought. *They got there by going along, avoiding risk, and attributing their own fuckups to the honest suckers subordinate to them.*

"Look, with you and me, it's water under the bridge as far as I'm concerned," O'Neil said.

"I appreciate that. Sorry you got blindsided."

"Nah. I would have done the same thing if I were in your shoes. But I'm telling you, as a friend, to stay away from this shit. They're red hot about it on the seventh floor. And if they catch you *in flagrante,* pursuing leads or whatever, I'm telling you, they are gonna fuck your shit up."

After O'Neil hung up, Arkin sat with the phone still pinned between his ear and shoulder, listening to the dead air on the line. Eventually, the "please hang up and dial again" recording kicked in. He muttered, "assholes," dropped the handset back into its cradle, closed his eyes, and once again fell asleep in his chair.

*****

Some time later, he awoke with a start as if something had jerked him back to consciousness. To his surprise, his mind was as clear as it had felt in days. As he gazed out his window and down upon the river, he realized the source of his new sense of clarity: without trying to, he'd come to a sort of resolution.

He reached into his pocket, took out his keys, and clumsily sorted through them until he found the one for his file drawers. As he tried to insert it into the lock, he dropped the whole set, and, in reaching down to pick them up again, realized his hand was trembling. He closed his eyes, took a deep breath, found the proper key, and unlocked the uppermost file drawer. He opened a folder, extracted the grainy black-and-white 5x7 print Lucricia Burris had given him years earlier, and tacked it to the corkboard next to his desk so that the Priest's haunting, fanatical eyes were staring down at him. Arkin met the Priest's gaze. "That's right," he said to the photograph.

He took the Wyoming LLC filings back out and went over them once more, hoping to catch something he missed the first time around. But there was nothing else. Just the name and address of the agent for service of process: some schmuck named Dustin Drake. He sat there thinking. What could he do now? How could he track down the LLC owners? He couldn't subpoena Drake for contact information without it getting back to headquarters, and he couldn't risk losing his job with Hannah being in the hospital and needing his medical insurance coverage. *Think!*

He decided to run Drake's name through NCIC, and then a trio of government financial data and personal asset databases. Maybe his queries would reveal something—some connection to the Priest's group that would get things moving again. There was a negligible chance someone at headquarters might see the log entry of his search and question him as to what it involved. But he could probably concoct some cover story over it being for one of his legitimately assigned cases. Anyway, he'd worry about that later. It was worth the risk.

Unfortunately, within 15 minutes, he'd queried the database only to learn that Drake was clean, and that there was no data on him that would lead to the company in Canada. Arkin was tempted to pound his keyboard to pieces with both fists. Instead, he settled for knocking his empty water cup clear across the room with a violent sweep of his arm, sending it crashing against the wall.

TWENTY

"I can't believe you did that," Morrison said across the table at Carver's the next morning, after Arkin told him of his running Drake's name through the databases. "I cannot fucking *believe* that you did that. Just plain stupid. Dale Cooper would never have done something that reckless."

They were just finishing up their Mexican scrambles and coffees.

"What about when Cooper crossed the Canadian border to go undercover at One-Eyed Jack's?

Morrison just shook his head.

"Hey, give me some credit. There was serious temptation there to do far riskier things."

"What, like forge subpoenas?"

Arkin stared back, silent.

"Are you kidding me, Nate? You're the one guy who has always done everything by the book. Stayed inside the lines, out of some dubious sense of morality that's apparently so divine you can't even explain it in normal people words. Now what are you telling me?"

"You're overreacting. There's very little chance the queries will be noticed at headquarters."

"Are you joking? Almost in the same breath, you told me your management was up in arms over your dabbling in this very case. Something or someone has obviously rocked your management's boat on this. Has them running scared for their continued hold on power. You're being uncharacteristically naive if you don't think there's a good chance they'll check your NCIC log."

"Uncharacteristically? When did you learn that word?"

"Your fatigue is making you dumb. I could have run that search for you. I have 27 active cases I could choose from to bury it in. Nobody would ever have known. Next time you need something like that, you come to me, understand?"

"Thanks."

"Thanks yourself, moron. You're buying." Arkin fell silent and stared down at his coffee, looking glum. "Oh, come on. Did I hurt your feelings?"

"No. It's Hannah." He shook his head. "I feel so helpless."

"You are helpless."

Arkin looked up. "Thanks. That helps."

"No, really. You're helpless. You have no control over this. And the sooner you come to terms with that. . . ."

"What?"

"The sooner—I don't know—the sooner you'll find a certain solace."

"Solace? Really? And then what? I'll be as happy as you?" Morrison opened his mouth as if to speak, then closed it. "Right," Arkin said. "Thanks for nothing, Dr. Freud."

Morrison's lips almost, but not quite, formed a grin. "Point," he said at last, and they shared a mirthless nostril laugh.

As they walked out the door, Arkin's cell rang.

"Mr. Regan. What's the good news?"

"The good news is that the initial analysis took less time than expected. You're looking at a .50 caliber fired by a Zastava. The striations match those of the Cortez bullet. And I'm guessing that doesn't come as a surprise to you."

"No, it doesn't."

"A copy of the report is in your email inbox. Got to bring the feds in now."

"Sure. Hey, Paul, I owe you one. Thank you."

"You bet."

"Cortez gun?" Morrison asked as they walked along Main.

"Cortez gun."

*****

That afternoon, Morrison insisted that Arkin accompany him to the range, despite Arkin's protests over being dangerously fatigued.

"There's no better way to blow off steam than by putting some lead downrange," Morrison had said. "And anyway, nobody else is scheduled to be there, so the only one you're going to accidentally shoot is me."

153

*****

When he got back to the office, he had a voicemail from Killick asking him to call back.

"What's up?" Arkin asked when Killick finally answered on the 6th ring.

"I told you I was going to give you the highlights of those FBI 302s."

Killick went on to describe two witness interviews—already corroborated by security video—that placed a man from Phoenix named Karl Heinz at the gas station two blocks from Pratt's house just about 10 minutes after the shooting. Heinz was a person of interest for two reasons. For one, the witnesses saw him lashing a long, hard-sided black plastic case down into the back of his pickup truck as he filled up. For another, the man's name came up on a roll of donors to Egan's church.

"What color is his hair?"

"What?"

"Heinz's hair. What color is it?"

"Hold on. His DMV photo is in here somewhere. Shit—it's a black-and-white. Fucking FBI. But it looks like he has fair hair. Could be gray, could be blonde. Close-cropped. Why?"

"The Cortez shooter probably has dark, curly hair. And long."

"Really?"

"That should have been in one of Pratt's weekly case summaries."

"I'll go back over them. Anything else I should know?"

"Pratt was shot by the same Zastava that Egan was."

"How do you know that?"

"Turns out the bullet was recovered, but there was some sort of miscommunication and it was accidentally taken to the state lab for analysis instead of just being handed over to the FBI. But the chain of custody is solid, so no worries."

"Damn. That's awfully damned sloppy. And anyway, I thought you promised you were going to hold off and let us work this case."

"I am, for the most part. It's just a small community here, law enforcement wise. Word gets around."

"What do you mean 'for the most part'?"

"Well, you know me. I can't just command my mind not to think about it. But what about on your end? Were you able to recover the Priest file from INDIGO backups?"

"Not yet. They're still trying.

TWENTY-ONE

It was finally dark. Morrison was back in position at his observation post above Arkin's house, having hiked over the ridge and down through the woods two hours earlier. There was a chill in the air, but he was wearing his winter BDUs and was quite comfortable.

He hadn't rotated though his observation cycle more than four times when something caught his eye to the south. Movement. A man on foot. Solo. Not a jogger. Someone walking. For the moment, on the darker side of the road where trees blocked the light of the moon. Good technique or just coincidence? Morrison would know in a few more seconds when the other side of the road became the better, darker option. Sure as shit, just before the west shoulder of the road passed a gap in the trees exposing it to bright moonlight, the walker switched to the east shoulder.

Tally-ho.

The stranger's pace slackened as he approached. He appeared to be looking toward the tree line on the side of the street opposite Arkin's driveway, directly below Morrison's position. After a moment, the stranger ducked into the trees, climbed a few yards up off the road, and began setting up his own observation post not ten yards below Morrison. Morrison stared with a predator's intensity. The man had his own set of small night vision binoculars hanging from a lanyard around his neck and a small two-way radio that he set against the trunk of an aspen. He didn't appear to be armed, but

Morrison couldn't be sure. As the man reached to plug a tiny cord microphone and earpiece into the radio, Morrison caught a quick look at his left hand. His pinkie finger was missing. It was the jogger from the other day.

Morrison watched the stranger for a good half hour without so much as twitching his own toe. The stranger never moved either. He just kept watching Arkin's house. Waiting. For what, Morrison could only guess.

Fuck this.

With glacially slow movements, Morrison rose to a crouch, picked up his night vision binoculars, and began, step by step and quiet as a cat, to close the short distance between himself and the stranger. So much adrenaline coursed through his veins, Morrison thought he might burst. But he was well-disciplined, and kept his movements slow, fluid and silent. He only wished he'd thought to bring his night vision headgear, in addition to his binoculars, so that he could see where he was stepping.

Stupid. You're losing your edge.

As careful as he was being, it took him nearly 20 minutes to close half the distance to the stranger. But then, when he was no more than nine feet away, his foot cracked something. Maybe a dry twig. He froze in place, staring at the stranger's silhouette, barely visible against the moonlit road down through the brush and trees. The stranger remained still. A minute went by. Had Morrison dodged a bullet?

Without warning, the stranger sprang to his feet and ran for the road. *Shit!* Morrison flung his binoculars and took off after him. The stranger was fast, and Morrison had to chase him so hard that he decided to wait on trying to un-holster his .45. They sprinted back down Carson Road half a mile before turning onto County Road 1822 and then on toward Highway 550.

Though his thighs and legs burned with fatigue, though his lungs screamed for more air, Morrison focused his thoughts on the pursuit to help block out the pain. *Your ass is mine. Your motherfucking ass is mine.* Thirty feet back, he wasn't gaining, but he wasn't losing ground either. And he was sure the guy had left his radio behind, so he couldn't call for help. *Give it up, meat. You're mine.*

As they burst from the narrow county road onto Highway 550, the stranger crossed to the far side before turning right. But as Morrison followed, his own tunnel vision locked on the stranger, he found himself illuminated by a southbound car bearing down on him from the left. He heard the tires screech as the driver locked up his brakes. Morrison was moving too fast to change direction in time. *I'm dead.*

But he wasn't dead. The car, in an uncontrolled slide and turned nearly sideways, passed within a foot of his left arm, blowing his hair back as it passed. It caught up to and hit the stranger with a low thud before at last screeching to a loud and dusty stop. The car—a big 80s sedan—sat there for a moment, its motor still running, its lights still on. Then it peeled out and fled the scene at high speed. *A hit and run. Unbelievable,* Morrison thought, still catching his breath, bent over with his hands on his knees.

Looking up, he saw the stranger lying on the pavement on his back, still moving, but barely. Morrison forgot his fatigue and ran over. The man—a tall Nordic blond in black pants and jacket—was still alive.

"Who are you? Who the fuck are you?"

The stranger didn't seem aware that Morrison was there. He just squirmed slightly, looking up at the sky with crazy eyes. His nose was bleeding from both nostrils.

Morrison looked from side to side. For the moment, there were no other cars on the road. He gave the stranger a cursory pat down and then picked him up and slung him over his back like a wounded soldier. The stranger offered no resistance. Morrison carried him off the highway and a few yards into the woods, laid him on the ground, and handcuffed his arms around a stout aspen before setting off to retrieve his own car.

*****

It was just after midnight when Arkin's phone woke him from a disturbing dream in which he'd found dozens of drowned dogs floating down a wide, brown river.

"This had better be good."

"Buddy, you need to meet me at my place right now."

"Why? What on Earth—"

"Just get your private boarding school ass over here right now."

*****

Fifteen minutes later, Arkin found Morrison waiting in front of his carport as he drove up.

"I have someone you just have to meet."

"A social call?"

Morrison opened the trunk of his car. In it lay the stranger, now conscious, but gagged with duct tape and bound with handcuffs and belly chains into a fetal position. He was tall, blonde and blue-eyed. Nordic blood, no doubt about it. His left pinkie finger was missing—an old wound with old scars. His left leg was clearly broken, his foot pointed in an unnatural direction. The left side of his pelvis seemed crushed inward. And a large white bone protruded three inches from a long and bloody tear in his mangled left forearm. It was the worst compound fracture Arkin had ever seen.

"There's a man in your trunk."

"Yes, there is. We were just about to get acquainted. He's going to be our new star witness."

"Is that right?"

"Caught him surveilling your house this evening. Flushed and chased his ass down to Highway 550 where he had a close encounter with a speeding car. It's just not his day."

"Surveilling my house?"

"About an hour ago."

"You were watching my house."

"I told you, I've got your back, buddy."

Arkin gave a soft snort, still staring down at the stranger in the trunk. "Didn't you promise you weren't going to do that?"

"You made me promise not to set up an observation post next to your house. I set it up well *above* your house, so we're good."

"You are so—" Arkin broke off and shook his head. A weak smile appeared on his face.

"I think that's the first time I've seen you smile in a week."

"Am I smiling?" His voice sounded weary.

"I think you are."

"You might be right."

"Always am."

Arkin nodded. "Thank you for this."

"De nada."

Arkin's expression hardened.

"Did he have any ID on him?"

"Not even so much as initials penned onto the tag of his shirt."

Arkin stared down at him again. For a moment, he felt a pang of compassion and consequent urge to get the man to a hospital right away. But then he thought of Pratt's family, reached down, and tore off the duct-tape gag. Blood and bile spilled from the corner of the man's mouth.

"Who are you?"

The stranger's eyes met Arkin's but he said nothing.

"Who are you? Speak!"

Arkin gave a hard yank on the elbow of the man's fractured arm. Any normal man would surely have screamed out in pain. All this one did was pop his eyes a little wider and breathe a little harder.

"Let me get my blowtorch," Morrison said. "It's just over on my workbench. In thirty seconds I'll have him singing 'Ave Maria.'"

The stranger didn't react.

"Why are you here?" Arkin asked.

The stranger's breathing was labored. He pursed his lips as if about to speak, then didn't.

"One more time. Who are you and why are you here?"

The stranger closed his eyes. "To save. . . ."

"What?"

"Save you from yourself." His accent was foreign—maybe Dutch?—his voice weak. His tone struck Arkin as sincere and sympathetic. Almost apologetic. Almost sad. Like that of a father reluctantly reprimanding a frightened child whom he dearly loves. It was unnerving.

"What the hell is that supposed to mean? Open your eyes!"

The man's eyes stayed closed, prompting Arkin to yank his broken arm even more violently than before. Then he twisted and bent it backward with all his strength.

"There's that dark side I've been waiting to see," Morrison muttered.

The man no longer appeared to feel anything.

"Did the Priest send you? Wake up, asshole! Did the Priest send you?"

At this, a faint smile appeared on the stranger's face. His eyes opened a crack and, just audibly, Arkin heard him whisper "Priest." Then he lost consciousness.

Arkin punched the man's wounded arm as hard as he could. The man didn't move. "Let's get him to the hospital."

"I think we're too late for that, brother."

The stranger had stopped breathing. Morrison pressed two fingers against his carotid artery, held them there for a moment, made eye contact with Arkin and shook his head. Arkin had a sudden, desperate urge to shout, as if the man could still hear him, *Can you see anything? What can you see?* But he got hold of himself, as embarrassed as he was surprised at his flash of irrationality. Then he frowned, clenched his fists, looked up at the night sky, and sighed.

Half an hour later, convinced they hadn't the time to arrange a more professional and untraceable disposal, they dumped the body in the woods 50 yards off a deserted stretch of Florida Road, far from any homes or driveways, knowing coyotes would probably have at it in short order. That would be that.

TWENTY-TWO

As he stood watering the bonsai tree in his office the next morning, Arkin reflected on what had happened the previous night. It was now abundantly clear that he was a possible target, and that he was probably being watched by a whole surveillance team of some sort. There was no doubt in his mind that this was the same group he was chasing when he led the Priest case for DCI years earlier. It was also clear—from the engineered disappearance of the INDIGO files, to the mysterious pressure being brought to bear on MWA with sufficient gravity to scare them off the Pratt case—that this group had operatives holding high-level positions in U.S. intelligence and law enforcement agencies. And he was beginning to suspect that the group had been behind his demotion, humiliation, and banishment all those years ago. That it was they who'd destroyed his career, upended his life, and pulled the strings that sent he and his wife packing to this remote mountain town.

The more he thought about it, the angrier he got, the hotter his face felt, and the faster his mind raced. Names charged at him from years back. Seemingly innocuous events in the past took on sinister significance through the dark lens of hindsight. How long had they watched him? Who was involved? How much did they know about him? What vulnerabilities could they exploit? What should he do now?

An idea formed. There was a remote chance it would get him to the finish line. It might even serve to bring him some form of redemption by bringing the whole Priest organization down. But it was a one-way ticket. Once he went forward, there would be no going back until he cracked the case open. And he would have to crack it before his tactics caught up with him, because if and when they did, the world would come crashing down on him. So much so that he could end up being taken away from Hannah.

Beads of sweat formed along his hairline. His stomach began to turn. He tried his breathing exercises—inhale deeply, hold it for ten seconds, exhale through the nostrils, and repeat. Repeat. Repeat again. He recited, five times, the Bene Gesserit "litany against fear" from his favorite novel, *Dune*. He recalled a line he once heard from a motivational speaker, along the lines that fear couldn't exist without prolonged indecision, or something like that. That if you could picture the worst possible outcome of the decision you faced, and could then resolve to live with that outcome if it came to pass, then in making your decision, in committing to a choice, your fear would melt away. But the worst possible outcome of his idea was that he would be taken away from his ill wife in her hour of greatest need. He didn't think he could live with that. And it was a very real possibility.

He stood up and stepped back from his desk. Then, desperate for some sort of release, he began to do, of all the inane things, jumping jacks, counting boot camp style as he went: "one-two-three-one, one-two-three-two, one-two-three-three. . . ." It wasn't helping, so he picked up speed, his tie flying this way and that as he flailed maniacally. "One-two-three-fifty-seven. . . ." His pulse thumped in his ears. Then, without premeditation, he spin-kicked the door of his closet with a loud crash, splitting it in half vertically. He watched the broken half fall to the floor, went down the hall to the open cubicle of a young Forest Service inspector where he knew there was a phone that blocked its own caller ID.

Within minutes, he'd tracked down the appropriate phone company official. An attorney in their compliance department.

"What did you say your name was again?"

"John Pratt."

"And you are a sworn L.E.O.?"

"Yes, sir. I'm a special agent with the U.S. Department of Homeland Security, Directorate for Counter Intelligence."

"I haven't heard of that one."

"It's relatively new. Post-9/11. I can fax you a copy of my credentials, along with the subpoena. I can also give you the address of the agency web site."

"A fax of your credentials would be helpful. And I assume you'll mail the original subpoena today?"

"Yes. You should get it shortly."

"Okay. So let me get this straight: you need this guy--what's his name?—Drake. You need the numbers of Drake's outgoing calls placed in the next 24 hours?"

"That's correct."

"And you have a subpoena for this."

"I can fax it to you in the next 10 minutes."

"Yes. It's just that something about this troubles me."

"Yes?"

"I mean, philosophically, this is almost like doing a pen register, which would require a court order, as you know."

"The difference is that I would not be getting the information in real time."

"You almost would."

"If it would make you feel better to check the applicable statute, if memory serves, I believe it's 18 U.S.C. section 3127. It's also addressed in the 1979 U.S. Supreme Court case of Smith versus Maryland. I can get you a court order if you need one. But I'd prefer not to, given the exigency."

The lawyer seemed to be deliberating. "Okay, just fax me the subpoena and we'll go for it. I'm assuming you want me to have our tech people fax you the results right at the 24-hour mark?"

"That would be perfect. Thank you very much."

"And you'll mail me the original subpoena."

"Today."

In 10 minutes, Arkin was faxing the phone company attorney a forged subpoena, along with a photocopy of Pratt's credentials he'd kept in a file after using it for a gun range rental application a year earlier.

*****

Sitting in the same Forest Service employee's cubicle that night, having waited until well after business hours in Wyoming so that he wouldn't have to talk to the guy, Arkin dialed the land line phone number for Dustin Drake, CPA. It rang and rang. At last, an antiquated answering machine kicked on. "This is Dustin Drake, CPA. I'm not able to take your call. . . ." Arkin was ready for the beep.

"Hello, Mr. Drake. This is Special Agent Chad Rhodes with the Federal Bureau of Investigation. I'm the agent-in-charge of the Redding, California, field office, and I'm trying to track down two companies for which you serve as registered agent in the state of Wyoming. The companies are called V-TAC and Star Dynamics. It is imperative that you give me a call back, as this concerns an urgent matter in a federal conspiracy and murder investigation. My number is. . . ."

Arkin made sure he gave the real number and name for the agent-in-charge in Redding, just in case Drake did any superficial checking. As long as he didn't actually get Rhodes on the phone, the cover story would work.

But he doubted Drake would even bother. With any luck, he'd simply call his client to pass the message along.

TWENTY-THREE

The next evening, as Arkin sat in the dark waiting, Pratt's fax machine chirped to life, printing out a one-page list encompassing the numbers for 17 outgoing phone calls from the office of Dustin Drake, CPA. The very first one, placed at 9:06 a.m., had an area code of 250, which, as Arkin would never forget, covered much of British Columbia, including Vancouver Island.

Bingo.

He took the printout home and called Killick after opening a cold beer.

"Go to a payphone and call me back."

"A payphone? Do we even still have those in America?"

"Just do it."

"Screw you, bud. It's like 28 degrees outside. And dark." Arkin waited, silent. "Nate, this is a secure line. If there's a problem with eavesdropping, it's at your end."

"Humor me."

"You're being ridiculous. The line is encrypted. Now, my extremely late dinner is sitting in front of me on my desk, getting cold, so I'm going to eat it while we talk."

Arkin sighed. "Got something for you." He gave Killick the British Columbia phone number.

"What am I supposed to make of this?"

"Just check it out. Find out who pays the bills for that line. I'm guessing

164

it will be a Chinese-Canadian formerly known as Zhang Zhou, now living under an alias. A one-time resident of Port Hardy, BC."

"And dare I ask, where did you—"

"Don't worry. I was just looking through a box of old photos and found that number on a scrap of paper at the bottom of the pile."

"Looking through a box of old photos."

"It has a British Columbia area code."

"So?"

"I think it's a number I jotted down when I was working the Priest case."

"And you just found it. Just now. In your house."

"Just check it out. I'll bet you my whole retirement fund that the bills for that number are still being paid, even though the billing address is probably for some sort of derelict storefront, warehouse, or factory that has been abandoned for years, and that the guy paying the bills will lead you to the Priest."

"Have you told the Bureau?"

"I'm going to call them first thing tomorrow. It's late."

"No shit, it's late. I'm on Eastern Time, you inconsiderate ass."

*****

Arkin was jolted awake by a shrill whistling. *The fire alarm.* Out of habit, he first turned to check the alarm clock. 3:37 a.m.. He turned a lamp on and rolled from bed. There was no smoke in the bedroom as yet, so he threw on a pair of pants, a sweatshirt, and shoes, shoved his cellphone in his pocket, and got up to check his door. It was warm, but not hot. He opened it to find the far end of the hallway in flames. He was cut off from the rest of the house. The first thing he thought of was the British Columbia phone number. But the fax was in his briefcase on the kitchen table. There was no way he could get to it. And for the second time in his life, he cursed himself for not thinking to memorize the number.

He stood for a moment, wondering how the fire had progressed so quickly when the alarm had only sounded a minute earlier. There must have been an accelerant. And that could mean only one thing: arson. Attempted murder by arson.

He pulled his gun locker from under his bed, spun the combination, and took out a holstered .45. He climbed out the window, executing a paratrooper's roll as he landed on the ground. Before bothering to get his bearings, he ran for cover into the clump of pine trees at the back edge of the yard, in case anyone was waiting to take a shot at him. He attached the holstered .45 to his leather belt, waited for his eyes to adjust, hopped the fence, and ran through the trees along the edge of the forest toward the hospital, making his way by moonlight.

*****

Morrison was already at the hospital, standing guard at the door to Hannah's room, by the time he got there. "She's fine, brother. She's sleeping."

"Thanks for coming," Arkin said, short of breath. "Sorry to wake you. I owe you one."

"Shut your mouth."

"I think it was kerosene. There was that oil lamp smell."

"All that matters right now is that we get you the fuck out of Durango."

"I'm not going anywhere."

"Nate, someone just tried to burn your house down with you in it."

"I'm not leaving Hannah."

"We'll bring her."

"She's in bad shape. I don't want to try to move her right now."

"What about somewhere close, like Telluride? I'll drive you both there today."

He thought for a moment. "No. No, I need to stay here."

"Why?"

"Network access. My weapons. You."

"Hey, look, I've got your back as much as I can, but—"

"We'll be okay. I'm sure DPD will be willing to put a security detail on Hannah's room."

"I think that's a bad decision. But it's your call. Anyway, here." Morrison took a new cellphone from his pocket. "This is for you. It's a burner. Just in case anyone is tracking your mobile." He handed it to Arkin.

"Thanks. I think I'll hang onto my old one in case I need a decoy."

" Well, at least take the battery out when you aren't using it. Do you have an active cover?"

"An old one. But it should still be viable."

"Then let's swing by the office and get your ID, make a few moves to drop any surveillance, and then go get you set up in some shitty motel on the south side of town. Let's get you a different car and then leave yours at the office so nobody finds you by searching parking lots."

*****

Later that morning, after borrowing a truck from one of his Forest Service buddies, executing clean off maneuvers to make sure he wasn't being followed, checking into a south Durango motel under a pseudonym, then driving up to Rim Drive and pulling to the shoulder to take care of business using his new phone, he updated O'Neil and Killick on the situation—in

Killick's case, only after insisting that he find a payphone to call back on this time—and gave them his new cell number. Killick sounded shaken.

"Holy shit. Is Hannah okay?"

"She's fine."

"I'm sorry. I should have—look, let me send a team out to cover your back."

"That isn't necessary. And I don't want to risk scaring these people off until I can figure out who they are and where they came from. Anyway, we still don't know who the traitor is in DCI. An operation like that could be compromised from the get-go."

"Well shit, then. What can I do?"

"I need that phone number back from you. It was lost in the fire."

"You don't have it saved anywhere else?" Arkin's silence answered his question. "Shit, I gave it to the tech guys so they could get started on running down the owner."

"I need to give it to the FBI."

"I'll try to get it back. I'll call you at this number."

"Good."

*****

An hour later, Arkin and Hannah were in her hospital room after discussing what Arkin had learned from a phone call with their homeowners insurance agent, as she lay in bed, sipping at a cup of apple juice. Arkin was now staring at the wall, quiet.

"Nate."

"Hmmm?"

"Where are you?"

"Sorry. Far away."

"It's alright. What were you thinking about?"

Arkin shook his head. "Historical noise."

"Tell me."

"It's nothing relevant."

"Nate."

He paused. "You remember the operation we ran against that neo-Nazi down near Appomattox, Raylan McGill—the meth dealer who castrated and killed an Ethiopian Jewish convenience store clerk in Richmond?"

"The guy who was planning to bomb the Holocaust Museum."

"It was a huge operation. Maximum priority. Sheffield himself ran the command post in Lynchburg. I was partnered with Killick on surveillance."

"I remember."

Arkin paused again. "There's an aspect to the story I've never told anyone before."

"Yes?"

"Killick and I, we'd been staked out in the forest, watching this guy's trailer for a few days, getting nowhere. It was obvious he was expecting surveillance. All we'd seen him do was slap his wife around. Of course, we couldn't sandbag him for that because our mission was to observe all comings and goings, to identify all his co-conspirators in the Holocaust Museum bombing plot. So Killick and I are out there in the woods one night in our static post, watching, when McGill flies into this rage and really starts to go to town on his wife, well beyond anything we'd already witnessed. A brutal beating."

Arkin's face took on a look of revulsion as he remembered. Hannah waited for him to go on.

"It's just that. . . ."

"What?"

"Killick started talking about how we would never win against the endless procession of people like McGill until we were willing to cross the line."

"Cross the line?"

Arkin paused again. "He wanted me to shoot McGill."

"That's frustration talking. He was probably just—"

"No, he literally begged me to. At first I thought he was joking. He wasn't. Believe me."

"Well. . . ."

"And he seemed genuinely frustrated when I didn't. Angry, even."

Arkin could still picture the scene as though it were yesterday. Could still feel the crisp autumn air on his cheeks, could still smell the fallen leaves. And he could still feel the nausea that hit him as he watched McGill beat the living hell out of his wife—could still feel the burning temptation to flex his finger just enough to exert 3.5 pounds of pressure on the cold steel trigger of his rifle and blow McGill's brains out.

Two hours after the beating, Arkin and Killick had been spelled by the reserve surveillance crew. Using night vision gear, they made their way through the dark Virginia woods, down to the tent they'd set up as a staging point 50 meters off a lonely country road that wound through a hollow and on south to the state highway. They cleaned the black greasepaint from their faces, changed back into their street clothes, and got in their unmarked pickup truck to make their way back to their base at an ancient hotel in old Lynchburg, where Sheffield waited to debrief them.

They drove for two miles along the dark, forest-flanked road that followed a small winding creek, down to where it merged with the road that came down from McGill's property. Taking a left toward the highway, they drove another half mile before happening upon McGill's wife, walking in the same direction along the gravel shoulder, in her bloodied tank top and jeans. No coat, despite the cold air. Her exposed arms were heavily tattooed.

Crosses. Citations to the Old Testament. A Nazi SS symbol. Arkin pulled up alongside her and lowered the window. Her swollen nose, lips, and chin were covered in dried blood, her shoulders slumped. She looked straight ahead, dazed. Didn't stop walking.

"Miss? Miss, are you alright?" No response. "Miss, were you in an accident?"

At this, she seemed to almost grin. She stopped and turned to face him, her face a battered, blood-darkened mess.

"Can we give you a lift into town?"

Without answering, she grabbed the handle of the crew cab door and jumped in. Killick shifted his body, ever so subtly, until he was in a position to keep an eye on her and, if necessary, strike with his dominant hand if she produced a weapon. He stole covert glances, scanning her clothing for telltale bulges, concluding that she probably didn't have a gun on her. A knife was another matter.

"Miss, can we take you to the hospital?" Arkin asked. No response. "I think this little lady might be in shock, George."

"Yeah, I think you might be right."

Should they make a pass at her? It was outside of their game plan. But McGill had just beaten her to within inches of her life. Could she possibly be motivated to betray him?

She was silent. They drove on.

"I don't know, Hank," Killick said. "I think maybe we oughta take her to the police station. I think maybe she's been attacked."

"Jus drop me ah mah sisuh's place," she said in a sad, weak voice, through her purple swollen lips. "A mile up on thuh righh."

"Miss, have you been attacked?" Arkin asked, in as kind a voice as he could muster. "Who did this to you?" He watched her in the rearview mirror. She was slumped, cowering, meek.

"Mah husbann," she said at last, her chin resting against her chest as she stared down at her own lap.

Bingo. Keep her talking. Say anything. Just keep the dialogue going.

"What happened?"

"Where ah you from, Hank?"

"Near Charlottesville."

"Near Charlottesville? Me too. Whereabouts?"

"Miss, I think we should take you to the hospital."

"How abow you, George? Where ah you from?"

"Miss, can you tell us what happened?"

She nodded to herself, as though in affirmation of something. Then she looked up and met Arkin's eyes in the rearview mirror. "Mah husban say I was a dirty ho."

"Did you have an argument?"

"He said I was a whore. Pull over here," she said, her speech suddenly clear.

Arkin did as she asked, bringing the truck to a halt at the end of a winding and potholed gravel driveway that disappeared into the forest. "Miss, I think we should get you some help." As he said this, the first hint of realization began to set in. Something had changed in her voice. The pain and fear in it had gone. Even the distorting impediment of her swollen lips seemed to have vanished. Her voice was icy and clear.

She opened the door, jumped out, then walked up to Arkin's open window.

"Yessir. Said I was a whore." Her face had grown dark and hateful. "But I'll tell you one thing I've never heard him say. I never heard him say, while we were laying in bed on a Tuesday night a couple of months ago, 'tomorrow I'm gonna cut that Jew nigger grocery clerk's balls off and push them one-by-one down his throat with my thumb and make him swallow them before I shoot his Jew nigger ass.' No, he definitely *never* said anything like that." Her eyes bugging out, she burst out laughing, a loud, dry, and sinister heavy smoker's cackle. "No, sir. Never heard him say anything about how we're gonna burn all the Jews and niggers and Arabs and faggots." She laughed again, a laugh of sheer homicidal insanity. "Well," she said, giving Arkin's door a couple of *see-you-round* taps with her knuckles, "thanks for the ride, *George* and *Hank*. Y'all run along home to Washington now. We'll see you again soon, when we march on your city with the armies of the Lord. And there won't be nowhere for you Jew lovers to hide." She turned to walk away.

Arkin jumped from the truck and had her handcuffed, face down in the prone position alongside the truck, in seconds. Keeping one knee pressed into her back with far more pressure than was necessary, he reached over, grabbed a radio from under the driver's seat, and called in the emergency takedown code. "Harpoon One Actual, Harpoon Two. Kayak, kayak, kayak!" He repeated his transmission, still kneeling on her back, the truck still running, parked in the middle of a lonely country road under a cold canopy of stars.

"Harpoon Two, Harpoon One has solid copy on kayak. Over." It was the somber voice of Sheffield's radio operator. Sheffield was still MIA, but it no longer mattered. In a matter of minutes, McGill and all his known co-conspirators, from Maryland to South Carolina, would be in custody.

For a long time afterward, Arkin would wonder whether the whole beating had been an act, premeditated by McGill and his criminally insane wife, to draw out the surveillance they must have suspected. And he would wish, far more than he would care to admit to himself, that he'd taken that shot.

*****

"Why are you telling me this now?" Hannah asked him as he continued to stare out the hospital window.

"I don't know. It just sort of popped into the forefront of my mind."

"You look troubled."

"Dark days."

"And you have a lot on your plate right now."

"Yes."

"Nate?"

"Yes?"

"You're going to be okay."

Arkin turned from the window and met her eyes. Here was his wife, lying in a hospital bed, her body stricken, focused not on her own well-being, but his. She never ceased to amaze him.

*****

As he left the hospital, Arkin called Paul Regan to see if there had been any progress in the arson investigation.

"Hey, I was just about to call you."

"What's up?"

"Well, uh. . . ."

"What?"

"We—we have a little problem."

"What is it?"

"Did you have anybody at your house last night?"

"No. Why?"

"DF&R found a body in your basement."

"A body."

"Face charred beyond recognition. Hands burned so badly we'll never get a usable print. But there was enough of him left to tell he was a Caucasian male, approximately 6-foot-2, 190 to 200 pounds, with a lot of broken bones and a missing left pinkie finger."

Holy shit. "Maybe it was the arsonist."

"That would have been my first thought too, except it looks like he was bound to a chair, gagged, and shot through the liver."

"Shot?" Arkin processed the implications, his first thought being that a shot through the soft part of the body where the liver was would probably mean DPD would find a largely intact bullet to analyze. Whether that was good or bad depended on the thoroughness of whoever was setting him up.

"We recovered a .45 bullet from an exposed pine joist. So I need your gun. Just to eliminate you as a suspect. For the record, Nate, I know this is bullshit. I mean, I know you didn't shoot this guy, and that there is something funny going on here. But I have to follow procedure."

171

"It's okay. Can I bring it by around lunch time?"

"That would be fine. Do you have another gun you can carry while the lab has your .45?"

"I have my .40, a short barrel Remington 870, and an MP5."

"That ought to hold you."

"I'll be alright. Hey, listen, let the coroner know that he should check for evidence that the bullet wound was post-mortem."

"Sure. But why?"

"If I told you, you wouldn't believe me. Let's call it a gut feeling."

"I'll do it. By the way, they still have to test the swabs, but it looks like you were right. Someone poured kerosene all over the place before lighting your house."

"Well, lucky for me, when you see how worthless my insurance is, you'll know I didn't torch my house for the payout."

*****

As Arkin drove toward his office, he got another call from Scott O'Neil.

"Scott, what's the good news?"

"The news is bad, Nate."

"What's wrong?"

"Seventh floor ordered me to suspend you."

Arkin was half expecting this, but not so soon. "Should I ask why?"

"Your NCIC and other database logs were audited."

"What a coincidence."

"There were a lot of queries under your I.D. that didn't appear to tie to names listed in your assigned cases. You'll have an opportunity to explain. But for now, your access is frozen and you're on administrative leave. You can hang onto your guns."

"Super."

"I warned you about this."

Troubled at the rapidity with which his MWA superiors had learned of his unauthorized activity, Arkin was nevertheless thankful they apparently hadn't yet learned of the subpoena forgery: a far more serious infraction.

*****

"Already?" Morrison said, after Arkin told him of his suspension. "What's it been, maybe 48 hours since you queried NCIC?" They leaned against Morrison's ATF Tahoe, on a rutted dirt road alongside the Animas, watching a lone fly fisherman casting across the trailing edge of a riffle 80 yards upriver. The air smelled of sagebrush and dry grass.

"Presumably," Arkin said, "there is someone either in or somehow affiliated with DCI who has enough clout to make the political appointees at MWA do his bidding."

"Or her bidding."

"Of course, it's possible the Priest group has penetrated MWA as well."

"What about Killick?"

"Nah."

"How well do you know him?"

"We've been friends since Basic Recon. Things got a little awkward after my banishment, but he's a decent enough guy. More importantly, I don't think he has the chops to run something like this. Something this complicated."

"He's DCI's director of operations."

"Morrison, please. Since when was promotion based on merit or ability in the federal law enforcement community?" He smiled weakly. "I'm starting to sound like you."

"You're getting smarter, is what it is. My point is does his rank and his access, not to mention your sharing information with him, make him the logical suspect."

"Hard to believe."

"Harder than anything else about this case?"

Arkin nodded. "You have a point. How would you test your theory?"

"Let me set up a perfect static post somewhere fairly remote, with only one access road. Then you call him on his encrypted line. Use your new burner. Tell him you've got the name of the Canadian company, and then tell him where you are."

"If Killick's the mole, and if I don't come out and give him the name of the company, he'll smell a rat."

"Then just tell him where you are. If he's the mole, then at the very least, he'll dispatch a team to keep an eye on you."

"Where are we going to do this?"

"How about Sundial Ranch, on Road 243, up above Lemon Reservoir? They have a long access road that curves up through the woods, and you can't see the parking lot for their cabins until you get way the hell up there. It's perfect. Plus, it's low season for tourism, and hunting season is closed, so there aren't too many people who will have a good reason to be up there on that access road. Should make a tail easy to spot."

"That works."

"You don't even have to be there. Just make the call. I'll be up above the road, with eyes on."

"When are we going to do this?"

"How about first thing in the morning?"

*****

173

"Nate, it's Paul Regan again."

"Regan. Don't tell me my .45 is the murder weapon. That'll ruin my whole evening."

"No, but someone red-flagged it. Next thing we knew, some fed came and took it right out of our inventory as Dominique was boxing it up for the state lab."

"A fed? But it's a state case."

"I know. I don't know what they told Ops, but they let them take it."

"A fed with what agency?"

"I don't know. I wasn't there. But there's more."

"More?"

"Feds brought a dog. They're saying it keyed on your car."

"Keyed for what? Cocaine?"

"Kerosene."

Arkin digested this. "This is getting downright spooky, Paul."

"Yes, it is."

"Did you review my insurance?"

"I did."

"So you know I have nothing to gain by burning my own house down."

"Look, Nate, I know you're being set up here. Some crazy fed conspiracy like in the movies. I just know it. But you gotta come in for questioning. I gotta cover my ass, even if this is total bullshit"

"I know."

"I don't like this."

"I don't either."

"I have a bad feeling the feds are going to toss us an arrest warrant." Regan sighed. "Go spend time with your wife. Don't come in until tomorrow."

"Thanks, Paul. Thanks for the heads-up."

*****

That evening, Hannah looked worse. The skin of her face was colorless and sagging. She looked like she'd aged twenty years in a week. She wasn't eating, and strange bruises had appeared along both of her forearms. Arkin had brought her a large bouquet of brightly colored flowers from City Market, but it did little to cheer her.

"We've got to get you out of here. To the city. To somewhere where they have more treatment options." She just gazed at him from her bed with a weak smile on her face. It was obvious that the altered chemo regimen was breaking her down. But he wasn't about to say that. Nor did he have any intention of troubling her with his situation at work. It would only add to her anxiety. And she'd be upset with him for taking such stupid risks. Anyway, his medical insurance was still active, despite his suspension. For the moment, that was all that mattered.

TWENTY-FOUR

Sometime that night, Arkin had a dream involving himself, Sheffield, and Killick. In it, Arkin recalled part of a real conversation they had many years earlier—when he and Killick were still colleagues and Sheffield was their boss. The three of them sat in the U.S. Department of Justice cafeteria, at the headquarters building off Constitution Avenue. Arkin had been awarded the National Intelligence Distinguished Service Medal in an elaborate ceremony that morning. As he woke from the dream, he relived the rest of the conversation.

"Magnificent work," Sheffield had told him. "I'm sincerely proud of you, Nathaniel."

"So proud that we're celebrating by having lunch in the DOJ cafeteria."

"Don't be a mope," Killick said.

"A mope? They just handed me the law enforcement equivalent of the CMH. I should be at the head of a tickertape parade."

"Glad to see it hasn't gone to your head," Killick said.

"Hey, at the very least, you two should be buying me hundred-year-old scotches at the Capital Grille right now. It smells like my grandmother's nursing home in here."

Sheffield smiled at him. "In due time, old boy. In due time. I have to meet with the notorious inter-agency steering committee in an hour. Can't be floating in there smelling of single malt and cigars. How about tonight? And

176

you can bring your lovely wife."

"That sounds wonderful."

"In the meantime, how about a green JELL-O cup?" Killick asked. "They're fresh."

"Really though, Nate, excellent, excellent work," Sheffield said.

Arkin poked at a lump of gluey Department of Justice mashed potatoes with his fork. "Thanks."

Sheffield and Killick glanced at each other.

"You don't sound all that enthusiastic," Killick said.

"No, I am."

"You are?"

"Sure. Yes. I guess I just find it a bit incongruous that they gave me this medal, at least in part, for the Appomattox operation."

"Why?"

"Because technically, the operation was blown. McGill smoked us out. He baited us with his savagery, and we fell for it."

"You saved hundreds of lives."

"We got lucky. We were lucky in that we'd already been watching him long enough to know how to disrupt the immediate conspiracy. We were lucky he didn't smoke us out earlier. But. . . ." Arkin stopped himself.

"Go ahead," Sheffield said. "Get it off your chest."

Arkin looked up. "It's along the lines of what I told you at the debriefing in Lynchburg. Bottom line, McGill's tactics beat our tactics."

"Like hell," Killick said. "McGill's in prison. His plot was foiled."

"But he flushed us out. The operation wasn't over yet. Things happened on his schedule, not ours."

"You're splitting hairs."

"Some of McGill's co-conspirators may still be out there, regrouping. People we hadn't picked up on before he flushed us, out there re-plotting the bombing. It may not be a serious possibility. But my point is that the McGills of the world are going to beat us more often than they should. Why? Because you and I are hamstrung by morality. Because people like McGill have no remorse for their actions, so there's nothing they won't do. It's hard to beat someone who doesn't have to play by the same rules you do. Worse, people like McGill inspire others to their own acts of evil. Things they wouldn't have otherwise done."

Arkin looked up from his potatoes to see Killick staring at him with an accusatory glare, as if to say, *That's exactly what I told you. So why didn't you shoot McGill when you had the chance, you spineless Boy Scout?*

"You certainly have a point," Sheffield said.

"We can't win. We'll have small victories here and there. But in the big picture, we'll never prevail. Not against the greater dark tide."

"Let's not be melodramatic," Sheffield said.

"I agree that we use inferior tactics," Killick said. "Would it be immoral to match the tactics, match the morality, of our individual adversaries?"

Arkin didn't bother to answer, and nearly rolled his eyes. "Sometimes I just feel as if we're fighting cancer with aspirin here, you know?"

"You don't feel like our work makes a difference?" Sheffield asked.

"I do. It does. In an immediate sort of way, anyway."

"What do you mean by that?" Sheffield asked, with a curiously pleased look on his face.

"I mean sometimes I think we're only dealing with the symptoms."

"As opposed to what?"

"Causes. Sources. The fountainheads of all this evil, to put it more sensationally."

"Ah-ha. And where do you think it comes from?"

Arkin shrugged. "I'm not sure. It's case-by-case. But taking down a Raylan McGill isn't going to keep more Raylan McGills from coming along. It's what creates the Raylan McGills in the first place—*that* should be our target."

"Yes!" Sheffield half shouted, pounding the table with his fist, startling Arkin, Killick, and a nearby booth of haggard-looking DOJ lawyers. "That should be our target. Absolutely, positively right. You may not know exactly what's doing it—what's creating the Raylan McGills, the Hitlers, the bin Ladens—but you know there's a deeper universal cause, hidden below the surface of things."

"Universal?"

"And you know that it's that *cause*, and not its hapless, deranged victim-agents, that is the real target in our battle." He clapped a hand onto Arkin's shoulder. "That awareness, my young prodigy, puts you light years ahead of the common man."

"Both of us, or just Arkin?" Killick asked with a grin.

"You aren't like all the 'world-is-flat' cromag knuckle-draggers in this town who are stupid enough to think that by doubling the conventional law enforcement budget, or building walls along our borders, or bombing the Middle East into radioactive glass that we're going to somehow make appreciable progress against the *cause*."

"He's going deep on us," Killick said to Arkin.

"And pedantic."

Sheffield took a long drink of his iced tea, a thoughtful expression on his face. "Let me ask you a question, Nathaniel," he said.

"Sure."

"Would you have gunned down Hitler or bin Laden?"

"Of course."

"No, I mean before they rose from obscurity."

"Before they'd done anything?"

"Exactly."

"This is an unusually hackneyed question. Even for you."

Sheffield smiled. "Fine. What stayed your hand in Appomattox?"

"What do you mean?"

"Why didn't you shoot McGill?"

Now it was Arkin's turn to smirk. "Oh, I get it. So now McGill is a future Hitler or bin Laden. Okay. The oracle at Delphi told you that, did she?"

"Answer the question."

"Why I didn't gun down McGill? I guess I wasn't in the mood." Looking up from his food, he saw that Sheffield was staring at him, waiting for more. "Was that a serious question?"

"Deadly," Sheffield said, his face turning hard. "If 9/11 taught us one thing, it's that humanity is running out of time. Don't you see that, Nathaniel? Don't you see that these people will destroy us all?"

"That's a bit of an attenuated—"

"What was going through your mind as you watched McGill through your rifle scope as he brutalized his wife?"

"I don't know."

"You wanted to shoot him."

"Part of me did, I suppose."

"But something held you back."

"Of course."

"You were afraid you'd be held accountable."

"No. I mean, yes, I'm sure that was on my mind. But not at the forefront. Just in the background noise."

"Then what was it? Let's establish a logical baseline. Why didn't you shoot him?"

"Maybe because it would have been wrong?"

Sheffield looked irritated. "Wrong? What does 'wrong' even mean anymore?"

"Huh?"

"The world isn't black and white."

"Some things are."

"In our world? In the shadowy world of intelligence and counter-terrorism? No, sir."

"We're sworn law enforcement officers now. This isn't SOG."

"Now you're *really* splitting hairs. McGill was a murderer and a terrorist."

"Okay, but—"

"Do you know what McGill is up to these days, Nathaniel?"

"Besides fighting to preserve the viability of his sphincter?"

"He formed a book club with fellow maximum security inmates of USP Lee."

"That's nice."

"He and his ring of deranged sycophants meet twice weekly to discuss white supremacist and anti-Semitic literature."

"Oh."

"Indeed. And get this—none of the fellows in the book club were part of McGill's Holocaust Museum conspiracy. No, these are *new* recruits. He's spreading his ideas to a new flock of crazies, several of whom will be released inside of fifteen months. Loosed on society to do heaven knows what, with McGill's teachings poisoning their hearts and minds. Maybe they'll murder other Ethiopian Jew convenience store clerks. Maybe they'll try to blow up the Holocaust Museum. Who knows? But rest assured, Nathaniel, they'll do something. Something terrible. And do you know what the stink of it is?"

"What?"

"It's that you could have stopped it from happening. You could have nipped *les fleurs du mal* in the bud. Could have stopped the growing storm when it was still a puff of cloud on the far horizon."

"Lovely metaphors, Roland."

"So I ask you again, why didn't you shoot McGill when you had the chance?"

"I don't know, professor. You might as well ask why we have laws. Or why we have a judicial system. Anyway, you can't hold me responsible for McGill further sowing his seeds of evil."

"Can't I?" Sheffield stared at him for a moment, then said, "Ah, I'm just jerking your chain, old boy." But his shoulders slumped forward just noticeably, and he stared down at his lunch without raising his fork. Arkin thought he looked defeated—altogether unusual body language for Sheffield. Maybe something else was eating him.

It was the first of several conversations they would have on the same theme over the following months, right up until Arkin's exile to Durango. Sheffield presented different hypothetical scenarios each time, and would quiz Arkin and Killick as to whether vigilante justice might be called for, and why. But no matter how Sheffield changed the facts, Arkin never changed his position that there was, absolutely and without exception, no place in federal law enforcement for extrajudicial killing. And despite the improbability and absurdity of it, Arkin swore that with each passing conversation Sheffield's seeming bewilderment and disappointment over his inflexibility appeared to grow until it bordered on genuine despair. It perplexed Arkin to no end.

The strange memory was interrupted by shrill beeping from Arkin's Durango motel room alarm clock. Dawn light was just beginning to peek through the crack between the drapes as he lay in bed, already wide awake. It was going to be a long day, he was certain of that. Morrison had called before dawn to let Arkin know that he was in position to watch the Sundial Ranch access road for any surveillance operatives dispatched by Killick. Arkin remained skeptical that Killick was involved but saw the wisdom of eliminating him as a suspect.

Arkin allowed himself a long, hot steam in the flimsy and mildew-stained motel shower, drank a canned espresso, and suited up. Then, leaving the Forest Service truck behind out of an abundance of caution, he set out for his office on foot, keeping to the fringe of the scrubby hillside that ran along the highway, doing his best to stay out of sight.

Being suspended, his only reason for going in was to call Killick from a phone he was sure nobody was monitoring. But after sneaking in through the back door of the building, he decided to grab a couple extra boxes of bullets and shotgun shells, just in case. After shoving the ammunition in his gym bag, he went down the hall to the same Forest Service cubicle and ID-blocked phone he'd used before. Leaving the lights off, he dialed Killick's encrypted line while standing by the window and watching the parking lot and surrounding area through a small gap in the blinds.

"Where the hell have you been?" Killick said. "I've been calling your cell every 10 seconds since yesterday."

"Battery. I think my charger was in my house when it went up."

"Where are you now?"

Arkin decided to play it cool. "I'm still in bed."

"Hungover again?"

"Suspended. Or hadn't you heard?"

"Suspended? What did you do?"

"Long story for another time. So did you get the phone number for the Canadian company back from your tech team?"

"Still working on it."

"You mean the Director of Operations can't just pick up his phone and get a simple scrap of readily available information from his lackeys in about five seconds?"

"Don't be an ass. Your needs aren't the only ones on my plate right now. I have political masters who need to bolster their crap self-esteems by making me dance like a monkey every half hour."

"So what did you need?"

"Let's start with where you're staying. Not in the ruins of your house, I hope. Can you give me a number for wherever you are so I can call you if there's an emergency?"

"Sure. I'm staying at a place called Sundial Ranch. It's northeast of town, out in the woods a bit. I don't have the number on me, but I'm sure you can Google it."

"Alright. Well, look, the lead agent on the Pratt investigation needs to take a statement from you. He can do it over the phone."

"That's why you've been calling my cellphone every 10 seconds since yesterday?"

"Plus, we want to set up a college fund for Pratt's kids. I just wanted to confirm that he had four, right?"

"Yes. There are four of them." The thought saddened Arkin. He could picture them climbing all over Pratt—all over their dad—as he rolled around on his family room carpet with them, rough housing, tickling them, pretending to bite their ribs as they laughed hysterically. Happy kids. What would become of them? The LDS church would probably take care of them. They were good about that sort of thing.

In thinking about Pratt's kids, something else occurred to Arkin. "I just thought of something."

"What?"

"I think I know where to. . . ."

"What? You know where to what?"

A dark blue Nissan Altima went down the road, passing the driveway to the building, just a hair too slowly. It was the second time Arkin had seen it in the past five minutes. *Damn.* "I have to run."

"No, wait."

"I'll call you back."

"Wait, Nate. Wait!"

He hung up, un-holstered his gun, and chambered a round, then topped off his magazine and slid it home so that he was loaded for duty-carry. He slipped down the hall and down the stairs, emerging on Pratt's floor. Pratt's office was still wide open. Arkin stepped inside, turned on the light, and saw what he was looking for. The Strawberry Monkey notepad was still lying on Pratt's desk. Arkin grabbed an old-fashioned graphite pencil from Pratt's desk caddy and began rubbing the oblique side of the lead on the notepad—thinking, as he did so, that he probably first learned the trick from, of all things, the Hardy Boys and Nancy Drew mystery stories of his youth. Faint text began to appear on the notepad. *Please, yes.* A word. 'O-R-G....' The words 'organic 2% milk' became visible. But there were more words beneath them. Hopeful, Arkin kept on with it, his rubbing revealing the words 'maple-brown sugar oatmeal,' 'carrots,' 'peach yogurt,' and so forth. Nothing more than a grocery list. Arkin's shoulders slumped as he set the pencil back down and stared at Pratt's desk. There were conspicuously clean squares and rectangles on the dusty surface where Pratt's computer monitor, printer, and phone had sat. Meager, ephemeral vestiges of a good man's life. Dispirited, Arkin gave Pratt's chair a quarter turn as he prepared to leave. But, giving himself a moment to sigh before he stood up, facing the wall to the left of Pratt's desk, he found himself momentarily transfixed by the empty jack where the cord to Pratt's phone had once been plugged in. A little, black, square hole, in an old off-white plate soiled and streaked with the finger oils and filth of untold generations of users of what had been Pratt's office. Soon a new user would move in, and all traces of Pratt ever having worked there would vanish. As he thought about this, about the seeming futility, the certain tragedy and needless waste of the whole Priest affair, it struck Arkin as rather odd that a fit of depression could seemingly be triggered by, of all the trivial things, the emptiness of the phone jack. But then something else occurred to him, and he took a deep breath, rose, and strode down the hall to retrieve a telephone from a different office. Back in Pratt's office a minute later, he plugged a phone into the jack for Pratt's unsecured land line, then dialed the operator.

"Hello. I'm hoping you can help me. I misplaced a phone number I need quite urgently, and I was wondering if you could tell me the numbers I dialed on this line on a particular date." He gave the operator the day before Pratt was killed. As he waited, he considered the long odds against him. Chances were slim that Pratt had made a rookie move like looking up and dialing numbers for any persons or entities he'd found mentioned in the INDIGO file—to confirm a number's accuracy or the existence of a number's alleged owner—taking the chance of prematurely spooking their quarry into flight to a new hiding place. It would have been far too risky, even if he'd planned to use the old trick of pretending he dialed the wrong number if someone answered.

The operator was breathing heavily through his nose as he took his infuriatingly sweet time processing Arkin's request. The sound drove Arkin half mad. Finally, the man muttered, "Okay. Here we are. At 8:47 p.m., you dialed...."

The first number was for Pratt's home. No doubt he was calling Ella to tell her when she could expect him. The second number began with area code 604, which, as Arkin knew very well, covered Vancouver, British Columbia. *Holy mother!* Barely able to contain himself, Arkin stayed on the line until the tortoise-speed operator gave him the other three irrelevant local numbers Pratt had dialed the day before he was killed. As soon as he hung up, Arkin ran to his own office, booted up his computer, and did a database search for the area code 604 telephone number. Up came the name "Seastar Aquaculture," and it all came back to him. He could picture the name of the company on his new yellow pad back in his office in Washington, D.C,. all those years ago. His heart was racing. He scribbled the name and phone number down on Pratt's Strawberry Monkey notepad, tore off the page, shoved it in his pocket, and slipped out of Pratt's dark office while muttering to himself, "Seastar, Seastar, Seastar, Seastar. . . ."

As Arkin emerged from the back door of the building, a strong breeze kicked up, blowing leaves across the parking lot. As he turned to pull the door shut against the force of the breeze, the door was knocked back with a sudden violence and a deafening crack ripped through the air. He dove for cover behind a cigarette-butt-filled concrete planter box, landing flat on his belly. He glanced over his shoulder to see that a large hole had been blown through the door. His mind went into overdrive. An armor-piercing .50 BMG round would penetrate the planter box, concrete or not. He crawled forward, on knees and elbows, to the better protection of a parked Forest Service pickup. There, he un-holstered his .40, rotated into a squat, and popped up for a quick peek of the area before dropping back down into cover just as quickly. He didn't see the sniper, but saw enough of the surrounding land to make a rough guess as to where the sniper was. He couldn't be too close. Probably across the river. The far bank afforded an unobstructed view of the building and parking lot, as well as good cover among clumps of scrubby trees. The breeze kicked up again, and Arkin realized it was probably what had saved him, blowing the bullet a hair off target. If the air had been still, or the sniper a few dozen yards closer, his lifeblood would already be soaking into the gray industrial-grade carpet tiles of the first-floor hallway. He took another quick peek to assure himself that the shooter was a good distance away. Assuming the shooter was across the river, it would be exceptionally difficult for him to hit a fast-moving target. With that in mind, Arkin made a crouching break for the trees at the north end of the parking lot, and when he reached them, kept going, never looking back, using all available cover—trees, bushes, buildings, cars, roadside berms—as he made his way toward the hospital as fast as humanly possible.

Twenty minutes later, he flew past the DPD officer standing guard at Hannah's door and burst into her room. She was sleeping but woke to the sound of his panting.

"Are you alright?"

"Yes." He knew he couldn't lie to her. But he didn't have to tell her everything. "Someone took a shot at me while I was leaving work," he said, pausing to take a breath.

"Just now?"

He nodded.

"Call the police."

He shook his head.

"Why not?"

"I have to call Morrison."

But as he took out his phone and began to dial, a tiny rivulet of blood started to run from one of Hannah's nostrils down to her upper lip. He put the phone back in his pocket, grabbed tissues from a small utility table, and ran to her side to clean it off, only then seeing that she held a white towel already blotched with blood in several places. Her body smelled sour and slightly metallic, the odor leaving an odd flavor on the very back of Arkin's tongue.

"It's been doing this all morning. Just little nosebleeds. No big deal."

But even as she said this, Arkin saw something he'd never ever seen in her eyes before, and it took everything he had not to choke up. It was fear. Not the common, everyday variety, but a profound, dark, terrible fear. He got into

184

bed next to her, and with teeth secretly clenched behind his tightly closed lips, he lay there stroking her bare head until they both fell asleep.

*****

Barely 30 minutes later, the burner cellphone chirped, waking them both. It was Morrison, his voice tense.

"Are you at the hospital?"

"Yeah, but listen to what—"

"I know. Someone took a shot at you. Listen, did you give anyone else this phone number?"

"Hang on a second."

"Wait, Nate!" he heard Morrison shout as he lowered the phone and pressed it against his chest. He rose from the bed and whispered to Hannah, "I'll be right back," squeezing her hand as he got to his feet. She held his hand for a moment before letting go, holding his gaze with her own. The terrible fear was still there in her eyes. But after a couple seconds, she did her best to smile, blinked slowly, and then let him go. He went into the hallway and, feeling the urge, made his way past the DPD officer, who was now chatting with a young blonde at the nurse's station, and on toward the men's room down the hall as he raised the phone to his ear.

"What's going on?" he asked Morrison.

"Did you give this number to anyone?"

"No."

"Get the fuck out of there."

"But—"

"I'll explain later. Just get the fuck out of there, and lose that phone. Meet me at the library." That was their joke code for the Diamond Belle Saloon, from the days when Arkin used to jerk Morrison's chain by pretending he had to hide their fraternizing from Hannah.

"Tell me what the hell is going on."

"A ten-second summary. I just got back from watching the road at Sundial to find a courtesy copy of a U.S. District Court arrest warrant for *you* rolling into my fax in tray. Some trumped-up false statement bullshit. The complainant is an FBI agent whose name I've never seen before. Consider armed and dangerous. You've got to lose that phone. If Killick is—"

"Yeah, yeah." He peeked out the window of the bathroom. Four officers in full body armor and SRT tactical uniforms were stepping out of two patrol cars as a third car pulled up to the curb behind them. "Oh, shit."

"Get out of there."

Arkin tossed the phone into the trash can, then cracked the bathroom door to observe the officer still standing at the nurses' station. He heard the short burst of static as the officer's radio came to life. The officer said something into the microphone lashed to his upper chest, then turned and walked toward Hannah's room while un-holstering his gun. As he passed through her doorway, Arkin, knowing this was his only chance, took one step forward, but then froze, thinking of Hannah. Thinking of her lying in there, terrified and bleeding. He couldn't leave her. His mind raced. If he stayed, they'd catch him and cart him off to some far away federal prison, assuming there wasn't an "accident" in store for him. And even if he lived to see a trial, he was sure they'd have enough fabricated evidence to put him away. But if he ran, and by some miracle found a way to clear his name, then he could come back. He knew it was a long shot, but it was his only chance for getting back to Hannah. He took one last look down the hallway toward the door to her room. Then, with tears blurring his vision, he ran for the door to the rear stairwell, threw it open, flew down the stairs and out the back fire door just as a half dozen police went in the front.

*****

Morrison didn't waste time with pleasantries at the Diamond Belle. "Here's money," he said, shoving a wad of cash into the chest pocket of Arkin's sweaty shirt. "Almost 300 bucks. My damned ATM card will only let me withdraw $200 every 24 hours, but I already had some cash in my pocket. Here, take the card too. The pin is 1234."

"You're joking."

"Bear in mind that they might be smart enough to trace your movements by it, knowing that I'll be inclined to aid and abet. Stay off the roads, even after you get away from town. If I got a courtesy copy of the warrant faxed to me, it's a good bet it's being circulated far and wide. And you know damn well that if anyone gets hold of you, you're as good as dead because they're gonna be under orders to hand you right over to whoever just took a shot at you. Right? You got a gun?" Arkin nodded. "Okay. You're sure you don't want me to come with you?"

"Are you joking? If they think you're on the road with me, they'll just fabricate another arrest warrant and you'll be a fugitive too. You'd probably be more use to me here anyway, at least for now. I'll call if I really need you."

"Alright, fair enough. You know Skyquest Condominiums, up by Baker's Bridge?"

"Yes."

"There's a dumpster apron at the back of the parking lot there. It's enclosed by a high wood fence. If I can make sure I don't have a tail, I'll head up there this evening and drop off a backpack, camping gear, proper clothes, a stove, fuel, and as much food as I can jam into the pack. I'll double wrap it in black garbage bags and leave it behind the wood fence where nobody but you will find it. I'll try to have it there before nightfall. So if you somehow get there before me, just sit tight and stay out of sight."

Arkin gave him the name and Vancouver, B.C., telephone number for Seastar Aquaculture, just in case, and then went quiet, staring at his own feet.

"What?"

"Hannah."

Morrison put a hand on Arkin's shoulder. "Nate, I've got you covered. I'll take care of her. Best thing you can do for her right now is to get the fuck out of here until you and I can sort this thing out. And here, take my jacket. There's a pepperoni stick and a chocolate bar in the pocket. I would have brought more if I'd had time."

"You'll tell Hannah."

"Yes, yes. And I'll spend time with her every day. Every day. She'll get sick of me."

Arkin nodded. "Thank you."

For a moment, an expression flashed across Arkin's tired face that Morrison interpreted as a sign that he was seriously considering giving up.

"You'll get it done. You always do."

"You must be thinking of someone else. I'm a fraud."

"The hell are you talking about?"

"I'm the fool who failed to see the threat to Pratt." In his mind, he added that he was the guy who failed to negotiate the obvious pitfalls of his career. Who let his wife follow him into an exile he'd accepted like a coward, to career Siberia, where the sum total of what he could call his own amounted to marginal equity in an ordinary house and an unimpressive retirement account. Who failed to get his wife the best possible medical care before it was too late. Just then, it seemed to Arkin that the accomplishments of his life amounted to shit. The only truly good thing he'd ever done was marry Hannah. And now he was useless to her.

"Don't be melodramatic. It makes you sound like a douche bag."

The expression on Arkin's face had grown even more hopeless. With sudden fury, Morrison stood up and punched him, hard, in the chest, startling him out of his malaise.

"Buck up, jarhead!"

Arkin's face hardened.

"There he is. There's the stone-cold killer I've been looking for."

"It's a façade, Bill. Behind it, I'm still the boy who was terrified by the Wicked Witch of the West and her hourglass with its orange sand. The boy who wished his mother had lived to hold his hand and whisper in his ear that the flying monkeys would never come for him."

"What the ffff?" For a moment, Morrison was at a loss. He punched Arkin again, harder, and yanked him out of his chair. "On your feet, puke! You have business in the Great White North."

PART II

SHADOWS

TWENTY-FIVE

That night, Arkin found the stash of gear Morrison left for him behind the Skyquest Condos and made camp in the trees another two miles further upriver, barely fifteen miles north of town. Knowing it would be wisest to camp somewhere quiet, where he might be able to hear the footfall of anyone approaching, he nevertheless opted to camp close to where the Animas roared through a narrow canyon, thinking the white noise of the river would soothe him. Instead, he found himself waking up several times throughout the night, the sound of the racing waters filling him with anxiety. A constant reminder that time was running by.

The next morning, he got up with the sun and resumed his journey, finding the grade of the Durango & Silverton Narrow Gauge Railroad by midmorning. That made the going easier. He walked the rails, taking to the trees only when he heard one of the old black steam trains rolling up or down the line, which at this time of year was only a concern until he passed to the north of Cascade Station.

Over the next two days, he followed the rails past Molas and Coal Bank passes, and finally up into the old mining town of Silverton, elevation 9,318 feet. There, he slipped into a touristy restaurant and pretended he'd left a cellphone there the previous day. Without a hint of suspicion, the hostess, in Old West period dress, pulled out a black Samsung and asked if it was his.

Minutes later, as he was walking down Greene Street, oblivious to the risk, he tried to call Hannah's room. She didn't answer. Perhaps she was away somewhere being tested or treated. He couldn't allow himself to worry.

He left Silverton not via the main highway, U.S. 550, but by a dirt road that led deep into the mountains, where rutted Jeep trails of the Alpine Loop zigzagged their way north and west, through the high peaks of the San Juan Range, passing the mining ghost towns of Howardsville, Middleton, Eureka, and Animas Forks. Each of the ghost towns had been lively settlements in their day. But now, a scant century later, the best preserved of them was little more than a hodgepodge of collapsed wooden buildings and abandoned, rusted mining equipment. Soon enough, Arkin thought, the relentless cycle of sun, rain, wind, and snow would erase all traces of the ghost towns and the lives that had been lived in them.

At his next campsite, several miles north of Animas Forks, Arkin faced a strangely discomforting discovery. There, in a deep, shadowed mountain valley littered with the disintegrating debris of long-failed gold and silver mines, he realized he was camped beside the very origin of the Animas River. The Animas—the beautiful, interminably flowing river that, even in a man as proudly rational and skeptical as Arkin, had, on very rare occasion, inspired a pause to wonder, for a fleeting moment, whether it was possible that there was perhaps something more to the universe than atoms, molecules, and cold, empty space. Whether there could perhaps, just maybe, be some sort of *beyond*. Yet here was where the river began. And though he didn't expect otherwise, he was nevertheless disappointed to see that it did not spring forth from any sacred or magical source. The unpleasant truth was that, fed by insignificant trickles of melt water, it started from a lowly gravel bed strewn with discarded beer cans, spent shotgun shells, and broken bottles. Nothing more than a polluted ditch.

*****

By his fourth day on the run, Arkin had rejoined Highway 550 and was at last descending from the high San Juans, down toward the town of Ouray. He was having great difficulty staying out of sight on a mile-long stretch of road that had been chiseled out of a sheer cliff face. On his right, a cliff climbed straight up a mountainside, while on his left it dropped hundreds of feet to the headwaters of the Uncompahgre River. He played the disinterested hitch hiker, praying that nobody who was looking for him would happen by. The silver lining to traveling exposed and in the open on this stretch of road was that as he neared Ouray, he found a long, flat strip of scrap aluminum in the gravel on the shoulder of the roadside. He tucked it into his pack, figuring he might be able to fashion it into a makeshift lockout tool that he could use, if necessary, to break into cars.

Once Arkin passed through Ouray, the country opened up again, and he was able to speed up his pace. He took a midday breather in a stand of pines 200 yards from the highway and tried to call Hannah's room again on the cellphone he'd grabbed in Silverton. Again, there was no answer. He made another quick call to check his office voicemail, mindful of the fact that he didn't have a charger to re-energize the battery once it ran out of juice. There were two messages. One from the phone company attorney saying that he hadn't received the subpoena, and could Agent Pratt maybe double-check that it had been addressed properly. The other was from Morrison, though he didn't identify himself and had called from an unrecognized number. Probably some random payphone or borrowed cell. Solid tradecraft. His message would have sounded irrelevant to any uninvited listeners. He said his name was Clark, and that he was trying to reach Devin about the canisters advertised on Craigslist.com. But Arkin understood. As the message played on, he recognized a word code giving him the Vancouver street address for Seastar Aquaculture. Morrison's message raised his spirits. He'd felt so alone the past several days. So desperate to get back to Hannah. Now, at least, he knew there was someone out there trying to help him. And he was sure Morrison would have mentioned if there were anything wrong with Hannah. Still, it troubled him that he couldn't get hold of her. He tried not to dwell on it, redirecting his focus to the fact that he was nearly halfway to the rail yards of Grand Junction.

He powered the phone down and resumed his trek north, hoping to make Montrose by nightfall. But then, ten minutes later, something happened that caught him off-guard. As he was climbing a small and thinly forested hill, he heard a crunch of gravel, and turned around to see a plain maroon Impala pulling off Highway 550 back down at the base of the hill, very close to where he'd stopped to check his voicemail. He dropped to the ground, crawled behind the biggest tree trunk he could find, and peeked around it to get a better look. The car had dark tinted windows. He was too far away to see whether or not it had any special antenna or license plate. Regardless, he had a very bad feeling. Could these people have the means to triangulate his cellphone signal—from a phone he'd only recently acquired and had only used to call Hannah's hospital room and his office voicemail system? Were they so hot on his trail that they could have a vehicle on his ass barely 10 minutes after he'd powered down his phone? And if so, was it the assassination conspirators or just conventional law enforcement tasked with looking for an officially wanted man?

As to who it was sitting in the Impala, it hardly mattered. What did matter was determining whether his cellphone was already compromised.

Arkin sat tight behind his tree, concerned that the occupants of the Impala could be scanning the hillside with heaven only knew what sort of optical equipment—anything from simple binoculars to infrared scopes. When the car finally drove off after sitting and idling for ten minutes, he doubled his pace as he hoofed it up toward the small town of Ridgeway.

Hours later, on a tree-lined street in a small neighborhood, he climbed to the top of a white three-board fence, turned the cellphone back on, and set it in the rain gutter of a tiny yellow house that appeared to be unoccupied. Then he jogged up a grassy knoll to a small, old, red-brick school overlooking the neighborhood. School was out, it being a Sunday. But Arkin tried the first door he came to. To his relief, it opened. He stepped inside, finding himself in a small but high-ceilinged assembly hall. It smelled of chalk dust and old varnished wood, and bright sunlight poured in through its tall windows. A worn but lovingly polished old Schimmel medium grand piano sat in the center of the floor.

He sat down at the piano and stared at the keys. He hadn't played since he graduated boarding school and moved to Annapolis. Though many who'd heard him play insisted he had a gift, it was something he'd always hated. Something that had been a constant magnet for criticism from his perfection-demanding father. Something his father had forced upon him. As he sat, he remembered playing his favorite piece for his father. It was the sadly beautiful Prelude and Fugue No. 1 in C major, from Johann Sebastian Bach's Well-tempered Clavier Book 1. He'd been practicing it for weeks, night and day, hoping beyond hope to please his father. And he'd nailed it, every subtlety of every note of every single arpeggiated chord. He'd played perfectly. Yet all his father had said was that any trained ear could tell that his performance was still amateurish.

Arkin slumped forward on the bench, the weight of the memory pressing down on his shoulders. Adrenaline drained out of him in the quiet of the assembly hall. At the same time, fatigue seemed suddenly to take hold. The heavy awareness that a long and uncertain journey awaited him. That he was being hunted, and that his hunters would never give up. That there was little chance he'd be able to clear his name and return to Hannah's side. He yearned to go to sleep right there against the piano, the soft sunlight warming his back. But he had to go on. Somehow, he had to find the strength of body and mind to continue forward. There was no other direction for him to go.

With his eyes shut, he let his fingertips probe the smooth, cool surfaces of the keys. Almost involuntarily, his left index finger hit Middle "C," and the note filled the room with clear, beautiful sound. He hit it again, his eyes still closed, listening to the way the sound hung and then slowly faded from the room. The rest of his fingers slid up onto the keys, and nearly 20 years out of practice, they began to play Bach's Prelude and Fugue No 1. He played almost perfectly, from memory and with little focus or effort, as his mind wandered back to a vision of Hannah's frightened face, looking to him for support and comfort, as he promised her he would "be right back." It could have been the last time he would ever see her. As his fingers picked out the

10th measure—to Arkin, the most gloriously melancholic part of the song—he opened his wet-blurred eyes, willing them to dry before any tears could fall. And he kept playing, not pausing until he heard the distant wail of approaching sirens. Then he paused just long enough to establish that several police cars were en route to the small neighborhood at the bottom of the knoll. He finished the piece, lingering as the final note slowly echoed and died in the auditorium, then strode to the windows and watched the scene unfold as uniformed patrolmen swarmed around the little house where he'd hidden the phone. Poorly trained patrolmen at that, Arkin thought, given that they'd blown any chance of tactical surprise by rolling in with their sirens screaming. Maybe Ridgeway PD. Maybe Ouray County Sheriff's deputies. Whatever the case, just locals. That was a good thing. But just as Arkin was feeling lucky, the unmarked maroon Impala pulled up alongside the first house. Nobody got out. They just waited. And they, Arkin was sure, were not locals. *Shit.*

*****

His extreme caution slowed him. But at a roadside gas station, he was able to stow away in the debris-filled bed of a northbound pickup truck that took him all the way from Eldredge to Delta. And by the middle of his seventh day on the run, Arkin reached the outskirts of Grand Junction, where he bought two bags of beef jerky, whole wheat tortillas, and two liters of water from a corner market. Desperate to get in touch with Hannah, he tried his lost cellphone trick again, telling the clerk he thought he'd left it there the prior week. The clerk said he was sorry, but that he hadn't found any cellphones. Just someone's leather appointment book with an attached silver pen.

Arkin considered using Morrison's ATM card to draw more food money, but thought better of it. If his pursuers had the resources to identify and track cellphones, then it was a good bet they'd already be watching Morrison's bank account. It wasn't worth the risk. For the same reasons, he decided his own ID and bankcards held nothing but danger for him, so he pocketed his remaining cash and dumped his wallet in the first garbage can he came to, shoving it down into the refuse where it wouldn't be seen by a casual passersby. He'd just have to get by on the money Morrison had given him.

He made his way north, through woods, fields, and small pocket neighborhoods, toward Grand Junction proper—his route roughly paralleling U.S. Highway 50. Along the way, to his surprise, he spotted a functioning payphone at the edge of a weedy, cracked asphalt parking lot of a dusty, long-defunct car wash. He stared at it for a moment, pondering the risk of trying to contact Hannah—the same risk that had just caused him to dump his wallet— yet yearning, aching to hear his wife's voice. He entered the phone booth, closing the bi-fold door behind him. It was warm inside, the air smelling of dust, metal, and sun-baked plastic. The breeze howled in the booth as it slipped through small unseen gaps in the ceiling. As he stood still, weighing the risk, the old black handset tempted him to the point of psychological agony. Looking up to watch two cars pass—people driving by oblivious, going about their business on what for them was a perfectly normal day—he was struck by an odd feeling of detachment from the world around him. He had the sensation he was being carried along in a tiny whirlwind. Outside of it, the routines of other people's lives went on.

He called the hospital collect, concocting a story about it concerning a potential medical emergency, and requiring that he remind someone of an allergy to certain medication. The hospital operator bought it, and attempted to connect him to Hannah's room. He held the handset against his ear as the line rang and rang. The breeze raised a small dust cloud in the parking lot—a swirl of bleached, powdery earth, dried bits of grass, and a crumpled green gum wrapper. Standing there in the old phone booth, watching the swirling dust cloud, listening to the repeated ringing, and thinking of how far he was from home, he felt all the more isolated. Eventually, a man answered. Another patient. He had no idea who Hannah was and knew nothing of her whereabouts. So Arkin called the main hospital number once again to ask if she'd been moved. But this time the operator stood firm, explaining that she couldn't share such information over the phone but would pass his message on. Next, he tried Morrison. He got voicemail. He hung up and stood in the booth for a moment, leaning his forehead against the top of the cradled handset, crestfallen, knowing that from here on he'd probably have to refrain from trying to contact Hannah or Morrison, since any call might reveal his intended route and destination, making him easier to capture and possibly warning or scaring off his quarry. In fact, he figured it was safe to assume police would be on their way to the phone booth in minutes. He set off once again, feeling more alone than ever.

*****

Eventually, he crossed the Colorado River via the footbridge in Eagle Rim Park and followed the curve of Riverside Parkway toward the town's large rail yard. To scout the security of it, he walked its length, ducking in and out of side streets dead-ending at the rails. He crossed the rails at 29 Road, and then approached the yard once more from the east via a dusty access road paralleling Interstate 70. There was no visible video surveillance. And while there was a small glassed-in booth atop a short tower amid the parked railcars, there did not appear to be a security guard present.

Arkin jumped a broken fence, slipped into the long lines of coupled train cars, and quickly found what he was looking for: A Union Pacific train oriented for west-bound departure. The Union Pacific main line ran into

Utah, where another line turned north, into Idaho, and then northwest toward the Columbia River, running along the border of Oregon and Washington. There—Arkin knew from having familiarized himself with rail lines during a manhunt several years earlier—he could jump over to a northbound train of the Burlington Northern Santa Fe Railroad, which would get him within striking distance of the Canadian border. Better still, this westbound Union Pacific train looked to have several dozen autorack freight cars loaded with brand new pickup trucks that might offer some modicum of shelter—even comfort. But just as he was feeling that things might finally be turning his way, an engine blew several short blasts of its horn, and the train jerked and began to move. Arkin immediately began to jog alongside, watching for a freight car door without the usual giant padlock. The train was slowly gaining speed, and Arkin was running out of train yard as its many sets of side tracks began to converge into the main line. He could hear the clang-clang of a crossing signal bell as the engine approached a cross street. Soon he'd be plainly visible to motorists waiting at the crossing. He broke into a sprint, huffing and puffing as he ran. Just short of the first cross street, he spotted an unlocked door. He grabbed hold of the cold, dirty metal of lowest rung of an access ladder, hauled himself off the ground, shimmied around the corner of the car, and scrambled up onto the narrow coupler. There, he balanced precariously as he caught his breath and studied the door. Puzzled as to how to unlatch it, he decided to simply give the door a pull and was relieved to find that it was unsecured and swung open. In moments, he was inside the freight car and unlocking the door of a big, American made, double-cab truck, using the lockout tool he'd made out of the aluminum strip he found outside Ouray. A minute later, he was lying down across the big back seat of the truck, his gear stowed out of site, as the train continued to roll forward, gaining speed, into the West.

*****

His first night on the rails was a fitful one. The train seemed to move at a snail's pace. He knew it was going faster than it felt. But it still frustrated him, and his frustration, in turn, kept him awake. Still, he knew it was a lot more secure than trying to hitchhike so many miles, risking attention—or a potential ID check—from a passing cop.

When he finally did nod off, he dreamt that he was back at Hannah's hospital. But it was different. It was much larger, and seemed mostly abandoned, with entire wings empty, the power off, the doors of antiquated rooms hanging open, their old-fashioned steel-frame beds unoccupied and covered with dust. He was trying to find Hannah. He had no shoes on. Empty, dim hallways disappeared into impenetrable darkness in all directions. When he was able to chase down a doctor or nurse, nobody could help him.

Nobody knew anything about Hannah. Nobody could even direct him to the information desk. He grew frantic, running down seemingly endless halls, short of breath, shouting her name into the cavernous dark. But there was no answer.

*****

Waking from the dream, in a cold sweat, to find the train at a temporary stop on a side track in the middle of nowhere, he gave long, pained thought to jumping off and, come what may, finding his way home to Hannah. But he held tight, and soon the train began to move forward once again.

TWENTY-SIX

Four days and three freight trains later, Arkin's thumb was in the air as he walked north on Washington State Route 9, on a bridge over the Snohomish River, having just hopped from the slowing train as it passed a small airfield busy with prepping skydivers. It was a cool, damp, overcast morning, the fresh northwest breeze carrying a hint of the nearby Pacific Ocean. Arkin managed to hitch his first ride—in a Volkswagen Westfalia van driven by a young couple wearing frayed alpaca wool sweaters and smelling of patchouli—before reaching the far end of the bridge.

Shortly after midday, he left the road and, checking that nobody was watching him, ducked into a stand of poplars. With great reluctance, he ditched his gun and spare magazines, burying them in a plastic bag in the off-chance he might come back this way. Then he hoofed it through a series of muddy cow pastures, climbing over half a dozen rusting, barbed wire fences, before crossing the grassy ditch, string of slightly leaning telephone poles, and small two-lane road marking the approximate location of the U.S.-Canada border. Three more miserable miles of walking in the rain, one more hard-earned ride, and he was on the outskirts of Vancouver where, on the north bank of the wide Fraser River, he found a small marina with coin-operated showers and cleaned himself up.

By evening, in a park on the southeastern edge of Vancouver's Granville Island gallery and shopping district, and with a free tourist map in hand, Arkin stowed his pack in a thicket of bushes and reconnoitered the area, noting the best escape routes and hiding places. With the approach of dusk, a sprinkle of rain began to fall from the gray overcast sky. The air smelled of the cooking in the vast food halls of the public market, just upwind, near the other end of the small island-peninsula. An exotic variety of frying pierogies, Asian noodles, smoked salmon, sausages, hearty soups, waffles, tacos, pizzas, and more. He remembered the food halls well from a time, years ago, when he and Hannah wandered the city after disembarking from an Alaska cruise ship. But he had neither the funds nor the free time to visit them now.

On his left, on the opposite side of a relatively quiet street lined with small galleries, workshops, a glass blower's studio, and small offices for architects and wine distributors, the address of record for Seastar Aquaculture was coming up in a few dozen yards. Warm yellow light emanated from its tall windows. Arkin made a slow pass, pretending to peer through the windows of the shops opposite the address, all the while studying the address in the reflection. A sign—with letters formed of bent rebar welded to a rectangular backing of rusted carbon steel floor plate—read "Liber." It appeared to be an art gallery of some sort. Arkin could just make out frames on the walls, as well as indeterminate shapes of sculptures here and there about the showroom. He continued his stroll, playing the gawking tourist, even stopping in a wine shop for a quick tasting of British Columbia chardonnays, before coming to a dead end and doubling back on Liber's side of the street. Reaching the address, he peered through the window, doing his best to look lost. The gallery was lit, but he could see nobody inside. He tried the door. It opened. He went in. The air smelt of drying acrylic paints. An artist was at work, somewhere. He wandered the floor, examining each piece. The works were anything but cheerful. Several gray sculptures of grotesque, melting humanoid forms, their mouths agape in seeming agony, eyes looking upward, arms raised to the sky as if in earnest appeal to some unseen deity. One labeled "Srebrenica." Another, "Truth." Then there were the paintings. The first he saw appeared to be some sort of interpretation of a sunset before a great storm. A last, narrow band of red sunlight disappearing below the black horizon, dark and ominous clouds blotting out the sky everywhere else. The next painting he came to was large—maybe six feet wide, four feet tall—dominating the entire left wall of the gallery. It depicted a dark landscape of bare rock and crumbling stone structures under a twilit but starless sky. Colorless, fiendish humanoid creatures—naked, with emaciated bodies, their faces the very picture of horror and suffering—stood in clusters around bonfires of white flame that looked as though they provided no warmth. As with the gallery's sculptures, many of the humanoids in the painting were looking skyward, their faces raised up in sorrowful, deeply fearful pleading, but with nothing above to answer them. Arkin's attention zeroed in on one of the figures who stood out from the others. He, assuming he *was* a he, sat on a broken stone wall, his hands resting in his lap, facing not the sky, but the horizon. His skin seemed to have at least some trace of color. Just a hint perhaps, but more than the others. Perhaps it was Arkin's imagination. Arkin looked closer. Was the figure smiling?

"What do you think?" a heavily accented female voice asked.

Arkin, startled, suppressed the urge to spin around, and instead turned, with forced casualness, to see a tall woman with long, straight, brunette hair tied back, leaning against the frame of a narrow doorway to a back room. How long had she been there?

"What is it?" Arkin asked, ostensibly returning his attention to the painting, but keeping close tabs on the woman in his peripheral vision.

"The piece depicts the consequences of man's refusal to accept that there is no God."

"Yes?"

"It is inspired by Lord Byron's poem 'Darkness.' Are you familiar?"

"I know of Byron. I don't recall that particular poem."

"'The brows of men by the despairing light wore an unearthly aspect, as by fits the flashes fell upon them.'" The woman began to take slow steps toward Arkin as she recited the poem. Arkin pretended to be transfixed by the painting while his mind raced through the most effective options for a hands-on counterattack if the woman turned out to be one of his shadowy pursuers. "'Some lay down and hid their eyes and wept. And some did rest their chins upon their clenched hands, and smiled. And others hurried to and fro, and fed their funeral piles with fuel, and looked up with mad disquietude on the dull sky.'" She paused as she came alongside Arkin, seeming as lost in the painting as Arkin was pretending to be. "What is your impression of it?"

"My impression?" he asked, turning to look at her. She had crystalline green eyes, their color brought out all the more by dark eye shadow. She also wore a pair of overly large golden ankh earrings that were probably expensive but certainly ostentatious and corny. She stared at Arkin with a penetrating intensity.

"What do you feel or think of when you look at the painting?"

Arkin thought for a moment. "Evil."

The woman smiled. "Precisely. To the extent that such a thing as evil exists—then yes, evil."

"It exists."

"You sound certain."

As they both stood facing the painting, Arkin had the urge to ask if there were any other businesses at this address, or if the woman had ever heard of Seastar, or whether her accent happened to be Balkan, or whether her employer, boyfriend, or husband happened to be a sniper and murderer.

"This one figure here," Arkin said, pointing to the humanoid that faced the horizon and was possibly smiling. "He's different."

"He represents men who are ruled by reason."

"As opposed to what?"

"Animal instinct."

Arkin considered that. "But animals aren't conscious of their mortality." The woman shrugged. "And you are the artist?"

"No. The artist is the magnificent Andrej Petrović, owner of this gallery."

Her use of the word magnificent struck Arkin as more than a little odd. "And what is the magnificent Andrej Petrović asking for this piece?"

"I'm afraid this one is not for sale. But works of similar size and quality generally sell for around $40,000."

"Canadian?"

"Yes."

"I imagine that art of this, ah, uniqueness appeals to a limited number of potential buyers. What sorts of people purchase these works?"

The woman's eyes conveyed a sudden loss of interest in talking with Arkin. "I don't understand your question."

"It's just that these works are very. . . ."

"Dark."

"Yes."

"The buyers tend to be people who appreciate the beauty of truth. Sometimes the truth is dark."

"So it is."

Arkin made a brief inspection of the gallery's other works, all the while stealing furtive glances to study the layout of the room, of the building. Of the windows, doors, and locks. There didn't appear to be any motion sensors. That was good.

"Thank you," Arkin said, and he opened the door and stepped back out into the rain-wet street.

*****

Electing to conserve the remainder of his cash, Arkin spent the next two hours scavenging a meal of sourdough bread crusts and half-eaten fruit from the garbage dumpsters behind the public market. As it grew dark, he positioned himself on a park bench that offered a distant view of the Liber gallery storefront. He pretended to read a discarded Vancouver Sun newspaper by streetlight, all the while keeping his eyes on the gallery.

The flaws of his vantage point worried him. For one thing, it looked like there were ways someone could slip into the gallery without him seeing him or her. Worse, there were too many places from which someone else could keep a lookout over the gallery and remain concealed. Unfortunately, unless he took the excessive risk of breaking into a nearby building, the park bench was about the best he could do.

A 'closed' sign appeared in the gallery's window at 8 p.m., and the lights finally went off just after 10. Shortly after that, a ludicrously tiny European car emerged from a parking access alley two doors down from the gallery. As it turned away, in the direction of the Anderson Street Bridge, Arkin was reasonably certain he saw the silhouette of the sycophant art gallery docent at the wheel.

Intending to let another 30 minutes go by before approaching the gallery once again, he found himself torn over his next move. If he could afford the luxury of proper tactics, he'd surveil the gallery for at least a couple of days, figuring out patterns, best ingress and egress routes, and so on. Ideally, with a team of at least four operatives. He'd have blueprints of the layout of the interior of the target and surrounding buildings. NCIC printouts and DMV files on any employees or owners. Phone records. But time wasn't on his side. He had to make due. Had to take risks. He wanted to rush in without bothering with surveillance. Still, the rough voices of innumerable instructors roared at him from the Virginia, South Carolina, and Georgia training courses of his past. Scarred, leather-skinned, barrel-chested trolls of men, chewing on the soggy butts of long-dead cigars, bitter for having been withdrawn from the field of operations before they were ready to hang it up, for having to endure the diminishment of coaching the generation that would replace them. Howling at him from the shadows, berating him for rushing, imploring him to take his time. *What's the first cardinal principal of ops recon, dumbass? There are old eyeballs, and there are bold eyeballs, but there are no old, bold eyeballs!*

At last compromising with himself, he settled on a delay of 24 hours. Twenty-four hours, most of which would hopefully be spent surveilling the gallery. Having made his decision, he worked out a plan for keeping watch, from concealment, through the night and next morning.

*****

Almost exactly 24 hours later, having taken a brief nap in the bushes just after dawn, having spent nearly $30 of his precious remaining cash after finding a store, many blocks away, that sold a flimsy and barely adequate folding mini lock pick set, and otherwise burning up time circling the area and observing while trying to be inconspicuous, he was sitting on the same bench, wearing a change of clothes and wide-brimmed hat he'd shoplifted, having just watched the same mysterious gallery hostess depart in her miniature car. He rose, stretched his stiff knees, and began his first pass. As he drew closer, walking along the opposite sidewalk, he saw that the interior was completely dark, just as it had been the same time the previous day. Instead of walking right up to the front door, Arkin slipped down the alley from which the car had emerged, turned right, and stood before a series of dingy, unmarked doors—the third of which was clearly the back entrance to the Liber gallery. Nothing seemed to have changed in 24 hours. Arkin scanned the area. All was quiet. He walked up to the door. An un-keyed knob and a common deadbolt. Piece of cake.

Despite his confidence, it took him a good 10 minutes of raking the proper pick tool back and forth across the deadbolt's lock pins before they were all in the open position, allowing him to turn the lock open with the set's detachable torque tool. But at last, he opened the door, slowly and quietly, stepped inside, shut the door behind him, and switched on a small but impressively bright LED keychain light he'd snagged from a tourist junkshop. Scanning the room with the keychain light, he saw that he was in what appeared to serve as the office and workspace—the room from which the hostess had emerged yesterday. A semi-finished painting stood on an easel at the center of the room. Streaks of black over a thin band of red. Perhaps another doomsday sunset painting to be. A long table against one wall held cans and tubes of paint, a rack of brushes, and unfamiliar instruments Arkin could only assume were sculptor's tools. There was a tall wardrobe in the corner to the left of the back door, but no storage cabinets anywhere. In one corner, a small desk. Arkin went right to it and began searching though papers in its in-tray. Receipts for paint, sculpting clay, canvases, and the utilities for the studio. Rough sketches of projects to come. Articles torn from art magazines. Nothing out of the ordinary. Nothing useful. No phone or fax machine. The desk had one shallow drawer that he pulled open to reveal more papers under a small paperback book titled *The Denial of Death*. Arkin flipped through the pages of the paperback. It was well-worn and yellowing, with many dog-eared pages and underlined passages. He came to a page that was bookmarked. Notes scratched in a foreign-looking hand in the margin said *Awareness and fear of death = destructive yearning for false feelings of immortality provided by myriad sources—power, control, victory, an enduring legacy, fame, a place in one of the afterlives promised by the world's religions = evil!* Then he thumbed through the papers. They were a stack of identical copies of what looked like some sort of newsletter from a group calling itself "Sapere Aude." Though his Latin was abominable, Arkin thought the name meant something about knowledge or wisdom. The lead article had to do with qualities of childhood that facilitated the development of strong self-esteem, eventually fortifying people against anxiety over mortality. He closed the drawer, then dumped out the contents of the waste basket next to the desk. Crumpled receipts. Used coffee cups. Again, nothing of use.

Arkin sat down in the desk chair, frustrated, and tried to think. Was this place just another letter drop? Was it just another address of record for another voicemail box that someone accessed from elsewhere? No. This was different. His gut told him the artist gallery owner, the magnificent Andrej

Petrović, could be the assassin. Perhaps tomorrow Petrović would drop by to touch up a painting or sculpture, and Arkin would track him home after work. Perhaps the day after tomorrow Arkin would drive his thumbs through the man's magnificent eye sockets.

Then he noticed something. The back room seemed slightly narrower than the gallery space of the front half of the building. Yet from the outside, the building appeared to be of uniform width from front to back. He studied the wall that the long table and wardrobe stood against, then the opposite wall against which the desk stood. The wall by the desk was painted brick. But the other was finished with drywall. He slipped out the back door again and examined the side of the building. No other external door. He went back inside, opening the wardrobe to find a black wool overcoat, a smock, and several aprons on hangers. He slid them aside and tapped a knuckle against the back panel. It made a hollow sound, as if the panel were unusually thin.

He fiddled with the wardrobe for several more minutes before discovering that the middle third of the inside right panel could be pressed inward, unlatching the secret door that the rear panel really was. He stepped into a narrow wooden stairwell and climbed to a small, unlit, five-by-five room in the center of the roof, far enough from the front or rear edges of the building to be out of sight from the immediate surroundings. It looked like an old greenhouse of some sort. Probably built by a long-vanished, small-time pot grower. The ceiling and two of the walls encompassed large glass windows of many panes. In one direction, the room looked out across the waters of False Creek to the beautiful twinkling skyline of downtown Vancouver.

Tempted to flip the light switch that presumably lit the single bare bulb in the ceiling at the top of the stairs, but worried it would announce his presence to anyone who could see the building, he opted to examine the room with his keychain light. All the room contained was a small table with a fax machine and telephone on it. The fax machine was a similar looking model of the same brand as the one he had in his office back in Durango. It was on. In the in-tray, a fax titled "salmon harvest projections," the first page of which contained unintelligible columns of numbers. A code? The second page consisted of nothing more than a hand-scribbled address in the town of Stony Plain, Alberta.

He picked up the telephone handset, pressed the redial button, and listened. The number dialed had many digits. An overseas number. He listened as a foreign sounding ring tone began to cycle. A man answered.

"Hola. Buenos tardes."

Arkin stared out the window distractedly. *Mexico? Spain? South America?*

"Hola?" the man said again.

Arkin hung up, took a pen and scrap of paper from his pocket, then pressed redial several more times, hanging up before the ring ever commenced, until he deciphered the entire number from the pattern of dialed tones. Then the hairs on the back of his neck went up. He sensed he was being watched. He quickly pressed the proper combination of buttons to print a full report of the numbers for recent incoming and outgoing faxes, shoved the report and the faxes in the "in" tray into his pocket, unplugged the machine to erase any electronic trace of what he had done from its temporary memory, then plugged it back in. As he turned to go back down the stairs, he heard the back door of the gallery squeak on its hinge. He stepped back off of the upper landing, back into the room. What to do. The surrounding windows didn't appear to open. He took a quick peek down the stairs, just long enough to register the image of a man's face—a man with long, dark, moderately curly hair—peeking around the corner at the bottom, and an arm aiming a gun back up at him. It fired, but not until Arkin was back behind cover.

Shit.

"Now hold on there, partner," Arkin shouted with a confident tone intended to give his attacker pause. "I just want to buy one of your psycho paintings. The 'Darkness' one. I have a perfect spot for it in my beach house. Why don't you come on up and we'll haggle."

The man didn't seem to be coming. Perhaps—as Arkin hoped—he thought Arkin might be armed too, and knew better than to get caught in the fatal funnel of a narrow stairwell. But his assumption would soon change if Arkin didn't return fire. Arkin picked up the fax machine and threw it through the windows. Then he picked up the small table it had sat on and used it to break out more of the glass and framing to make a bigger hole. As soon as it was big enough for him to jump through, he threw the table down the stairs, provoking another two gunshots, with one bullet grazing the stairwell wall, splintering the wood trim and sending bits of plaster flying.

Arkin dove out the hole in the window and onto the flat tar roof of the building. Knowing his assailant would be up the stairs in a blink, he ran around to the opposite side of the rooftop room, taking cover behind its windowless side. He was maybe 12 feet from the edge of the roof, at least 30 feet above the ground. The next building over stood across the gap of the alley. It was too far to jump. He went to the edge and looked over. No dumpster full of soft trash to break his fall like in the movies. But there was a tin downspout that ran down from the gutter near one end of the building. Arkin knew it was his only chance. His palms wet and his hands nearly trembling from his sudden fear of the height, he ran to and straddled the downspout, lowering himself onto it while holding the flimsy edge of the gutter. Down, down he shimmied, until, without warning, the section of downspout he was holding came loose and, bending at a point at least 15 feet down, tipped out over the alley. Arkin hung on, still high in the air, until the top of the loose section of downspout hit the brick wall of the building on the far side of the alley. The bottom end still held fast to the wall of the Liber gallery where it had bent, and Arkin slid down it like a fire pole until he was low enough to jump. The fall was at least 10 feet, and the soles of his feet burned from the impact. But otherwise, he seemed okay.

He took off running, heard the pop-pop of his pursuer's gunfire, and watched a large storefront window explode into shards on the far side of the street before he rounded the corner. His pursuer was out on the street now and had the angle on him—had him cut off from the bridge off the island, unless he miscalculated, which he wouldn't. So Arkin sprinted for the nearest access to the water. To get there, he would have to cross a narrow alley that might give his pursuer a clear shot. Still, the alley couldn't have been more than 15 feet across, and at the speed he was running, the chances of his being hit were next to zero. But as he came out from behind the cover of the building on the near side of the alley, he heard another two pops, and felt a bullet rip a burning hole through his side just below the bottom edge of his rib cage. His torso rotated in response as he clamped one arm down over the wound, the other flailing to keep him balanced. He managed to keep his feet, recomposed himself, ran down onto a dock lined with moored yachts and sailboats, and dove straight off the end of it, into the frigid waters of False Creek Inlet. He swam the breadth of the waterway without once coming up for air, though his lungs burned and the bullet wound in his side screamed with pain. He limped ashore in front of a line of new row houses, looking over his shoulder to see a single car racing across the bridge. His pursuer, surely. He ran up into the streets of the neighborhood, all the while hoping beyond hope that the ink of the printed fax reports didn't bleed out now that they were soaked with saltwater. Glancing over his shoulder once again, he spotted the glow of a rapidly growing fire back over on Granville Island, in the vicinity of the gallery. Of course.

Two blocks up from the water, he turned a corner and stopped to catch his breath, pressing his back against the side of an old brick apartment building. He was beginning to feel faint. He pressed his hand against his side, then held it up near his face for a look. It was covered in blood. His time was running out. He listened for the sound of the car. All he heard was the begging meow of a cat. Peeking back around the corner, he spotted his pursuer down at the intersection with the road that ran along the water. The man stood just in front of his car, and appeared to be studying the ground with a flashlight. Just as it occurred to Arkin that he'd left a clear trail of wet footprints, the man abruptly looked up, straight at him. Arkin pulled his face back around the corner, hoping he hadn't been seen, and took off running again. Hoping to conceal his tracks, he ran within a sidewalk planting strip, off the pavement, and then through the community green space of a new low-rise condo complex, stepping in several piles of dog shit as he went.

Three blocks further, he dove into a deep, tall laurel hedge behind an old row house, crawling through until nearly emerging in the home's backyard. There, he crouched, short of breath, exhausted, growing lightheaded. For a moment he lost his balance and, leaning forward, would have fallen onto all fours, or maybe even his face, had the many small branches of the hedge not held him suspended, nearly upright. He shook his head in a futile attempt to wake himself up. Then, certain he'd already lost a lot of blood, and despite the great pain it caused, he used the palm of his hand to try to put direct pressure on his wound. Through the leaves, branches, and twigs of the hedge, he could see occasional fragments of whatever was being illuminated by his pursuer's flashlight beam. While still half a block away, the man appeared to be making his way up the street, slowly drawing closer and closer.

Arkin could feel his consciousness beginning to flag. His eyelids were heavy. As quietly as he could, he squirmed down lower against the ground, maximizing his concealment. Then he heard a growl that sounded like that of a small dog. It was somewhere in the yard flanked by the hedge, but up closer to the house. He froze, but the dog began to bark anyway. It must have been chained or fenced off as it didn't come any closer. But it would be enough to alert his pursuer as to his location. Seeing no further point to hiding from the residents of the row house, he used all the energy he had left to crawl out of the hedge and fall into the backyard. The dog was now barking wildly, but Arkin was too tired to care. The firm earth cradled his body as he began to pass out. He was strangely comfortable. He thought he heard rustling on the other side of the hedge, as if someone else were trying to crawl through. But he'd lost his bearings and couldn't be sure. Inexplicably, as he let his eyes close at last, a vision of a smiling Hannah flashed across his mind. She was sitting behind the wheel of a tiny green convertible they'd once rented in the British Virgin Islands, a sugar sand beach and the turquoise waters of the Caribbean behind her. The sky was clear blue, and an extraordinarily brilliant sun bathed them in bright yellow-white light. Then everything faded to black.

TWENTY-SEVEN

Arkin began to come to. He opened his eyes a crack, his blurred vision affording him a distorted view of a small white room lit by painfully bright lights. His side throbbed with a dull pain. *What is that oily smell?* As he struggled to reassemble his awareness, nausea rose up and overwhelmed him. He clenched his abdomen and vomited down the front of himself, realizing as he did so that something was restraining his left wrist. He looked around, squinting his oversensitive eyes, to see that he was in a hospital gown, in a hospital bed, an IV attached to his left arm, handcuffs binding his left wrist to the steel railing of the bed. *What the hell?*

Fighting through the fog and nausea and pain, he began to piece things together. He'd been shot fleeing the gallery. He'd been chased. He'd lost consciousness as his pursuer was probably upon him. But by some twist of fate, here he was, alive.

Perhaps his pursuer had been scared off by a neighborhood police patrol summoned by the homeowner whose dog had sounded the alarm. Or perhaps his pursuer had simply lost the trail and assumed the dog was barking at him. Whatever the case, at some point someone—probably police—had found Arkin and arranged for his delivery to the hospital.

He lifted his sheet to find that his abdomen was dressed with a very large bandage. He tried to sit up, but was immediately hit by another wave of nausea. He turned onto his side and managed to puke over the side of the bed instead of onto himself.

At that moment, a rotund and scowling old nurse came in through the open door.

"Oh, aren't you a mess. I'll have somebody come clean you up."

"Where am I?"

"You're in Vancouver General Hospital."

"What happened? Why am I handcuffed to this bed?"

"You've been shot through the side. Lucky for you, the bullet missed your vitals. We sewed you shut and pumped you full of donated blood. Now we have you on an analgesic drip, so you may feel a little dopey. Looks like we better give you something for that nausea too."

"And the handcuffs?"

She shrugged and turned to go. "You'll have to ask the police about that. The officer had to step out but should be back in a minute or two."

Arkin caught another whiff of the odd oily odor in the breeze of the closing door, though it was hard to smell over the acrid aroma of his vomit. Then it hit him. The odd odor was kerosene again. It was coming from the half-open closet—probably his clothes. Now he knew why he was handcuffed. He'd been set up as an arsonist who torched the Liber Gallery. But how had they gotten the kerosene on his clothes? And if they could do that, why hadn't they just killed him? It hardly mattered. It was a good move by the group. In one fell swoop, they were taking him out of circulation and probably destroying all traces of their presence in Vancouver. By now, the shooter was surely long gone. Arkin would probably never find him again.

He took several deep breaths, trying to focus, trying to think through what to do next. He looked at the handcuffs, then at the IV. He tore the IV from his arm and cracked the hard plastic sheath surrounding the cannula port, snapping it apart with his fingertips. He took one of the broken pieces of plastic and went to work on the handcuff keyhole. In 10 seconds, he sprung the release. Moments after that, he found his damp and bloody clothes in the closet and, having positioned himself behind the door in case anyone came in, was dressing as fast as he could, not even bothering to button his shirt. As he bent down to pull his shoes from the closet he began to sway and thought for a moment that he was going to pass out. He steadied himself against the closet doorjamb, then took three deep breaths as he willed away the tunneling of his vision. At that moment, the door swung open and a young police officer walked in, staring at the empty bed as he processed the scene. Before the officer could react, Arkin shouldered the door shut behind him, checked the officer's turn with a quick stiff-arm to his left shoulder blade, and stunned him with a flat-palm strike to the brachial plexus origin nerve bundle on the side of his neck—using just enough force to stun the man, but not enough to risk damage to his spine. The officer collapsed, falling to the floor, with Arkin wishing he'd had the energy to catch the man and ease him down, making sure he didn't hit his head. But it had already taken more than he knew he had in him to execute the brachial stun move. Arkin jammed his feet into his untied shoes, stepped over the officer, opened the door for a peek, then slipped into the hallway. Walking with as much speed as he could manage without looking suspicions, and holding his shirt closed with one hand, he made his way for the stairs. Passing the open door of another room, he spied a smartphone on the lamp stand of an apparently unconscious patient. Checking that the coast was clear, he stepped into the room, pocketed the phone, and slipped back out.

Popping out a back entrance and into the early morning light, he found himself at a four-way intersection. A car and then a garbage truck waited for the light to turn. He looked up and down the sidewalk. The only other pedestrian was a block away and facing the other direction. He walked as casually as possible behind the garbage truck, reached for a handlebar, and pulled himself up into the back of it, feeling a tightness and then a sharp pain and tearing sensation in the skin of his abdomen as he did so. Once aboard, he lay down in the bottom of the receptacle and did his best to cover himself with trash that hadn't yet been scooped and pressed into the holding chamber by the compactor door. It stank like putrid meat. Like the fetid gray water of French Quarter sewer backflow after a New Orleans rainstorm. He saw movement out of the corner of his eye, and turned to see dozens of tiny white maggots feeding on a small chunk of unidentifiable decaying matter six inches from his face. He started to dry heave as the garbage truck began to move.

After retching nothing but bile-tainted spit for several minutes, he realized the truck was leaving town. There were probably cars following close behind the slow-moving truck, so he didn't dare sit up. But he was able to rock his head back and forth until a small gap in his garbage cover yielded a peek-a-boo view of the passing cityscape. He caught sight of passing street signs, and was relieved to see that the avenue numbers were increasing. 16th, 17th, 18th. . . . It did nothing to help him determine his location. But at least he appeared to be on his way out of the city center. *What now?*

He pulled the smartphone from his front pocket. As the screen lit up, he saw that it was smeared with his blood. Not daring to uncover the bullet wound in the filth of the garbage truck, he used the light of the screen to eyeball the exterior of the bandage. There was significant bleeding, but it wasn't too heavy. With any luck, it would stop without need for re-stitching. He pressed one hand against it while using the other to pull the received faxes and fax reports from his pocket. The paper had held up amazingly well for having been soaked with saltwater, kerosene, and blood. It appeared that someone—presumably the police—had opened it for examination, refolded it, and put it back in his pocket. It was still damp. But it was readable. Arkin used the smartphone browser to search for the number he'd written down after listening to the redialed tones on the handset back in the secret room at the gallery. It did not lead to a name. However, he was able to ascertain, from a handful of searches of phone numbers with the same first seven digits following the 011 international dialing code, that it was for a listing in the old colonial port city of Valparaiso, Chile. He turned to the fax report. There were only two numbers in it, repeatedly appearing for both inbound and outbound faxes. Again, the first didn't lead directly to a name, but Arkin could see that the area code was for the island of Montserrat, a small British Overseas Territory in the Leeward Islands of the Caribbean Sea. However, the other fax number turned out to have an Oregon area code, and he was quickly able to link it to a business in the city of Eugene called Bluefields Data Dynamics.

As if Arkin needed any further confirmation that the fax numbers were relevant, the report revealed that faxes came in from Eugene and Montserrat several days before the killings of Egan and Pratt, and went out to each location a few days after. Otherwise, there was almost no fax activity at all. That couldn't be a coincidence. It looked like someone in Eugene, Montserrat, or Valparaiso was dispatching a Balkan-Canadian homicidal lunatic artist on assassination missions in the United States.

Then, he did a search for the hand-scribbled Alberta address included on one of the faxes. It linked it to a man named Ted Wright. A follow-up search revealed that he was a fiery First Nations activist who was hell bent on stirring up his local tribal population to violently oppose the construction of a luxury resort on lands they claimed as ancestral. Arkin was able to find several photographs of Wright, including one, from a Calgary newspaper, showing him exiting a corner grocery, hand-in-hand with a little girl who must have been his daughter, each of them holding ice cream cones. Arkin had little doubt Wright was the assassin's next target.

Finally, he began a search of State of Oregon business entity records for Bluefields Data Dynamics. But before the Secretary of State website was fully downloaded, the phone ran out of battery power. Arkin dropped it into the garbage.

Though the painkillers, his blood loss, and his overall fatigue had him feeling lightheaded and dull, he did his best to think about what he'd learned. The last known link he had to the group was the water-stained pages of numbers, only one of which appeared tied to a U.S.-based location. Eugene, Oregon, was the most logical next stop. He considered going to Calgary to shadow Ted Wright, with the idea that he might be able to catch a member of the group as they circled for the kill. But he knew his chances would probably be better if he could catch them somewhere where they weren't already going to be on an operational footing—hyper-aware, hyper-observant. He just hoped the group really had some sort of physical presence in Eugene. That it wasn't a red herring, like another mere voicemail location. As he considered his next move, his condition gradually caught up with him and he nodded off.

*****

A loud, echoing crack and roll of thunder deafened Arkin. A flash of light from an approaching electrical storm illuminated the high sandstone walls to either side of him and the dry sand upon which he stood. He looked up in the next lightning flash to see that he was at the bottom of a narrow slot canyon, no more than 10 feet wide, its path twisting and turning away into the darkness ahead of him. A sandstone walled chasm cut, over millions of years of erosion, a hundred feet deep into the high Colorado Plateau. The air smelled of damp stone. He was wearing a full suit of dark wool, but he couldn't tell the color.

Between flashes of lightning, he stood in a complete and total darkness that added to his sense of confusion. Where was he, exactly? And how had he come to be here?

A sudden, howling gust of cold wind at his back got him to turn around and face the upstream direction. He knew that such gusts sometimes preceded deadly flash floods in slot canyons like this one. He squinted, wishing he could see through the darkness, when another lightning flash revealed a tall, dark figure standing near. At least 10 feet in height, the mysterious figure wore dark robes decorated with broad vertical and zigzagging white stripes. Its large and faceless black head bore a crown-like adornment with two pair of radiating spokes that projected outward as if representing antennae or beams of a magical light. But when Arkin saw the eyes—the empty, menacing, red glowing eyes—he knew exactly who he was looking at. It was the priest from the Anasazi pictograph he'd found in shadow below the canyon rim alongside the Animas River.

The priest stood staring at Arkin. A silent, ominous sentinel. *Who are you?* Arkin wanted to ask. But he couldn't draw breath to speak.

In the darkness between lightning flashes, the priest vanished. Arkin looked all around, but saw no sign of him.

"Who are you?" he finally managed to yell to the surrounding darkness. "Who are you?"

But the priest was gone. Rain began to fall, cold drops landing on the top of Arkin's head. Then he heard it. A low, distant rumble. Like a train. Coming closer. Coming from the upstream direction of the slot canyon. The rumble getting louder. In moments, it grew to a deafening roar, and in the next burst of light, Arkin saw a high wall of churning flash-flood water rounding the corner of the canyon and bearing down on him. He screamed as the cold water hit him.

*****

A filthy, overweight, jumpsuit-clad garbage man was staring down at him, holding an upturned beverage cup over his head.

"Come on, guy. Wake up. Free ride's over. Let's go."

Arkin stared up at him, dazed. He was still in the back of the garbage truck. His head and shoulders were soaked with cold lemon-lime soda.

"Come on, now. Out of my truck."

Arkin sat up. The garbage man saw the blood.

"Oh. Hey, man. You're messed up pretty bad."

Arkin didn't bother to respond. He rolled out of the truck and limped, dazed and aimless, down a potholed street between what appeared to be small warehouses or industrial buildings. He didn't stop until he'd put a couple of blocks between himself and the garbage truck. When he did, he looked around to find that he was only a few hundred yards from a body of water. A channel, it appeared. Probably some branch of the Fraser River. Without giving it any real thought, he hobbled down to the water and made his way along its bank, passing several warehouses and a large vacant lot fronting a collapsed pier lined with seagulls, before finding a small marina full of sailboats.

A plan took shape in his mind. Stowing away in a motor vehicle was out of the question. From where he was in Vancouver, it would be far too difficult to make an accurate guess as to what vehicles might be headed across the border. Even if he lucked out and found himself a southbound ride, there was an unacceptable risk of being discovered by U.S. Customs. Customs always inspected trains as they crossed the border too, so travel by rail wasn't an option. And he was in no condition to sneak through the woods to make the crossing on foot. But a sailboat offered a relatively low-risk, low-strain, and immediate option to get him moving south.

Doing his best to look sure of himself, to look as though he belonged, he gritted his teeth against the stabbing pain in his side, stood up straight, and entered the marina. Walking the docks, he found an old sloop-rigged Cal sailboat, maybe 29 or 30 feet long. It looked seaworthy, well-maintained, but also had enough salt film and dust on its decks to tell Arkin that it hadn't been used in a while, and probably wouldn't be immediately discovered as missing by its owner. There were only two other people in the marina, both on a boat a few slips over, fiddling with its halyards. They paid Arkin no mind. He went aboard, snapped an old padlocked hinge from the cabin door with little effort, and made a quick inspection of his ship. There was a good mainsail, a good Genoa foresail, and an ancient jib. No autopilot, but it did have a Washington State registration sticker, which would draw less attention once he was back across the border.

In five minutes, he'd fired up the engine, backed out of the slip, and was headed downriver. Putting along as he made his way toward the open water of the Strait of Georgia, he thought out his next moves. He could sail down past Seattle and head to the southernmost extremes of Puget Sound, down near Olympia, and then hitchhike from there. But hitching always invited scrutiny and suspicion from passersby and law enforcement officers alike— especially if he couldn't get all the blood washed out of his shirt. The safer play, at least with respect to the risk of getting picked up by a cop, would be to sail down the Pacific Coast until he was as far south as Eugene, and then hitchhike the short remaining distance inland. But the journey would probably eat up the better part of 300 sea miles. So even if he could maintain decent speed, with minimal tacking or beating to windward, and despite moderate assistance from the south-flowing California current, a nonstop journey would take more than two full days. Too slow. No, he'd use the sailboat to cross the border, hopefully avoiding customs, then put in at a marina near the main north-south rail line—which ran straight from Vancouver, through Seattle and Portland, down to Eugene—and catch a waiting southbound train. Again from his travels with Hannah, he remembered that the line ran along the water much of the way, and that trains had to stop at various points along the line to wait their turns to cross bridges, transition single track stretches of the line, and sometimes drop or link up with train cars in the bigger towns. Going by train, he could probably get to Eugene in less than a day.

As he emerged from the Fraser River and entered open water, he tied off the steering and went below to see what he could find. There was a well-insulated, foul weather sailing jacket in the cabin that he would put on as soon as he went back on deck. There was also a small first aid kit in a wall-mounted holder just inside the door. In it, he found various bandages, an iodine swab, and antibiotic ointment. Reluctantly, he peeled back the blood-soaked dressing to examine the bullet holes in his side. One entry and one exit wound, from the same bullet. They were relatively clean. But he had torn half the sutures out of the exit wound, still oozing with a pink, semi-transparent liquid. At least the major bleeding had stopped. As delicately as he could, he cleaned off the wound with the iodine swab, squeezed a large blob of antibiotic ointment onto a barely large enough square of new bandage, slipped the new bandage under the old hospital dressing, and then stuck the old hospital dressing back on. They had no doubt pumped him full of antibiotics back at the hospital too. Still, at some point in the very near future, he would need more.

He was pleased to find NOAA and CHS nautical charts covering the entirety of his likely route folded up in a holder next to the console. The nearest U.S. town in which the north-south train line ran, and that had a marina where he could tie up, was Bellingham. But if he was going to sneak onto a waiting train, he preferred doing so under cover of darkness. So he'd sail south during the daylight hours, and then put in and jump a train after sundown. Promising ports included Edmonds and Everett. But Everett was much bigger and more industrialized, so there was a better chance it might have side tracks with trains waiting their turn to head south.

Having plotted a rough course, he raised the sails, catching the 15-knot wind. The boat healed to starboard as he chose a southwesterly tack, close hauled, toward clearing skies. He trimmed the sails to a perfect 45 degrees off the wind, and the ship began to slice through the water with impressive speed and grace. It struck him, as he filled his lungs with the fresh sea air, that the best thing he ever learned at Annapolis was how to sail.

*****

The sun rose higher in the clearing sky, and both the San Juan and Gulf Islands grew on the horizon off his bow. By lunchtime, he was crossing the U.S.-Canada border somewhere between Saturna and Patos islands, shooting for President Channel, and he celebrated his uneventful transition to U.S. waters by drinking a bottle of lukewarm spring water he'd found in the cabin. His course would take him close to Friday Harbor, immensely popular with boaters of every imaginable sort, where he could lose himself among innumerable craft—ferries, barges, sailboats, motor yachts, fishing boats, kayaks. In the unlikely event that his movements were being casually observed by border agents, Coast Guard patrols, or vessel traffic radar operators, and even if someone were pursuing him in earnest, they'd have a hell of a time remotely tracking him through the crowded channels and radar shadows of the San Juan Islands. By the time he came out the other end of the archipelago, he'd be just another unidentified boat of unknown origin and unknown destination, looking as common as anything.

Midway through the islands, the wind began to die. To maintain his speed, he fired up the engine. But ten minutes later, a temperature warning light came on. He checked the gauge and was chagrinned to see that the needle was well into the red. He shut down, giving the engine time to cool, fired it up, and tried again. The temperature again climbed into the red in only a few minutes. He loosed the main and jib sheets, spilling his wind so that he could go below to take a look at the engine compartment. Opening the hatch, he found, in the immaculate and bone dry compartment, what he thought might be a bypass hose. He put a small clamp on it, hoping it would force more water through the engine block. It didn't make any difference. For the next half hour, he went through another three cycles of running the engine for a few minutes, letting it cool, and then running it again. But on the fourth attempt, it refused to start. He was sure he hadn't run in the red long enough for the engine to have seized. Perhaps he'd somehow flooded it. Whatever the case, it wouldn't start, so he limped along under full sail, with an anemic breeze pushing him along at a disappointing two knots. As he passed between islands, his empty stomach groaned for mercy as his nose caught the inviting smell of deep-fried something—maybe crispy fries, maybe cornmeal coated fish fillets, maybe both—drifting across the water from some undoubtedly quaint and welcoming island pub.

As he eventually passed the southern end of San Juan Island itself, heading out into the wide Strait of Juan de Fuca, he eyed the grassy pasturelands behind him and to starboard where, in 1859, the United States and British Empire almost went back to war over a land dispute brought to a head by something as trivial as an American potato farmer's shooting of a trespassing Hudson's Bay Company pig.

Halfway across the strait, the breeze died completely and the boat bobbed along on glassy water at the mercy of a rising tide that seemed to be pushing him backward. The conditions remained unchanged for an hour. Then another. Arkin grew restless, his lack of progress eating at him. Worse, whatever painkillers they must have pumped into him in the hospital were wearing off. The pain was strong enough to make him grit his teeth. Regardless, he took the opportunity to strip and wash the blood out of his clothes with saltwater. It took some scrubbing, but they came passably clean.

Remembering one of the instructors in his first Navy survival course telling him that in such situations one had to keep his mind occupied such that it didn't stray to troubling and demoralizing thoughts, he forced himself to recall, in every material detail, his most recent chess matches with Gregori Zhukov. Move-for-move, he replayed the matches in his head, pinpointing exactly where he'd made mistakes, and exactly how Zhukov had exploited them. Then he imagined alternate endings, in which he caught and corrected himself before making each key mistake, visualized making different moves than the ones he had actually made, and then contemplated how Zhukov might have responded to them. In his mind's eye, he played entire matches, move by move, until he began to play Zhukov to a draw. Until he eventually began to win. He began to state his moves aloud, just to break the horrendous quiet. "Bishop takes pawn. Knight to king six, checkmate."

In time, the well of imaginary chess matches ran dry. As it did, and between the pain, hunger, and utter exhaustion, Arkin's control over his conscious mind began to waver. His fears began to intrude, no matter how hard he tried to focus on other things. He was desperate for sleep. But fearful that the breeze might pick up and slam him onto the lee shore of Whidbey Island, to his east, if he were to heave-to and go below for a nap, he decided to try to sleep on deck, upright, in the captain's chair. He squirmed and squirmed, trying to make himself comfortable. But it was a short chair, and there was no support for his head. He tried lying against the stainless steel wheel, but that was no better. Chin resting on his chest, he might have nodded off for a moment. But then his head rolled to one side and he woke with a start, jerking his head back to the vertical.

In his frustration, he made the mistake of looking back over his terrible month. Three weeks earlier, he might have been sharing a quiet meal with his wife, gardening, making a pot of coffee, maybe fly fishing with his friends. Now one of those friends had been gunned down, his wife was in the hospital, and he was a hunted man. A fugitive in his own country. Stealing to get by. Dead in the water on a stolen boat more than a thousand miles from home. And for all the miles he'd run, all the ethical lines he'd crossed, all the pain, fear, exhaustion, and hunger endured, all he had to show for it was an abdominal gunshot wound and a pitifully short list of phone and fax numbers that might or might not somehow be connected to a conspiratorial priest who might or might not even really exist. It was absurd.

*****

Sometime later, he woke with another head jerk to see some sort of flotilla headed straight for him, maybe two miles away. He grabbed the boat's binoculars through which he observed three U.S. Coast Guard vessels—a coastal patrol boat mounting three .50 caliber machine guns, and what looked like identical high-speed, rigid-hulled inflatables with large aluminum crew cabins. *Holy shit.* He had no way to run. No way to even get out of their path. Through his binoculars, he could plainly see that they were observing him with theirs. However, a moment later they began to turn south, away from him, and he saw that they were not pursuing him, but were instead escorting an inbound Ohio class ballistic missile submarine, probably on its way to its homeport of Naval Base Kitsap. The sleek, black sub was hard to spot, with only its conning tower and the barest fraction of its 18,000-odd tons visible above the surface. Despite knowing better, he still found it hard to believe such a quiet, unobtrusive vessel was capable of launching 24 missiles with hundreds of nuclear warheads, single-handedly unleashing Armageddon.

*****

Around 4 p.m., the breeze at last picked up, and Arkin made the most of it, running before the wind with the main and genoa sails trimmed wing-and-wing. By nightfall, he had rounded Possession Point and sailed into the Port of Everett. It had one of the biggest marinas he had ever seen. He tied up the boat in a vacant slip and hobbled ashore. The train line indeed ran along the waterfront. But the train would have to wait. A few blocks into town, he found a drug store. Strolling its aisles, he collected large bandages, a standard screwdriver, a bag of ten Styrofoam coffee cups, a bottle of rubbing alcohol, and a cigarette lighter. He stuffed the bandages in his back pocket. Then he set the bag of cups on the ground behind a magazine rack near the pharmacy window, sprinkled alcohol on it, and lit it on fire. By the time he circled around to the other side of the pharmacy area, an impressive column of dense black smoke was rising from his small blaze. The fire alarm went off, sprinklers kicked on, and the two-person staff of the pharmacy evacuated with the rest of the employees and store patrons while Arkin kept out of sight. They had locked the pharmacy door. But Arkin was able to pop the latch with the screwdriver in a few seconds. Inside, he grabbed bottles of Ciprofloxacin and Metronidazole capsules. He found the prescription painkillers too. But they were inside a glass cabinet with a heavy-duty lock. He weighed the risk of attracting attention by breaking the thick glass, then left, grabbing a bottle of ibuprofen, another tube of antibiotic ointment, and a box of candy bars as he did.

*****

Arkin rolled south through the night in a freight boxcar, half freezing despite the foul weather jacket he'd taken from the boat, hidden in a cramped hollow atop bags of lawn fertilizer. The powerful chemical stink of the fertilizer put an unpleasant metallic taste in the back of Arkin's mouth as he ate candy bar after candy bar. And the cold, the pain of his wound, and the unrelenting fear of discovery and capture rendered his brief and woefully insufficient periods of sleep unhappily fitful. But for all his exhaustion and misery, he made it to Eugene by the next morning, gingerly stepping off the train as it slowed near the center of town. There, he found an open restroom in a park on the south bank of the Willamette River where he washed his head, face, and hands in a sink in an effort to make himself look less suspiciously filthy and haggard.

TWENTY-EIGHT

Putting on the mask of a careworn law student—a look he knew all too well—Arkin strode into the University of Oregon School of Law library. He sat down at an open computer terminal—one of many in a long bank—and began an internet search for Bluefields Data Dynamics. An examination of State of Oregon business entity records gave Arkin the street address, and revealed the company's owner to be a "Dr. David Tillman," Adjunct Professor, Sociology, University of Oregon. The name struck Arkin as familiar, though he couldn't say why and couldn't find a photo of the man. He racked his memories of the Priest case, but to no avail. A satellite image of the address revealed that it was not in a business park or office building, as one might have expected, but in a residential neighborhood, on a hillside to the southwest of the University of Oregon.

As he did a handful of follow-up searches to make sure he had as much information on Bluefields and Professor Tillman as was publicly available, a conversation at the far end of the bank of computers yanked Arkin from his trance.

"No, Jacob. It's effective upon dispatch," a male voice said with the forced pomposity Arkin had come to expect of the deeply insecure.

"Acceptance is effective upon dispatch?"

"That's the common law simplification. The Second Restatement says acceptance made in the manner and medium invited by the offer is operative and completes the manifestation of mutual assent as soon as it's out of the offeree's possession."

"Plimpton said it has to be received by the offeror."

"No, he said it *doesn't* have to be received."

"No, no. Think about it *logically*. Here's a hypothetical. If the offeree sends the acceptance and a rejection at the same time—"

On and on they went. Arkin wanted to pull his own hair out. Here he was, a wounded, half-starved fugitive, his far-away wife's health failing as he raced to clear his name, break a multiple murder investigation, and expose an international conspiracy of Hollywood proportions. And he was stuck listening to two posturing first-year law students carry on a trivial argument over the mailbox rule of contract law—something neither of them would probably ever encounter in the real world even if they didn't quit the legal profession, disillusioned and miserable, within five years of graduating. Though he'd fallen for it himself, it never ceased to amaze Arkin that people freely chose to go to law school.

Content that his search had been thorough enough, he took the stairs to an upper floor where he found exactly what he was looking for—private study rooms with locking doors. Inside one of the small, windowless rooms, he locked the door, turned out the lights, and lay down on the floor under the desk to catch a brief rest before nightfall.

*****

Arkin sat in darkness, observing, from ten or fifteen yards inside a dense stand of trees and bushes off the end of the backyard, the residence that served, at least on paper, as the headquarters of Bluefields Data Dynamics. The night air carried a penetrating, chilling dampness, and smelled of evergreens and ferns. From somewhere down in the south Eugene neighborhood in the valley behind and below him, a large-sounding dog was barking. Otherwise, aside from the soft white noise of the city, all was quiet.

He was lying as flat as he could, propped up on elbows to watch the large, 1920s-era Arts and Crafts style house through a small set of shoplifted binoculars. He was looking at the back of the house. The lights were on inside. There was a large glassed-in sunroom that the resident seemed to be using as a den or reading room. In it, a tall bookshelf filled with elegant hard covers, a large wingback chair of dark brown leather, and a jade green reading lamp. It was a warm and inviting room. A great place to curl up and read a book. There was a black-and-white photo of a mountainside waterfall framed at one end of the wall, an oil painting of an old sailing ship at the other. Being a sailor, and interested in all things maritime, Arkin lingered on the painting. It was a man-o-war. A three-masted heavy frigate, circa late 1700s, clearly of American design.

No.

As the wires connected, channeling old memory into his conscious mind, Arkin's body went rigid. He was back in Nag's Head, North Carolina. He was in the den, having been dispatched to retrieve cigars from a small bookshelf humidor while Hannah and the others lingered over dessert. He hadn't been snooping. The passport had simply fallen out of a false panel in the lid of the humidor. Dr. David Tillman, born in Livingston, Montana, 28 August 1951. Arkin assumed it was just another work identity. There was nothing odd about that. He himself had three active identities at the time, complete with drivers licenses, credit cards, and so forth, to be used, as needed, for undercover or covert work. The only odd thing was that it wasn't being kept in a safe at headquarters as required by DCI standard operating procedures. Arkin could still smell the cedar of the humidor, the roasted garlic aroma of the dinner they'd just finished. Could still picture the exact position of the same wingback chair and the grand, old hardwood desk that stood under the same painting of the heavy frigate U.S.S. Constitution in the study of Roland Sheffield's North Carolina beach house.

The first drops of a chilling Oregon rain brought him back to the present. "Roland?" he whispered. As he grappled with the implications, realizing, for the first time, that Sheffield might actually have orchestrated Arkin's disgrace and banishment to keep him from making further progress in the Priest case, a dark sadness took hold of him. Made his arms and legs go weak. He blinked, and blinked again, still half believing, half hoping it was an illusion, but knowing that it wasn't.

He rose to his feet with utter disregard for concealment. Part of him yearned to run to the house, kick the door in and embrace his old mentor, ask him what happened, demand an explanation. Doubt held him back. Doubt, a trace of reason, and a suddenly overwhelming fatigue that had come with the discovery that, instead of being his dear friend, instead of being a genuine source of long-yearned-for and treasured affection, Sheffield was, perhaps, his enemy. But Sheffield couldn't be with the group. There was just no way. Arkin knew him better than he'd ever known his own father. There had to be more to the story. There had to be some explanation.

In a daze, he turned away from the house, half stumbled out of the woods, and made his way back down the hill to a small city park. He sat down at a picnic table in the dark and lay his head down on his arms. A cold breeze began working its way under his clothes, but he couldn't have cared less. He didn't know where to go. He was too tired, too confused to think. His mind turned to Hannah. Hannah, surely watched by people hoping to catch him. Hannah, going downhill fast. He began once more to despair that Hannah would die long before he would ever be able to get back to her. That there was no hope for ever seeing her again. He had no desire to stand back up. He closed his weary eyes.

*****

When he next opened them, he found that he was walking on a broad, dry, colorless mudflat. A stiff wind was blowing across the hard ground, and dust in the air obscured everything more than a hundred or so yards away. Yet while he'd never been there before and could hardly see, he knew exactly where he was: the parched alkaline delta where the Colorado River once flowed into the sea.

The wind howled as it tore along the godforsaken earth, whipping his face with sand, stinging his eyes and forcing him to squint. He was turning his back to it when something yellow caught his eye. It was lying in a small depression, like a dried mud puddle, a good 50 yards away. He walked toward it, the color growing more vivid as he approached. It was a cluster of bright yellow aspen leaves, just like the one he'd seen floating down the Animas River so many weeks earlier. But what were they doing there? How did they get there? Before he could reach them the wind shifted, scattering and blowing them away. In moments, they'd vanished without a trace, and Arkin again found himself surrounded by a colorless, lifeless wasteland.

Then something else caught his eye, startling him. A figure. A person standing at the very edge of his field of view. "Hey!" Arkin shouted. "Hey! Over here!" he called. But the figure, its back to Arkin, didn't move. Didn't respond. Arkin began running toward it. The figure was robed and enormously tall. When Arkin had covered half the distance, he looked up to see the figure moving away from him. Its motion was odd, as if it were sliding away instead of walking on legs.

"Bryant!" Arkin shouted into the roaring wind. "Father Bryant!"

At this, the figure paused and turned its head around to look at Arkin. It was then that Arkin once again saw the mask of the Anasazi priest from the pictograph, his face dark, his eyes glowing red, pairs of spokes protruding from either side of the crown of his head.

"Wait!"

But the figure didn't wait. It turned and resumed its course, pulling farther and farther away from its pursuer. Soon Arkin was out of breath. His stamina gone. "Wait," he said sadly, at a breathless, barely conversational volume. "Please."

He dropped to his knees and watched as the figure moved beyond sight, disappearing into the haze of dust. Exhausted, Arkin dropped onto his side on the hard, dry earth and fell asleep.

*****

Later, there were voices in the dark. Gentle voices. The gentle touch of someone's hand on his back.

"Come on, brother. Put an arm over my shoulder and I'll lift you. Freeze alert's on."

TWENTY-NINE

Abruptly conscious of the fact that he was in bed, lying on his side, Arkin heard a pair of hushed voices mumbling something about extra blankets. The air smelled of acrid body odor, dried urine, and, to Arkin's perplexity, simmering vegetable soup of the bland and briny sort that came out of a can. He opened one eye, then another, only to find, across a three-foot gap between their parallel cots, a filthy man with a long and scraggly beard and unkempt hair staring at him. He could have been Arkin's age. But it was hard to tell through all the hair and beard and filth. He lay on top of his bedding and wore fingerless brown gloves, brown corduroy pants, an insulated polyester vest, and, of all things, a thoroughly worn out, full-length cashmere Brooks Brothers overcoat with belt loops but no belt. Arkin figured it would have been at least $2,000 when new.

The man's expression was placid and resigned. Tired. But his pale blue eyes bore a penetrating intensity. After taking a quick glance around the room—which appeared to be a temporary homeless shelter set up in the linoleum-floored coffee room of an old church or community center of some sort—Arkin stared back at the man, lacking the energy or will to speak, let alone move.

"Why bother, right?" the man muttered at last. "What's the point? The darkness is coming for all of us," he said as he rolled onto his back to stare at the cold, underpowered, humming fluorescent lights overhead.

Arkin took another glance around. His cot stood in a corner alongside a bank of windows, outside of which a cold Pacific rainstorm raged in a gloomy, gray morning, gusts of wind whipping the panes with heavy drops. There were maybe a dozen cots in the room, a third of them occupied by sleeping men. Double doors opened out to a wide hallway that surely led to wherever they were heating the soup. Arkin's eyes returned to his neighbor. At the foot of his cot sat a soiled, threadbare assault pack component of a Marine Corp ILBE backpack system with desert variant MARPAT camouflage. A large tear in it had been sown shut with what looked like green dental floss. He wondered whether the mysterious hairy man had stolen it.

Next to his pillow, a bottle of water and a bowl of what looked like quick oatmeal sat on a small PVC table. He considered eating or drinking. But his appetite left him the moment he pictured Hannah as he'd last seen her, lying helpless in her hospital bed. He moaned for a moment, then fell asleep again.

*****

Again he came to in the bed. It was night. His blanket had been changed. The oatmeal was gone, replaced by chocolate chip cookies. Again he stared at the food without the least temptation to eat, wondering how long he'd been there.

*****

Sometime the same night, he was pulled from the darkness by the sound of a woman's voice asking if he could hear her. Was he dreaming?

She asked again, "Can you hear me?"

He willed his crusty, tacky lips apart. "Yes," he whispered

"Will you drink some water?"

He didn't answer, but complied with her efforts to sit him up as she stuffed another pillow behind his head. She held a plastic cup near his lips. The smell made him realize how thirsty he was. He could imagine nothing better than a large glass of cool, fresh water. He ached with desire for it. But he didn't drink.

"What's the matter? Do you feel ill?"

He shook his head, a vision of Hannah anchored in his mind's eye.

"You need to drink. You haven't had food or water since you arrived."

He closed his eyes and shook his head again.

"If you can't drink, I'm going to call an ambulance."

Ambulance? He opened his eyes. *No.* "Wait."

She held his head as he sipped, paused as he nearly choked, then drank the whole cup down. It felt like it was pouring out a hole in the bottom of his empty stomach. All at once he felt a stabbing hunger. But it wasn't enough to overcome his greater wish to escape the pain altogether.

*****

The next morning, he woke to the spectacle of a beautiful cream yellow butterfly sitting motionless just outside his window. It was a sight to behold, its spectacular wings seeming, almost, to radiate their own light. But as his eyes cleared, he realized the butterfly was caught on the edge of a spider's web, and that the wretched brown-black arachnid was closing in for the kill.

An unwelcome vision of Pratt's terrified and blood-speckled wife and children flashed through his mind. Then came a vision of the group's probable next target, Ted Wright, the Canadian First Nations radical, walking hand-in-hand with his little daughter as the two of them licked ice cream cones. Finally, there was Hannah, helpless, frightened, and alone.

His eyes refocused, and he saw that the spider had already bound the butterfly in silk and delivered its venomous, fatal bite. It was too late to save it. All the same, from deep within, Arkin felt the urge to rise. To rise up and crush the spider with his fist.

Someone jostled Arkin's cot. "It's time for you to wake up, friend," he heard a voice say. He turned around to see his hairy neighbor standing over him, holding two paper plates.

"Wake up," the man repeated, setting the plate on the floor under Arkin's nose. It held a large baked potato, piled with sour cream and shredded yellow cheese. The aroma brought Arkin back to life. "You gotta eat something and get your shit together. The weather warmed back up. They're going to close the temporary shelter and flush us out of here pretty soon."

"Where is here?"

"South Hills Christian Academy. One of the volunteers must have found you and brought you in when they issued the freeze alert."

"I fell asleep in a park."

"There you go."

Arkin sat up and dug in with a fork. He looked down at the man's ILBE assault pack. "Where do you get a pack like that?"

"In Hell. Best pack there is, but it's not worth it." The man began eating his own potato. "I'm glad you're finally up and eating something. I was starting to worry. You look like shit, friend."

"You look like Osama bin Laden."

The man grinned. "Maybe I am."

"All the same, thanks for the potato."

As they finished, Arkin studied the man.

"What?" the man asked.

"Why are you in here?"

"Because I'm homeless, man. Why do you think?"

"Bigger picture."

"Bigger picture? Because I'm mentally ill."

"You don't seem too mentally ill to me. Cynical, maybe. But not mentally ill in any material sense."

"Only on paper. Only according to the DSM-V. No, I have a completely rational, crystal clear view of the reality of the world. But *that*, friend, is why I don't fit in the paradigm. *That* is why I don't function in society. *That* is what makes me mentally ill," he said in a sudden agitation, his fingers scratching quotation marks out of the air.

"I see."

"You see. That's good. It's all about seeing. Because once you *see* the truth, exposed, under the harsh sun of the high-altitude wastes, how can you ever go back? How can you ever convince yourself to bother?"

"With what?"

"With everything."

Arkin wondered whether the high-altitude wastes where the man had discovered his idea of the truth was in the same Hindu Kush mountain range where Arkin had found his own. He also wondered whether the man came from the same tree as Morrison.

"Everybody wants more," he went on. "The rest of humanity be damned. That's all any of it's about, friend. That's the big secret." He stood, slung his pack, and made to leave. "But you know what they say: the *Danse Macabre* unites us all in the end. In darkness. You take care now, friend."

"You take care too." *Friend*, Arkin thought as he watched the man walk out the door.

*****

He slipped his shoes and coat on, drank a full bottle of water, pocketed two more, and strode out of the cot room and into the hall. "Does someone have a phone I could use to call for a ride?" he asked one of the volunteers seated at a collapsible table in the sterile hallway. A minute later, he was down the hall, just out of earshot, dialing the number of an extraordinarily messy and disorganized U.S. Forest Service biologist who worked down the hall from Morrison. When she answered, Arkin put on the heaviest Texas accent he could manage.

"Hey there, young lady. Is this the ATF office?"

"No, that's just down the hall."

"Oh, shoot. I musta written it down wrong. Can you transfer me?"

"I'm sorry. Our phones can't do that."

"Or maybe you could give me the number?"

"Hold on." Arkin could hear drawers opening and closing. Papers moving about. "Oh, hold on. I'll just go down the hall and bring someone to the phone for you, okay?"

"Oh, now, I don't want to tie up your phone. Know what? If you could just tell that agent guy—Morris, or whatever."

"Special Agent Morrison."

"Yeah. If you could tell him to call Lurker at this number, I'd be obliged."

"I will."

A misdirected call from Lurker was part of a long-running training scenario all operative recruits went through in the intro course at Camp Peary. It was a code unique to that scenario, and was meant to alert the recipient of the need to go and find a safe telephone and call back on the number being called from. It was a distress signal. A call for help where both the handler and the operative were presumed to be in environments of extreme risk. Arkin prayed that Morrison had been through the same course and remembered the same scenario.

A few minutes went by. Then the phone rang. A Colorado area code. Arkin answered.

"Nate? Where in the hell—"

"How is Hannah?"

Morrison paused. Arkin stopped breathing. "She's hanging in there."

"Still in the hospital?"

"Yes, but she's a tough cookie."

"How soon can you meet me in Bend, Oregon."

"Let me see what the internet thinks. Hold on. Bend, Oregon. Okay. Sixteen hours and 38 minutes."

"There is a small park there, right on the Deschutes River."

"Go on."

THIRTY

It took Arkin nearly twelve hours to hitchhike his way across Willamette Pass and up old U.S. Route 97 into the high desert town of Bend, Oregon. As he did, he second-guessed his decision to call Morrison. He'd been comforted by the idea of him watching over Hannah. But then, she had many good friends who would keep her company. And as for her security, if the group was going to try something, Arkin reasoned that they already would have. They had no reason to harm her, as she was certainly no threat to them. And while it was possible that they might try to kidnap her to get to him, the group probably figured that the risk of trying to pull off such an operation outweighed the risk that Arkin posed. It was a weighing of probabilities, and there was little reason for them to think he'd obtained any useful information in Vancouver, having been chased off so quickly. By the time they realized he had, they'd be too focused on hunting him down to mess with Hannah.

With a few hours to kill before his rendezvous with Morrison, he wandered along a bike path on the Deschutes River, filling in the details of the tentative plan of attack he'd come up with on his journey from Eugene. As the sky eventually began to grow dark, Arkin made his way back to the riverfront park where he spotted a white Toyota Prius pulling to the curb on the quiet road that bordered it. "Hey, douche bag!" he heard Morrison shout as his window came down. Arkin strode to the car as Morrison got out and stretched. "That was a long damned drive."

"A Prius?"

"I was in a rush. It's what I could get from a friend of a friend of a friend. Anyway, can you think of a better statement of the strength of my self-esteem? And what cop is going to bother hassling a dude in a hybrid?"

"Point."

"Come look," Morrison said as he popped the hatchback. "I brought toys."

All Arkin saw was a large golf bag next to a ratty green blanket. "Are we going golfing?"

"In a sense," Morrison said as he glanced around the immediate area, removed a golf towel, and drew out an SR-25 sniper rifle.

"That the latest thing in putters?"

"They say you can't miss with one of these. But wait, there's more," Morrison said, pulling aside the green blanket to reveal a jumble of equipment. Ballistic vests, radios, one pair of thermographic binoculars, one set of image intensifier night vision goggles, and two handguns—the smaller of which, in an ankle holster, he handed to Arkin.

"This is for you. Merry early Christmas. A P239 loaded with Federal HST."

"No extra mags?"

"You ungrateful ass."

"Thank you."

"De nada. And here's another phone," Morrison said, handing Arkin a smartphone in a pink leopard print case.

"Cute."

"Compliments of an especially absent-minded diner at Barnaby's Truck Stop, Mountain Home, Idaho." Morrison stretched again. "So, here we are, in exotic Bend, Oregon. This is starting to feel a bit like an Ian Fleming novel, isn't it?"

"I'm a much more believable character than James Bond."

"Yeah, but come on. We're chasing an outrageously sophisticated transnational cadre of phantom bad guys. An international conspiracy run by a shadow priest. Smells like SPECTRE."

"You're the one who just pulled an SR-25 out of a Callaway golf bag. Did Q Branch fix that up for you?"

"It's improvised low-profile. Again, I was in a hurry," Morrison said as they got back into the car.

"Cut back through downtown and head east. What did you tell your boss?"

"That I have mono. That should buy me a couple of weeks at least."

"And they won't mind that you borrowed their $20,000 IR binoculars, among other things?"

"What they don't know won't hurt them."

233

"You amaze me, sir. And to think I always assumed that because of its battery requirements the Prius had no cargo space."

"Well, you know the saying: when you assume, you making an 'ass' out of 'u.'"

"And 'me.'"

"No, just 'u.'"

For a moment, Arkin considered telling Morrison about Sheffield. But he didn't.

"Alright Bill, out with it."

"Huh?"

"How is Hannah?"

"Oh—I got Paul Regan and a couple of buddies of his to rotate guarding her room. And her friend Diane from the legal aid office, she and a bunch of their buddies have damn near a full platoon keeping her company. She's in good hands."

"I mean, how is she?"

"She's tough."

"Don't sugarcoat it."

Arkin watched Morrison's hands squeeze the steering wheel. "She's not good."

"What level of not good?"

Morrison sighed. "Time. . . ." His jaw clenched as he swallowed hard. He couldn't finish his sentence.

"Time is of the essence," Arkin said solemnly.

"Yes."

Arkin sat still for a moment, then nodded.

THIRTY-ONE

Heading east, out of the pines and into the patchwork of lava fields, sagebrush, and grasslands that made up much of Eastern Oregon, they took turns filling each other in.

"This should come as no surprise," Morrison said, a giant wad of chew tobacco making a disfigured lump of his cheek, "but friends in our nation's glorious capitol tell me the word in federal law enforcement circles is that Killick bolted. Just up and disappeared in the middle of the work day. Left his computer on, his car in the parking lot, and a full cup of coffee on his desk. I thought I should pass that along in case, with your incredible capacity for self-delusion, you held out any shred of hope that Killick wasn't really involved. Oh—and Hannah said that a load of red cedar arrived for you at that big freight yard south of town. I was planning to go pick it up with my truck until you summoned me to Oregon, posthaste. What are you going to build with all that wood?"

"An ofuro."

"What'd you call me?"

"It a type of Japanese soaking tub. I was going to build it in the upstairs bathroom."

"*Are. Are* going to build it."

"Anyway, aside from getting shot, I've accomplished very little over these past weeks. Before Slobodan Milošević Jr. flushed me out of his grim excuse for an art gallery and shot me, I managed to figure out the last number dialed from a telephone, and was able to print sent and received reports off a fax machine I found in a secret room behind a hidden door."

"Of course. A secret room behind a hidden door. Did I not already say that this whole thing smacks of Ian Fleming? And our bad guy is a Serb? That, sir, takes the cake."

"What are you talking about?"

"The Serbs make such great bad guys. The big, bushy eyebrows. The spooky accents. All that hair. Someone is obviously going to want to option this story for the movie rights. But I'm putting the cart before the horse."

"The phone call was to a number in Valparaiso, Chile. The fax reports showed two numbers—one on the Caribbean island of Montserrat, and—"

"The island with the active volcano on it?"

"The same."

"Huh! I actually flew by that thing on the way to a night drop once. You could see the lava glowing orange."

"A night drop where?"

"Never you mind."

"Right. So the one is on Montserrat, and the other is in Eugene, Oregon. Both numbers were involved in isolated clusters of fax traffic before and after the shootings of both Egan and John."

"So why aren't we on our way to Eugene?"

"Because I don't want them to know that I know about Eugene—or Valparaiso or Montserrat, for that matter—until I have more information. Eugene could be a red herring. But our going there could alert the group and flush them out of all present locations. And then I'd have no remaining leads. So I want to sandbag the shooter first. If we can take him alive, find out what he knows, great. If not, at least we'll have eliminated the threat." Arkin thought, once again, that he really should mention his discovery of Sheffield. But he didn't.

"But you were already in Eugene. What did you find?"

"The fax number traces to a residence. A house."

"So, priorities being what they are, we're getting away from Eugene, and heading to a remote location to draw out and ambush our Balkan-Canadian artist psycho killer. Will I get to torture him for information?"

"For information, and for pleasure."

"Oh, Nate. You're making me giddy. So where exactly are we going?"

"To the Alvord Desert. To the eastern flank of Steens Mountain. There's a hunting cabin I know."

"I have to ask. Why the ass end of Southeastern Oregon? Why not Palm Springs or Maui or something? And is it far enough away that it won't arouse suspicion of your possible awareness of the house in Eugene?"

"I don't have time to search for something farther afield. It's a plausible hideout for Nathaniel Arkin, fugitive. And terrain-wise, it's perfect. The cabin sits in a gully below the towering eastern slope of the mountain. Lots of places for you to hide and still command a view of the long access road and entire surround. Plus there's nobody out there. And there's very little cover down in the valley. His approach will be entirely exposed. Anyway, you'd hate Palm Springs. It's all golf courses and gated condo communities."

"And you're going to get him there by attracting attention to your cellphone?"

"Yes."

"Is there even cell reception there?"

"Believe it or not, yes. There's a tower on the summit of Steens."

"Won't the group just tip off unwitting local law enforcement like they did before?"

"No. They know I've been to Vancouver. I might know something now, unlikely though they may find that to be. They can't take the chance that I'll pass along information that could expose the group. This offers them what they will think is a relatively low-risk way to take me out."

"But didn't they tip off law enforcement after you'd been to the gallery?"

"I don't think so. The son of a bitch definitely meant to shoot me dead. I think maybe somebody else called the cops because of a barking dog, and the locals got there just in time to scare off Slobodan Milošević Jr. and save my unconscious skin."

"Then why did they bother with the kerosene?"

Arkin paused. "I have to admit, I'm a little perplexed by that. Maybe the shooter came to the hospital to finish me off, only to discover that I had a police chaperone. Maybe he got hold of my clothes while I was in surgery. I don't know."

"You don't know. But you don't think this is too obvious? You don't think Slobodan will smell a trap?"

"He can't risk not taking a shot at me."

"What's Slobodan's real name again?"

"The magnificent Andrej Petrović."

"Played by Viggo Mortensen. Love it. But I'm still skeptical, Nate. I have a gut feeling this jerkhole is never going to show up."

"Viggo Mortensen is Danish, not Serbian. And have a little faith. I'm a law enforcement genius."

"See, I knew that would go to your head the moment I said it."

*****

In the next town, they stopped at a small sporting goods store to buy isobutane canisters, camp stoves, and freeze-dried food for their stakeout.

"The beef stroganoff is the best," Morrison said.

237

"I concur. Here, let's get this one."

"I like this other one. Plus it's a bigger serving size."

"No, Bill."

"Why not?"

"Because, first of all, with that one, you have to pour the stuff into a pot."

"So?"

"Then you have to wash the damned pot every time you cook. It's an inferior system. With the one I want, you just pour boiling water into the pouch, seal it up for a few minutes, and eat. When you're done, you toss the pouch and still have a clean pot. Plus my brand tastes better."

"Is it that big of a deal?"

"It is if you're on surveillance and don't want to carry extra water for doing dishes. And this one is $1.05 cheaper."

"It's my money."

"Doesn't mean you should be stupid with it."

Morrison grinned. "It's funny."

"What is?"

"You're a fugitive. I'm an accessory. We're in a bona fide battle against evil. Our lives hang in the balance. And here we are, in some two-bit sporting goods store a hundred miles east of nowhere, and you're arguing with me about which brand of freeze-dried beef stroganoff we should buy."

"Yeah, well. Sometimes focusing on minutiae shrinks the universe a little. Makes it less terrifying."

"Amen."

"And at least we aren't going to be eating MREs."

"Double amen. Shit, did you ever have the chicken fajita one?"

"Spectacularly awful."

"At least it came with a moist towelette. How am I supposed to wash my hands, Nate, without a moist towelette?"

"I'll give you a moist towelette. But probably not in the sense that you mean."

*****

They pulled off U.S. Highway 395 to refuel at an isolated service station in the grasslands east of Burns. Morrison manned the pump while Arkin did his best to wash the smeared guts of innumerable insects from the windshield. Meanwhile, they watched and listened as a goateed man wearing a Hank Williams, Jr. T-shirt and duck workpants that were so clean they may have only been worn for costuming purposes filled an enormous, immaculate Dodge Ram pickup truck on the other side of the pump island and berated his teenage daughter over her request for two dollars to buy a Hostess fruit pie in the station's mini-mart. "All that shit's going to do is make your ass even fatter than it is already. Is that what you want? To have a fatter ass than you already do?"

Arkin couldn't hear her subdued response.

"So you want a fatter ass? That's what you're saying, right? You want a fatter ass?" As the man returned his attention to the gas pump, he glanced over at Morrison, seeming to zero in on the Marine Corps tattoo on Morrison's right shoulder. "Did you serve?" the man asked.

"Yes," Morrison said after a pause, in a tone that all but said *no, dipshit. I got this tattoo at the county fair*.

"Thank you for your service. You and all the other heroes."

Morrison sighed and turned to Arkin, his face bearing an expression Arkin knew only too well. *Please don't,* Arkin wanted to say.

Morrison turned back to the man. "Does it make you feel good to say that?" he asked.

"Well, I—come again?"

"What the hell do you know about me, buddy boy? For all you know, I could've been in it for myself. I could be the type of guy who uses cuss words and is mean to puppies."

"And for all we know," Arkin added from the other side of the car, "you might actually be a great guy, and not just some creep who takes out his own shitty self-esteem on his daughter."

"The point being," Morrison went on, "if you over-apply a word, it loses its meaning. And who are you to go around watering down a word like 'hero'? Wait, let me guess. You work for Webster's Dictionary. You're here on assignment, collecting middle-of-nowhere Eastern Oregon slang for the next edition. Your stupid ass attention-begging truck and double-strength redneck clothes are just part of your cover so that locals will speak to you as if you were one of their own. Am I right, or am I right?"

Morrison stood staring the man dead in the eyes. For a moment, it looked as though the man meant to take a swing at Morrison. But then Arkin saw the slightest twitch of his eyebrows—a peek through a crack in the facade at the hardly contained fear within. He turned away without a word, finished fueling up his truck with a forced nonchalance, and took off.

"Good one," Arkin said. "That ought to help keep our profile low."

"We should team up more often."

*****

They drove for several hours, the roads becoming smaller, the passage of other cars growing less and less frequent. Eventually darkness fell, and the high desert came alive with its nocturnal host of creatures. The headlights illuminated pair after pair of luminescent eyes, reflecting gold, orange, sometimes green. Some large, some small.

239

It had been at least half an hour since they'd passed another car by the time they turned off the now unpaved main road, onto a long dirt driveway that was so badly rutted Arkin worried they might high-center the Prius and get stuck. They took it at a crawl, eventually rounding a gradual bend around a hillock where a tiny cabin situated up on the flank of the gully came into view, illuminated by their headlights.

"Thar she blows," Arkin said. "Home sweet home."

"Or the Alamo."

Morrison parked behind the cabin, just out of sight of the driveway. They got out of the car under a canopy of stars so clear that the Milky Way was plainly visible. Morrison grabbed their gear from the trunk as Arkin picked the lock of the cabin door. It swung open with a loud squeak from its dust-contaminated hinges. The stale air smelled of ancient sunbaked pine planks and the smoke residue of a thousand fires in the wood-burning stove.

"Well, this is cozy," Morrison said, following Arkin in. "Surely cozier than where I'm going."

"You want to trade places?"

"No, you're better bait, and I'm a better shot."

"Keep telling yourself that if it makes you feel better. And speaking of bait. . . ."

Hoping to set the trap without making it too obvious, Arkin turned on his new cellphone and dialed Pratt's office voicemail. He entered his passcode and listened to another two increasingly frantic messages from the phone company attorney who was still asking after the original of the nonexistent subpoena. Then he dialed Morrison's office number and hung up after the voicemail greeting, but left the phone powered up for another few minutes before shutting it off and removing the battery. If the group was as on top of it as he expected they were, that would be enough. They'd lock onto the cell number. They'd learn the call's point of origin in remote Southeastern Oregon, consider the oddity of it, and conclude that Arkin was hiding out. He hoped they'd have good enough cellphone locating capability to zero in on the cabin. He hoped they'd dispatch their killer.

Arkin and Morrison spent an hour going over their basic plan with respect to the most-likely scenarios. Plans of attack. Escape routes. Back up signaling methods in case either of their radios crapped out or were otherwise unavailable. Arkin, keeping a handgun, would remain in the cabin as bait—a warm body, in case whoever came had IR equipment. Morrison would keep watch, with his own IR gear and binoculars, from a hiding place among the boulders a few hundred yards up the mountainside. He'd be armed with his long-range sniper rifle.

Once everything was settled, they suited up, each putting on body armor and a radio headset. Morrison shouldered his pack and picked up his rifle.

"Bill."

"Yeah?"

"This guy winged me with a handgun from 50 yards away as I was sprinting across a narrow alley in the dark."

"Don't feel bad. Everybody gets a little bit slower and dumber at your age."

"He's good. He definitely read chapter two of the manual."

"Please. I'm the best there is."

"After me. Just be care—"

"Hey, hey, hey! Don't jinx us."

THIRTY-TWO

"Barnacle 2, radio check," Morrison said, his voice startling Arkin who had the volume of his headset turned up too high. He'd fallen asleep on the cabin's old, threadbare couch.

"Barnacle?"

"It's our operational call sign."

"Copy that, Barnacle 1. Your signal is five-by-five."

"And yours."

"Are you in position?"

"Yessir, I be. There's a metric shit-ton of IR clutter out here. Lot of little animals running around. Some bigger ones. One coyote. Two something-or-others with horns."

"Are you comfortable?"

"Up yours."

"That bad, huh?"

"I'm lying on volcanic scree, Nate. A zillion sharp little chunks of shattered basalt. And, to borrow a line from William Shakespeare, it's colder than shit out here."

"*Hamlet*?"

"*Romeo and Juliet*."

"Put on your coat."

"Thanks."

"I think, to properly play the part of bait, I should light a little fire in the stove here. Maybe read one of these paperbacks while reclined on the cozy couch."

"Bastard."

*****

A day went by without either of them seeing another human being, the highlights of the long hours being the breaks they took to cook freeze-dried beef stroganoff. On their first morning, a chill wind tore down the face of the mountain, bending the tall grass of the surrounding land, whistling around the cabin. To keep warm, Morrison had wrapped himself in a makeshift cocoon of two wool blankets and a sand-colored tarp. "I don't know how I ever had the patience for this shit when I was in the Corps," he said over the radio. Arkin didn't respond. "Nate?"

"What?"

"Did you hear what I said?"

"Was I supposed to say something?"

"Oh, that's nice. Just ignore me." Again, Arkin didn't bother to answer. "Nate, I feel like we never talk anymore."

"You sound like one of my ex-girlfriends."

"I'm just saying. It would be nice sometimes, you know, to talk about things."

"What do you want to talk about, Ms. Winfrey?"

"Our feelings."

"You're going to wear down the battery of your radio."

"Which is your dysfunctional way of saying that you aren't comfortable talking about your feelings. I hear you. Of course, our words usually just come out wrong anyway, don't they? Maybe if we expressed ourselves in song."

"Song?"

"Here, I'll be Barbra Streisand and you can be Neil Diamond." Morrison began a slow rendition of *You Don't Bring Me Flowers*.

"Bill," Arkin interrupted after the first two lines.

"Yes."

"Would it make you angry if I shot you just a little bit?"

*****

The following days were gray and windy, the nights exceptionally dark. Once in a while, coyotes would cry lonely signals back and forth across the hills. But for the most part, it was dead quiet. Arkin found the silence oppressive, but didn't want to wear down his radio battery chatting up

Morrison. The inactivity made it that much worse. He could hardly stand it—waiting in the dark, waiting in silence, standing still as time ticked by. The conditions were opening the door to his anxieties, and he was hard pressed to keep his concerns about Hannah from hijacking his mind to the point where he'd have trouble staying focused and ready for action. For once, it was he who broke radio silence. "So, Viggo Mortensen for the assassin," he said to Morrison. "Who plays you? Christian Bale?"

"Matthew McConaughey."

"Please. How do you figure?"

"Whoever it is, they have to be at least almost as good-looking as me. Plus, he can put on an accent. It's a slam dunk."

"Whatever. So who plays me?"

"Wilford Brimley."

Arkin laughed for the first time in days. "Thank you. But really, how about Josh Brolin, or that Brad Pitt?"

"That Brad Pitt? You sound like my grandmother back in Hattiesburg. She prefaces people's names with *that*, and puts *the* before the names of diseases. Like 'that Myrtle Scruggs got the diabetes.'"

"And?"

"You can't put that many superstars in one movie."

"Why not?"

"Simple physics. You put too many of them on one soundstage, and they start to spontaneously combust."

"That a fact? Then what about *Glengarry Glen Ross*? Or *Ocean's 13*."

"Anomalies. And for that matter, did you know Marlon Brando was contracted to play one of the characters in *Glengarry Glen Ross*?"

"Which character?"

"Fluffy."

"There's no—"

"But he burst into flame the second week of filming. They had to completely drop his character from the script and then go back and re-shoot all the scenes."

*****

With all the downtime, Arkin plowed through seven of the paperbacks, all of which he'd previously read. *The Sun Also Rises*, *We the Living*, and *The Right Stuff*, among others. He and Morrison would switch positions shortly after dawn so that Morrison could take a sleep break. The weather remained dry but cold. In the middle of the third night, Morrison was pouring boiling water into an unappealing pouch of freeze-dried red beans and rice. "Ugh. This stuff smells like the dirty dishwaters of the Mississippi truck stop luncheonettes of my youth."

"Say again?" Arkin mumbled.

"This food."

"You woke me up to complain about your food?"

"The red beans and rice. It smells wretched."

"I told you that one was bad."

"I can't eat beef stroganoff for every meal. I'll get constipated."

"That's your problem."

"Is that it?"

"No, I don't mean *that's* your problem, as though you only have one. I mean that's *your* problem, as in it's not *my* problem."

"Have you ever had curry laksa soup, Nate?"

"Can't say that I have."

"Oh, it's just wonderful. A Malaysian dish. Coconut milk. Curry, of course. Chili paste, coriander. You let the base ingredients simmer all day, and all those flavors blend together."

"Please stop talking."

"Throw in some fresh shrimp, fish, maybe some bean curd puffs and bean sprouts. Then you serve it steaming hot, over noodles. It's even better the next day, after those flavors have time to intermingle."

"Wait, did you just say intermingle? And you gave me a hard time about using the word terroir?"

"Terroir is a hundred times more ridiculous than intermingle."

"Oh, sure it is. And yet somehow I can already picture you in a MARPAT apron on the Food Network, a little jar of Herbes de Provence in one hand, a Williams-Sonoma copper saucepan full of Rocky Mountain oyst—"

"Movement!"

Arkin hopped to his feet. "Where?"

"Stand by one. Okay. West-Northwest, about 20 degrees up from your position. A solo. Looks like he's coming down off the ridge, maybe making for the cabin. But I'm not for sure."

"You're not for sure?" Arkin said as he took a peek out the window, up toward the ridge. "That's the first southern expression I've heard come out of your mouth since—"

"He has a long gun."

"Heavy rifle?"

"Can't tell yet. I'll update you as needed."

"Copy."

A few minutes later, Morrison's voice came over the radio again. "He's definitely making for the cabin. Definitely carrying a rifle. Not long enough to be a Zastava M93, but still a good size. No apparent night vision gear."

"Any other targets?" he asked, strapping on a hip holster and gun.

"Negative."

245

"I'm going outside."

"Copy. I'm coming down."

Their preplanned strategy for neutralizing a single operative approaching on foot was to close in from two different angles, with Morrison doing his best to get behind the person and into a good position from which to shoot his legs. And as the unidentified man made his way down the mountainside toward the cabin, they slowly positioned themselves to do just that.

"Talk to me," Arkin radioed in a whisper.

"Target is about 200 meters west-northwest of your position, still closing on the cabin."

"And the gun?"

"I can't get a clear view. It's strapped tight across his back."

"Copy."

"Nate, he just crouched down. Stand by."

"Is he setting up to shoot?"

"Hold on." Arkin held on, listening hard to the overbearing silence. "He's just crouching. Gun is still on his back. He's either looking at the cabin or the car. I see a good approach for you. If you shift to your right, you'll be behind a shallow ridgeline, just below his line of sight, almost all the way to his position. Do you see what I'm talking about?

"Roger."

"Make your move, and I'll keep eyes on. That approach should get you almost parallel to his position before you'd have to break cover."

Arkin began his shift to the right, and gradually made his way up the hill behind the ridge Morrison had pointed out. At the same time, Morrison continued his descent behind the man, pausing periodically to try to get a better look at what the man was up to and precisely how he was armed. After three such pauses, it looked as though the man was eyeballing the Prius, but Morrison still hadn't had any luck getting a good look at the rifle. When he got to within one hundred yards of the man, he dropped into a good firing position and took another look—this time through the night vision scope of his rifle. He could see Arkin now approaching from the man's left, his handgun drawn and aimed, his every step silent and sure. A vengeful predator, ready to shoot. Shifting his gaze back to the man, Morrison saw that the rifle was finally in clear view. It was nothing but an old bolt-action hunting rifle. It didn't even have a scope on it.

"Nate, wave off. Wave off."

"Copy." Arkin lowered his gun and took a deep breath.

*****

Arkin and Morrison sat still in the dark, waiting for their hearts to quit pounding. Waiting for the man to leave. When he finally did, disappearing, on foot, around the long bend of the driveway, they broke cover and rendezvoused in the spot where the man had been crouching. "And a good time was had by all," Morrison said, offering Arkin his canteen.

"Must have been poacher," Arkin said.

"Why do you think that?"

"He was worried about the car. Probably worried it was a BLM game officer."

"In a Prius?"

"In a white car that, in this darkness, he probably couldn't see well enough to determine the make or model of." Arkin kicked at the dirt. "Let's get out of here."

Morrison looked mildly surprised. "You sure you don't want to give it one more day?"

"If anyone was coming, they'd be here by now. It's only a long day's drive from Vancouver."

"Maybe he wasn't in Vancouver when you sent your clever signal. Maybe he was starting from somewhere farther away. Or maybe the group's footwork isn't always as quick as we've come to expect."

"Or maybe they didn't even pick up on the phone call. Whatever the case, I don't have time to sit around. I can't take it. Let's get the hell out of here."

"Eugene?"

"Eugene."

THIRTY-THREE

Several hours later, they were driving south on U.S. 97, along the eastern flank of the Cascade Mountain Range, with the high, glaciated summit of some old, extinct shield volcano—maybe Mount Thielsen or Diamond Peak—flashing between gaps in the trees ahead of them. "I have to confess something," Arkin said.

"If it's that you shave your testicles, I already suspected as much. You hardcore bike riders all get a little weird with the whole body hair remov—"

"I found Sheffield."

Morrison licked his lips. "Roland Sheffield?"

"He's alive. The Eugene fax number. It's his house."

"Huh. Well. Good to know, Nate. So you saw him, then?"

"No. But it's definitely his house."

"So he's involved."

"On some level."

"What do you mean, 'on some level'? He's the man."

"I can't. . . ." Arkin shook his head.

"Holy shit, Nate."

"He and his wife were as good as family to Hannah and me. I know him. There's just no way—"

"Bless your heart. Listen to yourself. You're starting to sound like one of those terrified souls who refuse to face the flaws of their religious beliefs.

Where is logical Nate when we need him?"

"There's a chance his involvement is peripheral. Maybe he's unaware of the assassinations."

"Unaware? He's the former director of operations of DCI. Has he ever not been aware of anything in the entire world? He's an all-knowing intelligence demigod."

"He's good people."

"And, according to your many stories, he's an extraordinarily gifted agent handler, which is trade-speak for gifted manipulator and liar." Arkin had no response. Morrison shook his head. "I can't believe you kept that from me. You're conflicted—no, no, you're deluded. Deluded because you're so damned desperate for affirmation. You have daddy issues."

"Look, I'll grant you there's a possibility that some of my more irritating obsessive and perfectionist behaviors might be rooted in a subconscious desire to please my father, but—."

"Which is obviously no longer possible. So switch it off."

"That would be a neat trick. After that, maybe I'll command each beat of my heart with a conscious thought."

"You know what I mean." Morrison paused, fuming. "I have to find a gas station or somewhere to take a dump."

"Let's hope they still have 3.4-gallon flush toilets way out here."

"That'd be funny, except that I'm not very happy with you right now."

"Bill, I didn't want you to—"

"In fact, I'm thinking of a word that describes you perfectly. But I don't want to cuss, so I'll just give you clues. It's a word that starts with an 'a' and rhymes with asshole."

"If I could just talk to him. If there could be some sort of explanation for—

"Explanation?"

"Before we. . . ." Arkin went quiet, then shook his head.

Morrison gave him a sidelong look. "Damnation, Nate. You look like you shrank by a third just now, like someone just told you there's no such thing as Santa Claus. And you're pale. Is your blood sugar alright? Snap out of it, man. The finish line is in sight."

They found a gas station with a mini mart, and went inside—Arkin turning down the snack aisle as Morrison sought out the toilet. But when Morrison emerged five minutes later, Arkin was gone. Morrison stood by the car, scanning the area in all directions, but to no avail. He nodded as though he'd known all along that Arkin would pull some sort of idiotic kung fu movie, Jedi knight *I-must-face-my-master-alone* bullshit, and would ditch him. Could someone as rational as Arkin really still harbor hope that Sheffield would offer some explanation absolving himself of guilt, thereby preserving himself as the good and honorable father figure Arkin so desperately longed for? The innumerable, twisted variations of father/mentor-son/apprentice relationships would never cease to amaze him for their power to make reasonable people do incredibly stupid things. With tremendous force, he kicked a loose rock across the parking lot, then went back inside to buy himself a fresh pouch of chew.

THIRTY-FOUR

Over the years, a number of people who'd known that side of Arkin had commented that he had liquid nitrogen for blood—or something along those lines. Indeed, in past lives he'd jumped out of innumerable airplanes in total darkness, operated alone in hostile territories for weeks on end, and killed people in a half dozen different ways. Yet now, as he fumbled with his cellphone, trying to push the right numbers, he was disconcerted to find that his hands were trembling. Actually trembling.

Standing in the gravel roadside turnout where his last hitched ride had just dropped him off, he was attempting to dial the home number for a Professor David Tillman, who Arkin knew was actually Roland Sheffield. The one man he'd ever truly looked up to. The man whose affection and approval had stood in for that of his own father. His heart pounded in his ears as he tried for a third time, finally getting it right. After an infinite pause, it rang—once, twice, a third time. He got a generic voicemail greeting. "You have reached 541. . . ." Then came the message tone, and the subsequent silence as the system stood by to record Arkin's words. It took a second before he could speak.

"Rol—" Arkin cleared his throat. "Roland, it's me. It's Nate." He took a breath. *Keep it simple.* "I need to talk to you. Call me back." He left the number. Barely a minute later, his phone rang.

"Roland?"

"Oh, Nathaniel. My boy. Is it really you?"

He sounded tired. Almost feeble. And significantly older than Arkin remembered. But then, of course, he was. And feeble or not, hearing his voice sent a chill up Arkin's spine.

"It's really me." *Now what?*

To Arkin's relief, Sheffield took the lead. "I'm sorry, Nathaniel. I'm so sorry. You must think me quite a coward."

"I—no. I don't know what I think."

"No. I suppose not. But I'm astonished! Utterly astonished! How on Earth did you find me?" A pause. "How is our dear Hannah?"

"Not good. She's not good." *Don't get distracted.* "I would really like to catch up."

"Yes. Yes, of course. An explanation is the least I owe you."

"Are you willing to meet me?"

"Nathaniel, it would be my absolute privilege."

"I'm actually at a cabin just north of Florence, out here on the coast."

"You're in Oregon? Ha! What serendipity. What on Earth are you doing all the way out here at the edge of the continent? Something for work? I'm guessing it isn't for a beach vacation like in the old days."

Sheffield promised to head to the cabin, estimating that he could get there by 10:30 p.m. Arkin gave him the address and hung up, perplexed by Sheffield's convincing kindness, sincerity, and ostensible ignorance of Arkin's state of affairs. Could the man possibly not be the assassin's puppet master after all? Could his fax number being on the machine on Granville Island actually be a consequence of something innocuous? Was Sheffield truly the good man Arkin always thought he was? He'd soon find out.

THIRTY-FIVE

Arkin crouched in the bushes and trees a few yards off the path that led down to the vacant beach cabin he'd picked from a list on a vacation rentals web site and then broken into. The cabin itself was perched on a bluff overlooking the Pacific, just south of Heceta Head. Remote, but convenient enough for his purposes. And there were plenty of escape routes—with good cover provided by the dense coastal forest all around—in case it turned out he'd miscalculated.

He'd been waiting there in the dark roughly six hours, having gotten situated at the earliest time he figured Sheffield could possibly have gotten there. He had the small gun he'd snatched from the Prius stuck in the back of the belt of his pants, its cold steel pressed against his skin, concealed by his shirt.

Just as he began to contemplate urinating again, a distant crunch of the gravel of the path sent a shot of adrenaline into his system. His senses went sharp. His heart began to pound. Before long, the silhouette of a lone figure appeared to his left, slowly, cautiously, making its way toward the cabin. No flashlight. As the silhouette drew near, Arkin could see that it was that of a man—a man of Sheffield's size and shape. He blinked his eyes, then blinked again, straining to see the details of the man's face. But it wasn't necessary. The stride alone told him all he needed to know. It was Sheffield. He'd had grown his hair long and wore a heavy moustache and beard, no doubt to make himself harder to recognize. But it was him, without a doubt.

Arkin's impulse, his yearning to run and embrace his old mentor, to ask him what happened, to demand an explanation, nearly got the better of him. But he managed to stay in control, and began to follow Sheffield down the trail with as much stealth as he could manage. He'd closed the gap to about 10 yards by the time Sheffield knocked on the cabin door.

"I'm behind you, Roland."

Sheffield spun around. And there he was, half-illuminated by the bare, low-wattage light bulb over the porch. "Nathaniel? Ha! My boy! You haven't lost your touch."

Arkin stood near enough that Sheffield could see him, but was careful to keep himself in shadow in case Sheffield had come armed or brought along a chaperone—like Andrej Petrović. "The door is open. Step inside but stay where I can see you. Leave the interior lights off and keep your back to me as I follow you in."

"Nathaniel, I—"

"Do it now."

*****

They sat facing each other in the cabin's pair of old plaid chairs, next to a cold cast iron stove. A single candle on the coffee table between them provided the only light.

"This is surreal," Arkin said. "I don't know where to begin."

"Why don't you tell me how you've been?"

"How I've been?" Arkin shook his head. "How could you do that to us?"

Sheffield's head leaned to one side, his sad face betraying confusion at Arkin's question. "Do you mean—"

"How could you let Hannah and me think you'd died? You were like a father. . . ."

"And you and Hannah were family to me. I am so, so sorry."

"I need you to do better than that."

"I was not myself."

"Which self? Never mind. Why did you leave, Roland? Why the staged death? I'll hand it to you, it was a convincing job. Your car going off the road and into the mouth of that creek. The feigned heart-wrenching despondency leading up to it, leaving questions about the possibility of suicide."

"It wasn't an act. The truth is that I was suicidal. Utterly and truly despondent after Claudia died. I suppose the price you pay for being an atheist is that eventually you have to confront death without any sort of candy-coating nonsense about eternal life. And that makes it all the harder to live with. At any rate, I couldn't stay there. I couldn't live in that house, sleep in that bed, walk those quiet and lonely halls, without Claudia. I had to go."

"But why not just move to a new home? Or retire? Why a staged disappearance? Why put your friends through hell like you did? We were devastated."

"Everything about my old life was a reminder of the past. I couldn't take it. I had to have a clean break."

"I don't understand."

"And I sincerely hope you never do. I hope you *never* know how that feels."

Arkin held his breath for a moment, rattled at the thought that he probably would know how it felt—soon. He wondered whether Sheffield was being sincere or trying to throw him off balance. "This is almost certainly insane, but I'm going to give you the benefit—just. . . . What's the extent of your involvement with the group?"

"Group?"

"Don't play me for a fool. There are too many connections for it to all be coincidental."

Sheffield held his hands out, his palms up, pleading. "Come on. You'll have to give me more to go on than that. What group? What involvement?"

"Roland."

"Look, Nathaniel, I can't refute anything unless you tell me what you think you know."

"What is Bluefields Data Dynamics?"

"What does that have to do with—"

"What is it?"

"My limited liability company."

"For what?"

"I moonlight. The University of Oregon doesn't pay adjuncts all that well, so I do some contract data analysis work. Same software packages we used at DCI and DIA. Most of it is for the Army."

"What about Seastar Aquaculture?" Sheffield looked blank. "In Vancouver, British Columbia. Granville Island, to be precise."

"You mean Sapere Aude? They're on Granville Island."

"Call it what you want. They dispatch that Balkan psycho to assassinate your quote-unquote future Hitlers and bin Ladens, don't they? That star chamberesque idea you were oh-so-subtly pushing on me all those years ago. Blinded by my affection, or maybe my need for affection, I never connected the dots. What a fool I've been."

"Steady, Nathaniel. You're mistaken. I don't know why or how, but you've made an error somewhere. I give you my word. Sapere Aude is a peaceful group. It's just a think tank."

"A think tank?"

"They promote academic discussion and disseminate materials pertaining to terror management theory. They send draft articles to me all the time. I edit them and prep them for their newsletters. That's all."

"Newsletters."

"Just newsletters. Scholarly articles. News of upcoming meetings and lectures. Requests for donations. All the usual paraphernalia of a nonprofit interest group."

"And what about Montserrat?"

"Montserrat? The island?"

"You don't know of a connection between the office in Vancouver and someone on Montserrat?"

Sheffield shrugged. "Maybe Sapere Aude has another editor. It's an international group."

At that, Arkin nearly questioned him about Valparaiso, but managed to hold back—his instincts telling him to play that card another day.

*****

Atop a promontory that poked out of the coastal forest and towered over the beach, Morrison was on his belly, observing the surroundings of the old, cedar-shingled cabin—watching for any movement, any heat signatures—though his thermographic scope. From his position high up on the rock, he had a commanding view of the area. To his left, his SR-25 sniper rifle, with a full 10-round magazine, sat ready on its bipod. A stiff, salty breeze was blowing in off the ocean. The sound of crashing Pacific surf roared up from the darkness to his right and below.

He knew Arkin was in the cabin. He'd watched him emerge from the back door and conduct a quick reconnoiter of the surrounding area—probably looking for firing positions, paths of approach, and, possibly for himself, paths of escape. Then he'd watched him slip off into the woods before, hours later, returning with somebody else. Now two glowing human heat signatures were visible through the wall of the cabin. *You sneaky son of a bitch,* Morrison thought. *Try to ditch me while I'm taking a crap. And now I'm starving, and probably going to get rained on, all to chase down and cover your stupid, ungrateful ass.*

As he thought about exactly what he would say to Arkin to maximize the jackass's sense of guilt, the image in his thermographic scope flickered. He ignored it. But less than a minute later, it happened again. *What the hell?* He'd recharged the batteries a day earlier. Still, he turned a dial to see his battery status and was enraged to see it down near zero. *Damn shit battery.* He switched back over to observe mode, hoping for the best, when movement and the glow of a distant heat signature caught his eye. Someone was approaching the cabin from the other side. Someone with a long gun. The man was skirting the area, probably looking for a place where he could see in though the picture window on the side that faced the ocean. That would be tricky—as there wasn't much land between the cabin and a steep drop-off to the beach many feet below—but not impossible. There was one outcropping of rock that appeared to offer the remote possibility of a suitable firing position. *Judas H. Priest. I hope Nate saw that too.* Just then, his scope clicked off. He went from watching the glowing orange and yellow image of the man to looking at a dead black screen. *Damn!* Morrison shoved the scope aside and grabbed his night vision binoculars. But by the time he got them turned on and lined up, the man was nowhere to be seen—probably crouched in the rocks somewhere, or concealed in the scrub brush. Morrison stared and stared, focusing on the rock outcropping that he guessed the man had been making for. It was no use.

Resigned, knowing there wasn't a moment to lose, he silently rose to his feet and began his approach—at a dangerous but necessary speed—toward the last known location of the gunman, hoping the man's attention would be focused on the cabin.

*****

Arkin stared at Sheffield long and hard, watching his eyes. There was, at least, a veneer of what looked like sincere perplexity. But then again, Sheffield was notorious for being hard to read, and legendary for his ability to put on false fronts.

"Could I trouble you for a glass of water?" Sheffield asked. "It was a steep walk down from where I had to park. And I don't know if you noticed, but I'm getting up there in years."

Arkin rose and crossed the great room to the kitchen sink, all the while watching Sheffield out of the corner of his eye. Filling a glass at the slow-flowing tap, he turned to see a long-familiar expression on Sheffield's face, intimating concern, esteem, and affection all at once. Glancing out the large picture window in front of the sink and kitchen counter, he was distracted by the view—or rather, the lack thereof. The total blackness. Though he couldn't see it, he knew he was looking out over the Pacific. The vast, dark ocean—often dangerous, entirely uncaring. "So," he said, still staring out the window. "Let me see if I have it straight. After holding one of the most powerful positions in the intelligence business worldwide, after dropping off the face of the earth and assuming a false identity, you're now a contract data analyst and volunteer newsletter editor for a peaceful little think tank."

"And adjunct professor of sociology."

"And you are honestly unaware of the group's dirty work. You had nothing to do with the shooting of John Pratt."

"I don't know who that is. Cross my heart, Nathaniel."

257

"You aren't a knowing member of a group that dispatches a psycho killer artist from Vancouver to assassinate rising fundamentalists and hatemongers, like the self-proclaimed Reverend Allan Charles Egan, Hassan al Nefud, and so on, or innocent bystanders like John Pratt."

"No," Sheffield said, startling Arkin by having crossed the room to stand within a few feet of him.

"Even though an assassination campaign of that shade would dovetail with your long-held position on the killing of your future Hitlers and bin Ladens. Even though the mechanism of your disappearance practically mirrored that of Father Collin Bryant."

Sheffield shrugged again.

"And you had nothing to do with my being sent to Indonesia all those years ago. It wasn't a setup. It wasn't a way to trump up an excuse for my banishment to Durango. You had nothing to do with it, even though you were DCI director of operations, seated at the right hand of the god of intelligence. The fact that I was pulled from the Priest case just as I was finally closing in—the timing of my banishment—was complete coincidence. The reassignment of the case to a green rookie. The disappearance of the files. The shooting of John Pratt just before he could give me the Vancouver location." Arkin's eyes widened with realization. "And the operation against Raylan McGill–the night Killick and I watched him take his wife apart—you didn't walk away from your radio while Killick begged me to shoot as some sort of test to see if I'd cross the Rubicon, take on your principles, accept your beliefs," he said, handing over the glass of water, watching Sheffield for the slightest hints of intent to attack. There were none.

"You know what they say about conspiracy theories."

"And there's really no Priest?"

At this, Sheffield's face changed. It was hard for Arkin to tell in the weak light of the faraway candle. But his lips might have held the slightest hint of a smirk. A smirk he was trying hard to suppress. Finally, as if relieving the pressure, Sheffield half groaned, "Oh, Nathaniel."

Arkin couldn't read the tone. Was it disappointment? Exasperation? Guilt?

"Really?" Sheffield said. "The Priest?"

"A mere phantom. A shadow wreaking havoc with my paranoid imagination." Sheffield didn't respond. "Roland."

Sheffield took a deep breath and stared at his glass of water. "Did you know, Nathaniel, that when the U.S. Navy SEALs found Osama bin Laden, they discovered video footage of him sitting in front of a mirror and coloring his gray beard with hair dye? Did you ever consider the implications of that?"

"Of bin Laden coloring his beard?"

"Damnation, Nathaniel," he said, sounding exasperated, shaking his head again. "If the human race would take one minute—just one damned minute's break from the hamster wheel to watch that video footage, to really think about it. The irony!"

"Roland, what the hell are you talking about?"

"I'm talking about all of the dirt we visit upon each other for the sake of our pathetic need to be a part of something enduring and bigger than ourselves. For the sake of our ridiculous illusory dreams of immortality. Because of our fear of death. Of oblivion. I'm talking about humanity not having enough time left to learn. I tried so hard to show you the light. It's the *exigency,* don't you see? The exigency is what justifies the method. Speaking of which, I've wasted enough time on this charade."

With that, Sheffield reached over to the wall and flipped a switch that illuminated a kitchen light over the sink, right over Arkin's head. Sheffield's face had turned alarmingly hard. Arkin began to reach for the gun he carried against his back.

"Roland, turn off the—"

At that moment, the window in front of Arkin exploded, shards falling everywhere to the loud bang of a heavy anti-materiel rifle. As he fell to the floor, he turned to see a newly punched hole, the approximate size one would expect of a .50 caliber bullet just beginning to tumble, in the fir-paneled wall to his left. In nearly the same moment, he heard a rapid series of rifle shots—nine or ten—of a lower caliber. Maybe 7.62 mm. Startled, he rolled away from the area of the window before springing to his feet. As realization hit home, he again reached for his gun. But as he looked up, he found that in his moment of distraction, Sheffield had drawn what looked like a .32 Beretta Tomcat from an ankle holster and was now pointing it at him. Sheffield fired three shots into Arkin's chest. Yet as he fell backward, his mind wasn't focused on the terrible pain in his abdomen, but on the frozen image of the expression on Sheffield's face. It was emotionless. Dead. And he knew then that Sheffield was a fanatic. Worse, that he had never really cared about him. Had never regarded him as anything more than a tool. A tool of potential use to the cause. Something to be exploited or discarded.

A deep sadness washed over him as he dropped to the floor.

THIRTY-SIX

Pain brought Arkin out of his daze. Tremendous pain, both in his chest and the old bullet wound in his side. He was flat on his back, on a bed of shattered glass. As he stared up at the light bulb over the kitchen sink, it struck him that while he was certainly sad, there was an unusual absence of any inner conflict or uncertainty. It was, in a way, liberating. A long-jumbled corner of his universe made sense again. Had a logical order to it. Effects connecting with their causes in a linear way, as with a family tree. Still, he felt as though he'd just been to a funeral.

But then Arkin heard a wholly unexpected and hugely welcome voice— more a whisper—coming through the open gap of the back window. "Nate," Morrison said, sounding deeply worried. "Nate, are you in there?"

"Yes," he answered, gritting his teeth as the effort to speak brought sharp pain to his rib cage.

"Talk to me."

"House is clear."

Morrison slid the window open from the outside and dove through, cradling his rifle. He looked up to see that the light switch was on the far side of the room, in front of the shot-out kitchen window. He grabbed an old hardcover thesaurus he found next to a bunch of worn crossword puzzle books on the shelf of an end table at his side and threw it at the overhead light fixture, knocking it out to a flash of light and the sound of breaking and falling glass. The room went dark.

"You're hit!" he said with alarm as he elbow-crawled across the floor to Arkin.

"Vest caught all of them," Arkin said, his voice strained. "It was just a little .32."

"Said the ultimate tough guy." Morrison pulled a pen light from a pocket to examine Arkin's pupils. "You're lucky the sea breeze kicked up when Slobodan fired that .50 cal, or I'd be scraping you off the floor with a snow shovel right now. Speaking of which, I emptied a magazine toward the point of the muzzle flash, but I can't be sure I smoked the son of a bitch. But I thought you might be hurt, so I didn't linger to figure it out."

"And Sheffield might still be in the neighborhood."

"You mean your surrogate father? Oh, good. Did you and Daddy have a nice talk? Did he finally tell you he loves you?"

"If three shots to the chest can be so interpreted, then yes."

"Love is complicated. And some folks have trouble expressing their feelings."

"It always boils down to communication."

"So say the self-help books." Satisfied with the reactions of Arkin's pupils, Morrison examined the three holes in the front of Arkin's shirt. "Wow. Daddy can still shoot. These are all in the five-ring. The range masters at FLETC would be proud."

"He was only six feet away. Even you could have done that."

Morrison's expression turned irritated. "Shit, Nate. To think I was starting to believe you had sense."

"I apologize."

"It's alright, I guess. When someone's as desperate to believe in something as you apparently are, the mind's capacity for self-delusion is limitless. Of course, if we take a good look at your childhood—"

"Hey, I couldn't be less in the mood. And I have a loaded gun. So whether I deserve a lecture or not, just send me the audio book."

"Would you listen to it if I did?"

"No. How did you find me?"

"How do you think, dummy? I put a tracking app on the smartphone I gave you."

"Didn't trust me."

"Should I have?"

Arkin couldn't quite suppress a groan as he sat up and slid himself back against the wall. "Now what?"

"I don't know. You're the genius who orchestrated this. I thought you always planned everything out ten moves in advance, like in your chess games."

"I think it's safe to say I let emotion cloud my judgment and planning this

261

time around."

"You don't say. So where does that leave us?"

"The cabin provides decent concealment, if not cover. If we wait in the northern half of this room, nobody can see us from outside. Of course, given that the Zastava could shoot clear through this cabin, we have to hope Slobodan is dead, incapacitated, or at least doesn't have IR gear."

"Wait until when?"

"Until daylight."

"Daylight? Won't they just call the cops on us? You're still a fugitive."

"We have to assume one or the both of them are still out there, and still functional, and we would probably also be wise to assume they at least have basic night vision gear. Speaking of which, where's yours?"

"The IR set is back up the hill. Thing ran out of power at the most inopportune possible time. Can you believe the luck?"

"Since you ask, yes, I can."

"I'll tell you, Nate, kingdoms will rise and kingdoms will fall, and it will all be determined by the damned brand of lithium batteries they bought."

"You're a philosopher."

"At least I have these night vision binoculars. But it's a cheap ATF set. Early generation. If those guys sit still in the bushes, I probably won't be able to see them."

"Great."

"So, what, we just hunker down until dawn, hoping nobody calls the cops, shoots us through the walls with that .50, or sets the cabin on fire?"

"Actually, we may have to move sooner than that," Arkin said, lifting a bloody hand from his ribcage. His shirt was soaked through.

"The old wound?"

"Every time it starts to heal, I tear open the suturing. The impacts of Roland's shots must have really ripped it wide this time. It's bleeding pretty good."

"I can see that."

"I don't suppose you have a needle and thread?"

Morrison shook his head. "There's a Rite Aid down in Florence."

"Okay. Let's think about this for a minute." A second later, Arkin caught a whiff of wood smoke. *Oh, no.* "Do you smell that?" Arkin asked.

"I do. I guess thinking time is over."

"I'm going to venture a guess that you didn't quite neutralize Slobodan."

"Or maybe Daddy came back to make s'mores with you. Plan."

"Give me the rifle and night vision. Slug that you are, you can probably still run faster than me today since you don't have broken ribs and a bleeding bullet hole in your side. You make a run for it. If and when either of them break cover to pursue or take a shot, I'll put some lead in them."

"Don't we want to take them alive?"

"I'll do my best."

"And you aren't going to hesitate if it's Daddy you find in your sights?"

"I will not hesitate," Arkin said, meeting Morrison's stare.

"Good times. Let's put some lead in them before they score in my five-ring, shall we?" Morrison said as he traded guns with Arkin. "You have a full 10-shot magazine there."

Arkin rose to his feet, gritting his teeth. They checked their weapons and took up positions to either side of the front door, left wide open by the fleeing Sheffield.

"Won't they be expecting us to come out the front door?" Morrison said.

"No, they don't think we're this stupid."

Smoke was beginning to pour in through gaps in the wood-paneled walls behind them, collecting along the ceiling. They peered at the area outside the door. A wall of dense forest—evergreens, maples, salal, ferns—offered excellent cover if they could just get across a 20-yard-wide clearing.

"Go straight into the woods," Arkin said.

"No, I think I'll stop and have a picnic in the clearing."

"Hopefully, he takes off after you, and I can get a clear shot from the door," Arkin said, extending the bipod legs of the rifle and dropping to the floor to take up position.

Morrison chambered a round in his handgun. "Whenever you're ready."

"Count of three." Arkin took a deep breath. "One. . . ."

On three, Morrison bolted for the woods. He made it across the clearing and into cover without a shot being fired. But barely a second after he'd disappeared into the trees, a black-clad figure appeared from the left, racing across the clearing in pursuit, holding some kind of handgun. Arkin lined up, aiming for the figure's lower abdomen, and fired. The figure continued on, unchecked, reaching the edge of the woods. Arkin lined up on him, just as he was disappearing into the forest, and fired again. He heard a groan of extreme pain, then heavy breathing. Alive. They'd bagged one of the bastards alive.

As he waited for Morrison to double back through the woods and assess their captive's status, he was startled by another unexpected bang, clearly of a small caliber handgun. Half a minute later, Morrison called to him. "It looks like you're clear to here. But I have you covered anyway. Make a run."

Reluctantly, Arkin set the heavy rifle down on the floor, took a deep breath, and, hand pressed to his bleeding wound, ran for the woods. When he got there, he nearly tripped over the body of Andrej Petrović. He scanned the body with Morrison's LED pen light. Petrović was on his back. There was a hole through the front of his pants, and they were soaked with blood. He was also holding a Glock to his own bleeding right temple. His stubbly face bore a final agonized grimace.

Morrison, his eyes still watching the clearing, said, "Looks like he didn't want to chat with us."

That much was certain, Arkin thought. With prompt medical attention, Petrović probably would have survived Arkin's hit. The shot looked like it went through his bladder or intestine. Yet the man hadn't let himself be taken alive. Arkin stood staring, frustrated but in awe.

As Morrison stood watch, Arkin searched the body, knowing he wouldn't find anything. He didn't. Then, dizzy, he dropped to a knee. "I got him though the guts there," he said. "But there aren't any other holes, aside from the one he put in himself with that Glock."

"So?"

"You missed him. All those shots, and you didn't even scratch him," Arkin said, panting

"I was shooting blind, jerko."

"You saw the muzzle flash. You knew where he was."

"I was a 100 yards away."

"Say it."

"Say what?"

"That I'm a better shot than you. I want to hear you say it."

"Haven't we been over this? And anyway, it's you who should be saying thanks, Bill, for tracking me here and trying to cover my stupid ass after I withheld information from you and made the ungentlemanly move of ditching you while you were on the pot. I owe you steak dinners for life, my best and only friend." Morrison looked down at the killer's face. "He doesn't look so magnificent now, does he?" he said as Arkin lowered himself, with a soft groan, to sit against the trunk of a large fir tree.

"All the great ones die young."

"So they say. Now let's get you some medical attention."

"I think you had better just stitch me back up with a needle and thread from that Rite Aid down in Florence."

"No hospital?"

"Too risky."

"What about the delightful Roland Sheffield?"

"He would have shown himself by now. He's probably on his way to Valparaiso, Chile, traveling under yet another assumed name. And speaking of names, I still won't be able to clear my own without capturing Sheffield. But I'm fresh out of North American leads."

"Well, you'll have to save South America for the sequel, 007. Sheffield is on the run. His group is, at least for the moment, probably in retreat and looking for a place to regroup. And you're needed elsewhere."

THIRTY-SEVEN

Against a yellow painted curb directly in front of the main door of the small Durango hospice, Morrison parked the medical services van he'd borrowed— using a friendly request, then guilt, then intimidation—from a man he sometimes played rugby with, who happened to own a dialysis center down in Farmington. He donned the white uniform top that he'd borrowed in the same instance, opened the side double doors, lowered the wheelchair lift to the level of the sidewalk, and rolled the wheelchair into the building.

"Can I help you?" the front desk secretary asked.

"Yes, ma'am. Here to pick up a Hannah Arkin for a radiology appointment at Mercy Hospital. I like your brooch. What kind of stone is that?"

"Oh, thank you. It's labradorite. My daughter gave it to me for my 50th."

"It's beautiful the way it plays with the light."

"I know. I stare at it all the time." The secretary flipped through the top several forms in a clipboard. "I don't see her out-sheet here. Who is the doctor?"

"McIver. 5 p.m. Here's the paperwork from our end." He handed over the convincing forgery.

"Well, okay. She's in room 4."

"Room 4. Thanks."

He rolled the wheelchair down the linoleum hallway and turned left into

Hannah's room. She was awake, wearing a pale pink hospital gown and with a blanket draped over her legs. Her face was colorless, sagging, dark around her eyes. There was a small bedside oxygen tank feeding a tube and cannula in her nose. Her eyes were directed at the television. There was a program on about dolphins. But her blank expression gave Morrison the impression that she wasn't really paying attention to it. Her head didn't move, but her eyes turned to him.

"Hey, good looking. I'm going to take you out and get you a little fresh air. Alright?"

*****

Having lifted Hannah and her oxygen tank into the wheelchair, and then into the van, he drove slowly, with uncharacteristic care, across town and onto northbound U.S. Route 550, taking a circuitous route to make sure he wasn't being followed.

"So how've you been, sweetheart? I've been thinking to myself, I need to take Hannah out on a little excursion. A little adventure. Now, what would she like to do? Watch some NASCAR? Do some whiskey shots down at the Diamond Belle? Have me read her tweener vampire fantasy romance novels all day long?" He glanced in the rearview mirror, and his heart warmed to see her smile a weak little smile. "Nothing seemed right. But then I finally came up with something good. And mark my words, Hannah, you're going to say to yourself, man, I had that creep Morrison all wrong. There's more to him than an obsession with high-capacity toilets. He's a hell of a guy, he is. All heart under that slimy, cold snakeskin. Yes, ma'am. That's what you'll say."

*****

After an hour of driving north, into the heart of the San Juan Range, with Morrison constantly checking his rearview for tails, he turned onto a well-maintained gravel road. It climbed and climbed, passing several cabins as it snaked up a mountainside. At last, as the sun was setting, he pulled into a driveway at the back of an old ski cottage framed by tall aspens and a spectacular view of the valley below. He lowered the wheelchair, lifted Hannah into it, and then wheeled her not to the old ski cottage but back down the driveway and onto the gravel road, which they silently followed a few hundred feet to the next cabin—an A-frame. The windows were dark, but a faint wisp of smoke curled from its chimney. He rolled her to the door, knocked, and then turned and left her as he went to stand lookout by the road. The door opened, and there stood Arkin. Unable to speak, tears in his eyes, he embraced her. And as awkward as it was for him bent over her chair, he didn't let go for a long, long time. When he finally did, he wheeled her over by the warm wood-burning stove, pulled a soft blanket up over her legs, and sat down in a chair next to her. There, they held hands and stared out the large windows, looking out from high above the Animas River Valley as the sky grew dark and the stars began to appear.

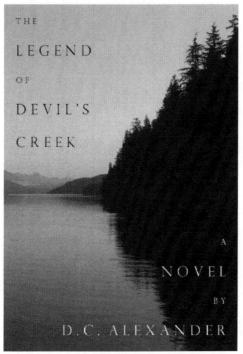

NOTE TO READERS:

If you enjoyed this book, **PLEASE** tell your family, friends, and acquaintances about it. It is *not* the product of a massive New York corporate publishing house, with advertising and distribution departments publicizing and supporting its release. It is a product of independent publishing and is supported by a marketing budget of exactly jack squat. If the author has any hope of quitting his day job and writing full-time, he is going to need your assistance in promoting his book via word of mouth. In fact, the author would be utterly grateful for your help. Thank you.

D.C. Alexander is a former federal agent. He was born and raised in the Seattle area, and now lives in Louisville, Kentucky. His debut novel, *The Legend of Devil's Creek*, was a #1 Amazon Kindle best seller. He welcomes your feedback. You can email him directly at:

authordcalexander@gmail.com

Made in the USA
Lexington, KY
17 December 2017